W9-BEL-253

# HANGING OUT *with the* DREAM KING

## Conversations *with* Neil Gaiman *and* His Collaborators

Fantagraphics Books

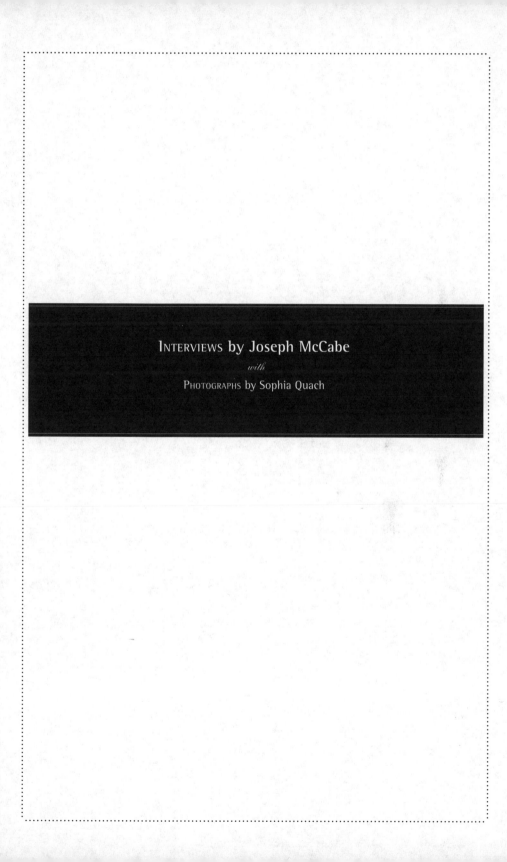

INTERVIEWS **by Joseph McCabe**

*with*

PHOTOGRAPHS by Sophia Quach

Fantagraphics Books
7563 Lake City Way
Seattle, WA 98115 USA.

Edited by Joseph McCabe
Editorial Liaison: Gary Groth
Art Direction & Design by Jacob Covey
Promotion by Eric Reynolds
Published by Gary Groth & Kim Thompson

 First Neil Gaiman interview originally published in *Chronicle*, issue #229, October 2002. Jill Thompson interview originally published in *Comic Book Artist*, issue #23, December 2002. Terry Pratchett interview originally published in *Weird Tales*, issue #335, March/April 2004. For a free full-color catalogue of comics and cartooning, call 1-800-657-1100. Our books may be viewed (and purchased) on our web site at www.fantagraphics.com.

First Fantagraphics Books edition: December 2004

ISBN 1-56097-617-9

Printed in Korea

THIS IS FOR

*Jeanne Marie McCabe*

———————

MY SISTER AND FIRST COLLABORATOR

## ACKNOWLEDGMENTS

...............................................................

Sincere thanks must first be extended to each of the individuals interviewed in these pages. They graciously shared their art, their thoughts, and their time. (Additional thanks are extended to the Fabulous Lorraine Garland, for support above and beyond the call of duty; to Tori Amos, for inspiring words and music; to Stephen Jones, for invaluable advice; and to Sam Kieth, for cab fare.)

Others who arranged interviews, contributed art, and provided much-needed assistance were Mark Wheatley, Mariah Huehner, Carol Kaye, Sandro Grancaric, Yoshi Segoshi, Lovern Kindzierski, Marilyn Mattie Brahen, Steven Tice, Greg Ketter, Allen Spiegel, Ken Meyer, Jr., Bill Sienkiewicz, Les Edwards, Herb Leonhard, Michael Whitehead, Eric Reynolds, Carys Cresny, Matt Silvie, and Kim Thompson.

Work on this book took a good deal of time away from my regular magazine assignments. During the last two years, my editors could have made my life extremely difficult. They did not. They are: Nick Setchfield, Steve O'Brien, James White, Brent Frankenhoff, and Simon Gerard.

Many thanks to the usual unwavering-support staff: Eric Cheung, Rich Rissmiller, Ed Burns, Patrick Killoran, David Angwin, Brian Roche, Jeremy Meyer, Kevin Neaves, Dave Severine, and Jane Wilson. And to Joan, James and John McCabe.

Warren Lapine, of *Chronicle* (formerly known as *Science Fiction Chronicle*), published the interview with Neil Gaiman that became this book's foundation.

Hy Bender is the author of *The Sandman Companion* – still the definitive book on *The Sandman*, and an invaluable reference.

Lance "Squiddie" Smith compiled the ultimate Neil Gaiman bibliography; and Davey Snyder updated it.

Jon Cooke is the editor of *Comic Book Artist* magazine. He kept me, and this book, on the right track.

Jacob Covey's skills as an art director are matched only by his patience with my tardiness.

Gary Groth, my editor at Fantagraphics Books, shepherded this project and took a chance on a punk kid with a head full of big ideas.

George Scithers and Darrell Schweitzer (who inspired this book's direction) are the editors of *Weird Tales*. They have also been my mentors. I owe them a great deal.

Sophia Quach is a gifted photographer, a tireless and unforgiving editor, an infinitely patient and supporting partner, and my own favorite collaborator. Without all of her hard work, this book would be much less than it is.

And, finally, my deepest thanks to Neil Gaiman, whose blessing and support made this book possible, and whose words created – and continue to create – a universe of dreamers.

[redacted]

NEIL GAIMAN'S STORIES HAVE ALWAYS CROSSED BOUNDARIES. THE BOUNDARIES between life and death, between reality and dream, between male and female, and between humans and gods. And the forms these stories take refuse to adhere to any strict boundaries of genre or medium. If an idea doesn't quite work in one medium, Gaiman does not abandon it like an unwanted child, but instead lifts it up and carefully examines it to see if it could work in another – be it a comic book, a movie, a novel, a short story, a poem, or a song.

This book, through the eyes of Gaiman and many of the talented individuals with whom he has worked, looks at the defiance of boundaries, the constant challenging of the notion that a writer must be only one *kind* of writer. My hope is that through its pages a greater understanding will develop of Gaiman's work and of the collaborative spirit in which so much of it has been created.

Some of the following interviews may cover ground familiar to longtime Gaiman fans, while others may offer a more in-depth examination of his work in an unfamiliar medium. Gaiman is fond of quoting Gene Wolfe's definition of good literature as that which can be "read with pleasure by an educated audience, and reread with increased pleasure." By the same token, the more familiar one grows with Gaiman's vast body of work, the more satisfaction they'll derive from referring to this book.

Only three of the following twenty-nine interviews have previously seen print. The first interview in this book, with Gaiman himself, was featured in *Chronicle*; and those with Jill Thompson and Terry Pratchett originally ran in *Comic Book Artist* and *Weird Tales*, respectively. (The latter two are edited from their original forms to focus on work created with Gaiman.) I'm very pleased to report that every other interview is exclusive to this volume.

Though not all of these interviews are presented in the order in which they were conducted (and so, for example, one will read Colleen Doran responding to a comment from Bryan Talbot, though Talbot's interview – with said comment – is presented after Doran's), I have attempted to present them, for the most part, in the order in which Gaiman worked with the interview subjects.

And now it seems we've come to yet another type of boundary. One it is always a pleasure to cross. A book's beginning...

Joseph McCabe
Bryn Mawr, PA
July, 2004

[redacted]

GARY GROTH, THE PUBLISHER OF FANTAGRAPHICS BOOKS AND THE EDITOR of the volume you are holding, has over the years accused me, probably quite accurately, of disingenuousness, and it would probably be considered the pinnacle of disingenuousness were I to describe my life and career today simply as "lucky," like the prelude to one of those *Reader's Digest* anecdotes which conclude "...and the harder I work, the luckier I am."

And yet I am, and have always been, peculiarly lucky in the people I have collaborated with, and the people I call friends.

The best thing about comics as a medium is the opportunity one has for collaboration, to work with other people, to learn from them; and in my collaborators in comics, from Dave McKean on, I've been astonishingly lucky.

About twenty years ago Alan Moore told me that when you write for specific artists you should write for them, and no-one else, play to their strengths, stretch them. "It makes you look good," he explained.

My friends have made me look very good indeed.

When Joe McCabe told me he wanted to interview the people I'd worked with, I rather doubted that he'd end up with a book anybody would want to read. I was, of course, wrong. The book is readable and enjoyable – a series of portraits of a diverse, brilliant and fairly motley bunch of people who have, as a common thread, worked with me at some time or other.

On a personal level I was fascinated by the vagaries and traps of memory: there are events and incidents in here that I remember differently; occurrences I remember (I am convinced) much, much more accurately, which are offset by circumstances and events mentioned in here that I can barely remember at all. There were several things that I had managed, until reading this manuscript, mercifully, to forget.

Reading this book was, for me, like spending time with old friends, learning new things and rediscovering old ones.

And, disingenuously or otherwise, it made me feel remarkably lucky.

NEIL GAIMAN
Bologna, Italy
August, 2004

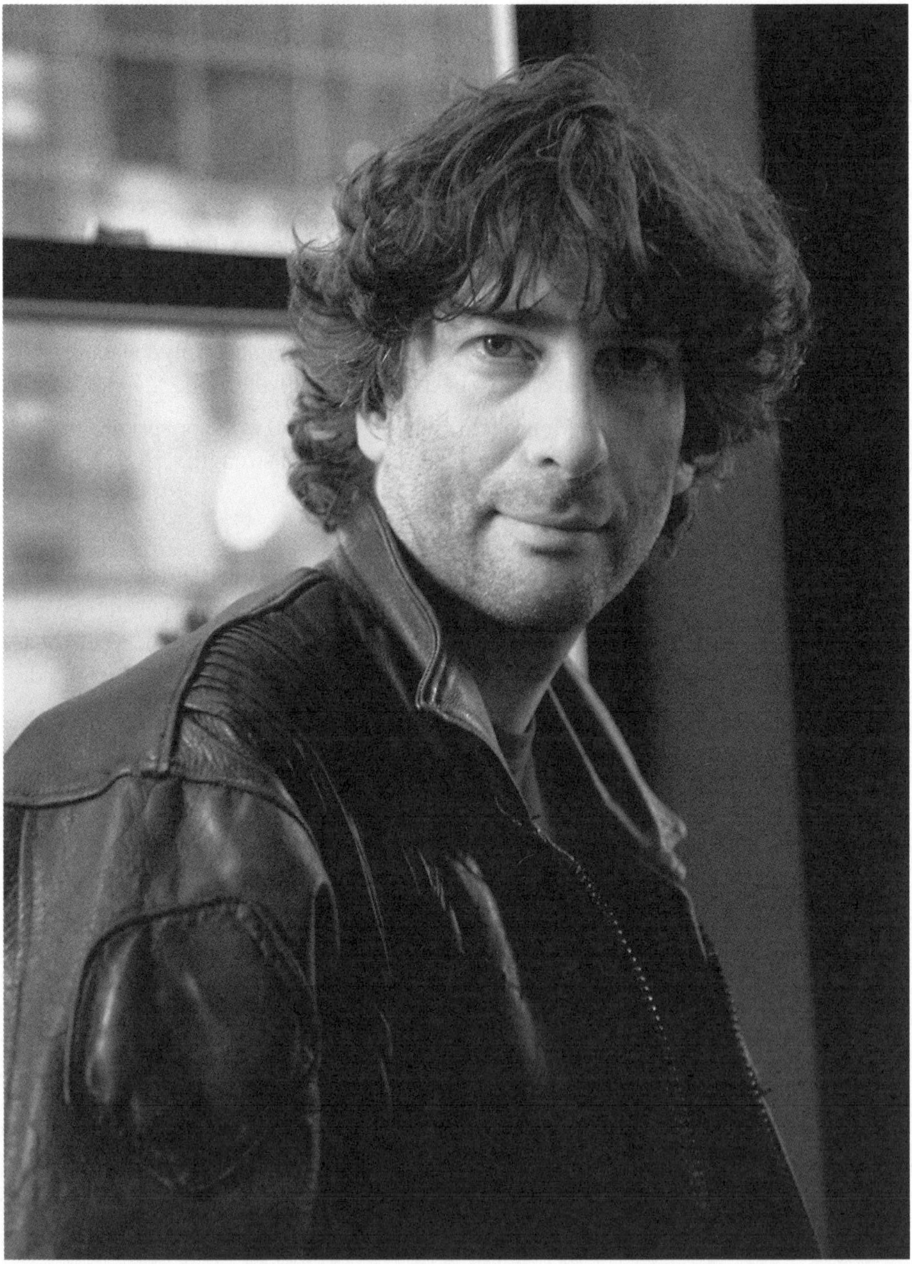

*Neil Gaiman*

---

THE FOLLOWING INTERVIEW WAS CONDUCTED AT BOSKONE 39 – THE ANNUAL CONVENTION OF THE NEW ENGLAND SCIENCE FICTION ASSOCIATION – AT WHICH GAIMAN WAS THE GUEST OF HONOR IN FEBRUARY OF 2002. DESPITE HIS BUSY SCHEDULE THAT WEEKEND, GAIMAN AGREED TO SIT DOWN IN THE CONVENTION'S HOTEL BAR AND SHARE A FEW WORDS OVER SUSHI. THE CONVERSATION THAT FOLLOWED EVENTUALLY BECAME THE CORNERSTONE OF THIS BOOK, EXAMINING AS IT DOES GAIMAN'S WORK WITH VARIOUS COLLABORATORS, AND IN DIFFERENT MEDIA. IT IS ALSO PERHAPS NOTEWORTHY IN THAT IT FINDS GAIMAN SPEAKING CANDIDLY ABOUT HIS EVER-GROWING SUCCESS AND THE ROLE IT HAS PLAYED IN HIS CONNECTION TO HIS FANS.

---

*I'd like to talk a little bit about your collaborations. You've worked with numerous individuals over the years, and the breadth of your collaborations is very impressive: artists, writers, musicians, and even, with the film* Princess Mononoke, *animator Hayao Miyazaki. I'd like to begin by just naming some of your collaborators, and getting your thoughts on working with them. Let's start with some of the artists you worked with on* The Sandman. *Such as Dave McKean, who did the cover of every issue.*

Well, Dave was one of my first collaborators, and he's still the one who is most exciting for me to work with. I think I said yesterday that the thing about Dave is that I never know what I'm going to get. But it's always cool, and it's always different than whatever I imagined. A Charlie Vess ["A MidSummer Night's Dream," issue 19; "The Tempest," issue 75] or a Craig Russell ["Ramadan," issue 50] are lovely examples of people who are brilliant and they will give you something that's like the kind of thing you thought they might do only it's better, but what Dave gives you is something that's nothing like what you had in your head, but it's still cool. In fact often it's cooler than the thing you had in your head. So I'm always fascinated by that. But I think very often there's a sort of creative tension with Dave that I don't necessarily get with other people because he's not doing it in the way that I expected it to be done, or would have done, or just naturally have assumed he would have done it. It's always done off of this sort of ninety degrees in Dave World, which gives you a weird kind of stretch.

*Charles Vess.*

Charlie's brilliant. Charlie's just fun. I mean Charlie's a lot like getting to collaborate with Arthur Rackham or somebody. There is this delight to dealing with Charlie as a creator, as an artist, and as a thinker. Because I know what his influences are and I know where he's coming from, a wonderful sort of Heath Robinson, Brandywine, Rackhamesque tradition. What was actually fun with Charlie was when we collaborated on the comic mini-series *Books of Magic* [Book 3, "The Land of Summer's Twilight"]. He was throwing in a lot of stuff in musical terms. He put together a tape for me of music he thought I should hear, all this English folk music that I didn't know, which I thought was lovely, a feeling of informing the thing. And that's with all of the collaborations with Charlie. I'd write something for him, he'd do something, and I'd say, "Oh, that's cool, I have to do more of that." The little hairy man was just meant to come on and go off, and I saw the drawing Charlie did of him in the first issue of *Stardust*, and it's like "Oh, great, we need more of him."

*Marc Hempel [The Kindly Ones].*

Marc was lovely. Marc was my second choice for *The Kindly Ones*. My first was Mike Mignola, and when it became apparent we weren't going to get Mike I said, "Well, Marc Hempel." I wanted a sense of form. I wanted a sense of everything reducing to light and shadow, of everything reducing to simple shape.

*His work almost looks like stained-glass windows.*

And what is interesting is that, as a monthly comic, it didn't work at all. Because as a monthly comic coming out over a period of about sixteen months, you have a month to read a bunch of other stuff, and then you pick up the Hempel and the artificiality of it – not that other styles aren't artificial – people would find it distancing. With the *Kindly Ones* story collected in a book, you're in there and it may be distancing for the first couple of pages but as it goes on, you are in *that world*. Everything becomes form, everything becomes shape. It becomes these stained-glass windows.

*How about Jill Thompson [Brief Lives]?*

Jill was just so much fun. Jill may well have been my favorite collaborator on *The Sandman*. Just from a personal point of view, the sheer amount of fun and delight we had working together. It was enormous fun. She'd send me these great little faxes… At one point – it was actually the only time this happened on *Sandman* – but she came and stayed with my family. And at one point she was drawing on one end of the sofa and I was writing several pages ahead on the other end of the sofa. Incredibly fun. And she brought a lot of herself to it, which I loved. And I also loved the fact that, when she began, nobody knew how good she was. She was sort of considered a minor *Wonder Woman* artist. I just saw some of her stuff and I saw so much potential and so much that was interesting about what she was doing and what she could do. And I feel like we got a lot out of the work we did together. I think, these days, her talent really has flowered completely. With things like her children's book, *Scary Godmother*, people can see for themselves what she does and how good she is. I loved working with her. She drew women who looked like women, which made me very happy.

*It was exciting to watch her find herself in* Brief Lives. *Whenever I think of Delirium, Jill Thompson jumps into my head.*

Jill put a lot of herself into the character.

*With all the praise it's been given, do you feel you achieved everything you wanted to with* The Sandman?

Well, you never achieve everything you wanted to. It's the simple act of writing. You begin with a platonic ideal that is a shimmering tower carved out of pure diamond, that is this perfect thing that stands there unfouled by gravity and the weather. And then, the thing that you build is this thing that you have to build out of whatever is at hand and you use empty sushi boxes and chairs and get friends to hold it up and try to make it look like it's standing. And at the end of it, people look at it and they say, "It's amazing." And you say, "Yes, but if only I could have done the thing that is in my head."

*What makes a good comic-book collaborative team work?*

In terms of comics, the joy for me is always looking at an artist, looking at what they do, what they do best, and what they don't do very well, and how I can write best to play to their strengths and minimize their weaknesses. For me, the perfect example of that would be Alan Moore writing his story "Pog" [in *Swamp Thing* 32] with Shawn McManus [*A Game of You*].

Shawn, at that time, couldn't draw very good people. They looked kind of lumpy and cartoonish. There was a lot of stuff he couldn't do terribly well. But Alan got Shawn to write a story that would break your heart. It's his *Pogo* story.

*With beautiful lumpy people.*

But rather than beautiful lumpy people, what you got was cartoon animals. It was a tale of these cartoon spacemen based on *Pogo*. And Alan completely avoided the issue of the standards of realism to which Shawn was working at the time. I still think it may well have been Alan's best-ever *Swamp Thing*, a remarkable piece of work. I always bore that in mind, that the smartest thing to do was to make an artist look good. To make them look good, because that would make you look good. To look at what they did. What do they do well? What can they do? And sometimes you'd do odd sorts of little extrapolative things. Looking at Michael Zulli [*The Wake*], who sprang to fame drawing animals in *Puma Blues*, and thinking, "What is important about Michael is not that he draws animals but that he draws what he sees." He's actually coming from a different artistic tradition than most people doing comics. Because they learned how to draw comics from drawing comics, and Michael came from a fine arts background combined with a sort of weird, wonderful bohemian-going-from-town-to-town-painting-things-for-people background. Which made me think, "I can do a historical story with him. He would be amazing at that kind of stuff." Just that sense of realism, the sense that somebody's there drawing what he sees, that became useful. With Kelley Jones [*Season of Mists*] – Kelley's a brilliant artist, but there is this wonderful wayward streak to Kelley, which could work against him in comics, where each drawing exists almost separate from any other. Not in terms of not moving – the flow of the comic moves fine – but he was much less concerned about making sure that a character looked like the same character from one panel to another. So in *Season of Mists* I made damn sure that while the angel might not have looked the same from one panel to another, you were always sure that was the angel. Thor's beard may have changed between one panel and the next, but it was only one huge, over-muscled Thor.

*How about writers collaborating with other writers? What makes those collaborations work?*

Well, many of the great collaborative teams have been comedians, comic writers, which is because the hardest thing to know in comedy is whether or not something's funny. The joy of writing *Good Omens* was we were two guys writing it and you knew if you could make the other one laugh it worked. It was that simple. There are so many, many great comedy-writing teams, particularly in the U.K. Going back to Frank Muir and Denis Norden; George and Weedon Grossmith, who wrote *The Diary of a Nobody*, an incredibly funny book; Sellar and Yeatman, who did *1066 and All That*; Arthur Mathews and Graham Linehan, who wrote *Father Ted*, a British TV series; and, of course, Galton and Simpson who, again, were English comedy writers who wrote *Steptoe and Son* and all the great episodes of *Hancock*. Comedy teams – Marty Feldman and Barry Took, who wrote an English comedy show called *Round the Horne*, which – as soon as Marty Feldman left – stopped working, although a lot of the funniest bits may well have been written by Barry Took. But it was the combination of sensibilities that worked. Even in *Monty Python*, you had two writing teams, because you had Palin and Jones as a writing team and you had Chapman and Cleese as a writing team, and then Eric Idle off on his own. *Fawlty Towers* was written by Cleese and Connie Booth. This isn't just meant to be a reductive list of names. My point is, particularly in comedy, collaborations are successful and easy because you're in a room with somebody and you can tell if the joke is funny or not. If the other guy laughs, it stays in. It's nice and easy. In novels, I'd be much harder put to find successful collaborations.

A nice example of where a collaboration works is in *The Talisman* and *Black House*, by King and Straub. Where it works, it works because it is not written by two people, it is written by one two-headed person. *Black House* was not written by Stephen King and Peter Straub, it was written by Stephen King-and-Peter Straub, who together have written a book that neither of them could or would have written. Not that way.

*The whole is greater than the sum of its parts?*

No, the whole is not greater than the sum, the whole is *different* than the sum. The whole is a new person. The whole is a different entity. And it has written a different book. Could Stephen King have written *Black House*? Yes. Could Peter Straub have written *Black House*? Yes. Would it have been that book? No. Why not? Well, partly because the act of collaborating gives you a specific audience. A lot of the time when you're writing your audience is either you or some kind of notion of the reader. The joy of collaboration is it's no longer you and it's no longer the reader, it is – in Stephen King's case – Peter Straub, and – in Pete's case – Steve King. So all of the sudden, Steve is going to be sticking in jazz references to make Pete laugh; Pete will be doing some splattery stuff and he'll say, "Ah, Steve will like this." My favorite moment in writing *Good Omens* was a bit where Terry Pratchett had written the first scene where Adam met Anathema. Terry sent it in, I read that scene, and I looked at it. He had just a line where Anathema mentions a book, and I said, "My God, he missed the ultimate opportunity." And I just went in and wrote a paragraph where Adam says something like, "I wrote a book once. It was really good, especially when the dinosaur came out and fought the cowboys." I just stuck in a paragraph in the middle of something Terry had written, and I sent it back to him and he phoned me up and he said, "I nearly pissed myself laughing." It was one of those perfect moments because I just wrote it to make him laugh in his bit.

*What was it like collaborating with Terry Pratchett?*

People arguing about and discussing *Good Omens* tend to pick the wrong thing to argue about and discuss, which is who wrote what and how much of us wrote which. Which tends to miss the point. The answer is of course that I actually wrote – and not a lot of people know this – ninety percent of *Good Omens*. But the trouble is that Terry wrote the other ninety percent. But what was it like for me, that particular collaboration? It was like going to college. Even at that point Terry was a master craftsman, like a Wedgewood chair-maker or whatever. He could do it. And I had never made a chair before, but I had some ability as a woodworker. So there was a lot of Terry and I talking about this thing that we were building, and Terry would send me off and I'd do my bits, and we'd talk about it. But it was very much a fifty-fifty collaboration between a journeyman and a master craftsman and that's very much how I viewed, and still view, *Good Omens*. It's not that it was my idea – at least fifty percent of it is mine – but for me it was an amazing learning experience: working with Terry, and the way that Terry worked, having no idea where the characters were going to go, stitching it together at the end. And it's not necessarily a method that I would ordinarily use. My tendency is to start at the beginning and then keep writing until I get to the end and then stop. Although it was fun with *American Gods* to have my little short stories on the side so I could go off and do something different.

*Let's switch gears for a second and talk about an entirely different collaboration. I'm curious about the work you did with Japanese filmmaker Hayao Miyazaki. You wrote the English-language script translation of his animated epic* Princess Mononoke. *In a way, you were presenting his work to America; yet there's a lot of you in that version of the film.*

One of the joys of collaboration is knowing when to shut up and let someone else shine. The most important thing in collaboration is not standing in the middle of the stage, showing off. With Miyazaki, I figured that my role was to try and take the subtitles and the literal translation and turn it into dialogue that people could say. The thing that always hurts in watching dubbings of foreign movies is when, all of the sudden, characters are trying to say things that sound stupid. Somebody's done some literal translation, and you know, immediately, if you're listening to something or watching something that's been translated because characters are going to say something like, "Look! Watch! Over there! The things come! Their spears are raised!" You scratch your head and say, "What was that? What did he say?" A lot of what I was trying to do was twofold. One of which was just dialogue that people could say, and the other was to try and fold in enough background surreptitiously. Like the moment when Ashitaka cuts his hair. For an American audience, that only meant one thing which is "He's leaving and he's thinking long hair will get in the way." They completely miss that this is something a samurai does when he becomes a monk. This is an act that literally means: "Once I cut my hair, I am dead. I am no longer." Which, when you understand that he is literally dead to the village, tells you why he doesn't come back to it at the end of the film. So I tried to fold in a little bit of dialogue about "You will cut your hair and become dead to us" and stuff. Just little bits that Miyazaki wouldn't have thought necessary for a Japanese audience, but that I could slide in for an American audience.

*Had you ever done any work like that before?*

No.

*It must have been a pretty interesting experience.*

It was a hugely frustrating, enormously fun, learning experience. The frustrating side of it was I'd keep coming up with lines of amazing beauty and subtlety and tenderness and brilliance and grace and poetry, and if only the characters had opened their mouths one more time I could have used them. You were sort of limited to lip flaps.

*But you were obviously very successful. Roger Ebert, after seeing* Princess Mononoke, *said it was one of the ten best films of 1999. I don't know of too many dubbed films that get that kind of praise in this country.*

It was very nice, having Ebert and having Janet Maslin of *The New York Times* singling out the script translation. It was very lovely.

*We've talked about books, comics, and movies, but you've also written songs, such as those for the goth-folk music duo the Flash Girls. How did that collaboration come about?*

Well, I've known Emma Bull about fifteen years. I met her and Will Shetterly when they came to the U.K. for a convention. I first met Lorraine Garland in about 1991 at a convention in Amherst. The two of them came out to my very first-ever Guy Fawkes party, when I moved to America. A lot of people had brought guitars and violins along and had come out to the Twin Cities and were playing music, and I hesitantly said, "Well, I occasionally write songs. Here's one." And I played them the song that they call "Tea and Corpses," but that I still call "The Tea Song." It was at that party that we tried to get a fire going. The fire didn't actually get going – I didn't know much about lighting fires at that point – and Will and Emma and Lorraine were sitting around playing music. Emma and Lorraine had already played together in Renaissance festivals and stuff, and somehow by the end of that evening Emma and Lorraine had formed a band. I said blithely, "Oh, you can have that song that I did." After that I remember giving Lorraine some lyrics, and saying, "Here's a couple of things that I've written that I don't have tunes for." And she went off. Some of the time I'd write music myself, and sometimes it would be Lorraine, or Lorraine and Emma, doing it. The "All Purpose Folk Song," for example, was just written because I was listening to them play one day at a Renaissance festival and I thought, "They need a song that does this, this, this, and this." So I just wrote one – wrote the lyrics, handed it over to them and said, "Here you go," and two days later it was already in the act. You'll have to ask them what it's like to work with me as a songwriter because, from my perspective, I'm easy-going and a delight to work with.

*Utterly charming?*

Absolutely. In every possible way. [*Laughs.*] And they, of course, would say, "Okay, is this on or off the record? He's a monster."

*Since we're talking about collaborations – in a broad sense, every written story is a collaboration between the writer and the reader. And every reading is a collaboration between the reader and the listener. How important is the connection with the audience to you?*

It's all-important, because if it's not there you're masturbating. There are writers out there who write for themselves. While I write for myself in some sense – I get to be the first reader and I don't like writing things I don't enjoy – the audience and the existence of the audience is the most important thing for me. I am happier with a poem that gets printed in one of the Windling-Datlow anthologies and that ten-thousand people will read than with a movie script that I'll get paid five-hundred times the amount that I get paid for the poem, but which will be read by three film executives and nobody else. It's always fun when it's read and there's that wonderful feeling of interaction, which does change what you're doing. It's fascinating for me doing any kind of live panel or live event or whatever, especially the ones where you just sit up there and you have no idea what's going to happen – you just do it. Because it is a collaboration with the audience. I did a question-and-answer last night, and it was completely a collaboration – you never knew where it was going to go.

*As you become more and more successful you draw larger audiences and bigger crowds to your readings. Does that fire you up? Does it give you more inspiration when you're doing a reading?*

No, it's much more fun when you're doing it out on your own and nobody knows you exist. This has been a very odd convention for me. On the one hand, Boskone is a lovely convention – great con, lovely people, well-run, a good convention – but on the other hand, it's very odd because I'm here but I'm thinking, "I am not at this convention." Normally, if you come to a convention as a writer, you're *at* the convention. And I'm having to come to terms with the fact that "Okay, it's a convention I would love to be at, but I'm not here." I'm working the whole time. If I wander into a room party, I'm not wandering into the room party as some guy wandering into the room party. I'm wandering into the "Hey, look over there... [*whispers behind his hand*]" And I'm sort of thinking, "Well, okay fine," and having to come to terms with the fact that I will probably have to rethink how and when I do conventions in the future – this *kind* of SF convention. I figured I would have one kind of convention and I'm thinking, "It's not working." If I'm going to do this kind of convention in the future, I may as well just do the equivalent of a World Horror or a World Fantasy, and then do things like the International Conference for the Fantastic in the Arts on my own time, where it's just academics and writers, and I can actually meet new people and have conversations in hallways without suddenly realizing that I'm drawing crowds. It's very odd. And not necessarily odd-bad, but odd in the sense of having to think, "I can't do this any more. I'm no longer one of the attendees." You know, Charlie Vess is having a wonderful convention. He's either at the bar or he's over at the art show or he wanders around the dealers room. He's having the kind of convention that I used to have, and can no longer have. So I'm starting to think, "Okay, I might just have to rethink this one."

*Stephen King apparently had similar convention experiences in the late '70s and early '80s.*

I remember Steve telling me the deciding thing about him not going to conventions any longer. He was actually sitting on a toilet and somebody pushed books under the door for him to sign. In the men's room. I think, certainly for him, that was the deciding factor.

*If someone told you that you could only work in one medium – comics, prose, screenwriting, poetry, music – what would it be?*

Is physical survival an option? By which I mean, does it have to be something that will at least pay my mortgage, or can I work in anything? Because if paying the mortgage were not an option, it would probably be radio plays. I'd go straight over to radio drama. I would, of course, have to send the children out in the streets to dance for pennies.

*Lemonade stands would probably be in order.*

Absolutely. But I love the fact that in many ways you're moviemaking, but you can make a movie in a weekend. You get to fuck with the inside of people's heads just like you do in a novel, you get immediacy, the kind of immediacy you can only get with a comic normally. And it's fast and it's fun and it moves in real time. And it's evocative. And your special-effects budget *is* unlimited. For me the greatest line ever uttered in radio is in *The Hitch-Hiker's Guide to the Galaxy*, where Arthur Dent says to Ford Prefect, "Ford, you're turning into an infinite number of penguins." But this is not a line that could or should ever be seen. They tried on the TV show. Suddenly the screen gets covered with penguins. It's like, "You know, that was stupid." If I were directing it, I probably would have just had strange sort of blotchy, smudgy colors going on and close-ups of people's mouths.

*You've mentioned numerous times that you love reading stories to your daughter.*
*Do you think this hones your ability to do public readings?*

I don't know. It certainly keeps a hand in. But the weird thing is, an awful lot of what people, I suppose, think is charisma is in some ways confidence. And, in some ways, is the confidence of knowing that you haven't fucked up too badly in the past when you've done it. You can stick me up on a stage in front of five-thousand people and I will be nervous for the first thirty-five to forty seconds, and then it all comes back. And I can do it. And I don't know how I do it, particularly. I didn't do it this well fifteen years ago, I didn't do it this well *ten* years ago. A lot of it actually came from doing the Guardian Angel Tour stuff for the Comic Book Legal Defense Fund. Actually having to get out there and fill up the air time on my own, and read stories to a theater full of people who had come there to see me and nothing else and it's like, "Wow!" And then doing question-and-answers with an audience and discovering that, on the whole, I could do it.

There are different kinds of panels. This morning's panel was great fun: me, Bob Sheckley, Emma Bull, and Ginger Buchanan trying to discuss the subject with not really a wish to reach a conclusion – although I think some conclusions were reached – but much more from a point of view of "There is a bunch of opinions from people who've done some of this and have something to say." Which is different from "Get up there and talk about stuff." Can I keep an audience entertained for several hours? Sure. How? I don't know. I've been doing it long enough now that the idea of doing it doesn't scare me.

When I was sixteen, I was in a punk band and I remember once getting a beer can in the chin – I still have a little scar under there – and being dragged off to a hospital to have my face stitched up. And I thought, "You know, it's never going to be that bad again." A lot of it for me is wanting to treat people as I would like to be treated. Some of this goes back to me saying some of the stuff about this convention that I'm not comfortable with. Alan Moore was always my standard to "How do you behave toward fans? How do you behave toward the professionals? How do you behave toward people?" One of the things I always liked about Alan was he didn't have one head for fans and one head for writers and one head for famous people. He just treated everybody the same, which was with kindness, politeness, and grace, believing very much that a cult of celebrity had some kind of elevation of status that was fundamentally wrong and fundamentally a lie. Which I think is true, and which is how I've always tried to behave. It's like, "Everybody's here at the convention." I'm always very flattered when anybody wants to get in line and stand there for several hours to see Neil and get something signed, because there's nobody I would stand in line for five hours to see. God could return, and I'd say, "What? Stand in line for five hours?" So I always think it's terribly kind of people, terribly sweet and terribly nice. What I'm starting to figure out though is that there is a weirdness whereby sometimes it's not necessarily up to you whether or not that sort of status thing is there. Alan's line, which I always thought was fascinating, was "Communication is only possible between equals." What I've always tried to do is maintain an equality, because that's where you get the communication. What I have misgivings about is if you get to the point where you have difficulty maintaining equality not because you're not trying to do it, but because people won't let you and they're not comfortable if you do – if you're sitting in a room party, *they* are not comfortable. Then it gets weird. Somebody sent me an e-mail to the website, to the journal, about AggieCon, saying, "Is there some sort of secret wave we could do to let you know that we think you're keen, and slip it in without bothering you?" "Well, actually," I said, "the best way is to just come over and say 'I think what you do is really cool and keen and neat and thank you very much.' Then if you say, 'Gee, what rotten weather we're having!' you might actually get a conversation out of it." [*Laughs.*]

*Darrell Schweitzer commented that, upon hearing you read your book* Coraline *at the 2000 World Horror Convention to an audience, he felt you could become one of this country's truly beloved storytellers. It was that powerful for the audience.*

They were such a nice audience. I started at eleven o'clock at night, and I said, "Look, I'm going to read the whole book to you." And, bless them, they stayed until two o'clock in the morning. They were still there – well, one guy fell asleep – and Darrell was one of them. I just thought they were very brave and very sweet because I got to stand there and find out what my book sounded like if you read it all through.

*Who are your favorite live speakers? What storytellers do you enjoy, and what do you think makes them connect with an audience?*

I love Alan Bennett, who, interestingly, is not a live speaker. He does his stuff in studios mostly. I love poetry read by poets. I love good stand-up. And, by good stand-up, I mean people like Tom Lehrer or Woody Allen. Or Lenny Bruce. You go back to some of these old Lenny Bruce albums and, my God, the acting and the performance and the timing is magnificent. English guys? Alexei Sayle, he's a fascinating performer, fascinating stand-up. Eddie Izzard, who has managed somehow to create an entire vocabulary that didn't exist before in terms of timing and beats. But much more important than any of that is my dad. My dad is a wonderful public speaker. As a kid, I used to watch him get up and talk and I would think, how does he do that? And Richard Curtis, who wrote *Black Adder* and *Four Weddings and a Funeral* and *Notting Hill*. I've been privileged occasionally to be around Richard when he has to get up in front of an audience, normally of major-league celebrities and things, and make a short speech. He says exactly the right thing, and it's funny and it's heart-warming and it's brilliant and it's from the heart. So Dick Curtis is definitely someone who I'd be influenced by as a speaker. But so much of it is just doing it long enough and finding your own voice. It's the same with writing. I know Jerry Garcia said it once, but I know many people have said it before him, which is "Style is the stuff you can't help doing." Style in some ways is the stuff that you do wrong. Because perfect technique would be completely without style. Stuff that lets everybody know that it's you playing is the falling away from perfect technique. So after you've written a few million words, the thing that lets anybody picking up a page read it and say, "Neil wrote that," is style, it's the stuff you can't help doing. You're not thinking, "How can I write this like a Neil Gaiman sentence?" You're writing a sentence. If you've been writing long enough and well enough, then it's going to be a Neil Gaiman sentence, because that's what they do.

*In addition to your creative collaborative work, posterity is going to remember you for the work you've done with the Comic Book Legal Defense Fund. You've raised hundreds of thousands of dollars for the Fund.*

I feel that freedom of speech is an incredibly valuable thing, coming from England, which has no freedom of speech enshrined under law. It has Obscene Publications Acts, it has repressive customs laws, it has all sorts of weird things – laws against horror comics, laws against this and that. Coming out to a country where freedom of speech is actually enshrined in the Constitution is incredibly important. And I felt like somebody coming to a country in which every citizen is, at birth, handed a large gold egg, and most of them find it an embarrassment, and lose it, or hide it, or think maybe things would be better if the gold egg were taken away from everybody and put somewhere where it's not going to offend anyone. It's just weird. And I think the Comic Book Legal Defense Fund is *right*; it's this really good thing. Literature has won most of its battles, comics is still fighting its battles. I'm going to be out on the front line helping it fight the battles. The price of freedom is not cheap in this country. The price of freedom *may* be eternal vigilance, but the price of justice is several hundred thousand pounds per annum, so I'm getting out there and helping to raise it.

BEGINNINGS

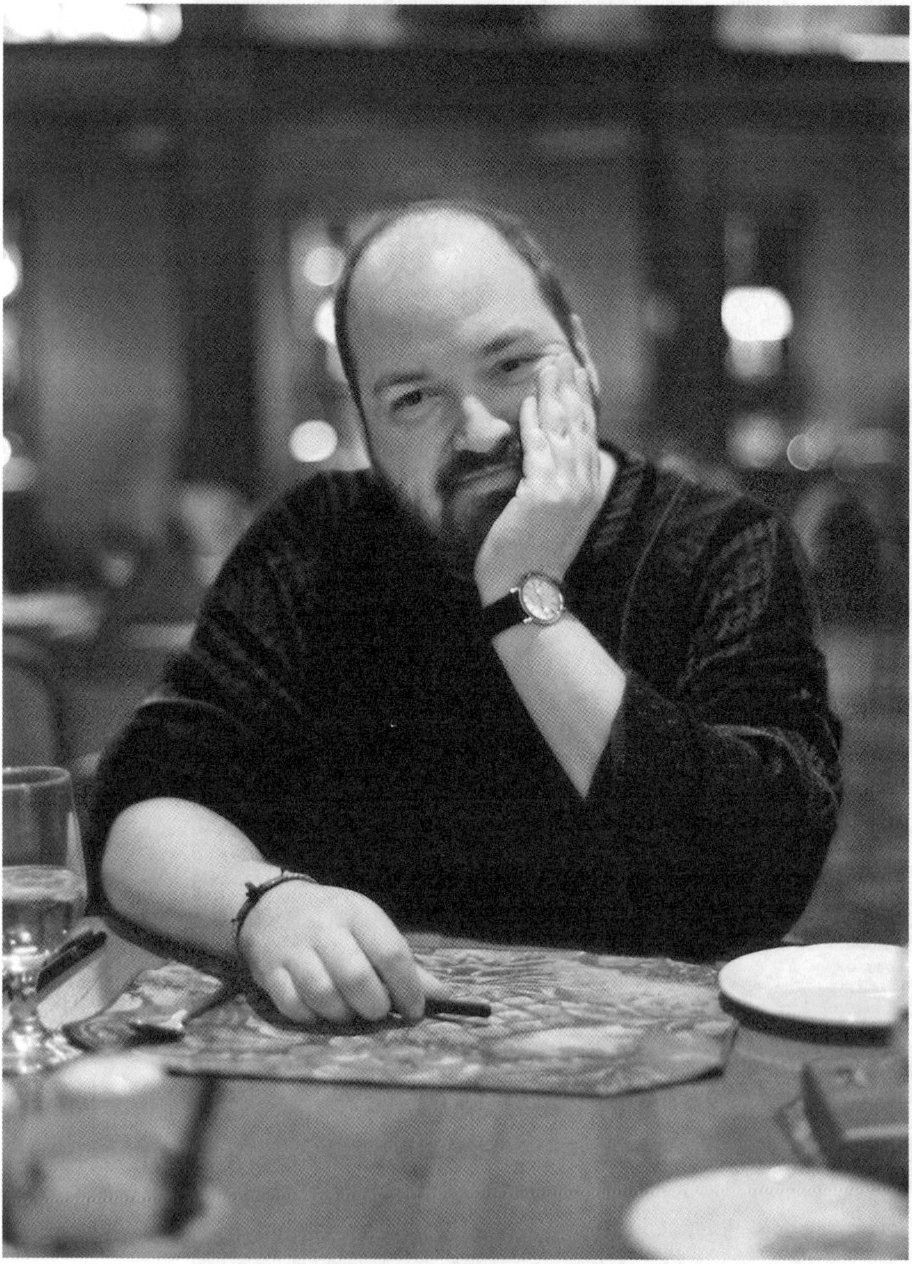

## Dave McKean

# IT'S DIFFICULT TO BELIEVE THAT THE SMILING MAN

IN THE PHOTO ACCOMPANYING THESE WORDS IS GAIMAN'S FIRST AND PERHAPS MOST FREQUENT COLLABORATOR DAVE MCKEAN. TRUE, MCKEAN'S ILLUSTRATIONS FOR GAIMAN'S CHILDREN'S BOOKS *THE DAY I SWAPPED MY DAD FOR TWO GOLDFISH* [WHITE WOLF/BOREALIS, 1997], *CORALINE* AND *THE WOLVES IN THE WALLS* [HARPER COLLINS, 2002 AND 2003, RESPECTIVELY] DISPLAY A SENSE OF WHIMSY. BUT MCKEAN IS ALSO THE ARTIST WITH WHOM GAIMAN CREATED THE DARK WORLDS OF THE GRAPHIC NOVELS *VIOLENT CASES* [TITAN/ESCAPE, 1987], *SIGNAL TO NOISE* [VG GRAPHICS AND DARK HORSE, 1992], AND *MR. PUNCH* [VICTOR GOLLANCZ, 1994], AS WELL AS THE THREE-ISSUE COMIC-BOOK MINI-SERIES *BLACK ORCHID* [DC/ VERTIGO, 1991] AND AN ASSORTMENT OF OTHER TALES FROM THEIR EARLY CAREERS. NEEDLESS TO SAY, MCKEAN IS THE ONLY INDIVIDUAL OTHER THAN GAIMAN TO HAVE HAD A HAND IN EVERY ISSUE OF *SANDMAN*, THROUGH HIS IMAGINATIVE COVERS.

ON HIS OWN, MCKEAN IS HIGHLY REGARDED IN THE COMICS COMMUNITY AS THE ARTIST BEHIND *ARKHAM ASYLUM* AND THE WRITER/ILLUSTRATOR OF *CAGES* AND *PICTURES THAT TICK*. LIKE GAIMAN, HOWEVER, HE WORKS COMFORTABLY IN A WIDE RANGE OF MEDIA. MCKEAN'S PRODUCED BOOKS OF HIS PHOTOGRAPHS (SUCH AS *OPERATION: CLICK* AND *A SMALL BOOK OF BLACK AND WHITE LIES*), CREATED COUNTLESS CD COVERS, WRITTEN JAZZ MUSIC, DIRECTED SHORT FILMS, AND RECENTLY MADE HIS FEATURE-LENGTH DIRECTORIAL DEBUT WITH THE GAIMAN-SCRIPTED *MIRRORMASK* FROM THE JIM HENSON COMPANY.

*You've commented, in past interviews, on how you define art. On how you consider it to be the cutting edge, the avant garde. And on how you feel that what you do is not art. How would you describe what you do?*

Well, I do think it's true. This stuff that's around…I think this is good or bad illustration, or painting, or drawing, or whatever you want to say. But I don't really consider it to be art. Because I think art is like an ongoing conversation. It's defining the language. It's like the difference between pure maths and applied maths – the people who are actually creating, or trying to explain, cutting-edge particle physics and all the people who use all of those equations, and use all that data, and use all that information in their work. I use all that information in my work, but I don't think

I'm necessarily creating the language. I'm the happy beneficiary of other people's creations.

Maybe a little bit in comics. I don't know. I think I've added a note or two. And I'm trying to do the same in film, but I've only just started that, so I'm just kind of trying to come up with some sort of tone of voice that feels like mine. But, no, it's just applied art, and I think it's silly getting hung up on pretending that it's not. It's a pleasure to do it, and it's often the work that communicates to the most people, and it has huge importance. But the only reason I make the distinction is because I have such high regard for the Francis Bacons and the Jim Dines, and, more recently, Picasso – the people who really created this. And it's all very well, when Jackson Pollock comes along and goes "plop, plop, plop," and everybody says, "Well, anybody could have done that." And the fact is they didn't do that. It's easy to have those ideas after somebody else has had the idea, but they didn't do it first, and they didn't do it very well. So that's the only point worth making. Everybody talks about art as if we all agree on what it is, and I think it's a personal thing.

*But how would you describe your work?*

Again, it's a personal thing. It's a way of kind of describing the world or coming to terms with the world or making sense of things. And people happen to find uses for that, so a book cover or a CD cover can be part of that inquiry. Some things are very commercial, they're things I have no real connection with. And to a greater or lesser degree I'll do those jobs or not, but most of it is a work in progress. We all have ways of dealing with life. We write stories about those things, or we have conversations with each other about those things. Or we have children, and we see how that works, and how that explains our relationship with everything. For me it's just making pictures that make sense to me. It feels to me like a nice way of doing it because I can cherry-pick all the things in the world that feel like me. And in a way it's a mirror. I start to see myself in a clearer way: that bit of music from Norway really feels right to me; and every time I visit Venice I feel at home; and every time I see a picture by Francis Bacon, or somebody like that, I understand that emotion. So put all those together, and that's me.

I saw Terry Gilliam in Telluride, and he was saying he let some people make a documentary about his failed attempt to make his Don Quixote [film]. *Lost in La Mancha* was the name of the documentary. And obviously everybody was asking, "Why did you let these people make this documentary?" Because it was completely hands-off, no control, complete access. He said the reason was that he saw a little bit of the documentary [*The Hamster Factor and Other Tales of Twelve Monkeys*] made on a previous film. (These [same] people [Keith Fulton and Louis Pepe] had come in and shot some stuff.) He was watching it, and there was this person jumping around and hysterical, with this ridiculous grin all the time, waving his arms. And that was him, he just didn't recognize himself at all. So he wanted somebody to come in and make a documentary so he could find out who he was.

*I've seen some of your own short films. They look like they cost much more than they apparently did.*

The fact that they look like they cost *anything* means that they look like they cost much more than they actually did.

*Is this due to your grasp of the possibilities of digital technology?*

I've just applied a lot of the things that I do in my still images to film. They haven't really contributed to my family's standard of living. [*Laughs.*] But all of the work has really evolved from my own personal projects. I haven't really come up with any preconceptions. I've pulled a lot of favors. (That's what everybody in the film industry does – the first job everybody does for nothing in the hope that when the next one comes in with a budget they'll call you again.) And I'm not hung up on reality. When you're trying to make everything hyper-real and photographic, that's expensive, because it's time-consuming to program all that stuff; and then the rendering time is huge. You're talking a lot of man-hours and that's expensive. And, at the end of the day, I don't have any connection with that stuff. It tends to just look flat to me. All the big *Star Wars*-y films and their huge technical exercises and very extraordinary effects…they don't tend to move me at all. Once the first few vistas appear on screen, I'm…kind of done, really. I've had enough. It's a bit like flipping through those books of air-brushed science-fiction pictures – you've seen a couple…

*You pretty much get it?*

Yeah. You've had enough, really. I don't need a whole film of it. I want some emotion and I want to be surprised. And I would like a non-literal and more expressive use of computers. And the fact is, computers can go anywhere, digital stuff can go anywhere. Why we're spending all this time on *Final Fantasy* creating live humans, as realistic as possible, with that slightly plastic edge which looks a bit strange… I think, at the end of the day, they're markers in time in a technical history of cinema. But I don't think they're really any place to go to put up a cul-de-sac. I think, slowly, *Amelie* and *Being John Malkovich* and *Fight Club* and some of these films really starting to build the digital technology into the narrative in a very seamless, translucent, expressive way, dealing with the emotions, not just pretty pictures…

*You recently had a chance to do some of this yourself in your first feature-length film,* MirrorMask. *How did this project develop?*

*MirrorMask* is a very commercial, family fantasy story, that I've written with Neil. The basic premise of the story is a very traditional fairy tale. It's an *Alice in Wonderland* type, *Wizard of Oz*-y – very traditional. The events that happen in the story are more unusual, but the basic frame plays with very traditional fairy-tale aspects.

What happened was somebody at Sony had noticed that *Labyrinth* and *Dark Crystal*, over the years, had made a significant amount of money. They went to Henson and did a two-picture deal. (One of the pictures is a Kermit movie.) Columbia-Tri-Star said, "Well, you've done these fantasy films in the past, which were Jim Henson's pet projects; if you can do one really cheaply, we'll just give you the money." And so they sat around and figured out, actually, that they couldn't do it. They could not. I mean, *Dark Crystal* cost about twenty million, twenty years ago. And they just couldn't do it. They couldn't make a Muppet creature thing, and kind of gave up on it. Lisa [Henson] saw my film *The Week Before*, and, during all of that, Lisa [Henson] asked Neil if he would write a film, and he said, "Well, no, I don't really want to do that. I'll just come up with a few possible ideas and you can give them to other writers." And then Lisa came back and said, "Well, actually, like *The Week Before*, what if [Dave] directed it?" And Neil said, "Right. If Dave's going to direct it, I want to write it." So we just put our cards on the table and started to do it. Even though the budget was minuscule and there was no real money in it or anything, it [was] a great opportunity.

*Did you and Neil first work together while you were still in art school?*

I was just coming to the end of art school. I was still in art school. It was about 1986. We were working on a magazine called *Borderline*, that never happened. The editor was a shady, flaky character, with a name that turned out to be not his name at all. [*Laughs.*] (I told [my wife] Clare who this guy was, and she said, "Wow. That's a great name" – and it really was – but she was so disappointed when she met him and couldn't believe that was his real name, and sure enough it turned out to be David Smith or something.) But the nicest thing about it was that we had these meetings every month. All the people involved would come over to London, and show what we'd been doing. Only a couple of the other people ended up going professional, which included a guy who calls himself D'Israeli.

*He inked a portion of* Sandman *[The Kindly Ones, Chapters 2-6, issues 58-62].*

He was one of that gang, and a couple of others. But Neil was obviously serious and I was pretty serious at the time. And we just liked each other's company.

*How much work did you produce together for* Borderline*?*

We weren't working together. Neil was writing, I think, two or three stories for other illustrators. And all of those got only between half and one chapter finished before we all realized it was never actually going to happen. And I was writing and drawing two stories – "Going to California," which I finished the first chapter of, and "The Fox," which I [also] finished the first chapter of. So I think I got further than most. Because I was self-sufficient, so I just got on with it. I was happy with what I was doing at the time. I'm glad it never saw print, I must admit. But Neil suggested that we work together on something, and he had *Violent Cases* all ready. He had written that as part of a writer's workshop. There's a real close little community of fantasy writers and science-fiction writers, and he was locked into all that. He knew them all. And they were all centered around people like John Clute, and that gang – and Colin Greenland was there. I think it was actually Colin who said, "This is really good," when Neil read it out. And I think it was actually Colin that suggested the name "Violent Cases." Neil didn't have a name for it.

*You chose to depict the narrator of that story as Neil.*

Yes, that was my decision. It sounded like it was in Neil's tone of voice, the narrative was written in the way that Neil speaks, which is quite precise – he goes, "Ummm," for a long time and then you get a precise text. I don't know many people who speak in perfect prose, but Neil's one of them. [*Laughs.*] And that seemed to be the tone of voice of the book. He was the ideal model for it, and his son was the little boy.

Violent Cases *is what led to* Black Orchid, *and* Arkham Asylum, *which you did with Grant Morrison.*

Yes.

*A lot of people still point to the "memory trilogy" of* Violent Cases, Signal to Noise, *and* Mr. Punch *as the finest work you and Neil have done together. Do you feel that's the case?*

Yeah, I think so. I like the kids' books as well. I'm very happy with the kids' books. But I think we started on the right side. We did *Violent Cases* first, and that kind of planted our flag.

*"This is who we are?"*

This is who we are, and we're not necessarily interested in genre stuff. We are interested in doing the kind of stories that we're interested in. Not huge marketing-concept-driven things, just these interesting little stories. And then running parallel to that were these commercial ventures. You know, *Black Orchid* was a commercial venture. We had to pitch them a character, and we had to try and come up with something about it that made it interesting for us, which at the time was some sort of ecological message. Which was pretty naïve, looking back on it, but we were kids really, and we were trying hard to please. We probably tried too hard. And *Arkham*, for me, was, again, on that rung. It was on the commercial rung. [I] was trying to buy a house. I was a working illustrator, and I needed a job. But none of these books were taken on with great reservations. We were happy to do them. I was happy to do an ecological book where, at the end, there isn't a big fight. It's just somebody saying, "No, I'm not going to fight." I was happy to do it. I was happy to do *Arkham Asylum* and spend a while trying to come up with something that was insane, and that took apart these overblown characters and tried to strip them back to a kind of mythological character. It's only with the benefit of hindsight that you look at these things and see all the stuff that Grant wrote, all these levels that Grant put in, and all this sort of visual baggage that I put in is based on this tiny little foundation. This tiny little foundation is Batman. He just can't support it, and it doesn't really work. The people who do Batman comics the best are the ones who just know that it's a sort of young boy's power fantasy entertainment and get on and do good fun ones of those. And great, they should be doing that. But I'm not interested. And really after *Arkham*, I was ready to pack up. I didn't want to do it.

*You'd had enough of the mainstream, high-concept book? It had left a bad taste?*

Well, yeah, I thought I wanted to be on one side, and wanted to be part of the club. And DC are lovely people. Karen [Berger] was great. Neil and I went over to DC – they wined and dined us. They introduced us around to everybody, and it was great. I went to a first few conventions; everybody suddenly was interested in my opinion and it was exciting. But…actually, that was not really what I wanted, and I was very happy to leave DC. Because what I really want to do is just do the work that I enjoy. And that's not really part of that. I mean, Karen is very supportive, but I don't consider them to be my publisher, in the sense of…when I've finished a book they'll come and say, "Right, what would you like to do next?" – it's not like I'm in a relationship – "Would you fancy doing a *Sandman* book, or is there some sort of Vertigo character we could do?" And if I do approach them with a book, they're enthusiastic, but it's tempered and "How can we make this work?" and "Why doesn't he just want to do a *Sandman* book rather than make our lives trouble?" So I don't consider them my publisher.

*Yet even if one were to only look at the work you've done for DC, they could still get a sense of your work's evolution.* Black Orchid *and* Arkham Asylum *featured some lovely painted illustrations, and your* Sandman *covers found you experimenting even more, with collage. Could you explain the direction your work took with those covers? For a lot of people, those covers were what first screamed "Dave McKean."*

A lot of that stuff started in art school, and a lot of it comes from the stories, and what I think is appropriate for the book. A lot of it was in the spirit of the times. That little group – Alan Moore and Jamie Delano and Grant and Neil and me and a bunch of others – we all felt that we…We had no awe of "We're working for DC Comics and aren't we lucky?" and all that. We really just wanted to break it all apart, and remodel it in our image. We were very happy to do that and they were very happy to let us do that, because the books were selling very well. And they didn't understand why, so they just said, "Go and do that…thing. Go and do what you're doing." It was a very lucky moment in time. But not now. You couldn't do that now, and you certainly couldn't do that before then. We just happened to hit the cusp, the golden window of opportunity, and pushed it as hard and wide as possible. The art style in *Black Orchid* was just appropriate – as far as I could see – for that, and all of the things after was just trying to find what was appropriate for that particular story or cover. So *Black Orchid* was about… Somewhere, back in 1940, the people who were drawing comics looked at real people, and this style was developed because they looked around at real people. The years passed and nobody looked at real people any more, they looked at those comics. And then the next one looked at *those* comics. I just wanted *Black Orchid* to say, "Let's start this back again. This is what real people look like, remember? This is what real people look like!" And it was never meant to be a style for life, it was just meant to be getting everything back to zero again, and then, "Okay, now let's expand and explode and we'll express the emotions of the characters, but from a point of reality. But not this sort of strange Galapagos-like evolution, on one track."

*Which of those old illustrators did you admire?*

The one I still really love – and I just think he's amazing – is Winsor McCay. I think he's brilliant. Every couple of years go by, and I'll see the book on the shelf and pick it up again. It's like rediscovering how great he is. So he's the man for me.

*Like yourself, he was both an artist and filmmaker. And he certainly was one who, as you said, "defined the language."*

Yeah, he was the pioneer in animation, and a terrific draftsman. He almost invented comics. The way those first comics evolved, he saw how to best use the grammar, almost immediately. And it evolved very quickly over a period of about one year. I think he was wonderful. And over the years, from being a kid and teenager, I've liked lots of different things and lots of different work, but none of them have really stayed I would say...

*Are there any comics artists presently working whom you admire?*

Well, I think the best comics artist who's ever been is Lorenzo Mattotti, and he's currently working. He's doing books still, and I just think he's in a league of his own. He's Italian, but his books are available in this country. *Fires* is available, his *Jekyll and Hyde* is available. But the best things are his own books. *Fires* is great, and he's done a couple of little black-and-white books: *The Man at the Window, Stigmata*. They are just extraordinary.

*What is it about his work that you respond to?*

He manages to draw the essence of the people. He manages to actually draw their motion, their movement. So you *feel* the movement. It's not a description of movement, it *is* the movement.

*That's a kind of holy grail for many comics artists. To capture that quality without distancing the reader with obvious mechanics.*

Really, yeah. And I love his painting. It's vivid and full of life and color, and typical Italian love of brightly-colored foods, and all that kind of stuff. It's all there. His books have a lovely rhythm to them. They start with one or two lines on a page, with people on the horizon, and then slowly more and more, and then the crowds come in, and there's more and more. And you really feel it right inside you. It's like music. It's comics like music, and I kind of aspire to that, really. I think he's wonderful. And many others. I'm trying to think of Americans…David Mazzucchelli…Art Spiegelman is terrific. Richard Sala I like very much, I think he's American. And then there are people all over the world. And there were these little groups – the Valvoline group in Italy is where Mattotti came from; there were a couple of others as well. There's a guy called Stefano Ricci, who's brilliant, stunning. Jose Muñoz, from Argentina, is brilliant. Lots of them. I just tend not to like this sort of mainstream stuff, and a lot of the painted work that's come since…again, I find it kind of stodgy and it doesn't really do much for me. But I still love comics.

*Getting back to your work with Neil for a moment – you were involved with* Sandman *from the beginning. The initial design for the Sandman character was conceived by Neil, but how much work did you do on the character's look?*

I think Neil had a pretty good idea of what he wanted. He had done little sketches, little doodle sketches, so I think a lot of it was coming from Neil to start with. I know a friend of ours at the time – who was also working on *Borderline* and ended up working at Titan Books: Leigh Baulch – did some drawing. And I did a couple of drawings, based on Bono, I seem to remember. I had just seen a U2 video, and Bono was dressed in a long black cloak wandering around the misty Irish countryside. I said, "There's the man! That's the Sandman!" So I did them based on Bono. No, I think the defining couple of factors were Neil's to start with.

*Neil said he felt very freed by your covers to take the stories anywhere he wanted to go.*

I think that was one of those rules that we were bucking. Once characters were designed, they became like animation templates – you know, "This is the character from the front, from the side; this is him happy, this is him sad" – and never strayed from that. Sandman didn't seem to me to be like Superman. He wasn't a visual thing, he was concept, a fluid thing. I think Neil kind of understood that, and that's what I wanted to do with the covers. But I always felt it a shame that a lot of the illustrators who came in felt hidebound by just one particular visual image. I think there were plenty of other places to go with the character. I'm not a big fan of manga or whatever, but I was glad at least that [Yoshitaka] Amano made him Japanese [in *The Dream Hunters*], and made it a manga kind of character. I think that's good. One or two others tried to play with it a little bit, but he could have gone so many other ways. Because he's an idea as much as anything. He's not a strict, real person. Not that Superman's a real person (I'm not that deluded), but you can see what I mean.

*I see your point. The Sandman could have been vapor or a particular shade of color.*

It really could go anywhere. There was opportunity for that, and that's certainly what the covers were trying to do. The covers, I think, were trying to be a filter. And that's what I try to do with *my* covers – *Cages* covers and things like that – they're a filter. You see the story through the filter of that cover – this is the sort of texture and color and area and emotion and feeling that you're going into. And it doesn't have to be literal. Then you're into the story, but you've entered the story through that filter.

*So no matter how the interior art appeared, it could never completely dispel the emotions first generated by the cover. The cover would say, "Don't get too comfortable."*

Yes. By the time the fan base was there, Neil was off and running and it was great. But I think the one thing the covers helped, initially, was peaking people's expectations, and attracting an audience that maybe would not pick up a regular comic.

*I asked Neil this question, and I'd like to ask you as well, since you've also worked in a wide range of media – out of all the media in which you've worked, if you could only choose one, which would it be? What tool would you choose?*

[*Laughs.*] It would be the piano. I really miss not being able to play the piano, if I'm away from home. Because I try and play every day. The immediacy of music and improvising or whatever...

*You find that's the shortest route to the brain?*

Yes... But it would probably just be drawing. Again, it would probably just be drawing. I could live without the computer, and I could live without the photography, I suppose. Just the drawing, a pot of ink, and a scritchy-scratchy pen.

*Of course, it's your use of combined media that gives a lot of your work its distinct flavor. Could you talk a little bit about your collage technique?*

It is a mixture. The things often have a bit of life of their own and they evolve in different ways, but usually – unlike [someone] who tries lots of things and then scratching the original idea and reacting to it – it's just different personal ways of working. If I have an idea that I think is right, that's my template. If I've got a box, that's my box. And I want to make sure whatever I'm doing *explains* that idea. It's the idea that's the key, it's the only important thing, really. And if I have any doubts about what I'm doing (especially if it's a book, or a long project, and I'm spending a year on something), if along the road I have any doubts about why I'm doing this, and I start to lose focus, I can always go back to that core idea, and that's the reason why I was involved, and that's what I'm doing it for, and that's what sort of keeps me on the straight and narrow – the content. The form, the way it appears, is up for interpretation and is up for play, and things can happen to change it. And that's fine, but so long as it expresses what I want it to express. I tend to know what the image is going to be made of, and I just go away and find those things. Some of them need to be objects, photographs, some of them need to be bits of type or bits of paper laid on the scanner, or some of them need to be drawings or paintings. And I just get them all together, and sweep them up and scan everything into the box, and then start seeing how they work off each other. And sometimes I was wrong and I need to go and do something else; sometimes the computer can add something. I try not to overuse the filters and the Photoshopy effects and all that kind of stuff. But sometimes they're very helpful and can make things work. It's fairly self-explanatory really. I mean, most of the images are pretty obvious I think.

*What has influenced your collage technique?*

People like John Heartfield, who was working in the '30s and the '40s, with photo collage, in a very basic way, without any of the tricks of the trade that people use now – you know, putting these photo collages together and then re-photographing them to make a sort of smooth image. You can still just see little bits of edges and little bits of how it comes together. But they weren't just for effect: he was doing very important work, anti-fascist stuff, working during the war. All of that had a real, powerful, important point. A lot of this sort of photocollage stuff around is really effect. John Heartfield's stuff was a big influence. It amplified to me that these things have a context – you can't just rip these things out of context. Surrealism *was* a political movement. You can't rip it out of the 1920s and just put it down now and hope that it has the same impact or effect. You're just playing with the surface, you're not dealing with the reason why it was there in the first place – the political systems that it was reacting against, the art, at the time, it was reacting against – these things *do* have a context. You can't just take the form and try and slant it and hope that it will be okay.

*With your short films, as you've said, you seem to have taken the lessons you learned from other media and very much tried to incorporate them into film. You're in a Dave McKean world in those films. You're inside one of those Dave McKean collages, and you can physically move around in it.*

I'm very glad that that's what comes across, because that's definitely the intention. I'm a big fan of Walerian Borowczyk, who's a very strange filmmaker. His most infamous film is *The Beast* (*La Béte*) but he started as an animator, and a poster designer. And his animated films are extraordinary – he did a film called *The Game of the Angels*, a short film, and it's generally considered to be one of the top-ten animated films of all time, a huge influence on Terry Gilliam. They're amazing, they're really exquisite. Then he started making live action, and the first one he did was a film called *Goto, Island of Love* – which is very strange, interesting, medieval; a big influence on *Monty Python and the Holy Grail*. Terry Jones loved those films. [Borowczyk] was always interested in erotica as well, and his early shorts had some of that, and they were fascinating. But slowly he started to become more and more like a French soft-porn guy, to his lowest point, where he was doing *Emmanuelle 5* or something. All of that disappeared – all of the interesting, fascinating stuff disappeared, and he just sort of ended up doing…that. I'd known his animated work, I knew his posters, and then I realized that he made feature films. I was so disappointed when I saw these loads of films. Because it had all gone, it had all evaporated. And, again, I'm determined that that shouldn't happen. I want the films to feel like me and everything else, the music and everything else. It's my world.

*We just live in it.*

Yeah. [*Laughs.*] Well, that's the work I love, when I feel like I've had access to somebody else's head for a while, and seen the world through their eyes for a while. That's a wonderful thing, I think. I mean Terry does that – Gilliam does that – and several others do that.

*You were Neil's first collaborator and he told me that, in some ways, you are still the most exciting for him to work with. Do you feel your working relationship with Neil has changed much over the years?*

I don't think it has really, no. We've both grown up as people. We started as very different people, and I think, if anything, we've probably gone in opposite directions to a degree. We're very different people.

*In what sense?*

We have very different tastes. I think we probably have different priorities in life. Inevitably we're just very different people. But we do have a sort of cross in common.

*I think Neil's said it's a Venn diagram.*

[*Laughs.*] A Venn diagram – we do have a big chunk in the middle that's common to both of us. And we do have a respect of each other. I think the other thing that's really helped us is we have lives away from each other. If we were like Simon and Garfunkel we'd be at each other's throats, but we have very happy lives away from each other. And, even better, when we've been away from each other for a while and we come back together, we've brought all this other stuff with us, all these other experiences back with us.

*Do you dump it on the table and say, "Look what I've got," to each other?*

Yeah, absolutely, and all of that I think is healthy and has worked in our favor. I love working with Neil. He's a complete professional writer – he can just write anything. And that's something I *can't* do. I can't just write anything. If it's something that really moves me or if something really affects me deeply, maybe I can do it. I can't sit down and write professionally. Maybe that's just a practice thing. It's a particular talent that Neil has that I admire greatly. And he's a very *honest* writer – all of his feelings are there on the page. We have a good time together.

The Wolves in the Walls *was the most recent children's book you worked on together, and* MirrorMask *is the first major film on which you've collaborated. Have you and Neil spoken about any other potential projects lately?*

Oh, yeah. We've talked about all sorts of things. Neil wrote some lyrics, and I wrote the music, to some songs. And I've started recording that, so at some point there will be a CD of songs. We've got another kids' book that we wrote as a sort of long poem that I'd like to do. I think I like the kids' book thing – just doing one kids' book every two or three years is nice. We have a lot of fun doing them. As far as longer form projects go, we're really looking more at films. Obviously *Signal to Noise* involves both of us, although I've kind of taken up the reins in a way. And *MirrorMask* is a co-production.

*Are there any other comics projects on the horizon?*

I loved doing that book of short comics – *Pictures That Tick*. I had such a lovely time doing it, it was a real pleasure. And I've been thinking about it. Over the next few years, if I did a few books, another volume of that and maybe a longer book, and a kids' book, I would have a very happy life. And if I choose to make these films, I'm going to be miserable and stressed out and depressed. But I'm going to make the films. I have to do it. That's my realization – I just have to do it. There's no logical explanation.

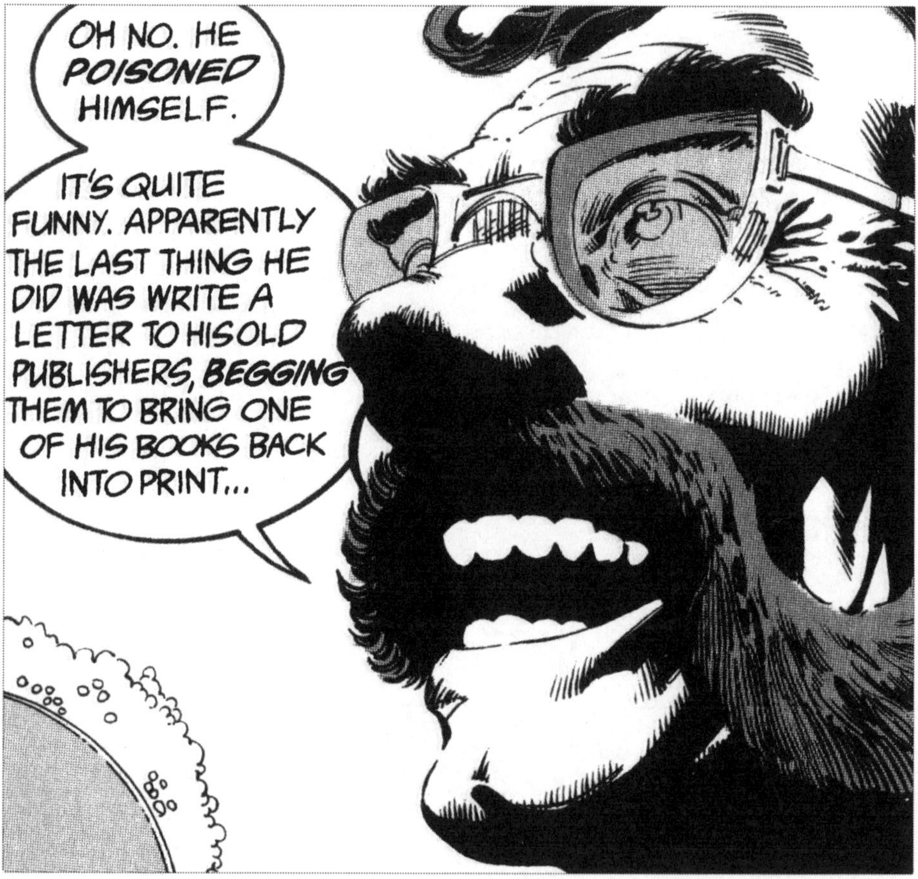
OH NO. HE *POISONED* HIMSELF.
IT'S QUITE FUNNY. APPARENTLY THE LAST THING HE DID WAS WRITE A LETTER TO HIS OLD PUBLISHERS, *BEGGING* THEM TO BRING ONE OF HIS BOOKS BACK INTO PRINT...

Kim Newman as the host of *The Book Nook*, from *Sandman* 17, "Calliope," page 15. Art by Kelley Jones and Malcolm Jones III. © 2004 DC Comics.

# KIM NEWMAN MAY BE BEST KNOWN TO *SANDMAN* FANS

AS THE VISUAL INSPIRATION FOR THE HANDLE-BAR-MUSTACHIOED HOST OF *THE BOOK NOOK* (AS RENDERED BY KELLEY JONES IN ISSUE 17, "CALLIOPE"), BUT NEWMAN'S CONNECTION TO GAIMAN GOES BACK MUCH FURTHER, AND DEEPER, THAN THIS AMUSING HOMAGE. LIKE GAIMAN, NEWMAN BEGAN HIS CAREER AS A JOURNALIST AND FILM CRITIC IN LONDON, BEFORE THE TWO MEN WORKED TOGETHER ON A SERIES OF HUMOROUS ARTICLES FOR BRITISH MAGAZINES, AND SOLD THEIR FIRST BOOK, *GHASTLY BEYOND BELIEF: THE SCIENCE FICTION AND FANTASY BOOK OF QUOTATIONS* [ARROW, 1985].

A PROLIFIC WRITER OF PROSE AND CRITICISM, NEWMAN CONTINUES TO SERVE AS CONTRIBUTING EDITOR TO SUCH BRITISH FILM PERIODICALS AS *EMPIRE* AND *SIGHT AND SOUND*. HE'S ALSO WON THE INTERNATIONAL HORROR GUILD AWARD AND THE BRAM STOKER AWARD (FOR *HORROR: 100 BEST BOOKS*, CO-EDITED WITH STEPHEN JONES); THOUGH HE IS PERHAPS BEST KNOWN TO FANTASY AND HORROR FANS AS THE AUTHOR OF THE BEST-SELLING *ANNO DRACULA* AND ITS TWO SEQUELS, *THE BLOODY RED BARON* AND *DRACULA CHA CHA CHA*.

*Your first published book,* Ghastly Beyond Belief, *was also Neil's – except, of course, for his biography,* Duran Duran: The First Four Years of the Fab Five *[Proteus, 1984]. But he may prefer we disregard that one.*

That's right. [*Laughs.*] I got him that job. In fact, my first published book was *Nightmare Movies*, which came out from the same publisher, Proteus Books. It's a book about horror films – though *that* particular edition is very hard to find. It was later brought out by Bloomsbury in a perfect – or, if not perfect, a *much-improved* – edition. Everybody has a bad time with their first publisher and we were no exceptions.

*Was* Nightmare Movies *published before* Ghastly Beyond Belief?

It was certainly the same year, 1985. Certainly it was written before. I was working with Neil on *Ghastly Beyond Belief*, because we did that *very* soon after we met… Proteus, who did *Nightmare Movies*, also did a bunch of books on rock stars and film stars, and I gave Neil the contact, so, for better or worse, it's my fault he did the Duran Duran book. I suspect none of the people involved in that are even in the publishing game any more. They certainly went spectacularly bankrupt, owing all of us money. [*Laughs.*]

*Had you and Neil met through the British Fantasy Society?*

Yes. They used to have, and still do in fact (I'm going to one this week), open-night things, which are meetings in pubs in London. I don't think it was the *first* one of those that I'd been to, but Jo Fletcher, who's now an editor, actually introduced me and Neil. Certainly she was the person who asked me to go along to that thing.

It was that evening that Neil floated the idea to do that book, *Ghastly Beyond Belief*, although he first wanted to call it *Beam Me Up, Scotty*. I volunteered to do half of it, and so it was that we met and agreed to collaborate within about twenty-five minutes. It was Neil, however, who made the contact who sold the book. Faith Brooker, who was then at Arrow, was as responsible for shaping what the book turned out to be. Neil wanted to do something that was almost a serious science-fiction book of quotations, with a humorous element. Faith guided it toward being a funny book. Probably, of all our books, it's one of the hardest to find. It may need a bit more explanation: it consists of mostly humorous quotes from science-fiction books and films. Neil did the books and I did the films; although the demarcation isn't quite as strict as that. I put in a few book things and he put in a few film things. We originally asked somebody else, a friend of mine, to do the comics, and he didn't deliver. Neil threw together a whole section on comics that ended up not being in the book, because the manuscript was vastly over length. I turned my stuff in, and then Neil, as is his wont, was late. I remember Faith calling me up and saying it was too long and we had to do something about it. I think Neil has still got tons of serious reference books somewhere lying around, that still haven't been used.

*That may explain why some of the book's quotes aren't really humorous. Was that due to the two of you putting in some quotes you felt were simply noteworthy?*

We thought that if it was called *The Science Fiction and Fantasy Book Of Quotations*, it needed a few. Neither of us were particularly interested in stuff like *Star Trek* or *Star Wars*, so that sort of stuff isn't really in there; which, probably, if you were doing that book seriously, you'd have to do. The few bits of science fiction that have actually entered the language in books of quotations are in there, mostly stuff from *Nineteen Eighty-Four* and *2001*, *Forbidden Planet*, things like that. So all that stuff is there – "Klaatu barada nikto." It was a quickie paperback book [*laughs*], and we would probably do it a bit differently today. Also, when we were doing quotes from rubbishy paperbacks, we over-relied a bit on Lionel Fanthorpe. He had to write his books over long weekends so it's only natural that some were not quite good. There were some supposed titans in the field whose prose was just as bad, and we should have included more of those. Probably, in retrospect, it's a good thing we didn't, because we would've made even more enemies at the beginning of our careers than we did.

*A curious thing about* Ghastly Beyond Belief *is that there were, supposedly, nine-thousand copies printed, seven thousand of which sold to New Zealand or Australia.*

No – I think they were *remaindered* to New Zealand or Australia. [*Laughs.*] That might be true. Even today, publishers very rarely tell authors things like print runs. I know we had a two-thousand pound advance but we never earned out. We got the advance, but we never got royalties. Actually, it was a paperback original, so that was a pretty good deal. [*Laughs.*] For us, back then, it was very good.

*But it was only published in the U.K.?*

Yes, there was only one edition. It was never even reprinted. And fair enough, in many ways. It was not that successful a book. It was a hard book to know where to place in bookshops. It was *science fiction*, but it wasn't *fiction*, so, yes, it ended up being mixed in on the shelves with whatever else was there. You would find it squeezed between the Asimovs and the Philip Dick paperbacks. Also, it was one of those books that *fans* like, but it didn't have much of a constituency outside people who knew this stuff already. It may well have been difficult to sit down and read a whole book of funny things without getting humor fatigue after a while. But I still occasionally pull it out and use it as a reference book. It's earned some kind of permanent place on the shelf. [*Laughs.*]

*With the success that you and Neil have enjoyed since then, has there been talk of a reissue? Perhaps among specialty-press publishers?*

I don't know if anyone's ever taken it to Neil. He actually owns fifty-one percent of it, so it's absolutely his decision. Faith, who bought it in the first place, at one point was thinking of doing it, after she got a job at another publisher. She liked working with both of us. She had the idea of mucking around and maybe bringing it out in a form which would have more illustrations (it didn't have any illustrations). It didn't get particularly far. Hey, if someone wants to bring it out again, I've got no problem. I certainly wouldn't want to go through the trouble of updating it, but it's a fun book. We particularly liked the cover, which is the only occasion either of us have had where we sat down at a pub and drew a little sketch and put all the things we wanted on a cover and they went and did it.

*As you said, you worked primarily on the book's film quotes. Do you have a particular favorite?*

"Take that, you thing from another world, you!" which is Porky Pig from *Duck Dodgers in the 24 1/2 Century*. [*Laughs.*] Actually, I like most of them.

*I've always had a fondness for "Decrucify the Angel or I'll melt your face off," from* Barbarella.

[*Laughs.*] I like that one, too.

*Some of them are intentionally humorous.*

Yes. "Decrucify the Angel" is *kind of* deliberately funny, and I'd obviously think that "…you thing from another world, you" is. And a few other things in there are. I think, sometimes, maybe moreso with film than with books, we were quoting jokes that the people who wrote them knew were jokes. There are also things like a big section of lines from posters, and there, I think, they are intended to be witty, or hyperbolic, or to provoke a reaction. So they're not inept. I know that was the first thing that was done on the book. The sample pages I contributed to the prospectus that sold it were the poster lines. That was before the book had really taken form, so I think it's probably more like a complete reference guide because it does include *Alien* and *2001* – serious, important films – as well as the jokier lines or the stupider lines.

*There's a perhaps intentionally tongue-in-cheek line in the book's biography section, which describes you and Neil as "aspiring writers."*

Yes, Faith wrote that. I personally would never have written that. [*Laughs.*] And I seemed to have been mildly taken aback when that turned up in print. That's not what I would describe myself as.

*Perhaps "aspiring fiction writers" would have been more appropriate.*

Yes, in fact, I think at that time I'd already sold fiction. I sold my first short story to *Interzone* and that came out in '84, a year earlier, while I was working on *Ghastly Beyond Belief*. Neil had sold bits of fiction about then as well.

*At this time, you also first discussed, with Neil and Faith, what later became your trilogy of vampire novels.*

Oh, that's right! I don't think that Faith or Neil even remember this, but certainly I remember that conversation. We were kicking around for things to do, and that particular idea spins off from a footnote to a dissertation I wrote at university on turn-of-the-century apocalyptic fictions. In discussing invasion narratives like the Battle of Dorking in *The War Of The Worlds*, I put in a footnote that said, "*Dracula* could be considered an invasion narrative." I filed away the notion that there was a way of doing a book like *Dracula* with that. So, yes, I do remember saying, "It might make an interesting trilogy." Then nothing happened. [*Laughs.*] I didn't actually put pen to paper for at least ten years. I did a novella version of *Anno Dracula* before doing the novel.

*"Red Reign," for Stephen Jones's* Mammoth Book of Vampires.

In 1990, 1991. And Neil and I talked about writing lots of things that we never did actually get around to doing. There was a horror novel called *The Creeps*, about tramps turning into monsters on the London Underground, with a hero who was an investigative reporter for a porn magazine; and a humor book called *How to Lose Friends and Irritate People*. We did lots of things that did actually appear, although mostly in very disreputable areas. The *Anno Dracula* thing was like yarning away at the pub, sharing our ideas. We did sort of feed into each other quite a bit. For instance, Neil wrote a story very early on called "We Can Get Them For You Wholesale." I wrote the last two lines of that. It was something like "We have to be asked." Yes, that's my line. But there are plenty of things in my stuff that are his. So I'm not claiming it. [*Laughs.*]

*Can you share one of Neil's contributions to your stories?*

Yes, well, there's a line about goat rapists in my novel *Bad Dreams*, which is Neil's. [*Laughs.*] That's something I lifted from one of the comedy articles we wrote together.

These were articles we wrote for porno magazines. Actually, we also wrote for a short-lived, humorous magazine called *The Truth*. I suspect Neil may have copies of that. We wrote some quite good things for that. And, actually, we wrote some quite good things for porno magazines; at various times we've thought about doing a collection of the stuff. It wasn't just me and Neil – Eugene Byrne, who is also a novelist and is an old school friend of mine, contributed to that a lot. The three of us would get together for long weekends and write five or six funny articles, or bits of things. We also worked on various other projects.

For instance, Eugene and I and an old friend of ours, Brian Smedley, wrote a musical which is called *Rock* 27 times. It's called *Rock, Rock, Rock, Rock, Rock, Rock, Rock, Rock, Rock, Rock, Rock, Rock, Rock, Rock, Rock, Rock, Rock, Rock, Rock, Rock, Rock, Rock, Rock, Rock, Rock, Rock, Rock.* The end of act 2 was written by Neil, and half of a song. [*Laughs.*] Because he happened to be in the room while we were doing it. That's just how we worked then. It was a comedy routine about the fad, at the time, of using old music in ads. But most of the funny stuff we wrote was very topical and of passing interest. You might get mildly nostalgic about it now, but there were some jokes in there that are still good, and so we're still using them. We did a whole run of articles where we would take a subject, like education or romance or writing a best-seller, and do gags on those subjects. We tied it together with a character who would go around interviewing people. I know this is a structure that we both still use – the sort of innocent person who goes around from place to place, meeting strange people, who answer questions, sometimes ambiguously. And there's always some trickster figure lurking around in the background prodding the audience surrogate through the plot. I've noticed that Neil uses that all the time, and so do I, as a kind of plot structure. We play that a lot. I'm not sure if you're familiar with my novel, *Life's Lottery*, which is an interactive, choose-your-own-adventure-type book for grown-ups. That's an enormously expanded take on a funny article of Neil's and mine from *Penthouse*. It was at the time when all those fighting-fantasy-type books were around, and the brief was to do a kind of sexy one of those. But in the end, we wrote a kind of cruel, absurdist-comedy one. My book is a much more serious take on that. I think I learned how to play with the form while doing that article, and, again, filed it away and didn't do anything with it for ten years, and eventually did. That's another thing that lingers from all that work.

*It's fitting that you tackled the film quotes in* Ghastly Beyond Belief, *while Neil tackled the quotes from books, because you had written numerous film reviews for the British Fantasy Society while Neil was writing a number of book reviews.*

Yes. I still work as a film critic for British magazines, fairly popular ones, fairly serious ones. And, actually, for a while, Neil did a bit of that. He worked for *Knave*. He said I showed him how easy it was to get into press screenings where you can get free sandwiches.

*Have you and Neil spoken about working together again some day?*

Whenever we get together, we sort of talk about it. Obviously, since he emigrated he's not around as much. We haven't actually got around to doing anything yet. I wouldn't rule it out, but we are both rather busy. Eugene Byrne, the other guy we were always with, points out that we were going to write a book together once, and he wrote his bit. So we ought, at some point, to finish it. [*Laughs.*] It was a kind of funny science-fiction novel called *Neutrino Junction*. It was conceived in the '80s, so it may be rather an '80s thing. It was a story about a guy who's a bit of a loser, in a future where everything is kind of horrible. Actually, it's rather like the world we've got – I think our main villain was a version of Ronald McDonald. There's a whole sub-plot about Michael Jackson, which we probably wouldn't be able to do any more. It was to do with a world of generic products and homogenization. It's very, very grim-sounding, but we wanted to do an absurdly funny, cyberpunk future – the heroine was a nun, who was an assassin. I think Neil ended up writing the synopsis, so I don't have it. Eugene wrote fifty pages of it. We never did get any further with that.

*There's another example to support Neil's belief that a collaboration between writers works best when writing humor.*

That's probably true. Eugene and I have written serious fiction together, and I've done it with Paul McAuley as well, but, yes, most of the stuff that I've written in collaboration has been funny. There's somebody to tell you when the joke isn't funny. In the days when we were doing humorous writing together there was a catch phrase, which was "That's a stupid idea, Neil." [*Laughs.*] It wasn't just because all of *his* ideas were the stupid ones – Neil often said "That's a stupid idea, Neil" to me or Eugene. We would go off on these crazy tangents. It would start out funny and then get bad, and that's when one of us would have to say, "That's a stupid idea, Neil." And we would just calm down and go on and do stuff that *was* funny. [*Laughs.*]

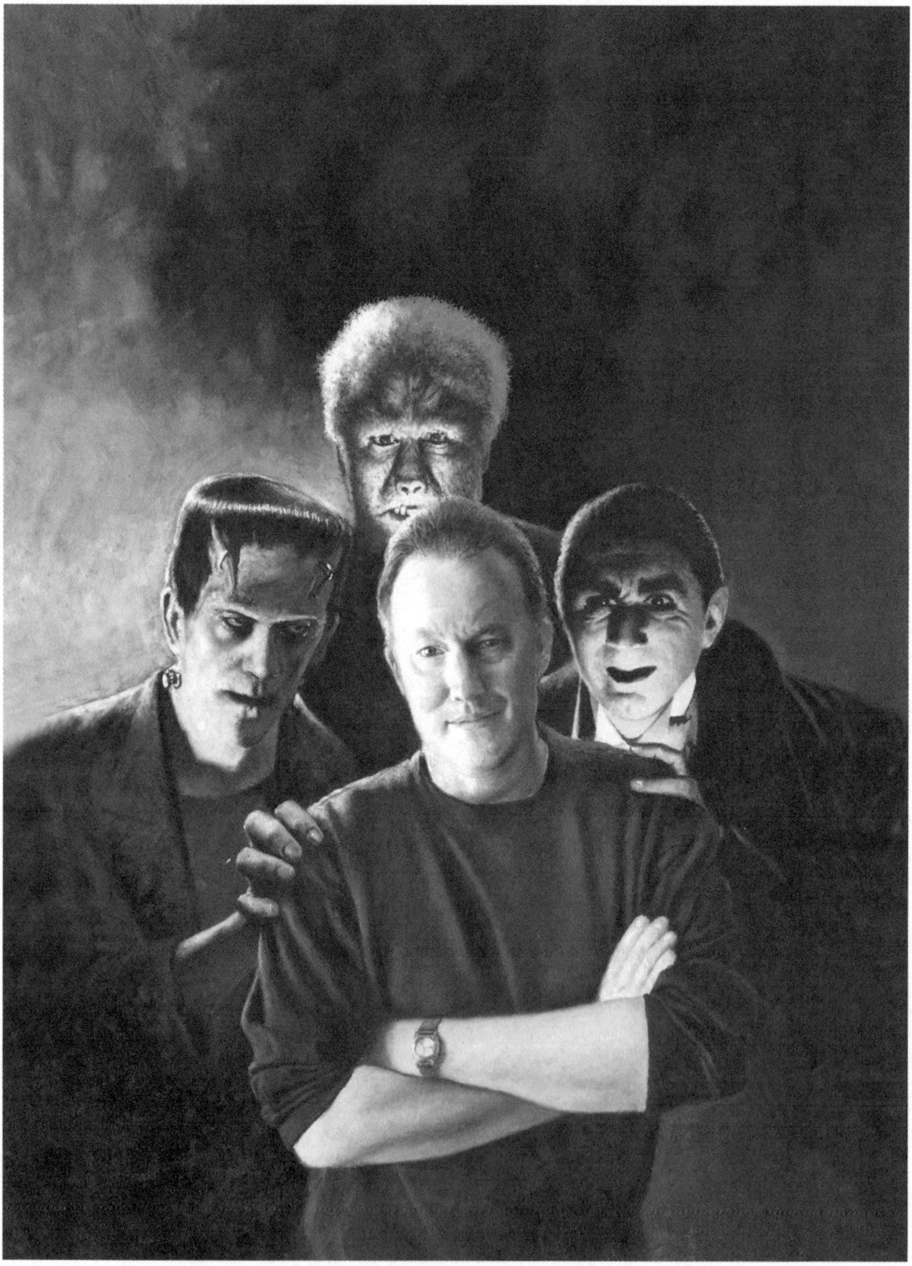

*Stephen Jones*

........................................

AS HE PROUDLY POINTS OUT ON HIS WEBSITE, STEPHEN JONES
SHARES HIS NAME WITH THE PROTAGONIST OF THE H.P. LOVECRAFT-HAZEL HEALD
COLLABORATION "THE HORROR IN THE MUSEUM." IT'S FITTING THAT HIS LITERARY
NAMESAKE SHOULD BE THE CHILD OF COLLABORATION, AS JONES HIMSELF HAS WORKED
WITH MANY OF FANTASY AND HORROR'S BRIGHTEST LUMINARIES – RAMSEY CAMPBELL,
BRIAN LUMLEY, CLIVE BARKER (MOST NOTABLY AS UNIT PUBLICIST FOR THE FIRST THREE
*HELLRAISER* MOVIES AND *NIGHTBREED*), AND, OF COURSE, GAIMAN, WITH WHOM HE
CO-EDITED *NOW WE ARE SICK: AN ANTHOLOGY OF NASTY VERSE* [DREAMHAVEN
BOOKS, 1991].

AS ENGLAND'S TOP HORROR EDITOR, JONES HAS WON TWO WORLD FANTASY AWARDS,
THREE BRAM STOKER AWARDS, TWO INTERNATIONAL HORROR GUILD AWARDS, AND FIFTEEN
BRITISH FANTASY AWARDS. AND HE'S PUBLISHED NEARLY EIGHTY BOOKS SINCE 1988, AN
OUTPUT HE EXPLAINS WITH HIS TYPICAL IRREVERENT WIT: "I AVERAGE ABOUT THREE OR FOUR
BOOKS A YEAR. THAT'S BECAUSE I HAVE TO PAY THE MORTGAGE. LONDON'S AN EXPENSIVE
CITY, AND I DON'T EARN AS MUCH AS NEIL OR CLIVE."

........................................

*You've known Neil for quite some time. But in addition to working with you, Neil seems
to have played a role in the direction your career has taken, along with two other well-
known fantasists – John Carpenter and Clive Barker.*

In the 1980s, I was really, really poor and had no money – I was poorer then than
I am now, which is hard to imagine! [*Laughs.*] But I was actually so poor, I had no work
coming in. Neil, at that time, was writing for a softcore "girlie" magazine in England called
*Knave*, and he very kindly helped a group of us out with work. We all got commissions
from *Knave*. It was what we call a "top shelf" magazine – those titles that are on the top
shelf so children can't get hold of them in newsagents. It was glossy and had naked
women all through it, but also all these great interviews with writers and musicians
and media people. Neil did that – he was involved and he got us all jobs. So I was in Los
Angeles with Jo Fletcher, and we interviewed John Carpenter for *Knave*. We went over
to the Twentieth Century Fox lot and my friend Dennis Etchison introduced us to John
Carpenter. At that point he was just finishing up work on *Big Trouble in Little China*. It
was a great interview, and we got paid very well for it. It helped with the questions that
I used to be a TV director.

*You got your start in television.*

Yes, for twenty years I was a TV director working in advertising and promotional
films. I got to work with all sorts of people – David Niven, John Cleese, Charlie Drake.

*How did you make the move from TV directing to print journalism?*

I didn't. For a while I just did the two together, basically working on magazines like *Fantasy Tales* and *Fantasy Media* in my spare time. Eventually I was doing more of the books and less of the TV – a bad mistake! But back then, John Carpenter said to me, "Well, Steve, why don't you come over here and work? You know what you're doing. Why don't you direct?" And I said, "Yeah, right! Good idea! There are so many people in LA who want to direct and produce stuff – I'd rather be a reasonable-sized fish in a small pond over in England." He then suggested that I look at becoming a film publicist. As a freelance journalist, I had worked for such magazines as *Starburst*, *Halls of Horror* and *Cinefantastique* and had visited many movie sets. Carpenter said that with my background in film and my TV experience I would make a perfect film publicist.

After I got back from LA, I called up my friend Clive Barker and I said, "Clive, you're doing some little horror film in London, right? Do you have a unit publicist?" He said, "Yes. It's called *Hellraiser*, and we can't afford a publicist." At that time I was a partner in a production company in London, and I said, "Well, let me be your unit publicist on *Hellraiser*. I'll just go on sabbatical from my company for three months. You don't have to pay me anything." Clive agreed to set up a meeting between his producer and myself. We met up in a wine bar in London and I got the job. They even agreed to pay me a weekly salary! So I became the unit publicist on *Hellraiser* – and all because of Neil, if you go back to the beginning of the chain of events. After that I worked on the first two *Hellraiser* sequels, *Nightbreed*, and various other films. I wish I was still doing more of that kind of work, but the books just took over.

*How did you and Neil first meet?*

Jo Fletcher and I were running the British Fantasy Convention, and this young journalist named Neil Gaiman called us up and contrived his way in to interview Robert Silverberg. After that, because of mutual friends, we just began to hang out at various events together.

*You mentioned that your books were what led you away from your work as a publicist – did you use any of Neil's stories in your anthologies at this time?*

No, not in those days. Neil, Kim Newman, Phil Nutman, and Stefan Jaworzyn worked together as a kind of writer's cooperative. They were all young guys, and they wanted to get involved in the field. Kim and I ended up editing *Horror: 100 Best Books* together. We had to find a hundred writers who would write about a hundred books. At the time we said to Neil, "Look, we will include you in the book, but you're going to be the last guy in." You see, he was already a professional and could be relied upon to come up with something appropriate. So we lined up our other contributors, and let them all pick their books first. Finally, Neil was the last to be included.

*With his essay on* The Complete Werewolf?

That's right. And he wrote a fabulous piece about it.

*That was the first contribution you received, as an editor, from Neil?*

That I can remember, yes. When *Fantasy Tales* went from being a small-press magazine to a professional paperback, he sent me a story and I bought it. At that time, Neil was a journalist – he was only just getting into writing fiction.

*And it was after* Horror: 100 Best Books *that you began putting Neil's short stories in your anthologies?*

During this period he was starting to write a whole bunch of short fiction that I would use – in such books as *Shadows Over Innsmouth, Dark Detectives*, the various *Mammoth* titles. Neil was becoming a really clever, witty and *intelligent* writer. Just as Kim Newman can take the tropes of genre fiction and make them his own, so Neil is capable of doing the same thing. He started doing it in *Sandman*. He even rewrote William Shakespeare's *A Midsummer Night's Dream* and won a World Fantasy Award for it!

*Around the time he won that award, in 1991, an* Anthology of Nasty Verse, *which you edited with Neil, debuted. How did* Now We Are Sick *come about?*

Neil had come up with a really clever concept: He'd ask a bunch of authors to write gruesome children's poems. He loves all that stuff – he's widely read, very erudite. He had come up with this cool idea and then, in typical Neil way, had kind of ended up with only half a book. "I've got this person, and this person – I've got something – but I don't know what I've got," he told me. So I agreed to look at the material he had collected so far. It was wonderful! I told him, "Look, you need to get some more authors after you find a publisher." He moaned, so I said, "Okay, what do you want me to do?" "Finish it off," he replied. So I did. He already had some really great people at that point, and some really wonderful poems. So we sat down, had a few beers, and threw some ideas around. And we eventually doubled the size of the book. We found a publisher through, from what I remember (it was more than ten years ago), Robert Garcia, the designer of the book. Originally Tom Canty was going to be the illustrator and designer. We had a very positive meeting with Canty in London, and Neil was really excited about that. But then he never got back to us. So after about four years we decided we'd better move on. We brought in Bob Garcia – who was an old friend of mine from Chicago – and I suggested another old friend, Arkham House artist Andrew Smith, to do the interiors. We used Clive Barker's frontispiece art on the cover of the hardcover edition, and Bob later brought Gahan Wilson on board to do the cover for the paperback. Greg Ketter's DreamHaven Books was going to publish the book anyway, and it just came together like that. We've been talking now for another ten years about updating and expanding it with a new edition. We're still talking about it, but I think it's eventually going to happen.

Now We Are Sicker?

*Now We Are Sickerer*. Right! [*Laughs.*] I have to say, I've co-edited with a lot of people and Neil is one of the easiest guys to work with. Unfortunately, few people seem to remember that I was involved with *Now We Are Sick*. [*Laughs.*] I ended up doing most of the business stuff. But, to be fair, it doesn't sell because I was involved – it sells because Neil's name is on it. It was his original concept. He came up with the initial material, which was enough of a book to make it work.

*It's curious that, with your involvement, it has never been released in a British edition.*

Originally, we tried to interest several publishers in a British edition. They said, "Poetry. Yeah, right. No thanks." When the book was originally published, Neil, myself and various contributors traveled around to SF conventions, reading the poetry on stage. It was a kind of touring live show, and that was really cool. The line-up of contributors would change from convention to convention. I would have loved to have done more of that. My inspiration for the book came from the late Stanley McNail, an American poet. He did one Arkham House book called *Something Breathing*, in the mid-1960s. That book is fabulous, and I wanted to recreate the whole tenor of that book in *Now We Are Sick*. It was serious, it was funny – sometimes it was funny-serious – and most important of all, it was scary. I love that tradition. I loved *Something Breathing*. And what I did on these tours was preface the performance by reading a Stanley McNail poem.

*Not to dwell too much on this, but I asked about a British edition because the macabre humor of* Now We Are Sick *strikes me as something that might be more readily accepted by a British audience, as opposed to an American one.*

We thought the same thing. Remember, in those days, I was just starting out as a professional editor. Neil wasn't even that well known. I'd been around the small press, and I'd had several books published by that point. Neil was still best known as a journalist.

You have to understand – Neil just exploded upon the scene. (It was the same with Clive Barker.) Neil had been around as a journalist, he was well known and well respected. But suddenly, he started doing fiction, and he started doing comic books. As I said earlier, Neil is a very well-read, very erudite writer. So he took tropes and ideas and concepts that most writers would use in books, and introduced them to comics. I'm a comic-book fan from way back, and nobody had ever done that before. And it was a brilliant concept, because the comics field was absolutely ready for it. They needed to attract a new, "adult" readership. He said, "Let's assume that the comics people don't know this stuff. It's a whole new market we can expand." And obviously it's been incredibly successful for him. It was a phenomenal marketing idea.

*You mentioned Clive Barker – you're in the somewhat unique position of having worked closely with both Neil and Barker. It seems that Neil's career trajectory is similar to Barker's.*

To a certain extent, that's probably true. They certainly took similar career paths. I hate both of them actually. [*Laughs.*] I hate the fact that I stayed on in Britain to fly the flag for the genre there. They headed off to America and made a fortune. [*Laughs.*] We all made different life choices in the early 1990s. Neil and Clive had both gone as far as they could in Britain doing what they wanted to do. I felt very much that there was more I could achieve. Not having their talent, I still wanted to be a medium-size fish in a very small pond. Anybody can do the job I do, it's not that difficult. In America, Ellen Datlow, Marty Greenberg – all sorts of people are already doing the job I do. Nothing much has changed since I talked with John Carpenter. In America I'd just be another editor, while in the U.K. I've managed to carve out some kind of a career for myself. Neil and Clive are both genuinely unique writers, unique individuals, and, I have to admit, much more personable than I am, so they get on with people better. They worked hard for their success. I still love being based in London, though. That's *my* strength.

With Neil, he came to America and made it his own. With Clive, he came here and made it his own as well. That's their strength – that's what they achieved. And they did it brilliantly. But I still hate them! They're millionaires, I'm not. [*Laughs.*] But

I guess if I die before them, then they will at least give me a good headstone. They've always been incredibly kind and generous to me. I still work with them both. And I see them both whenever I can, Neil particularly. Whenever he's in town we will try to get together, or when I'm in his neck of the woods. What I love about Neil is the fact that he lives in Minneapolis, which still seems so bizarre to me. If you're as rich and successful as Neil, why would you live in Minneapolis? I've visited his home several times, and it's always covered in snow! [*Laughs.*] But I must say that Neil has never lost his sense of identity – where he came from, who he works with, and who his friends are.

It's always a pleasure to work with him. There's no ego there. Neil is still a delight to work with. What I'm trying to say, I guess, is that he has not lost that "personal" touch. Anyone who has attended one of his signing sessions will attest to that. I don't know if you are aware of this, but – in America, moreso than Britain – when an editor goes to a publisher and says, "I've got this great idea for an anthology," the publisher usually replies, "Okay, I have a list of Big Names: Stephen King, Dean Koontz, Anne Rice, Clive Barker, *Neil Gaiman* ... You've got to get one or two of these people, and then you have a deal." I don't work like that. From me, you get my experience as an editor and a, hopefully, cool concept. If you don't like it, then I'll find another publisher. But the point is that I *would* ask Neil first anyway, or Kim Newman, or Michael Marshall Smith – whoever – there's a core of people I would approach to contribute. And more times than not, Neil will come through for me, or at least do his best to come through for me. But he's probably getting these requests every day, just like Stephen King – "Can you give me this, can you give me that?" Editors have to do this because their publishing deals rely on Neil's name being on the book. My deals (usually) aren't based on that. I like to include him because he's a bloody good writer. It's as simple as that. We also have an understanding about how we work together. The thing about people like Neil or Kim or Mike and a lot of other writers – Ramsey Campbell, Brian Lumley, Christopher Fowler – you just say, "Here's an idea, here's the concept. Run with it. I'm not going to limit you to what you can do with it." And most writers appreciate that kind of freedom. So when we did the *Shadows Over Innsmouth* book and we did *Dark Detectives*, Neil had some fun with his contributions ["Only the End of the World Again" and "Bay Wolf," respectively]. And I love writers who have fun with it, who take something and just go and see what they can do with it. Neil's done that in his comics, he's done it in his books. He does it with his own prose all the time. The man is phenomenal in that respect.

*So at its most intellectual, you find his work is still playful?*

Yes, but it's respectful as well as playful.

*I'd like to discuss genre with you for a moment. Your books usually seem to be labeled "dark fantasy" or "horror."*

It's one of those weird things. I started out as a fantasy and science-fiction guy. I read science fiction when I was a kid before moving on to dark fantasy with H.P. Lovecraft and Fritz Leiber and Robert Bloch and Robert E. Howard. Somehow I just ended up being a horror guy. I have no idea how that happened! I guess that was obviously where the affinity was. I've done a few other bits and pieces over the years. A couple of years ago, I put together a massive Clark Ashton Smith collection, which I'm very proud of. I've also done fantasy books in the past. But I guess they all have a dark edge to them. I would love to do a science-fiction book at some point. A lot of my friends are science-fiction writers, but somehow I don't see that happening now . . . I guess, like Boris Karloff, I was pigeon-holed. I've become "typecast." Actually, I don't mind it. Again, like Karloff, I don't mind being typecast. I'm very relaxed about it, and like Karloff I'd rather die with my boots on doing what I love. If I'm always known as "the horror guy," then I'm still happy. And I do my best to defend the genre. I try not to pretend that its "magic realism" or "dark suspense" or "light fantasy." It's *horror*. Pure and simple. That's what I do.

*What would you say to those who consider the idea of genre as a barrier to creative expression? There are those who would argue that in adhering to traditional elements and labels we restrict ourselves. For example, why is it necessary to include vampires? If the only reason is because it's fun, are we limiting ourselves to providing entertainment instead of stepping outside of definitions to create art?*

I would ask, "Why can't we do both? Why can't we create entertainment *and* art, and why would we need to step outside the genre to achieve that?" I have always found horror, and fantasy fiction in general, to be the most liberating of all genres. The only people who find it restrictive are those who do not understand it or who have not read widely within it. In the past, people like Clive Barker, Steve King and our premier critic in the field, Douglas E. Winter, have argued passionately for encompassment, and I totally agree with them. We can claim works by William Shakespeare, Mary Shelley, Robert Louis Stevenson, Charles Dickens, M.R. James, Henry James, Ray Bradbury and numerous other "respected" names for our genre. We should be proud of this heritage, not trying to deny it. It is only marketing departments and tabloid journalists who appear to think that "horror" is a pejorative term. Obviously, a certain amount of any genre will be rubbish, and it may well be that horror has more than its fair share of that. But that should still not prevent us from supporting the best any genre has to offer. I am proud to work in the horror field. The titles and the covers of my books reflect that enthusiasm, and I only wish that bookstores – especially in Britain – would reinstate the horror sections where such volumes can be properly showcased.

Nothing makes me laugh more than best-selling writers or successful film-makers who say something like, "It may be about a mutated cannibal serial killer, but it's not horror. It's a romantic drama about the modern human condition, unlike anything that's ever been done before." Yeah, right. Sure it is.

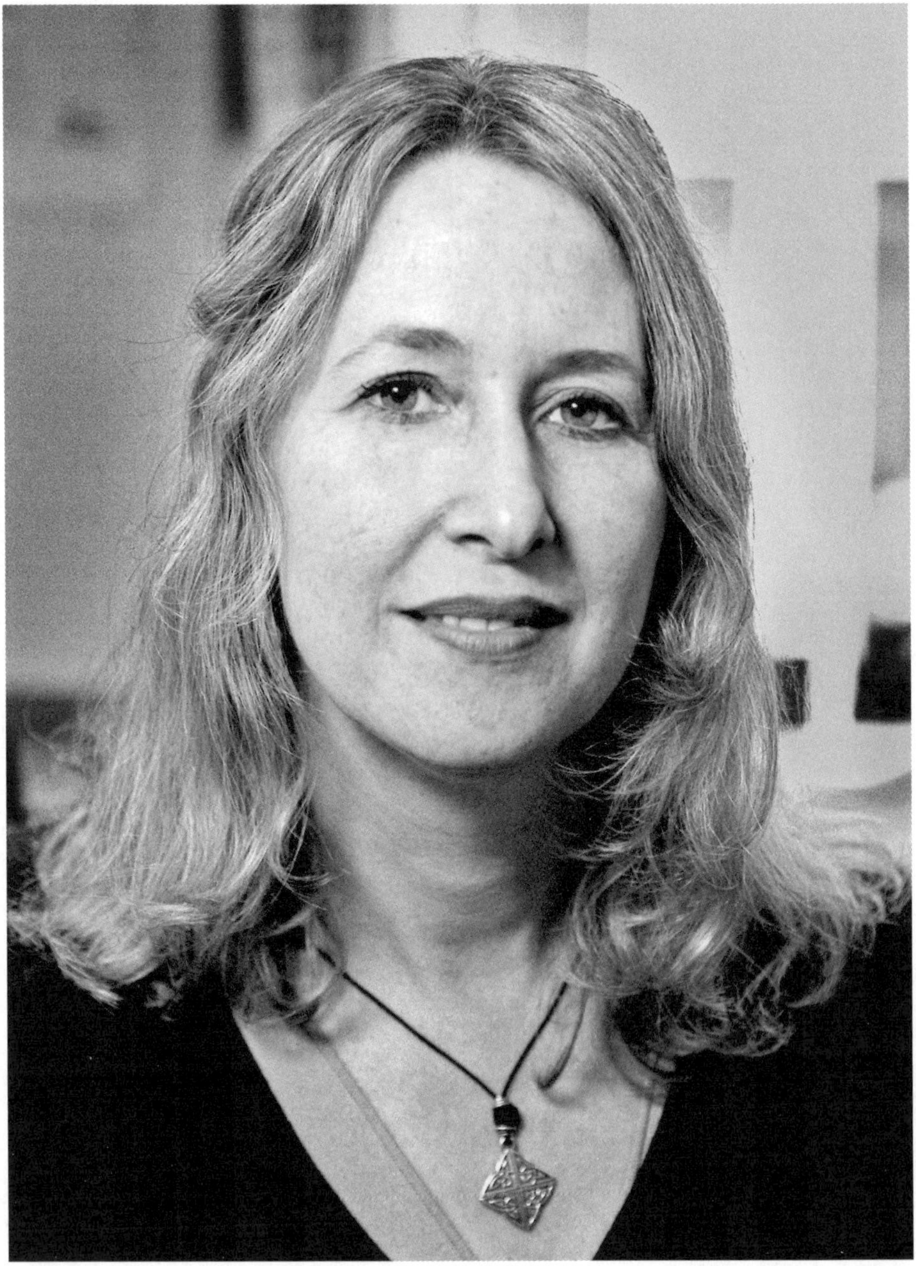

*Karen Berger*

## KAREN BERGER'S FIRST FULL EDITING JOB IN COMICS WAS,
APPROPRIATELY ENOUGH (GIVEN THE ROLE BOTH SHE AND DC'S HORROR/MYSTERY BOOKS PLAYED IN LAYING THE FOUNDATION FOR *SANDMAN*), *HOUSE OF MYSTERY*.

BEFORE THE ESTABLISHMENT OF DC'S VERTIGO IMPRINT IN 1993, BERGER EDITED A NUMBER OF TITLES, INCLUDING *THE LEGION OF SUPER-HEROES*, *WONDER WOMAN*, AND, MOST NOTABLY, ALAN MOORE'S *SWAMP THING*. AFTER WORKING ON *SWAMP THING* FOR SEVERAL YEARS, BERGER FOUND HERSELF IN THE POSITION OF DC'S BRITISH LIAISON, RESPONSIBLE FOR DEVELOPING NEW COMICS TALENT IN BOTH THE U.S. AND THE U.K. IT WAS ON ONE OF HER U.K. TRIPS THAT SHE FIRST ENCOUNTERED GAIMAN. BERGER EDITED GAIMAN'S FIRST U.S. TITLE, *THE SANDMAN*, AND OVERSAW EACH OF ITS SPIN-OFF TITLES. IN TOTAL, BERGER EDITED FIVE OF THE SIX BOOKS THAT INITIALLY TRANSFERRED TO THE VERTIGO LINE – *HELLBLAZER*, *ANIMAL MAN*, *SHADE, THE CHANGING MAN*, *SANDMAN*, AND *SWAMP THING* – WORKING NOT ONLY WITH GAIMAN BUT WITH HIS FELLOW BRITS JAMIE DELANO, PETER MILLIGAN, AND GRANT MORRISON.

AS VERTIGO'S EXECUTIVE EDITOR, BERGER NO LONGER EDITS INDIVIDUAL TITLES, BUT WORKS CLOSELY WITH THE LINE'S EDITORS AND DEVELOPS NEW SERIES THAT CONTINUE TO CHALLENGE THE COMMON PERCEPTION OF THE MAINSTREAM COMIC BOOK.

*You once mentioned, in a* Sequential Tart *interview, that when you first came to DC, Paul Levitz (then an editor, now DC's president and publisher) hired you as his assistant, in part, because he wanted someone who "wasn't a comics fan."*

Exactly, yes.

*Do you feel that this approach on the part of Paul, in a way, started your career as an editor of mainstream comics for people who might not typically read mainstream comics? Do you think it set you on that path?*

Yes. I thought working here was pretty interesting initially. Marc DeMatteis (J.M. DeMatteis) is a friend of mine from college, and he's the one who told me about the job, because he was first starting to write comics at the time – short stories, mystery and war tales. So that was how I found out about the opening. Marc is a few years older than me, but I had just gotten out of school, and Marc had started writing comics; and he knew Paul was looking for an assistant. Marc had mentioned, "I don't think she knows anything about comics." And Paul said, "That's fine. I don't really care that much." Paul was thinking a lot of the job was administrative and scheduling. (Half of it *was* assistant-editing him, but a lot of it was the scheduling of all the freelancers' assignments. DC was much smaller then than it is now, and Paul was editorial coordinator in addition to being an editor. The whole system was centralized then, so all the deadlines and the freelancer payments went through Paul. They didn't go through each individual editor.) I think Paul ultimately probably wanted someone who wasn't a fan, because they wouldn't be interested in doing that kind of stuff. I don't think he was looking at me, or anyone in that position, as potentially a new editor. It would have been nice if it turned out that way, but I don't think it was necessarily the main thing for that kind of job.

Even though I didn't know anything about comics, I was a quick study and I learned a lot to see what we were doing, but the stuff I responded to was not the super-hero books – it was the horror and the mystery titles. Ultimately, I wanted to edit books that I would like to read, so I guess bringing my sort of non-comics interest to comics was what I wanted to do. Pretty selfishly, at the beginning, but more broadly, obviously, as my career went on.

*During that early period, you worked on a couple of different books, of which* Swamp Thing *may have been the most groundbreaking. How did that begin? How did you come to work with Alan Moore?*

Actually, Len Wein was editing *Swamp Thing*; DC brought the book back when the first movie came out. Marty Pasko and Tom Yeates did it for a year and a half or so. Len had known Alan's work from some of his British comics work, like *V for Vendetta* and *Miracleman*, so he asked Alan to write the book. Alan had written a couple of issues, and Len's editorial workload was very heavy. He loved Alan's stuff so much but he figured if there was one book he could give up and know that it would be in the good hands of the writer, then that would be *Swamp Thing*. So *Swamp Thing* ultimately became mine. I edited it beginning with Alan's sixth issue, issue 25.

Swamp Thing *was fairly taboo-breaking for its time. How did the challenges that book presented compare with what you faced on Neil's* Sandman? *Was* Swamp Thing *a trickier book, in terms of what was allowed to see print?*

Probably, just because nobody was doing anything like it at all. *Swamp Thing* was the first book to really do intelligent, adult, literary comics. In many ways it was trickier because when you're on the one book that sort of carves the path, it's always a little trickier than on books to follow. *Sandman* obviously plowed through after the road was carved out, in terms of what could be done in comics. But *Swamp Thing* was probably trickier because it was the first. "Tricky" is not the right word – it was challenging the medium in mainstream comics. Both *Swamp Thing* and *Sandman* were series that showed that comics can stand side-by-side with contemporary fiction.

*After the success of* Swamp Thing, *was there a fair amount of pressure to find another book that was as successful, and to find another creator to follow Alan, to be the "next Alan Moore"?*

No, no. It was never "We must go out and find a new Alan Moore," but his effect was immeasurable. Alan blew the whole field wide open, influenced scores of writers, and really changed the face of modern comics. As an editor, I wanted to build on what

Alan had done, and push things even further. I wouldn't say it was a pressure, as much as a natural editorial follow-through and interest that fortunately collided with the sensibility of a fresh and daring bunch of new British writers: Neil, Jamie Delano, Grant Morrison, Peter Milligan and, a few years later, Garth Ennis and Warren Ellis. I first approached Jamie, who had also written a number of things in England, about doing *Hellblazer*. That book came out, I think, a good year and a half before the other pre-Vertigo books. But, initially, even for those first few years of *Swamp Thing*, I was just watching what Alan was doing. It hadn't even crossed my mind yet to say "Hey, let's try to bring in more writers who can write this edgy, smart material," because no one else out there was writing like him." It was after *Swamp Thing* and *Watchmen* that you really felt there was no going back.

*I suppose that was felt once more when Neil finished writing* Sandman.

To create a seven-year epic saga that we could collect and become a perennial and really have an influence? I think the influence of *Sandman* definitely points in that direction, but Vertigo was going at full strength by the end of *Sandman*. *Sandman* was the key book that really helped launch the line, because that book always did proportionately better than the other books. There were a lot of incredible Vertigo books, but, of those books, *Sandman* was commercially more successful and also reached out more to people who didn't read comics. It was a real crossroads book for us. It reached out to people who didn't read comics with its literary sensibility, endearing and provocative characters and complex mythology. It introduced people to the medium, who hadn't really read it before. That's a huge thing.

*Before Neil began work on* Sandman, *he and Dave McKean delivered several art pieces to you, just a few days after first discussing what became* Black Orchid. *Was it the efficiency they demonstrated that made the greatest impression on you at that time?*

They both showed they were ambitious and really serious about what they wanted to do with the character. And getting a really nice, well-thought out proposal with character sketches was just a great representation of how serious and committed they would be to this. It's what they're all about. So, yes, it definitely made a good impression. [*Laughs.*]

*What else appealed to you about Neil's work during that early period?*

I thought he had really good ideas, and I liked, with *Black Orchid*, how he was trying to subvert and change the character from how it was originally done in comics. That really appealed to me. I usually respond well to people trying to take some things that are status quo or a given, and doing something different with them; but something that makes sense and is interesting, creative, and exciting, not just doing something different for the sake of doing it. Neil is a very smart writer and has great ideas. I recognized that pretty early on. I think, as a writer, he matured more technically while he was writing *Sandman*. He was always a good writer, but I think his sheer quality as a storyteller and as a wordsmith evolved as he was writing *The Sandman*.

*You mention in your introduction to the latest edition of* Preludes and Nocturnes *that, in Neil's early work, "The craft was there, but there was a distance that kept you from getting emotionally involved –"*

It's true. There was sort of an emotional distance. I felt that he figured everything out, but somehow the connect to the characters, for me, was a little too distant. But when he first introduced Death, that was, to me, the most personal of stories. I really connected to the character, and I thought as a writer he really made that leap in being able to connect to a universal, emotional level.

*You've mentioned before that you feel the reason British writers have done so well in comics is because they have an outsider's point of view, and can be irreverent and subversive. Why do you feel British writers have this particular point of view?*

I felt that way more ten, fifteen years ago than I do now. Because when I first started working with British writers, the majority of American mainstream comics were pretty similar, tonality-wise. There was some good work being done, but nothing that really challenged the medium, that made you really think about the story the next day, made you really think, "I can't believe that story was done in a comic book." I think a lot of the way that British writers looked at American comics was different from the way American writers were looking at it. I think that if you look now, the way the whole medium has matured, a lot of it *is* because of Alan and Neil and Grant and Pete, and Jamie and Garth Ennis. Those guys made a huge impression in terms of what can be done in the medium, and it heavily influenced a lot of what's being done in mainstream comics today.

*Before* Sandman *debuted, one of the house ads had the slogan, "I can show you fear in a handful of dust." Was DC hoping the book would become more of a horror title than it eventually became?*

That was Neil's line; he ripped it off from T.S. Eliot. DC as a company has a great respect for the creative process and evolution of a series. No one was going to Neil and saying, "Give us a horror book." I think Neil was looking at what was done with *Swamp Thing*, which used horror as a backdrop to explore the world in which we live and how people relate and act and deal with it. Horror is a great backdrop or platform to explore a lot of relevant modern-day issues. Neil and a lot of the Vertigo writers used horror as a genre device to explore deeper things.

*The first artist to work with Neil on* Sandman *was Sam Kieth. What was it about Sam's early work that led to him becoming the book's original penciler?*

Neil and I were sorting through, mentally, and even with samples in front of us, many, many different artists. We really were looking for a look that was not a standard comic-book look. We were looking for someone who had a nice, illustrative style with a bit of quirkiness. Back then, Neil was a nobody, and doing a horror comic was still pretty much a risky thing. It wasn't as if well-known artists would even *want* to draw this book, so we knew we would have to go with someone fairly new. We both actually independently came up with Sam while we were meeting in London one time, trying to figure just who the hell was going to draw this book. We both had seen his work – I think it was in *Wandering Stars* – and we both really liked it. I liked his sense of composition a lot.

*Sam apparently felt uncomfortable drawing some of the early issues, and he mentioned he did extensive re-drawing on the first issue. One notices a greater synergy between art and story as* Sandman *progresses – did that early experience compel Neil to know exactly who would be penciling a story before he began writing it? And to know exactly what they liked to draw?*

Neil definitely wrote toward the strength of the artist working with him. I think he always intuitively had that ability. Neil started constructing different arcs and storylines after we couldn't find an artist who could draw a monthly book. Sam left the book because he wasn't happy with the work he was doing. We gave Mike Dringenberg the book; who did a wonderful job on it. He ultimately couldn't keep up with deadlines at all, and Neil, then I think, realized that probably the best way to do this [was] to use different artists for different storylines. At that point, he had a clear structure in his head of how he wanted the series to develop and then made that conscious decision to use different artists for different storylines. When we first started doing the book, we just figured, "You're my one and only" – whoever the artist was on the book. That was the norm for monthly comics: you didn't have people doing different stories. You might have had someone do a fill-in issue, but it was pretty much the same person drawing the book.

*Sam brought Mike on board. Did you bring on Malcolm Jones?*

I don't know how Malcolm came into doing it. I have no memory of it. I don't know if Mike suggested him, or if Malcolm came in to show me samples, or if Neil suggested him. It's been a long time.

*Was it difficult at that time to persuade DC to allow Neil co-ownership of* Sandman*?*

It's not a co-ownership. DC owns the character. Neil has equity in the character, he has participation in media on it, as do the majority of our equity agreements with creators on DC-owned properties which were created after 1976.

*I had the impression that* Sandman *was somewhat unique in its equity deal.*

Not really. When Neil created *Sandman*, we hadn't yet done creator-owned deals, and *Sandman* initially was clearly imbued in the DC mythos.

Sandman *does have a reputation for achieving several "firsts." For example, wasn't this the first DC book that was permitted to use the "F" word?*

I think it was probably tied! Neil was one of the writers who was asking to be able to use words of all kinds. [*Laughs.*] But it was around the same time as other Vertigo books.

*Of the* Sandman *stories, long or short, which do you feel work best?*

It's hard to choose, to be honest. I like the stories in *Worlds' End* a lot because they dealt with different time periods and different historical characters, and many were told in an unconventional way, by some wonderful artists: Alec Stevens, John Watkiss, Mike Allred, Michael Zulli… I also liked *The Kindly Ones* a lot, I like Marc Hempel's work immensely. The whole graphic look of his work is just beautiful, and he's a very powerful storyteller. *A Game Of You* is definitely up there, as well. I thought that Neil used a really fresh approach in storytelling, combining reality and fantasy plotlines. The story was also pretty controversial for the time – a transsexual, actually *pre-*transsexual, was a fairly central character. The issues dealing with gender and gender identity were written compassionately and beautifully. I thought that was really, really well done. I also loved the Cuckoo and Barbie stuff, and all those funny little animal characters that Neil likes to come up with. What was your favorite? [*Laughs.*]

*I like a lot of them, but I certainly appreciate Hempel's stuff, and the minimalism he employs. Neil told me he didn't think it worked as a monthly, but collected in one volume, he felt it worked better.*

Yes. It's interesting that *A Game Of You* and the Hempel stuff were probably least responded to by the monthly comic-book readers at the time. A lot of people weren't into *A Game Of You* as much, and a lot of the die-hard *Sandman* fans made a big stink about Marc Hempel's artwork as well. But, we stood behind him because we thought he was perfect for the storyline and really did a great job.

*Were there any artists you suggested to Neil?*

I think I suggested Chris Bachalo because I had just seen his work, and he was starting on *Shade* at the time. He was a really new, vibrant artist, and Neil really responded to it.

*Neil has mentioned that one of his reasons for doing* Endless Nights *was to show his gratitude to you. He dedicated it to you, as well as to Jenette Kahn and Paul Levitz. Another reason he mentioned was the opportunity to work with different artists from around the world. He was surprised that you rounded up these artists for him practically overnight.*

[*Laughs.*] It wasn't. It seemed that way to him, that's what good editors are for. But we [got] some of them quicker than others. Actually Shelly Bond, Vertigo editor extraordinaire who worked with me on the book, was the one who landed Milo Manara and Miguelanxo Prado, and she was very persistent in dealing with their agents. I was the one who got Moebius, and then Moebius eventually couldn't do it. I think, for the other few, we sort of went back and forth, but Shelly deserves equal credit if not more, in being able to get Manara and Prado. The other artists were people we knew fairly well, like Bill Sienkiewicz and Frank Quitely and Glenn Fabry. Again, it just points to the fact that people were really excited to work with Neil on what they knew would be a special book. It didn't happen as quickly or painlessly as Neil thinks it did [*laughs*], but I'm glad *he* thinks it did.

Sandman *helped pave the way for Vertigo, and it was the most popular monthly title when the Vertigo line began. How satisfied are you with Vertigo overall? Do you feel it has lived up to its initial potential?*

Totally, totally. I'm extremely proud of the work we've published.

*In the early years, did you feel that it was somewhat trapped by its roots (so to speak)? That it had to deliver horror or genre titles?*

Not at all. People love to pigeon-hole, it's just human nature. People like to find categories. I think people pigeon-holed us as a horror line or as a dark fantasy line. I've always thought Vertigo [is] less about genre fiction, and more about using those genres as backdrops to explore the world in which we live, and the real disturbing aspects about society and humanity, and everyday life. By just looking at the extraordinary in the ordinary world in which we live. I've always marched to the beat of my own drum, and the writers who work for Vertigo have, too. We're not following anybody's preconceptions or anyone's rules of what we should be doing. The whole reason why the imprint exists and why it's successful is because we're not playing by anybody's rules. If there's any rule, it is you can do anything, any kind of story, in comics. You can treat comics and write comics as a form of contemporary fiction, which is what it is, and not look at it within the confines of a super-hero, adolescent boys' medium.

*Both you and Vertigo were the focus of a* New York Times *article from last year [September 15, 2003]. You were quoted as saying that you felt female editors are "braver than men," that they're more likely to "take chances and push the creative envelope." Why do you feel this way?*

I think a lot of it comes down to what I was saying before: a lot of the women who work on comics didn't grow up reading comics. They're not part of the boys' club that is super-hero comics. As women they're bringing an outside perspective and more objectivity to the types of books that we do and are less likely to do something formulaic and to do something because of some fan interest. I'm not saying that every male editor is a fanboy or every male editor does things conventionally. I think there are a lot of good male editors out there. But in my experience, female editors have more guts. And the male editors that have guts tend to be the ones who work or have worked for me. [*Laughs.*]

DREAMS

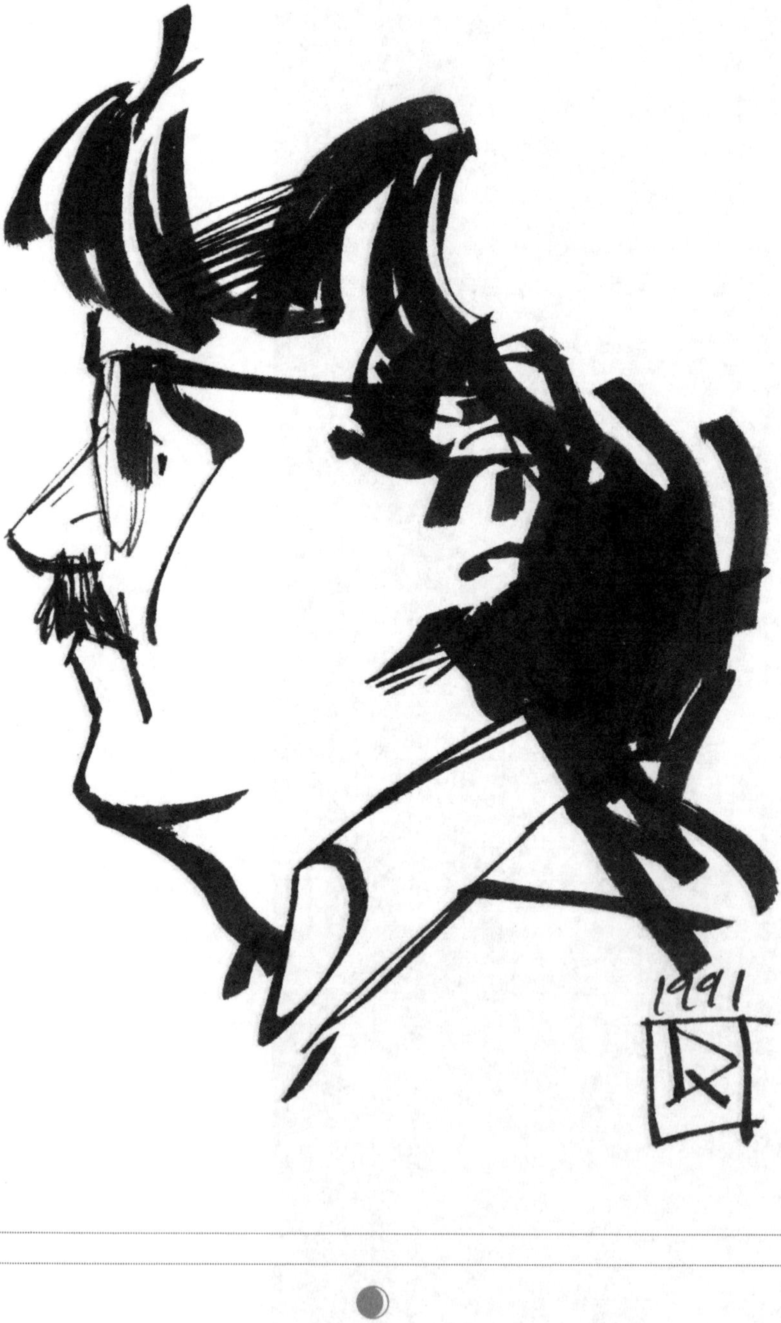
1991

Caricature of Sam Kieth by Mike Dringenberg. © 2004 Mike Dringenberg.

*Sam Kieth*

---

CREDITED AS ONE OF *SANDMAN*'S CO-CREATORS, SAM KIETH
WAS THE BOOK'S FIRST PENCILER. ALTHOUGH HE LEFT *SANDMAN* AFTER ONLY FIVE
ISSUES, KIETH'S QUIRKY SENSE OF HUMOR EVENTUALLY FOUND ITS WAY INTO HIS BEST-
KNOWN COMICS WORK, *THE MAXX*, THE SUCCESS OF WHICH LED TO ITS MTV ANIMATED
INCARNATION. KIETH HAS ALSO WORKED ON A VARIETY OF COMPANY-OWNED PROPERTIES
SUCH AS WOLVERINE AND THE HULK (HIS LATEST BOOK IS THE BATMAN MINI-SERIES
*SCRATCH*), AND HIS ORIGINAL CREATION (WITH WRITER WILLIAM MESSNER-LOEBS)
*EPICURUS THE SAGE*. LATELY, HE'S WRITTEN AND ILLUSTRATED *FOUR WOMEN* AND
*ZERO GIRL*. AS KIETH EXPLAINS: "IT'S OBSCENE, THE AMOUNT OF LUCK I'VE HAD. I
COULD BE HIT BY A TOMATO TRUCK TOMORROW AND BE PARALYZED FROM THE WAIST
DOWN, AND COME UP EVEN, Y'KNOW? I SHOULDN'T HAVE HAD AS MANY THINGS AS HAVE
HAPPENED TO ME. IT'S JUST GRAVY THAT ANYTHING ELSE HAPPENS..."

---

*You first spoke to Neil on the phone, when he and Karen Berger called you up out of the blue to discuss a little project called* Sandman.

Yup. I was trying to get work from Karen. I was bugging Karen, hoping that the current artist on *Swamp Thing* would die, because I wanted to draw *Swamp Thing*!

*May I ask what you were doing prior to bugging Karen Berger?*

Working for small black-and-white publishers, like Fantagraphics, and doing short stories.

*Did that immediately precede* Sandman?

No. I was inking an obscure book called *Manhunter*, but it wasn't Walt Simonson's version of the character. I was inking this book for DC, and for an editor named Barbara Kesel, and Karen wanted to steal me away from Barbara Kesel, which Barbara was just thrilled about. [*Laughter.*]

*I assume this was your first mainstream gig?*

Pretty much, yeah, for Marvel or DC. I was inking there and I was bugging Karen to do *Swamp Thing*, and I wanted to draw it like Wrightson, but she wouldn't let me. She wasn't interested in that.

*Who was penciling* Swamp Thing *at this time?*

I think it was Bissette and Totleben. I would have all these excuses to call Karen up. I'd use every excuse I could get from the freelancer's book. You know, you call up – "Oh, I'm sorry. Did I get ahold of you? I was actually trying to call somebody else. Well, as long as I've got you on the line..." The other one was "Did you get the submission package I sent?" (before it gets there); "Did you get the package I sent?" (when it gets there); "Did you get the package I sent?" (after it gets there). These were all of the excuses to call the editor. And it worked! Karen had two books. She kept talking about an unknown writer from England on a new book called *Sandman*. She thought I should draw that one, but I wanted to draw the other one. Who was the guy that used to do *Moonshadow*?

*J.M. DeMatteis.*

Yes, and he was doing a book that was published more or less at the same time as *Sandman*. I think Shawn McManus or somebody drew it.

*Doctor Fate?*

Yes, *Doctor Fate*. I'm pretty sure that happened around the same time. If it wasn't that book, it was another book at the same time, and it was a "name writer," not an unknown. And I was just...*dismayed* that I didn't get the name writer, because I hadn't heard of – nobody had heard of – Neil. She said, "I think you would be good for this other book, *The Sandman*." I remember thinking, "Aw, shit." She had called up to say, "Well, there's a book, and it's by this guy you've never heard of, and it's a subject you've never heard of. There's another one, though, I was thinking about, but we're going to get this known writer and this known artist. So you probably won't do that one – but you can get this unknown character and this unknown writer." "Well, is it a new character?" "Well, no, it's actually revamping an old character that nobody read." "Oh. Great. Yeah. Okay." Obviously I wasn't going to pass that up, but I remember feeling gypped that Neil wasn't J.M. DeMatteis. And, of course, he wasn't that thrilled with me either – I think – because, despite, I'm sure, his colored memory, I remember saying to him when I first met him, "Do you know who should draw this book? P. Craig Russell." He said, "Yeah, he'd be great."

But we just talked on the phone. Karen said, "Here's this guy who has this project." And the guy had outlined nine issues already. Clearly this was an ambitious thing. I said to Neil, "Well, you know, you're English, it's a Karen book, so it will sell." He said, "You're right. It's all kind of set up. It's part of that whole thing." I thought, "Well, it's one of those books where...it will have great writing, crappy art, and it will come out from Vertigo and it will have its following. So if I just don't get in the way of the writer, it will probably be fine. But if I do get in the way of it, I'm gonna be steamrolled right over. *Because that's the way the system works.*"

*You felt that was the established system?*

With *Hellblazer* and *Swamp Thing*, but especially with *Hellblazer*, where they had started out with the painted covers – really great covers – and...I don't want to say *bad* artists, because, actually, they tended to be more structurally grounded and have a better illustration sense than I did. They were illustrated stories, and they were great to read, but they weren't my cup of tea, visually.

*You were coming from the Frazetta-Wrightson school of illustration.*

Yeah, but in my case, all style, no content. Right.

*Well, I don't know if I'd go that far.*

No, it's true. My stuff's very cartoony. It's very ornate, and, often, you can actually coast by with very minimal illustration skills, which was what I was all about right then. So I was bound to fail on this book, because everything that was poor about me – my illustration skills – would be glaringly revealed, and all of my penciling would be shown to another inker, who, ironically, I chose – a friend, who had amazing illustration skills, but who I didn't mesh with, at that time, with that style of inking. So right off the bat, Mike Dringenberg should have been penciling *Sandman* – as he did so fabulously later, after I left – and I should have been inking it. But that's not what happened, because I insisted on learning to pencil on that book. I said, "This is not working, Mike." And Mike said, "Why don't you let me pencil?" I said, "I'm not gonna let you pencil it. I want to pencil it. I don't know how yet, but I gotta learn on this book. So I'm gonna try to *learn* how to pencil on this book." That was the least of it. But, yeah, that's how I met Neil. I was going to pencil the first forty-page issue of the *Sandman* book, this new book, with him. I said to him, "It's a P. Craig Russell story. You should get Craig." He said, "Yeah…I know." And I told Karen. She said, "Yeah. But he's too slow."

*So this was all discussed during a single conference call?*

No. I would just call each of them, Karen would call Neil…I don't know if we even conferenced. I think we might have over the sketches. They sent some sketches. Dave McKean did some sketches which looked exactly like Dave McKean sketches, at that time, which means they looked more graphically real and they looked like whatever photo model he was using.

*Dave had already sketched the Sandman character at this point.*

He had drawn a couple of pictures of a guy, with scratchy lines through the face – it was a Dave McKean picture. And it was a guy in a trenchcoat. He looked like the guy in *Hellblazer* [John Constantine].

*And these were based on Neil's original sketches?*

Right. I actually have the sketches Karen and Neil approved. I did two or three sketches of Sandman, a couple in the mask, which I inked and still have. Do you know why? Because they're in the same sketchbook as a bunch of other covers I did, for *Marvel Comics Presents*. That's the only reason I have them left – no vanity or "Wow, this is amazing!" thing. They're just stuck in the sketchbook, in the middle, because at that point, "…yeah, now I did this [*pretends to turn a page*]…yeah, now I did this…" It's a big thirty-page sketchbook and on a few pages there's a bunch of pictures of a freakin' gas mask. I did about eight gas-mask sketches of what he would look like in it, and then some pictures of him without it.

*These were the first sketches you did?*

Yeah. I sent them off, and nobody liked the first round. Then I sent a second [round] off and the one they chose is the one that we went with, the only inked one, which looked a little like David Bowie, a little bit of a cropped top, but from the beginning, the David Bowie/guy-from-the-Cure, whatever his name is…

*Robert Smith.*

Robert Smith. That look came in, and was really heavily championed and pioneered through Neil and Karen, I think. And I think Dringenberg played upon this, then later Kelley [Jones] came in. I would give him grease in his hair and have his hair matted to his head. I wasn't with the whole hip, trendy Sandman. I wanted the goofy Sandman.

*A little more cartoony?*

Right. And that was not the game plan.

*Your Sandman had an unusually large nose –*

Well, yeah, that's the only nose I can draw, so I was pretty much stuck. [*Laughter.*] We were all stuck. We battled with this mule we were calling Sam Kieth, trying to make him into this sprinter horse that he was never gonna be.

*Were your initial design sketches pretty close to what Neil and Dave had drawn?*

Dave's were basically just of a guy standing there. The first time I saw them, I remember thinking, "Why are they sending me a picture of Constantine from *Hellblazer?*" Because it was a short-haired guy in a coat, looking mysterious. I said, "What's this?" And [Karen] said, "Dave did some sketches of Sandman." All I did was just give him long hair and I drew a long face. All I was trying to do was rip off P. Craig Russell, just doing one of those gaunt faces that he did. That way of drawing a very thin, emaciated-looking character, but with the whole structure there. My drawing, often, was trying to have those thin, skinny-looking emaciated characters, but there was no structure underneath like [Russell] had.

*Your characters appeared more amorphous.*

Well, undisciplined. Poorly drawn. They lacked skill. They were amateur drawings by somebody who hadn't drawn a lot. But if I had my druthers, my favorite thing would have been to have P. Craig Russell pencil it so it would have some structure underneath, that I never had.

Nobody was anybody's first choice on this book. [*Laughter.*] It's true: Neil wasn't excited about me, I wasn't excited about him. But he decided that this drawing I did was the one they were going to use. I think the biggest departure [came with] Kelley. He gave him the moussed-out hair, though it's true Mike gave him the moussed-out hair, too. He got the mousse in him after I left. They put the mousse in and it got really big, and he looked like a rock star. That was what they wanted, and the fans liked that, too. I was clearly the weak link in that system, because I didn't want him to look like that, and I was out of touch with that.

*You mentioned that Neil had already outlined the first nine issues before you came on board.*

At least up to Death [issue 8, "The Sound of Her Wings"], and I think three or four issues past it. He had a paragraph for each issue: "Issue 8 – this happens; issue 9 – this happens…" as an outline for the whole series. I think he went up to ten or twelve. Then there was this specific first-issue script, which was quite a bit longer. I specifically remember when he called me up and said, "Okay, you're going to get the first issue. And I'm exhausted." I said, "What happened?" He said, "I've been through the whole script with Karen, and she went through every single page and made me trim the panels I had after I'd already written it. Every one of the forty pages." Sometimes he would have seven or eight panels on a page, and she wanted no more than five or six, and he sounded like he'd been through nine guys in prison. He was exhausted. I said, "Oh, God."

*Had you met Neil face-to-face yet?*

No, this was all on the phone. I'd never even met him. (I didn't meet him until after the whole thing.) When Neil was carping about Karen putting him through hell, I said, "Oh, hey, tough titties, dude. What can I say?" He said, "Well, now it's *your* turn!" I said, "My turn? You got your panels down, what could happen with me?"

I drew the first issue and, right around page 6 or 7, I had this idea in my head that something had to happen differently. Not differently from the panels he'd laid out, but a little sequence that would cross-cut back from the character who had his hands out – the magician who started the whole thing – to insert panels of the Sandman. And that became me facing off with Karen about whether my storytelling was competent, whether I had a right to try and challenge this. She was like, "No. This is the way it is." I had an enormous power struggle with Karen, and Neil sided with her. I felt really betrayed, but the reality was: that was the way. I didn't get it until then. So from then on I realized, "Well, okay, I need to do it exactly as they want." But by the time I had finished, say, the first twenty or thirty [pages], I think I had penciled pretty close to the whole first issue, and then Karen had me go through and redraw…probably the bulk of it, all forty pages. No additional money. "Okay, here it's been two months of whatever you've penciled, now, for another two months, pencil again." I thought, "So the deal in comics is you redraw everything you do, and you don't get any payment, and you go for another two months without income? That's how comics work? No, normally they don't. But because, apparently, I suck, they do." [*Laughter.*]

So I redid it. I remember Karen was really upset. I think Karen felt that this was a necessary discipline and – make this very clear – I think she was right! But I think the thing that bothered me at the time, that I wasn't able to express, was that I felt that every instinct I had, creatively, to offer – not just in panel arrangements, but just in terms of suggesting things – was being ignored. So it made me doubt the simple things I needed to draw, like "Here's a guy in a room." I would think to myself, "But can I draw a guy in the room? Here's an angle – but am I choosing the wrong angle? Or are Neil and Karen going to doubt me on this angle? Here he is picking up a cup – will this be the wrong cup?"

I remember Karen was going away to an editorial conference at one point, and she said, "I'm going to come back and we'll decide whether you're on the book or not." And I remember thinking, "Yeah, and I should decide whether I want to do it. Because I'm so fucking unhappy, maybe I shouldn't do it." Neil was trying to be the peacemaker – bless his heart – saying, "No, no. Come on. I want you to do it" and "Sam's the right guy." But basically it was just me and Karen butting heads, and what could he say at that point?

*Those early stories had a bit of an EC-horror-comics flair to them. Do you think that was, in part, Neil providing you with some material that you'd enjoy drawing, since you did come from the Wrightson school?*

The answer to that is yes. He was trying. It's true.

*Did Neil discuss this with you? Did he ask you what you'd like to draw?*

I think he might have thought of that, but I don't remember.

*Is it possible he'd just seen some of what you had already drawn at that time, and concluded – "Aha! Sam must like to do that EC and early-'70s-DC horror."*

Or concluded, "These are the things that would be about what this guy can handle, so we better play it up. I'm in a boat with one oar, so…"

*In either case, it's an interesting starting point for the series. Because the road for Alan Moore's* Swamp Thing, *for* Sandman, *and for the rest of Vertigo was paved by that early-'70s-DC horror. Do you think part of Neil's intent with those early issues was "Let's remember where we came from and let's start the book there?"*

Oh, God…that's a Neil question. I think he was stuck at one point, trying to figure out if the artist on this new book was *still* going to be [the book's] artist, that's all. [*Laughter.*] Sure, on the other hand, he was making some kind of diplomatic attempt to play to the strength of the artist he was writing for, while still keeping to the framework he had outlined long before that. The thing about *Sandman* was, it was largely a generous gesture on Neil's part to even give me my credit as co-creator. I think if anybody helped co-create anything in that world it was probably Mike. Actually I think Mike should be served an additional five percent above whatever he got, just for the Death merchandise alone. Because that look of that character, tapping into that world, was because of this guy in Utah that used to paint and draw like a motherfucker. Walking around town, he had a portfolio filled with work that was scary. Mike Dringenberg did two or three issues of a book called *Enchanter* – and that made people like Dick Giordano go, "Kid, anything you want to do here, it's yours." I mean he just blew people away with this amazingly mature body of work that looked like Jeff Jones had penciled it and Wrightson had inked it. He made everybody really jealous. I just knew that if I could hurry up and get fired from this book and Mike could take it over, it would be fine. [*Laughter.*]

*In the* Comics Interview Super Special: Sandman, *Neil commented, "…[issue] 4 was sort of like, 'Right, I'm doing this one for Sam.'"*

There was an issue ["A Hope in Hell"] where they went to Hell, there was a bunch of demons. That was the issue Neil started writing for me. Because I remember us feeling like the closest we ever got to some synchronicity was with that issue. Because he was actually bending over backwards to try to give me something that I wanted to do, and I spent a couple of weeks working on one double-page spread [pages 12-13].

*Was that the big shot of Hell with –*

A thousand demons. Right, yeah. And I inked it myself. (Bless his heart, Dringenberg, the ever-bludgeoned inker.) It was my attempt to say, "If I ink this book myself, this is what it could look like, Karen. *Now* can I do it?" And she still said, "No." Actually, though, I don't think I would have been able to make the book better if I had inked it myself. They were both gracious. Neil said, "Oh, yeah, I liked it." And even though I was crapping all over poor Mike, he said he liked it. Mike did pull me aside and say, "I'm not an idiot here. What am I not doing right? What am I not doing to contribute as an inker?"

*Why did he ask you that?*

Because I was telling him, "This looks like crap, and some of it's the inking. It's not working." We were good friends. Tough stuff, that.

*So you felt comfortable saying that to him?*

Yeah. I said, "Mike, this isn't working for me." I wouldn't actually say, "It looks like crap." I knew Mike was skilled and could ink circles around me. He was really, really good. I somehow said, "We're not working." And he said, "Well, tell me what to do, and be specific about it." I told him, "You need a thinner brush." I also realized that, again, our styles were such that he would draw a really realistic drawing and do a loose style on inking, and I would do a very tight, detailed cartoony drawing. We would be perfectly complemented if we reversed what we were doing. It's like a guy who's a good songwriter and a guy who's a good musician and they switched chores, and they found that they were weaker for it. It just was *not* working. I should have been inking the book and he should have been penciling it. I had developed into the kind of person that would fix things in the ink. My penciling hand was a weak left hand, and my inking hand was a strong right hand, and I had to hold everything with my weak left hand. The first issue sold really well – it was like eighty-thousand or something. It was a high-selling book for a DC book. It was up there. I remember seventy or eighty-thousand was what Karen told me.

*Had DC promoted it a great deal?*

There was a lot of energy around it because, at the time, of *Hellblazer*. There was an expectation that this would be, maybe, the new *Hellblazer*.

*How did you and Neil fare together on issue 5, after the synergy you achieved on issue 4?*

It was good, but, after issue 4, he had to go back to his [outline]. When I look back on it, I think so much of the problem was me trying to be what I thought they wanted me to be. Either I would try to be what I wanted – and then they said, "Well, you brought this big, pink elephant in here. This isn't gonna work. Because we got this system set up. We have these stories that he wants to tell and that people like." Then when I was finally able to *be* what they wanted me to be, in issues 5 and 6, I said, "Okay, how's it looking?" Karen said, "Good. You're doing what we say. It's all working out. It's looking fine." And I said to my wife, "What do you think of this?" And she said, "You seem so unhappy to me, and it looks like the closer you get to what they want, the less it seems like you to me. There's a lot of other people who can do this, and probably do it better, and probably not want to kill themselves." The feedback I was getting from other professionals in comics was that this was really bad work, that I really should quit the book. Looking back on it, even Mike's inks weren't the most garish part of the book. It was the color, too. But I have to place the bulk of the blame on my shoulders. It was just this magical chemistry of things that I don't think ever worked. This friend of mine, Albert Moy, was telling me the other day, "You know, I couldn't read *Sandman* in the beginning." He thought, "*Sandman* was crap. I'm not gonna read that." And this other friend of mine said, "You should have picked it up at [issue] 16 or 17. It was getting good. You should have read it." In retrospect, everybody goes back and reads it and says it was really good, but they weren't saying it was really good *art*, not at the time. When I finished, I was looking at the art for the first issue and I was thinking, "This is terrible. I should jump off a roof or something.

I really should kill myself." I was really upset, because I knew that Karen would not have said, "No, this is it. This is fine." It was like working on *X-Men* 1 and you're the weakest link. You're the one to whom everybody says, "It's great. Everything is great." But clearly the thing that's not working the most seems to be you.

I knew Dave McKean was a great artist, but I had some wounded pride about him doing the covers. Karen didn't say, "You have to get him to do the covers." She said, "You're the artist. If you want to do the covers it's fine. If you want to do the covers, I won't take them away from you."

*So you chose not to do them?*

Well, Neil and Karen said, "We'd like Dave to do the covers, but it's up to you." Well, what are you going to say? I went through the same thing with the *Aliens* covers, and they looked great.

*John Bolton wound up doing those, didn't he?*

Yeah, John Bolton. You can't deny that those covers looked great. I remember Neil saying to me, "Come on, you gotta let Dave do these covers." And I knew he was right, that Dave had skills I didn't have. And he would make the book look really classy. Even if the insides stunk, it would have these cool covers and good writing. So I said, "Okay, yeah, you're right." I am glad, because now when I go and sign something, it's got a cool cover.

I haven't talked about this in ten years, since it happened. It's not that this stuff is juicy, but it's interesting that it hasn't come out in ten years.

*Over ten years. Fifteen.*

What would be interesting would be [for you] to go back to Neil and have him put this in perspective. What's becoming clear to me now is: I had power struggles with Karen, and Neil was aligned with Karen but he consciously didn't do things to be cruel to me.

*How did you come to know Mike Dringenberg?*

I met him before those guys, back in the black-and-white comics boom. I was drawing books about adolescent, radioactive, black-belt hamsters. Mike Dringenberg drew a hamster series, too. We were all trying to break into color comics at the same time, together, doing embarrassing comics. Before we went off and did other comics that were embarrassing for Marvel and DC, we were doing embarrassing *black-and-white* comics. [*Laughter.*] Mike was one of the guys I met through Don Chin, who wrote the hamster book. Mike was just this guy running around San Diego with an amazing portfolio.

*And you brought Mike in as the* Sandman *inker.*

Yeah. Of course this whole thing is a road map to how I screwed myself. Poor casting. I asked him if he would ink it when he should have been penciling it. It's tragic.

*Well, tragedy sometimes makes for an interesting story.*

If your book features all of Neil's *Sandman* collaborators, you should save this interview for the end. Go backwards. Start off with the last *Sandman* artist and work your way back to issue 1. Most people will put down the book and go, "Man, the rest of it's great, but that Sam Kieth is just screwed up – what was going on with *that* dude?"

*I guess the book would resonate more strongly if it had a tragic ending.*

Yeah. [*Laughter.*]

*Regarding your situation with* Sandman*, you were quoted in several places as saying something like "I feel like Jimi Hendrix playing with the Beatles."*

[*Laughter.*] That was not my line. That was Neil's.

*That was Neil's?*

Maybe I said it…but I remember him saying it, and then people saying it back to me. So I don't know who said that [first]…but I doubt it was me. I said, "I felt like I was playing in the wrong band," and then I may have qualified it by saying "Jimi Hendrix in the Beatles." And then people would come up to me and say, "So you're Jimi Hendrix in the Beatles, right?" I'd say, "What are you talking about?" But I guess that's the line that stuck with people. I guess I was just trying to come up with a quasi-metaphor for saying that I didn't belong. It was two people that didn't belong together, yet were successful in their own right. Rather than saying, "I was like Ringo in the Beatles," I carefully chose Hendrix and the Beatles. [*Laughter.*] Because they were both popular, yet didn't…

*I'd like to talk about the issue of ownership of the* Sandman *character. Neil has managed to retain a share of the characters in the book, and he's also retained a share of the character for you and Mike Dringenberg.*

The nicest thing the man ever did. He made me and Mike a lot of money over the years. [*Laughter.*] There's seventy issues of *Sandman*. I did five issues, so out of a dollar I made five cents. And every couple of months you get a nice little *Sandman* check.

But Neil didn't have to do it. Frankly, I don't think Mike and I had a thing to do with creating that character. We were just artists on the book. I didn't create it. I do think that Mike co-created Death. And I'm not taking anything away from those issues that Neil wrote. At that time on the book, one of the last issues I read – that issue Mike started with – it was refreshing to see Neil make fun of that *Sandman* mythos with this other female character. [The Sandman] is always so melodramatic, you thank God [Neil's] mocking him a little bit.

*Death, oddly enough, humanized the book.*

And made it cheesy, too. I think Mike created Death ten times more than I ever created Sandman, and frankly Death is the outstanding character from the book. That's the one that Fairuza Balk keeps trying to make into a freaking movie! (She's wanted to be Death for a long time now, and Neil knows her.) But my point is that *Death* is closer to being made into a movie than *Sandman* was.

*The character has a very large following.*

Or tapped into what was already dormant. Even beyond her, just the idea of it, it just clicked with people. So I think a certain amount of the credit for Death, and her look, should go to Mike. I remember Neil calling me up and saying, "I told Karen, 'This is silly,' about us not owning Sandman." Because this other [Sandman], from the past, with the gas mask, was a totally different character. Clearly he had created something different. DC resisted. But I think that the leverage at that time had less to do with DC wanting to be nice or thinking it was the right thing to do, and more to do with the fact that Neil, by implication, wouldn't do any more *Sandman*s if they didn't do it. Bye bye, franchise. [*Laughter.*] I don't think he even had to say that, but I think it was clear that that's what was on the table.

*Do you remember the point at which this occurred?*

It must have been close to the time we published the first issue. I remember the conversation with him saying that, and then him saying that we were going to give [credit] to me, and if we were going to give it to me, we should give it to Mike. And me thinking, "Wow. That's generous. We're just two bumps on a log. We don't deserve that. But, fine – yeah!" Not relating, too, that one little fateful word, "credit." The two most consistent things in my entire life are *The Maxx* and *Sandman*. Thank God that one of them I'm actually responsible for! [*Laughter.*] *Sandman* was like a nuclear reactor I happened to be standing next to when it exploded. One of them, *Maxx*, I actually at least caused, or partly caused.

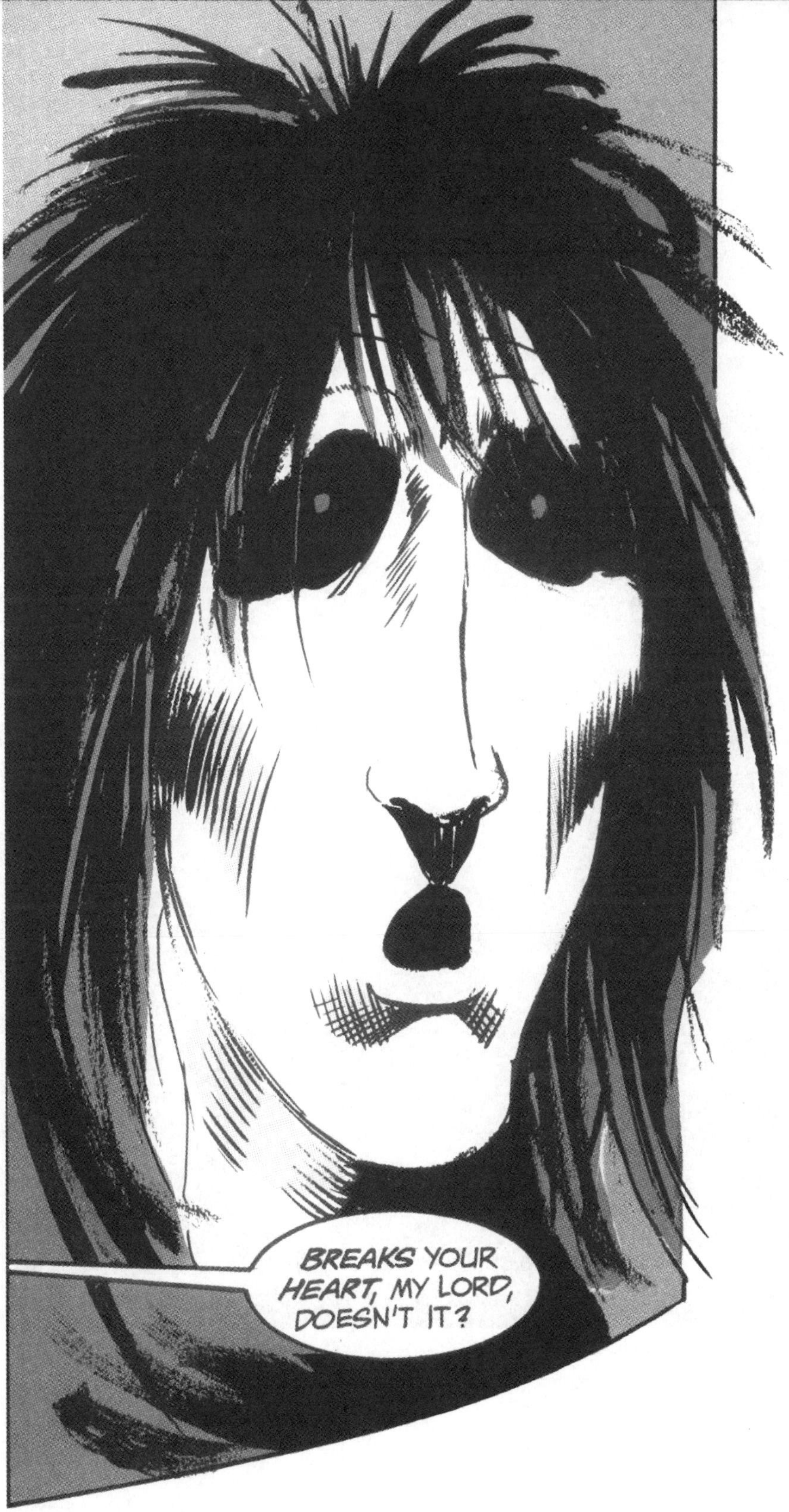
BREAKS YOUR HEART, MY LORD, DOESN'T IT?

"The goofy Sandman." From page 13 of *Sandman* 2, "Imperfect Hosts," page 13. Pencils by Sam Kieth and inks by Mike Dringenberg. © 2004 DC Comics.

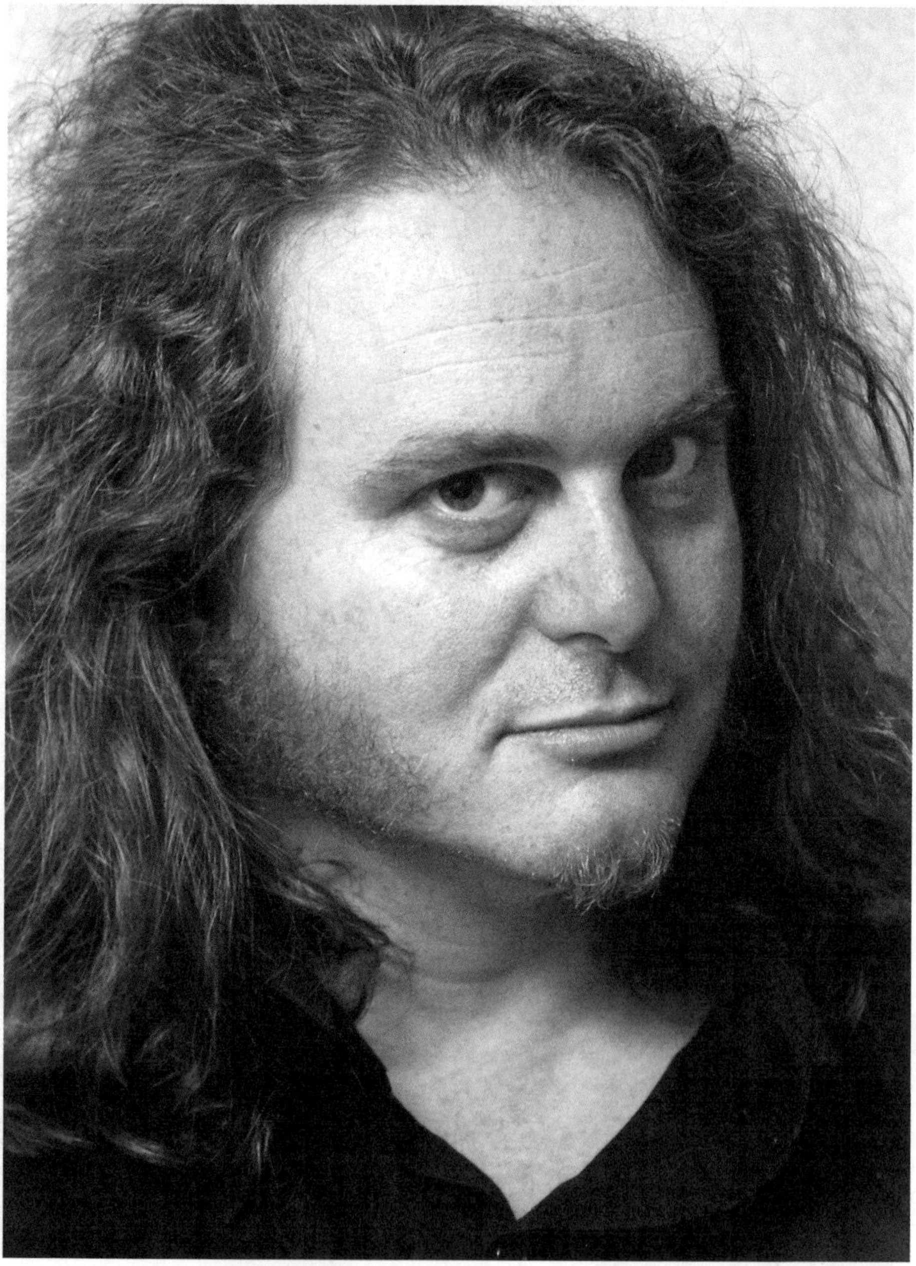

## Mike Dringenberg

MIKE DRINGENBERG, CREDITED ALONGSIDE SAM KIETH,
AS ONE OF SANDMAN'S CO-CREATORS, INKED THE BOOK'S FIRST FIVE ISSUES BEFORE
TAKING OVER THE PENCILING DUTIES. IN THE ELEVEN ISSUES HE ILLUSTRATED — INCLUDING
MOST OF THE DOLL'S HOUSE — DRINGENBERG DEVELOPED THE LOOK OF FOUR
OF THE SEVEN ENDLESS: DESIRE, DESPAIR, DELIRIUM, AND DEATH (BASED ON HIS
FRIEND CINNAMON). HIS SOMETIMES MOODY, SOMETIMES SEXY, ALMOST-ALWAYS
POWERFUL IMAGES SET A VISUAL TONE FOR MANY OF THE SANDMAN ARTISTS WHO
SUCCEEDED HIM.

AFTER LEAVING THE BOOK, DRINGENBERG WORKED ON A MARVEL GRAPHIC NOVEL, THE
WAY OF THE SORCERER. "UNFORTUNATELY," HE SAYS, "IT GOT ENTANGLED WITH THE
ICON-PERLMAN NONSENSE. WHEN THEY SHUT DOWN EPIC, WE WERE IN THE PROCESS
OF WRAPPING UP THE BOOK. WE HAD FINALLY, AFTER TWO YEARS, GOT TO THE POINT
WHERE WE WERE ONLY FOUR PAINTED PAGES AWAY FROM FINISHING THE PROJECT."

THESE DAYS, DRINGENBERG FOCUSES ON ADVERTISING AND BOOK-ILLUSTRATION WORK.
HIS COVERS GRACE THE LATEST PAPERBACK EDITIONS OF TOLKIEN'S SILMARILLION AND
SIR GAWAIN AND THE GREEN KNIGHT, KIJ JOHNSON'S FUDOKI, EMMA BULL'S
WAR FOR THE OAKS AND NUMEROUS OTHER BOOKS.

*A number of* Sandman *fans regard the first appearance of Dream's sister, Death [Issue 8, "The Sound of Her Wings"], as the point where the book really started to take off. Since you penciled that story, I'd like to hear some of your thoughts regarding the creation of Death.*

Actually, I always thought that Decay would be a good character to do. Decay is a natural process of the universe, and I was thinking that would be a lot more fun than Despair. Decay would be wandering around with little bits of things falling off of her all the time. It would have been a lot of fun to draw. I mean, imagine if she served somebody tea. [*Laughs.*] But, yeah, Death was certainly that. I mean, she was based on someone who was an absolute pleasantry to be around.

*I believe Neil initially came up with a little sketch of Death. How did he first describe the character to you?*

The way he originally described her – I have never seen the sketch – was very much a Louise Brooks kind of concoction. He wanted that look, with sort of a short, black bob, and much more stylish.

*So there was a jazz-age influence?*

Decidedly. And the way I saw it… I saw her walking down the street knowing she's it. And I knew it in the pit of my gut. Every bell rang as loud as you could possibly say it, from the haircut to that perfectly sculpted face to the little speck of glitter she stuck to her teeth with superglue. Little things like that, you know? That was it, she was it. And that was the way it went. The Sandman is an amalgam based on three or four different people I knew, and didn't want to know well. Death is based on, primarily, Cinnamon – who was a ballet dancer – but also a couple of other people I knew. My girlfriend, at the time, posed as the character on a number of occasions. She was also, like Cinnamon, bone thin. The kind of physique that, were she to ball her hand into a fist, you could see every single muscle running up and down her arm. Ballet training will do that for you.

*There's a close-up of Death on page 9 of issue 8. I suppose that was Cinnamon's portrait?*

Oh, yeah. [*Laughs.*] That was actually a pre-existing piece that I ended up using there. Malcolm [Jones] didn't ink that one.

*Was Death's ankh your idea? It's an ironic touch, of course, because the ankh was originally used as a symbol of life for the Egyptians.*

Death's ankh was indeed my idea. For two reasons, the first stemming from a line at the end of Philippe Druillet's "Yragael/Urm" (Dragon's Dream), which reads: "…Only mortals die forever," a line that I repeated on a tomb engraving in Death's page of DC's *Who's Who*. Also, since Death was "Endless," and since Cinnamon was prone to wearing a little silver ankh – a sign of immortality and rebirth – I thought it both a fitting tribute to a beauty and a lovely irony – worthy of such a deity, a kind of cosmic joke.

*One of the things I noticed about your Death and Dream, that I believe wasn't picked up by later artists, was the boots they wore – with the pointed toes that curled up.*

We all had pointy-toed boots that curled up in those days. Everybody had them, and if you've ever had a pair yourself, you'll notice they will quite naturally curl up at the toe after a while. And if you really wear them out, the only way to get them to actually stay in one piece is to wrap black electrical tape around the tips. [Laughs.] So that was just a part of it. It was just a part of the look. Baggy, soft clothing was just a carryover from the '80s, the '80s gone dark. I mean, when it came right down to it, the bunch of us were really more Grave-Wave than Goth, and were just as likely to wear silvery silk paisley as black. But the Goth scene itself, as we know it now, sort of turned up about half-way through my run of *Sandman*. The style, that is.

*Later artists changed Death's look a bit, giving her rounded-toe boots with buckles. What would you call that look?*

I would call that L.A. Rocker. They cuted her up.

*Do you think they made her more user-friendly?*

Oh, very definitely. Recently, I wandered around for a while in a comics shop with a friend of mine from the old days. We found a whole set of Little Endless statues, done in the classic manga, super-deformed style, based on Jill [Thompson]'s drawings. Here we were looking at the little Chibi-Death, and saying, "This isn't Cinnamon." Because we're thinking of Cinnamon with her thigh-high leather boots and her 42 piercings, with her shredded fishnet brassiere – if you can call it that – and her leather jacket and her purple hair and her purple pubic hair…[*laughs*] her little speed-freak scars; and saying, "You know, it's just as sweet as Cinnamon is, but this just isn't her." It's just the process of drift from reality to caricature to cartoon: taking a real person and just going further and further away from that source. But, you know, out of all the people who worked on *Sandman*, I'm the only person who's ever met Cinnamon. Some of the fans did when I did a signing down in Austin, and so there are some *Sandman* issues floating around that have been signed by Cinnamon.

*After Death came the other Endless. Could you briefly describe what went into the design for…*

For the characters? Well, Delirium originally came from a girl that Neil pointed out in a British body-piercing magazine, this ambiguous little photo that was taken at a club. The thing is, at the time, the girl in the photo bore an astonishing resemblance to a girl that I had recently dated. And I kind of went, "Oh, that's it!" And so I called her up and had her pose for the various Delirium pieces that I did. She was perfect for it. I mean, she was basically that character in a nutshell, every bit as delightful and every bit as weird. But Jill made the definitive Delirium, though.

*Let's talk about Desire for a moment. There's something in those early Desire images that bring to mind some '80s pop music stars…*

Like, for example, the great giant statue that she stands in looks a little bit like Annie Lennox?

*Kind of…*

It's more like the great giant statue that she's standing in was actually my girlfriend. [*Laughs.*] She was also the substitute Death, on many an occasion. She was a very thin, very graceful-looking woman. To this day, she's one of the best belly-dancers here in town. But I just wondered what she would look like with very, very short hair. That she ended up having exactly those cheekbones was coincidental. Neil's idea for Desire was essentially sexless and forever unsatisfying. And my Desire was the idea of being omni-sexual and perennially tempting. I saw Desire – and still see Desire, I guess – as a thing that can tempt anyone with anything. For example, mine has breasts and a bulge between the legs, and Neil's has nothing. So – different views of things.

*Since you drew most of* The Doll's House, *I suppose we saw your Desire throughout that story.*

That's the nice thing (or not nice thing, in some people's eyes) about being the artist – ultimately, you get to put the final stamp on whatever goes out. Neil saw Desire as being somewhere between David Bowie and Annie Lennox, but I always thought more in terms of Duran Duran – sort of two-dimensional and slightly vapid.

*Regarding Despair, you've mentioned before that when you first drew her, you found her difficult to draw, as, at that point in your life, you'd not yet experienced true despair.*

I'd never experienced it, nor had I ever really seen it in anyone else. Since then, I have seen it. And consequently, there are a few people I can think of, in drawing that character, that would come to mind, that would more readily facilitate my being able to relate to that character, to that mind state. I'm not a despairing individual. I'm a perennial optimist, to the point where it does sort of drive a few of my friends crazy. But, y'know, it's either that or overdose on a ton of heroin – edit yourself out of the narrative. Let other people do that.

*Yes, that's been done. It's passé now.*

Yup, [*with Liverpool accent*] that's been done. Yeah. I prefer the brighter side.

*You may have had trouble drawing her initially, but I should point out that on page 5 of Despair's first appearance in* The Doll's House *[issue 10] you drew a fairly disturbing-looking Despair. You already had a definite look for her.*

Thanks. Again, Neil found a picture, of a circus freak, with her sawed-down-looking teeth. I have no idea when the photo was taken. It was an old black-and-white thing that he had made a copy of and sent to me. So I fairly stuck to that, because it was a wonderfully creepy-looking image. I would probably handle it better now, but then I basically played it as rote. Nowadays, I could actually fill it with a certain amount of spirit, one way or another, and really get to where Neil was going with her character. Despair was always a little bit different in some ways, I think, because Neil took a rather patronizing approach to the whole idea of Despair.

*In what sense?*

He was always very sentimental toward it. I don't think that Despair was anything that he had personally felt, so he could only stand on the outside of that equation, look in and say, "Oh, you poor thing," and then move on. Whereas I was seeing people ruin themselves, and occasionally had very good friends ruin themselves; and it will tear at your heart like nobody's business. And I think from that experience I could probably handle it a little bit better now than I did then. Despair, at one time, if I recall correctly, was Neil's favorite of the Endless. I guess you could say Neil wrote from the viewpoint of whoever it was that wrote "All Tomorrow's Parties." Granted, that was Lou Reed, but I'm talking about the mindset that the song represents, which is to say, of an outsider looking in at someone else's despair.

*Was Destruction a little easier for you to depict?*

Very much. My concept of Destruction was based on my best friend, who's this six-foot-four son of Ireland – bright-red hair, huge beard, capable of leaping tall pitchers of Guinness in a single bound. The funny thing is, he very much matched up to Jill Thompson's boyfriend, as far as the physical profile went. So after I had done the character – in a couple of posters and a couple of odd scenes here and there – when Jill actually kind of did the majority of the work about Destruction, it just matched up anyway. It was just a very lucky coincidence. Her boyfriend was the primary model. My friend was also the model for Sir Gawain, on the cover of J.R.R. Tolkien's *Sir Gawain and the Green Knight*. He looks the part and his last name is Green, so the choice was obvious. [*Laughs.*]

*I'd like to talk about some of the work you did on the early* Sandman *issues, inking Sam Kieth. When I spoke with Sam, he mentioned this "amazingly mature body of work" that you were carrying around in your portfolio at that time. He said it looked like "Jeff Jones had penciled it and Wrightson had inked it"; and that he just knew if he could hurry up and get fired from* Sandman *and you could take it over, it would have that going for it.*

Well, I think it's safe to say that Sam and I were coming from the same direction. But we had actually crossed over into different directions about a year and a half or so, or maybe two years, before Sam got on *Sandman*. By the time we were on *Sandman* we'd already crossed paths, so to speak, and were heading in opposite directions toward inventing our own styles. The early issues of *Sandman* might point that out – as being sort of our fond farewell to Bernie Wrightson and Arthur Suydam and Frank Frazetta and "Ghastly" Graham Ingels, and the great tradition of horror that both of us came from. We were both off on entirely different routes – Sam to become essentially the Jimi Hendrix of comics, or maybe the Eric Clapton of comics, and me toward becoming its Jeff Beck. It's an easy summation that Neil became as Led Zeppelin, you know, its Jimmy Page. The early issues of *Sandman* are a little bit like the early Yardbirds albums, where you had Beck, Page, and Clapton all on the same tape.

It was one of those things. We were both extremely unique stylists. And quite frankly they just didn't have any place to put us – no stage to play on. Think about it – when Jimi Hendrix first turned up as a guitarist for a Little Richard tour, he was first reprimanded for upstaging Little Richard, and later booted off because it was the "Little Richard Tour," not the "Jimi Hendrix Tour." Eventually Hendrix had to form the Experience to do his own thing. At the time, both of us, Sam and I, were essentially looking to be session players and had no idea that either of us were essentially rock stars in our own right. Maybe that's exaggerating things, and I apologize to anybody who takes that the wrong way, but that's sort of the truth. We had styles. Sam says that my style was amazingly mature at the time; but I think he's being extraordinarily depreciative of his own. The basic point, though, was that we were unique enough that they had no idea where the hell to fit us. That Neil turned up when he did with *Sandman* was amazing luck. It was a remarkable coincidence. It was a situation where we were all right there at the right place at the right time – I knew Sam, and Sam had done some issues of *Manhunter* and was eager to cut his teeth as a penciler. They already had McKean in place to do the covers and wanted someone to do the guts who wouldn't too far compete with what they thought was going to be the next big thing, and dragged Sam in. And he didn't really like the inkers they showed him and suggested me, even though, frankly, the two of us had always worked the other way around, that is with him inking and me penciling.

The first time that Sam ever called me about the whole thing, he essentially said, "I know you're not going to like this because we always talked about you being the penciler and me being the inker. I know you're gonna turn this down." I said, "No, Sam, this is great. We get to work together." He said, "Well, I know you don't really want to do this..." "No, Sam, really!" "You mean it?" he said, "You really want to work with me like this?" I said, "Sure. We're working together. That's the important thing. It's what we always wanted to do!" "You mean it?" "Yes!" I had to convince him for half an hour that I was being serious. He's the most self-deprecating guy on the planet, and he really has no cause to be. I don't think, at the core of it, that he really is. But he's extraordinarily honest to the point of being rather funny. He'll probably take that the wrong way, too.

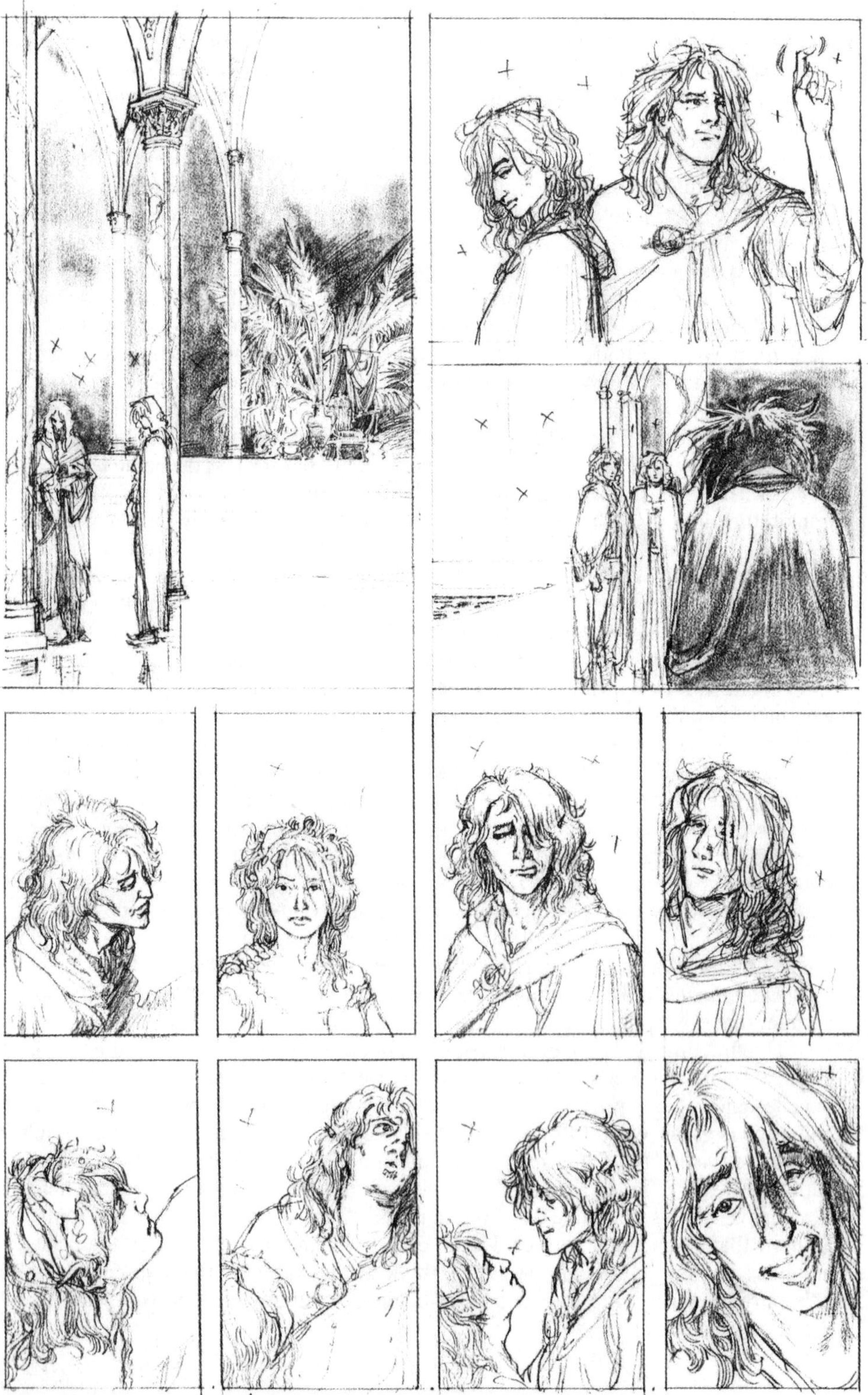

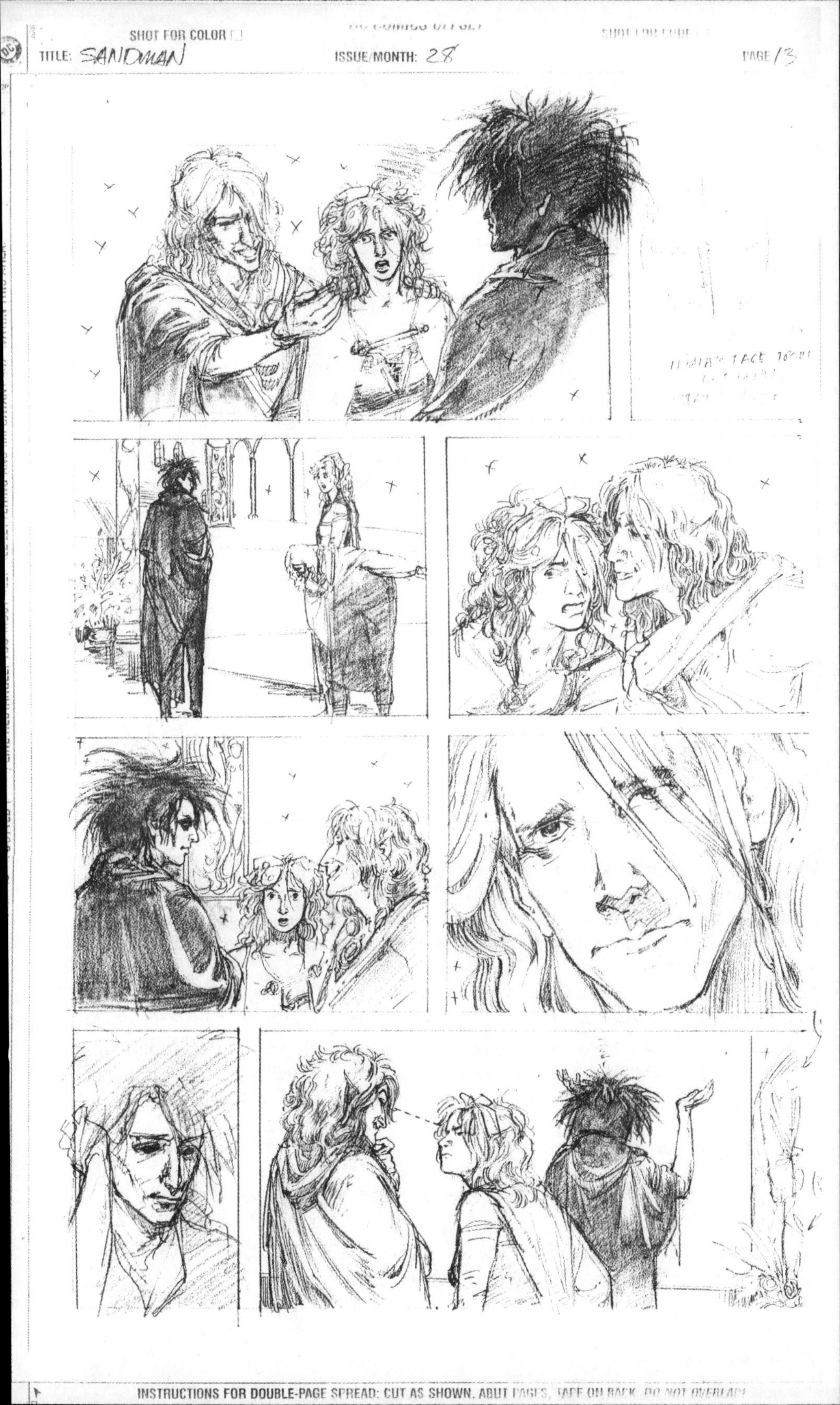
SHOT FOR COLOR
TITLE: SANDMAN
ISSUE/MONTH: 28
PAGE 13
INSTRUCTIONS FOR DOUBLE-PAGE SPREAD: CUT AS SHOWN, ABUT PAGES,

MIKE DRINGENBERG'S PENCILS FOR PAGES 12 AND 13 OF *SANDMAN* 27, *SEASON OF MISTS'* EPILOGUE. © 2004 DC COMICS.

*Or at least pretend that he is.*

He'll pretend that he is. Yeah, I think he has a little more confidence in how I feel about him, and in my admiration for his work, and of him as a person. He's kind of like the big brother I never had.

*You hold him in that regard?*

Well, Sam and Neil. Yeah, the funny thing is that Sam always thought that I was kind of like the big brother he never had. At one point we both kind of mentioned that to each other. It was like, "Wow! Really?" It was a very funny moment.

*And you regard Neil the same way?*

Oh, yeah. I think a lot of Neil.

*Did the two of you socialize much?*

Oh, yeah, back in the early days. I mean, Neil and I got on straightaway. I guess the difference between Neil and myself was that Neil was of the generation that listened to Lou Reed, and I was of the generation who listened to Nick Cave – to the musicians that themselves listened to Lou Reed. But Neil and I, even though we saw eye to eye most of the time, there was a little age difference, and even with that slight difference, although some of our attitudes are similar, there are others that suddenly change. We were all the difference between, say, the Eno and Bauhaus versions of the song "Third Uncle." I was essentially a punk rocker. Neil was still very much proto-punk. So there was always a slight difference in perspective.

*Neil actually played in a punk band for a little while, in the '70s.*

Yeah, he played bass. And though we never really did, we always talked about jamming a version of "Suffragette City."

*Do you play as well?*

Oh, yeah. I play guitar. I've played in a few garage bands and played a few live gigs myself. But the closest Neil and I ever got to it was irritating the hell out of the staff of Night Flight Comics in Salt Lake City, by both of us caterwauling the lyrics as we were crossing the parking lot one night. [*Laughs.*] But yeah, I think it would have been a lot of fun – taking out the instruments and just jamming for an evening.

*And I suppose you and Neil did tour together, in a sense, at this time, at least to promote* Sandman. *I heard DC treated you guys pretty well.*

Oh, yeah. They were treating us pretty much like rock stars – at least on tour. Anything we wanted they gave us. It was a total star trip. And with our leather jackets, sunglasses, and haircuts, we looked the part. It was something that Sam always kind of bailed out of. He said, "I always felt like Jimi Hendrix playing in the Beatles." He didn't have the haircut.

*He didn't favor a rock-star haircut for Dream either. He said he preferred the goofy-looking Sandman.*

His Sandman was a little more like Ron Wood or Keith Richards. My version of Sandman was more like Peter Murphy or Robert Smith.

*I'd like to hear your comments on a few of the images I encountered in your run on* Sandman. *One of the things that struck me is that you seemed to employ an interesting technique in rendering Nada, Dream's ex-flame whom he sent to Hell [issue 9, "Tales in the Sand"].*

Actually the technique I used there was one that I exploited more fully in some of the great "dream vortex" pieces, all of the great swirling purple vortices at the end of *The Doll's House* [issue 15, "Into the Night"]. What it is, is that you can get an effect very similar to a monotype by putting ink down on Mylar, the matte surface of Mylar, and simply letting it dry, and then wiping it off with a solvent, or, while it's still partially wet, spritzing it with the solvent. It'll bubble up and make some rather interesting effects. I wanted something that was amorphous and had the imprecise feel of a monotype, but obviously on a much smaller scale because, of course, a comic-book page is only 11x17 rather than, say, 35x35, and it has to bear several images rather than just one. So essentially you put the ink down as an emulsion and you lift out the different areas with a cotton swab soaked in 409. Afterwards, we ran the Mylar sheet as a K-tone. People ask me about that all the time, and to me it's just a simple technique I picked up back when I was in school. I'd used it on any number of occasions. I still occasionally do, but nowadays I have better materials for it.

*Why were Chris Bachalo and Michael Zulli brought in to cover two of* The Doll's House *issues (12 and 13)? Was that to give you some time to catch up?*

Yeah, I was in the doghouse at the time. Frankly, the editor and I never really quite saw eye to eye, from minute 1. Even from the earliest sample pieces I turned in, when Sam was quitting the book, we never really hit it off. (I was fine as an inker, because then I was essentially batting clean-up for Sam, and I could sort-of separate myself from the creative matrix.) Eventually, it got to point where I was taking all kinds of crazy chances with the look of the book and when I thought I had achieved a good effect, I would occasionally sit on the pages until it was too late to make corrections, which would drive her crazy, and then send them in. To which she would pretty much freak out and scream, "This wasn't in the script," and show it to Neil. Neil would say, "Oh, it's brilliant" [*laughs*] and she would have to eat a little crow and be completely angry at me. Then of course the thing shipped out and the fans loved it. Needless to say, this was not something she enjoyed [*laughs*].

There's a time in everybody's life when they know precisely what is right. And when I was doing that, when I was in the groove, I knew exactly what was right. And at the time, I felt very much like the tail should wag the dog, you know, like "The world is my oyster and I will do whatever the hell I like with it." Let's face it, I was a prima donna. It was absolute hell doing that. My mindset at the time was a little bit like…I can describe it as a sound. Have you ever had the brakes on your car wear out? Where you're grinding metal against metal? That's what my mind's state was like at the time – that sound. Between my extremely demanding model girlfriend and the editor and the demands of the book, I burned my candle at both ends and I burned myself hard. I essentially let all the pressure out through the book. Whatever I was feeling, I put into it in one way or another. It was really rather chilling when I was looking at *Sandman* 16 ["Lost Hearts"] about five or six years ago and really realizing that, if you had the code, if you were there at the time and knew me at the time, you could see literally everything that was going on around me in one way or another written into the art. It was chilling. There's a little scene in there where that glass heart shatters [page 14]. I felt it was my own heart shattering, because in some way I kind of realized that I had somehow crossed the invisible line, swum the Rubicon between being an illustrator and being an artist, in the sense that I was no longer fulfilling someone else's vision, and I was, in fact, communicating my own. And I suddenly felt stark naked in front of a hundred-thousand people. It was an amazing epiphany, and a scary one, and probably a good thing I didn't do a couple of issues after that, partially because we needed to catch up on the deadline, partially because mentally I had about had it. And shortly after that everything completely fell apart. When I did *Sandman* 21, I was in this very strange sort of state of shock, where everything was essentially just functioning on autopilot. I look back on it as being probably the most graceful issue we did. It was in fact the only issue we worked on where everything went right.

*That was the first issue of* Season of Mists, *the Prologue.*

That was, I think, the one issue we did where everything worked out perfectly. As another point, I never really got on with the colorist on the early issues. It was one of those things. For whatever it's worth, Steve Oliff [issue 21's colorist] very definitely speaks the same language that Sam and I do when it comes down to art and some of the various artists that we're all into. I could speak to Oliff in shorthand and he would understand exactly what I was after, and, consequently, we ended up with a stunningly, beautifully colored issue. It's always bothered me that if we'd had him on day one, the way that we initially wanted it, the way that Sam and I wanted it, every single issue of *Sandman* up to that point would have looked as beautiful. The way that we originally drew the book, more or less normal comic-book coloring would have been fine, and it was great for the early issues – issue 1, issue 2 – it worked fine for that. But as we started to branch out and started getting more experimental with the artwork, I don't think it quite kept up. I think the colorist fell back on what he knew as abstract painting.

You see, when I look at *Sandman* I see a whole series of maimed children. I see what might have been as opposed to what is. To this day, it's very hard for me to actually look at the issues, when I think of my conception for this or Sam's conception for that and say, "You know, there are a great many places where there's no way I could have inked what Sam had in mind" – he's a far better inker than I am and, in some ways, he's a much more imaginative artist. Then again, there are times when I look at it and I think of the Wagnerian scope that I had in mind when I was working on the issues, and I'm just lucky that Malcolm was there to pick up on it.

*You were pleased with Malcolm Jones's inking?*

Oh, yes. It's a big shame Malcolm never actually got to draw an issue himself. He was a fine penciler.

*Issue 11 ("Moving In") is dedicated to "Inell Jones."*

Malcolm's sister. At the time we did the serial-killers convention story, Malcolm's sister died. Also, one of my friends was attacked by a serial killer up in Canada. This was an amazing series of coincidences, but then the whole of *Sandman* was essentially founded on bizarre incidents of synchronicity. Issue after issue, month after month, it had a very, very unusual vibe, all the way around. The first letter that I ever received about the book – I opened it up and the song "Mr. Sandman" actually came over the radio while I was sitting there reading it. I knew from that moment that it was going to be one very strange ride.

*Neil called Jones "the unsung hero of pen, brush, and deadline."*

Yeah. Malcolm was an Iron Man. I met him at the DC commissary. We had an instant rapport. Both of us thought it was really amusing when we were formally introduced as people who would be working together, because we'd already met and hit it off about a half-hour beforehand.

*Your styles meshed pretty well.*

We had a lot of the same heroes. Malcolm had done a lot of very, very detailed inking work for various Warren publications. He had the technical ability to pretty well handle anything I could throw at him. It was like walking out on the stage and finding out that the guy who was playing sax with you is every bit as able as you are. It's an absolute delight that you don't have to hold back, or you don't have to try to play catch-up or something. You're on the same wavelength. And when that happens it's a kind of magic. I still miss him.

*You mentioned some of the trouble you felt you had on the book. Did Jones have any difficulties?*

Well, between my being an extreme prima donna and screwing up a lot of deadlines, which ate into his inking time, and various personal troubles of his own, Malcolm, I don't think, ever was really quite happy with the book. He felt very underappreciated, I know that. But the thing is, if he'd stuck with it, if he hadn't killed himself, if he'd stuck with it for another year or so, he would have won every award that an inker could win.

*Your depiction of the Dreaming at the end of* The Doll's House *[Issues 15 and 16] is somewhat desert-like. Was that due to the influence of your home environment, of Utah?*

Utah, if you've never been there, is like Dali's painting "The Persistence of Memory," even to the melting clock and the ants. But I think my most accurate conception of the Dreaming was probably the one that I did for the DC *Who's Who* [issue 15], in which I originally started at the bottom with a Columbus-era map. Essentially what happens is that the map gets folded about midway through, just crumpled; and the areas where the crumples are, at the end of it, just break out into all kinds of image fragments, until at the top, it becomes a collage. Some of it's people, some of it's faces. I had to throw a Dali melting clock in there someplace, just because. Neil never conceived of the Dreaming as being a kind of surrealist Daliesque place, or as anything even vaguely related to that. He imagined it much more akin to the way that H.P. Lovecraft imagined the realm of Dream – a definite sense of place. It's not a nebulous area, it's not a Freudian wilderland, although some of those paradoxes do exist there. It has a very definite sense of place, it's a very physical environment. It was something that I didn't quite understand at the time because I had never read any Lovecraft. I'd read Lautréamont, I'd read DeChirico, I'd read Rimbaud; but I had never read Lovecraft. At any rate, my conception of the whole thing was more along the lines of Artaud rather than Arthur Machen.

*What other aspects of your home found their way into* The Sandman*?*

I can say that *Sandman* serves as a kind of documentation of the Salt Lake scene at the time. Not the whole scene by any means, but I tried to get as many people to pose for it as I could. And there are various little icons from those days that I incorporated into the background, like the 24-hour diner [in issue 6, "24 Hours"]. There was a local diner here, now recently plowed under, unfortunately. It was the only 24-hour place in town. There are little things like that all over *Sandman*. For example, Rose Walker's house in Florida is actually my friend's who was the primary model for Rose Walker. In the story, Rose Walker had the top-floor apartment and, by coincidence, so did my friend. So it all worked out rather neatly. There are little bits and things like that – the mansion on 824 South Temple is the mansion at 824 in *Sandman*, and so on.

*Neil remarked in his weblog that the setting of Death's first appearance was originally to be Central Park, but that you changed it to Washington Square Park. How often did you find yourself changing things in Neil's scripts?*

I have some profound memories of Washington Square, and it's the heart of the Village. I set the action there for personal reasons, and for the dramatic and symbolic effect of the arch. I often found analogues for Neil's locations from my own experience. There's a German word, *stimmung*, meaning (approximately) "mood," or an "atmosphere," that doesn't quite translate into English. I sought a particular "stimmung" in the work, a certain "feel" that I knew was correct, with which I knew I *had* to imbue it (as Andre Breton put it, "Beauty will be *convulsive* or will not *be*") – I can't describe this in more rational, graspable terms – and that meant finding settings that would, at some level, free my emotions into the work. It required a certain juju.

The 24-hour diner was another of my location changes; Neil originally had the story set in, essentially, a classic English pub. Part of *Sandman*'s dynamic stemmed from Neil's discovery and fascination, as both a European and an Englishman, with America. There were, however, some gaping holes in his experience – like the fact that the phenomena of English-style pubs are somewhat foreign to everyday American life. The roadside diner is a better American equivalent, and if you've ever been fucked up and fired out in one at 3 am, or, say, read *Fear & Loathing in Las Vegas* (or, better, lived it), you know exactly what an odd environment it can be. So, with the relic diner as the locale ("Bill & Nada's," now a vacant lot after some fifty years of operation), I applied Hitchcock's method of taking a familiar setting and using it as a stage for the out-of-the-ordinary, and *Sandman* 6 was the result.

*Your final* Sandman *issue, 28, was also, as I mentioned, the epilogue of* Season of Mists. *Kelley Jones had drawn the bulk of that story, but were you still considered the book's regular penciler?*

At that point, the idea of having me back on the book as a regular artist was wishful thinking. The editor and I had not worked together for a period of about six months, and I had started to realize that, on the whole, it had been a pretty bad experience, and she had also realized, at least from her standpoint, that it had been a bad experience. So we gave it one last try just to see if anything would work out. And even as I started penciling the thing, I knew it would be something like my swan song. I very deeply cared about those pages and at the same time I was extremely demoralized about them. It took me an extra couple of weeks to do it, so I really ate into other people's deadlines. I suppose it was vain of me to do that, but it was my last issue, and I knew that it was going to be my last issue. So I tried to make the pages the best I could possibly make them. Afterwards, Neil still tried to get me back on to the book, tried to sort of sneak me in through the back door, but I flatly told him – and I think that he took this rather hard – that if I wanted a favor from him, I'd ask for one. I didn't ask him to try to get me back on *Sandman*. That was his plan, not mine.

There was a whole world of mental pain there that I didn't want to have anything to do with. I was off the book, and, for whatever it was worth, I've always been the kind of character who… If I'm going to burn a bridge, I'm going to burn it with gasoline. It's the punk rocker in me. I'll happily throw a brick through your front window if I happen to feel like it. But I was off the book and off the hook, and I really did not want to go back onto it, because although I loved working with Neil – it was a fun ride – I knew in some way or another if I had kept on with it, I would have gone bug-fuck. And I certainly didn't need that. So I stayed off of it, and that's just where it hung. To this day, I think it's something that Neil kind of holds against me in the sense that he really extended his hand while I was out there in the ocean, and I batted it away. The truth of it was, it's not that I didn't want to climb on board with him so much as that I rather felt like I needed to learn to swim. In one way or another, I had to find my own way out of the whole thing, to grow as a person. Neil has his destiny and I have mine.

*Lately you've been doing a lot of advertising and illustration work. Do you derive more pleasure from this work than you feel you would from comics?*

As far as I'm concerned, they're equally challenging, but for entirely different reasons. I function very freely in both mediums. I would rather work on single illustrations if I have to work on deadlines, simply because I've never grown attached to a single illustration in the same way that I have to a narrative piece. It's a much less intimate process. You work up a series of sketches, and you go through the formal process of design, which is a little impersonal, and you have to look at the image in a somewhat colder way. You can't become sentimental about any one thing. If you have a particular element in an image that's more troublesome than not, well, either you have to find a way to make it work because the client wants it that way, or you have to cut it simply because there isn't any way or time to make it fit. Or you may have to reexamine the concept in a completely different light. So you have to basically distance yourself from the work, in an academic way. You have to be able to look at it in a way that doesn't involve your personality, your likes and dislikes. Save your personality and your personal involvement for the final technique. Save that for the painting, but when you're doing the design, it has to essentially be kept at arm's length so that you're getting the best possible design you can, and the reward comes from a job well done.

But when you're dealing with a narrative, you live with it for a certain amount of time, and as a consequence, the work process becomes more subjective. I mean I lived with *Sandman*. I slept with *Sandman*. I ate *Sandman*. And as crazy as it sounds, for almost three years it was the biggest thread in my life. In this whole interview, I've described various aspects of it. My friends were in it, the various locations where things happened were in it, and so on. In that regard, it occupied a very fair-sized place in my life, moreso because I was young, and gave myself over to it wholeheartedly. Either as a mature professional or as a young dreamer, in one way or another, you live with that narrative. You associate with the writer, the inker, the colorist, every single month; with the editor, every single issue, with every single group of pages you send in, every line. The narrative becomes an environment, and there's an intimacy that develops with that. If you're working on a graphic-novel project, for example, you have to maintain a certain objective distance from the work in order to convey the narrative correctly. But at the same time, that's very, very difficult to do, simply because it does surround you all the time. It takes an artist of unusual ability and insight to excel in that environment, and its agonies and ecstasies are their own reward.

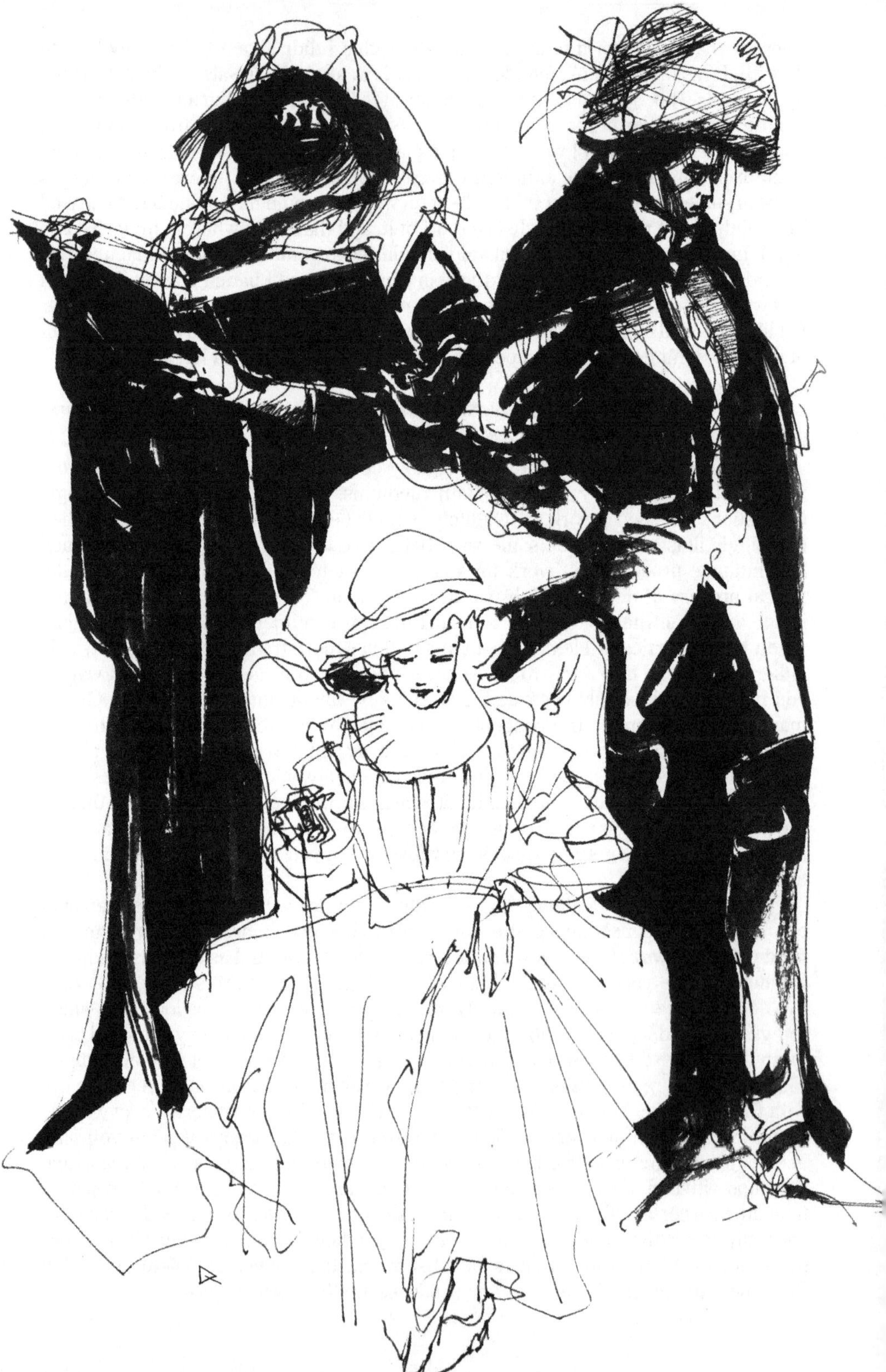

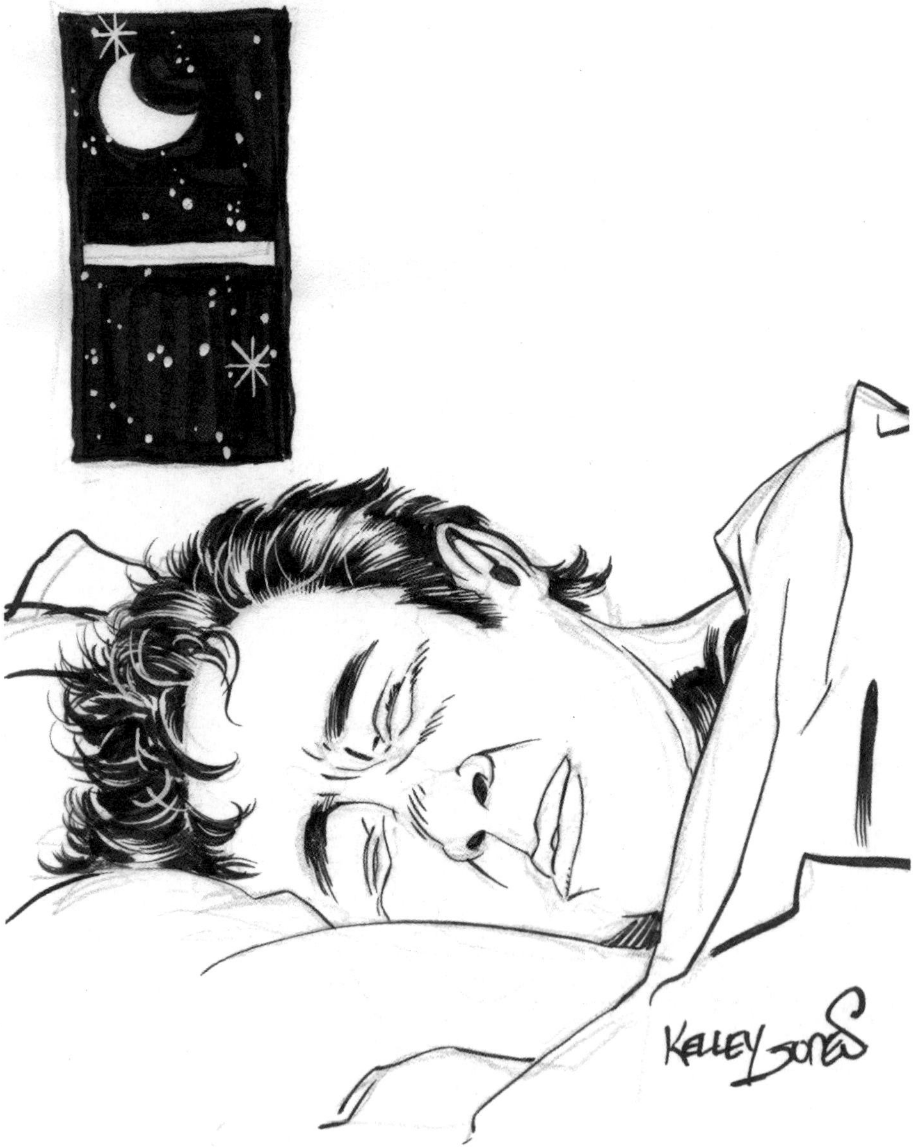
KELLEY JONES

SELF-PORTRAIT. © 2004 KELLEY JONES.

# GERARD JONES AND WILL JACOBS, IN THEIR 1997 BOOK

*The Comic Book Heroes*, refer to Kelley Jones as "the best horror artist in comics." Jones, with the ghost of "Ghastly" Graham Ingels haunting his pencils, first established his reputation by taking over the penciling chores on the weekly *Action Comics*' "Deadman" strip. Delighted with the chance to draw the DC character as dark and twisted as he wished, Jones followed this assignment with the prestige-format *Deadman: Love After Death*; which led to his *Sandman* debut "Calliope" [issue 17], the succeeding tale "A Dream of a Thousand Cats," and his five issues of *Season of Mists*. As the first *Sandman* artist (after co-creators Sam Kieth and Mike Dringenberg) to illustrate the bulk of an extended storyline, Jones demonstrated the adaptability of the *Sandman* mythos and helped craft, in *Mists*, a tale that more fully explored the Dream King's universe.

After leaving *Sandman*, Jones became known as one of the definitive Batman artists of the '90s, and created his own title, *The Hammer*. In recent years, he's reinforced his reputation as a horror-comics maestro by collaborating with writer Steve Niles on *The Last Train to Deadsville*. Jones is presently working on a creator-owned project with the working title *The 13ᵀᴴ Son*.

*When you began working on* Sandman *did you sense the kind of reaction the book was getting?*

When *Sandman* started this phenomenon happening, other artists were coming up to me, writers were coming up to me, people who weren't into comics were coming up to me, and they were saying, "You know, *these* are good."

I remember this nightmarish fellow wanted me to sign at several stores. I said, "Fine." He was nightmarish because he looked like someone from *Deliverance*. Here's this guy and he's telling me in this thick backwoods accent, *"That motherfuckin'* Sandman *is good. I'm really enjoying all these conflicts within his domain."* I thought, "Oh my God, Neil's reached *this* guy. He's reading this thing and he's *liking* it." I'd go to these places in the middle of nowhere, where you pray you don't run out of gas, because *they eat people out there.* I'd tell Neil, "I was in this place miles and miles into the foothills, the scariest country I've been through, the scariest damn people driving me there, and they're digging it. This is good. If you can get the people who practice incest to like your work, you have written and drawn something of note." [*Laughs.*] I would tell him all these things.

*You have described your attitude toward* Sandman *as being fairly "blue collar," regardless of how many people talk about the book's "artistry."*

Comics are kind of that way anyway. You have to go into them thinking that. Basically, you have to do your best work within twenty-one to thirty days. Not to exclude super-heroes, but anytime that isn't super-hero work you kind of have to give something a little more than perhaps that attitude would require. But still, all in all, it's blue collar. That simply means you gotta get a page a day done.

Super-hero comics have a lot of things they can rely on – a guy's posing or he's punching someone, flying through the air, using powers, that kind of stuff. *Sandman* was the opposite of that. It's guys standing around. And it's very atmospheric, because it relies so heavily on the writing. I tried to drag it more toward what comic books are visually, not trying to do something that would appear in a fine-arts magazine or some kind of hip, indie magazine. I tried to do straight comic-book stuff with it, but classically – you try to go about doing it in a classical sense. And since that was the case, I always thought, "Neil's writing something that's not entirely different." Because it reminded me, actually quite a bit, of the really classic Jack Kirby-Stan Lee *Thor*s of the early '60s, because you had gods interacting with people but with all of these personal problems. But what I admired was he would do these things, and it wouldn't come off like that. I thought, at that point, "People are maybe assuming that, so I'm going to go in there and do it with a much stronger graphic style, a lot of darks." Neil was not having the Sandman in it – in the first two I did, he's really not in it that much. In "Calliope" [issue 17] and the "Cats" one [issue 18, "A Dream of a Thousand Cats"], he's not in it that much. So I got a chance to play with more of a noir type of technique. "Old Universal horror films" was what Neil had remarked to me when he saw them; that's what they looked like. That's kind of what I was trying to do. So it wasn't like I was trying to look into the middle distance and create wonders. No, you want to stay out of the way of the story so that the impact is there.

*Was it your* Deadman *work that caught Neil's attention?*

Yes. What had happened was that I'd done that and DC at that point was saying, "We really don't want you to go somewhere else," so they gave me some *Swamp Thing*s to do as well. I did a few fill-ins for *Swamp Thing* that went over really, really well, because I couldn't do what Steve Bissette was doing, but I could go back and do the old Wrightsony thing. I did one of those, and I did a couple of little things here and there. Neil had heard, "Boy, this guy's really good," out of left field, and Sam was working with him early on – he kind of knew who I was from that. Neil looked at my stuff and thought, "Wow." He kept telling me that the stuff looked like a James Whale movie. I thought, "Well, that's cool," because I was into that kind of look anyway. At that point Neil said, "Would you like to do one?" It actually came through Karen Berger. Karen said, "Neil really likes this stuff, and I'm going to give him your phone number and see if you want to work together." Because she wanted me to stick around and do something there, and I really enjoyed doing it because I was getting to do my own stuff.

I sat down and read over what Neil had sent, the initial thing he threw out. It was something that was supposed to be called "Sex and Violets," but he never did that. I vaguely remember the outline of it. Neil said, "No, it was terrible, dreadful, forget about it. I'll get something to you." I waited and waited and finally it came. He kept apologizing. He had had writer's block, and then "Calliope" came. It was about writer's block, and it was a good angle – the whole thing about how a muse kept you writing so you don't have that, and how the worst thing is to have all your ideas taken away. Well, that was just terrific stuff. I read it over, and I know he had said, "Look, I know you'll be disappointed, because there really isn't much Sandman in it. He's only in a couple pages. It's really just for revenge purposes, so it's not about him." But I read the story over. At that time it was all critical, early-career making. *Deadman* was a challenge because everybody was going to compare it to Neal Adams, and then this came along. I said, "This is perfect, because the character's not in it that much, so its success is going to be based on how well it's done." I jumped at that. It came out and it was very well received. I wasn't supposed to do the following issue with the cats; it was just that they couldn't find any artist who wanted to do it. They had told me four or five artists (and I won't name them because I know most of them) didn't want to do it, because they didn't feel they could, because there were no people in it. It was like a *Charlie Brown* cartoon, or a Warner Brothers cartoon – you only saw their feet. They didn't want to do that, and I understood: when you hear that, all the visual things you use to draw a comic book are removed from you. But, again, I was at that point where I wanted to prove that I could not only draw a comic book, but that I could also *think* a comic book, that I could come up with the ideas. It was very funny, Karen kind of broached that to me. She said, "It's really, really late, and there's nobody in it. It's just this cat stuff." Neil called and said, "I apologize again. The last one actually had some Sandman in it, but this one has none. But nobody wants to do it, and I really think this is my best story." I said, "Okay." That sounded earnest to me, but I had already agreed. I said, "Yeah, I want to do it. I have a cat. I'll just draw him." It came, and Neil did a neat, neat thing in there where none of the adjectives are people adjectives, they're cat adjectives, like "his claws were winter sharp," or something like that. He did these neat things in there like that, and I thought, "Wow, that's really good." So I made a point to do things from a cat perspective and do the best kind of cats. Not a standard cat, but different kinds of cats.

When it was all done, one of the nicest things ever said to me – not from Neil, just in general – was said two or three years after the fact. It was the mid-'90s or something and I had not done *Sandman* for a long time. [Neil] told me, "That's still the best issue." Because, distilled down, it was his best story. It got across all the elements of what *Sandman* was without Sandman in it. I mean if you were to tell someone, "You have to write a book. Superman's not in it, but it's got to feel the most Superman there ever was. It's got to be really compelling…" I felt it was a real challenge for Neil to do that. And he didn't say, "I'm gonna write the best one," it just turned out. I remember him saying, "That was the one that got people into it. People were handing it around." I knew that because I was seeing that happen. I felt good because it was an overall good issue. I wasn't separated from the fact. It was like, "Man, the cats look great." I had lied to him and told him, "Yeah, I'm a great cat artist. I have no problem with it." I had never drawn cats. You always lie to get the job, but at that point it was like, "Okay, now, man, I gotta draw some damn good cats!" [*Laughs.*] My poor cat had to be held and positioned and…he was very happy when that was over.

*Dave McKean commented to me that he wished there were more instances in* Sandman *where the typical image of Dream, which he considered to be almost a sort of animation template, wasn't always present. I guess the "Cats" story is one of the first and strongest instances where it hits the reader that Dream isn't so much a personage as an idea.*

Yeah, Neil's thing was "Everything dreams." He is to everything what it understands, as he is to us what we would understand. I would only say that the thing I felt was, you have to kind of have the template, whatever it was. You're doing a comic book, and the things you do in a comic you can't do in a novel or vice versa, or in a film, so you have to have something there that everyone can hang their hat on. And that's always been difficult. I know in doing comic books you have to remind yourself, "Basically these are geared toward younger people." So that doesn't mean you write down to them, but that does mean you have to write and draw in the language everybody gets. [*Sandman*] is one in which you have to have something where people go, "Okay, there is our guy."

If you have, in the case of *Sandman*, whatever your main character is, if you have him do the great moment where he takes revenge, or he displays himself, comes into his full aspect, and he's really cool and terrifying and stuff like that, it's very meaningful because it's offset with him questioning himself in quiet moments. Having an anxious moment, having a moment of happiness or hope or something you can kind of relate to. So when you do something like the big release moment, the big moment which is generally the climax, then you get the full impact of that. If you have it be all big-impact moments then they all become meaningless. You don't have much to hang your hat on if you're doing a story that's just loud from beginning to end. At least with *Sandman* – and horror comics in general – one of the things that always felt good was that it was the quiet moments where all the real fun was. Because it's the anticipation, it's the tenseness of it, it's the building of mood – it's all these things that have been pretty much chucked from doing a book now. It's those things that make something work. It doesn't matter what the subject matter is. If you're going to criticize *Sandman*, it's probably too much of those moments. But I would rather have that, because when the big moment happens you remember it.

One of the neat things that happened at the end of *Season of Mists* was there was not this huge confrontation that everyone expected. It was like pulling out the rug from under it, and probably people would cry foul at any other title. But there it worked, and that's why it was satisfying. I remember Neil saying he was going to have it where, originally, Nada was grateful to be out of [Hell] after ten-thousand years, or however long she was there, after all this torture. I said, "Jesus, Neil, what women you've met, I would like to meet them, because I don't know of any woman that I screwed over and left in Hell who'd be happy about it. [*Laughs.*] Even if I came and got her out of there. You know what I mean? They're not going to like that..." I said, "Jeez, maybe in England they're nicer, but, well, I guess they're really mean in California!" He said, "Well, what do you think?" I said, "I think that he would have to do a lot more than apologize, he would have to give her back what he took. In the human world, it's buying them a really big ring or something nice, because they can always look at that ring. Think of something like that." And he did – he reincarnated her to have a life.

*So that plot element in the epilogue to* Season of Mists *[issue 28] came from that conversation?*

Yes, yes. Certainly I don't take credit for it, but we used to talk about those things. Bullshitting in the middle of the night (my time) and the middle of the day (his time) you'd get that.

*The design for the gate of Hell, in* Season of Mists, *also came from those discussions, didn't it?*

Reading a comic, I want something weird and evil, and as an artist I wanted to draw that. When I got the script it was a nice little wooden picket fence, a small stone wall, something like that, with little flowers and daffodils. It was sunny and nice, and it would be the opposite of what you'd expect. I said, "No. Let's make it bad and horrible. You don't get much of an opportunity to draw the gates of Hell – big, huge, horrible walls." At that time I was thinking, "Yeah, like we entered Mordor or something." I always loved that. I thought, "I want to do something like that, where it's just horrible and evil, and it should be ominous and you're ready for swelling, demonic armies to come down and…nothing's there. Because everybody's gone. So you think, "Well, are they just waiting to jump on me?" Well, you're not that important. That was how Neil wrote *The Sandman* – you're not that important for everybody to jump on. Those little things would happen. And then the fact that you found that basically Hell was not just a place of damnation, but a really sad place because everyone had lost their grace. It's an amazingly religious-but-non-religious type of thing, you know what I mean? It was a very, very religious, good interpretation, without…

*Being preachy?*

Not at all, and that's hard to do. You could feel pity for Satan, but you can't empathize with Satan. That's what Neil did. Because, okay, you feel bad that you're denied sundown. Does that mean you have to nail people to rocks? So it should be that way, just all the hideous stuff you see there. I thought that would be tremendously cool, to have it be everything you think it's going to be, but it's empty.

*At what point during your time on* Sandman *were you told you'd be working on* Season of Mists?

I was told after I did "Calliope." Neil called me and said, "I think you're the guy to do it. Would you want to do this?" I said I had enjoyed working with him, and that's why they felt comfortable sending me the cat one. That's why they called me, after four or five people, because they knew I was going to do it anyway. He said, "Okay, I'm going to send you what I have on it." It was a page-and-a-half overview of five or six issues, or however long it was. I told him that I primarily just wanted to do the ones in Sandman World and in Hell. I think there was one that Matt Wagner did [Chapter 4, issue 25], but I didn't want to work on that. Since Neil had different [characters] in that one, I said, "It's going to be a really tough plow for six months. I'd like to stay within that world, because I'm going to do a lot of referencing, and I'm not going to have time to switch gears as much as I normally do." He said, "Fine." He sent me this page and a half. You could see it was his big moment with this character: "Okay, we know who he is. Now I'm going to present who he is, and I'm going to present in relation to how he is received and understood and accepted by all these other great immortal beings and whatnot." I know when he did the Norse gods it was traditional, and then I took it and played with it, making fun of a lot of it – a really big, huge, steroided-out Thor with a teeny-tiny hammer. Neil didn't really describe something like that, it was just funny to do. There was a lot of that stuff.

Then there were other things that I didn't do. Other artists came along and obviously Neil wanted them to do it. For example, I didn't do the Escher-type library. I did more of a straight one. The only reason was that I didn't feel confident enough to do an Escher-type thing, and I liked that the Dreaming could be strange and weird, but I didn't like for it to be weird when it was normal. You know what I mean? Probably, I just didn't have the technical capability of doing it correctly. I didn't feel comfortable with something like that. I like odd stuff, but other artists did it and they did it much better, so at that point I just stuck with what I knew because I like the idea of a big, lofty, giant, old wooden library. Neil said it contained the books that weren't written, and it also contained the dreams that had been dreamed and the dreams that hadn't been dreamed yet. I loved that kind of stuff.

*You had some fairly noteworthy inkers on* Sandman *– Malcolm Jones, Craig Russell, Dick Giordano…*

It was one of those good things that happened. Malcolm had fallen tremendously behind. He had taken on other work and he hadn't told any of us.

*Was this work outside of DC?*

Yes, some stuff at DC and some stuff at Marvel. And, of course, I knew, financially, at the time, he needed to do it. He had told me he had done this, and he needed the money at the time, so I didn't rat him out or anything. But he was getting increasingly late. Neil made contact with some of these people, and said to me, "How do you feel about these different inkers?" I said, "That would be great, fine. I have no problem with that." Like you said, he got Giordano and Russell, and he was not going to go wrong with those guys.

*A number of pencilers seemed to appreciate Jones's inks a great deal.*

Malcolm Jones was as energetic as he was enigmatic. He loved being an artist, and that was what kept him here as long as he was. All my conversations with him but one were of a frantic and joyous type. And all of those, with no exceptions, were always late at night. That seemed to fit Malcolm. He said he couldn't think in the day. His conversations were like a jazz solo. You really had to just go with it. I remember having to translate a lot of them to Neil, who would always tell me he loved Malcolm's phone calls because he never knew what the hell Malcolm was talking about.

Malcolm gushed his loves and hates and his voluminous ideas. Anyone whom he inked, when they would get their original art back, would find the back of the pages filled with his sketches and drawings (some inked!). I kept those *Sandman* pages for what was on the back as much as on the printed side. We would talk about everything – his son, favorite books, what went best with coffee, favorite artists (he worshipped Norman Rockwell, and told me countless times that he wished he could live in the kind of world Rockwell depicted). I never made fun of that, as he always told of the shootings and mayhem in his neighborhood. Malcolm said being an artist didn't go down well there, and he told me several harrowing tales in passing. When I in response would say something like, "Jesus, Malcolm, no shit?" He would matter-of-factly say that it was okay to die if you are what you want to be. He said it as unpretentiously as was his way in most things.

Yet toward the end of his life, Malcolm would speak with people as if from the middle of a conversation they weren't involved in. They knew little of what he was talking about and this made him feel as though they were disregarding him and his ideas. He became angry at this. On top of that, Malcolm was a big guy and never took into account how that could scare anyone he was in a conflict with.

We had a falling out after DC had mistakenly sent me all the originals of a job back. When I phoned him that this had happened and I would send him his allotment, there was silence and then a torrent of accusations that I had done this on purpose in order to keep them all, he then told me how everyone in his life betrayed him.

I gave him an extra twenty pages or so, but he said it didn't matter. After some months, he called, he spoke about how much he loved what we did together, and how he'd like to do more. Since I knew he could work where he wanted, I felt this was his sincere way of making up. I told him that would be great. He hung up. It was the only time he called me during the day. Several weeks later he was dead from suicide.

*If I may go back to* Season of Mists *for a moment – were you told before you began that storyline that Mike Dringenberg would be doing the first and last chapters?*

Again, I think that all happened by chance. People were coming in and out. One of the things was that they'd offered me the book as a regular assignment. I just didn't think I could do that. Not that I wasn't up to it, but they were tough books to do. It was a thing where you were doing a monthly, which is relentless, no matter what, and you were switching gears a lot, which adds more to it. *Sandman* was a book where, when I read the script, it would take me three or four days of heavy referencing, getting a list of all the things you needed, getting in the car…because you couldn't fake a lot of stuff. Most comics you can kind of fake it. If you walk into the laboratory of a mad scientist or an evil supervillain, you can make up machines. You can make up spaceships and crap like that. When Neil would say, "a rococo-style drawing room," you'd say, "Oh, jeez – now I gotta go find that!" You had to do it. If he would reference a location in which something would happen, you would have to find it. I'm big on having enough reference to make up what I think it should look like, but not enough reference to hold me down. Well, that would take three or four days, every time. Both Neil and [*Batman* writer] Doug Moench were so big on their referencing that I built a huge library just from working with them. Every month I'd be going out to buy huge stacks of books. I would go to used bookstores, Tower Books, anywhere, and just come home with thirty to forty new books every month.

*Were you offered the job of penciling* Sandman *as a regular assignment after* Season of Mists?

It was right in the middle of it. They had seen the first few, and I was not that on-time, but I was way ahead of what everyone else was doing. They were taking two or three months to draw a book, and I was doing it in four or five weeks. But Karen would say, "I know these are tough. These are some pretty tough books." At that time, I had agreed that I would do a follow-up to *Deadman*. I had done a couple issues of *Grimjack*, I'd penciled and inked. I'd done those *Aliens* books. So I had done a lot of stuff, and I got to a point where not only did I have a lot of stuff to do – I like that, because I get bored pretty easily – but it was getting to be too much. And I also wanted to ink myself. I wanted to have jobs where I could do the full work. As good as inkers are – and there are some tremendous ones, and you just love them – even then it was becoming harder and harder to find good inkers, and a lot of the cool stuff I like to do came in the inking, not in the penciling. It came in the finishes. And Malcolm then said, "You really should be doing some Batman stuff." He knew those people and that was kind of a transition, because when somebody comes along and says, "You can spend a year on something again" – seven months or however long they were going to give me – "and it's monsters and Batman," you say, "Okay, I'll take a whack at that." I felt bad. I think I disappointed some people, I might have irritated them, but it wasn't a thing where I said, "Okay, I'm going to go off to greener pastures." I knew what it was. I knew it was a great book. When I was doing that I was coming off four or five really rough years, production-wise, and I didn't want to burn out. And I had never done Batman before, or I'd done nothing of note with it.

*Since we're talking about a character with a cape – one of the trademark elements of your Sandman was, of course, his own distinctive cape. What led to its design?*

Because he's a static character. He just stands there. In a novel, or in prose, you don't have to describe the action too much. It's really based on what they're saying and how well the writer gets that across. But for an artist, that's useless shit, because you've got to draw something for the reader to be interested in. Visually there has to be something more than just talking heads. You can do talking heads, but after five pages the finest talking heads are boring. I remember sitting there, thinking, "I really like this book, but there's not much to hang your hat on…"

Especially in *Season of Mists*. "Calliope" and "Cats" were strong one-shot stories. You got in, you got out. Like "Fall of the House of Usher – you don't have to go on and on about the house when a couple of paragraphs will do. But in a comic book, if you're going to do months of it, then you have to come up with something. I would sit there, looking the Sandman over, and looking at what everyone else had done. The one thing I thought was, "Well, no one has taken advantage of the cape yet. No one's done that." I couldn't just draw a draped cape all the time, so I took a sheet and I got it wet and I went in the backyard and draped it over a chair. And I started practicing getting the folds all over the place. A wet sheet, a wet blue or black sheet, is the best thing in the world, because you get real high definition. I just started drawing and drawing. I thought, "Okay, if you're gonna have a cape, it had better be different than the other capes you see drawn." So I'd go out there at high noon, when the sun was at its highest, because that was the best direct light I could get. I got all these wonderful shapes and shadows and folds and textures, and at that point I knew I had a character there. There was something *visually* as cool as rippling pecs. I had something with that. I used to kind of joke and give him a mood cape, so even in a still room his cape would be swirling around.

I know Neil always said [the Sandman] was based on Robert Smith of the Cure, but I just hated the Cure. I didn't want to hear that. That's like somebody telling me he's based on Roseanne Barr or something – bleh, you know? I can't have that, because I want to like the character I'm doing, and I want to identify with him so I can do a little of that method-acting thing, where you can get in their head and feel it come through the pencil. I *was* really into Peter Murphy at that time, the guy from Bauhaus. I didn't like Bauhaus, but I liked him on his own, and he had a song called "Cut You Up" or something; it was on the radio at the time. I bought the CD, and I said, "You know, with that big poufy hair, he looks like that guy." At that time, Murphy was very gestural. I don't think the guy ever had a picture taken of him that wasn't angled and in deep lighting. So I took that, too. I said, "Whenever I do him, I'm gonna do that kind of thing. And get into his face, don't *just* keep him in deep shadow all the time. He will be in deep shadow all the time, but I want to put across a guy who's clueless. Not stupid, but he's not understanding things." Because he's an immortal guy who…

*Doesn't completely get human beings?*

Yeah, when he's affected by an actual thing like screwing up a relationship with a girl, I wanted to get that across so you could kind of empathize with him. I wanted that cluelessness, and also I thought that that made him more visually interesting. I did a lot of stuff with his hands, anywhere I could show some physical movement or motion I would try to do that, and give him something you could look at. Every time I did him, I would try to get a composition that, if you didn't read the words, would make you say, "Okay, I can look at this. That's kind of cool. Let's go from there."

I also did something else. Poor Karen Berger probably thought it was because I didn't have any technical ability – and that's probably partly true – but I made a point to make Sandman (I never called him "Morpheus," he was always "Sandman" to me) like a dream: he kind of *distorts* a little bit. I never really wanted him to look the same from issue to issue. I wanted him to be a little vague and fuzzy, because generally, other than a handful, you don't remember dreams that well. And that was his world, so I wanted him to kind of alternate a little bit. Neil would have him wearing black-leather coats, and that's because Neil wore black-leather coats, and that's fine, but for me, I said, "Okay, I gotta put something of myself into this." So he was always taken aback by stuff, and a little vague. He would be just a little distorted here and there, with a little different shape to his facial structure.

The reason I did it was that I thought as long as I was consistent with everybody else, then that would make him look that much more impressive. I think the only time I had to follow direct reference from something was when Neil was *adamant* that the Devil was David Bowie. He just said, "He is. You *must* draw David Bowie. Find David Bowie, or I'll send you David Bowie. Because if it isn't David Bowie, you're going to have to re-do it until it *is* David Bowie." So I said, "Okay, it's David Bowie," which I never had a problem with. It's one of those things. When there's something like that, where somebody says adamantly, and they don't ever tell you anything else, okay, that's not a problem.

Getting back to the distortion thing, I remember Karen calling me and just saying, "He looks different from the last issue. Are you getting more comfortable with him?" And I said, "Well, he'll look different in the next one, too." That's what I was doing. And she probably thought, "[*Sighs.*] Another pretentious artist…" [*Laughs.*]

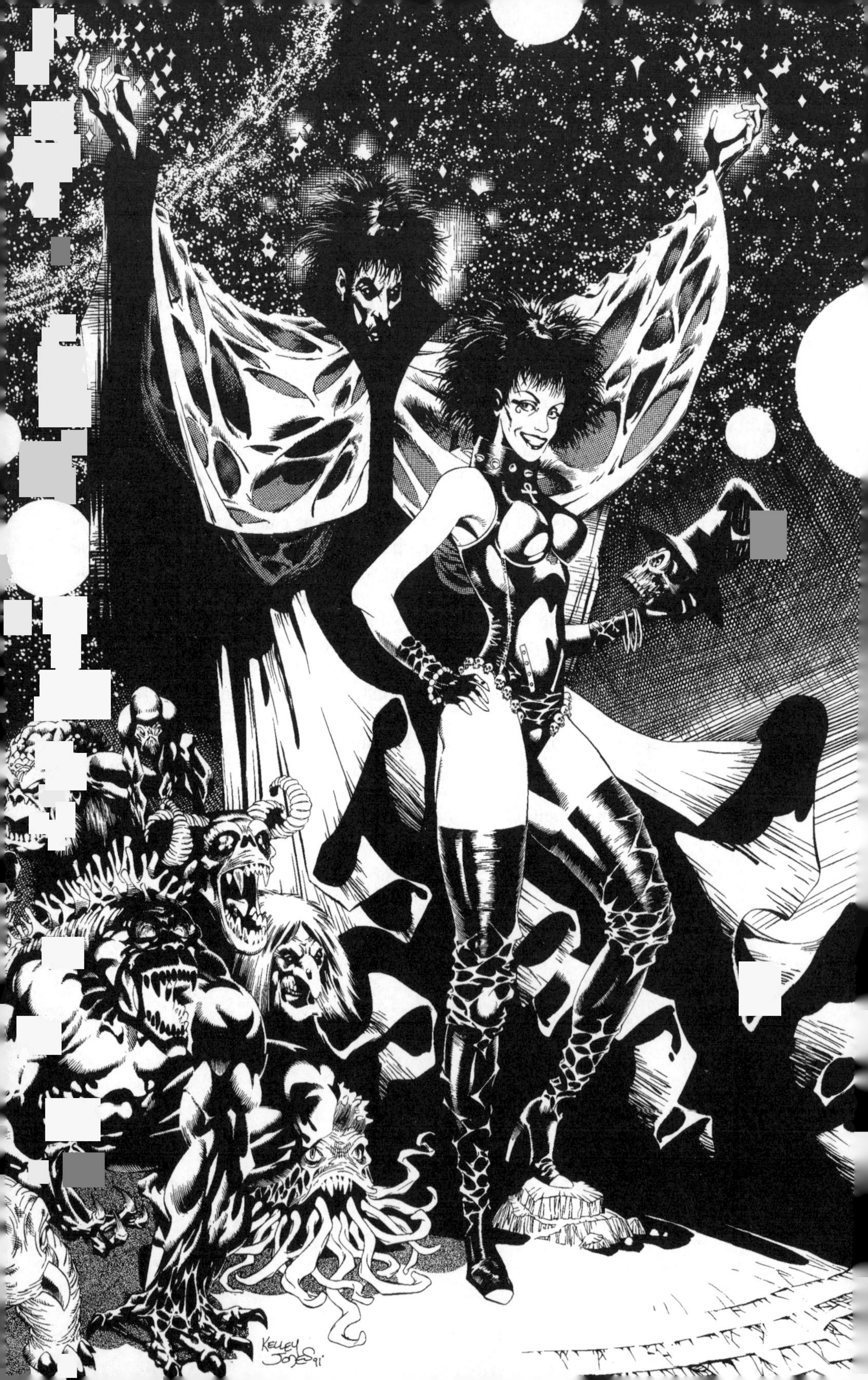
KELLEY
JONES '91

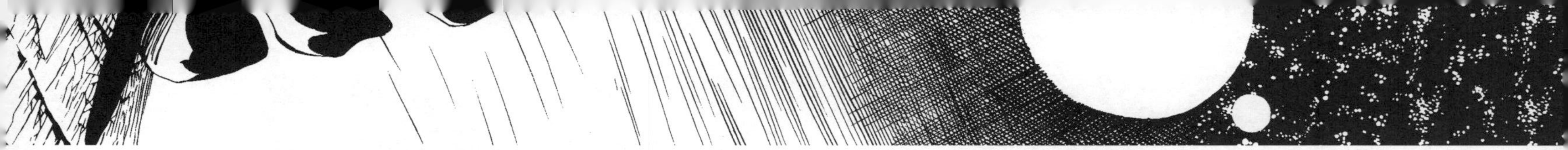

Pencils and inks for unpublished Dream and Death poster by Kelley Jones, commissioned by DC after the artist penciled *Sandman* 18. ("[DC] didn't want Death in the t-shirt and jeans," says Jones. "They said, 'Come up w[illegible] something you haven't seen before.' I thought, 'She's playfu[illegible] so I'll make he[illegible] that.'") © 2004 DC Comics.

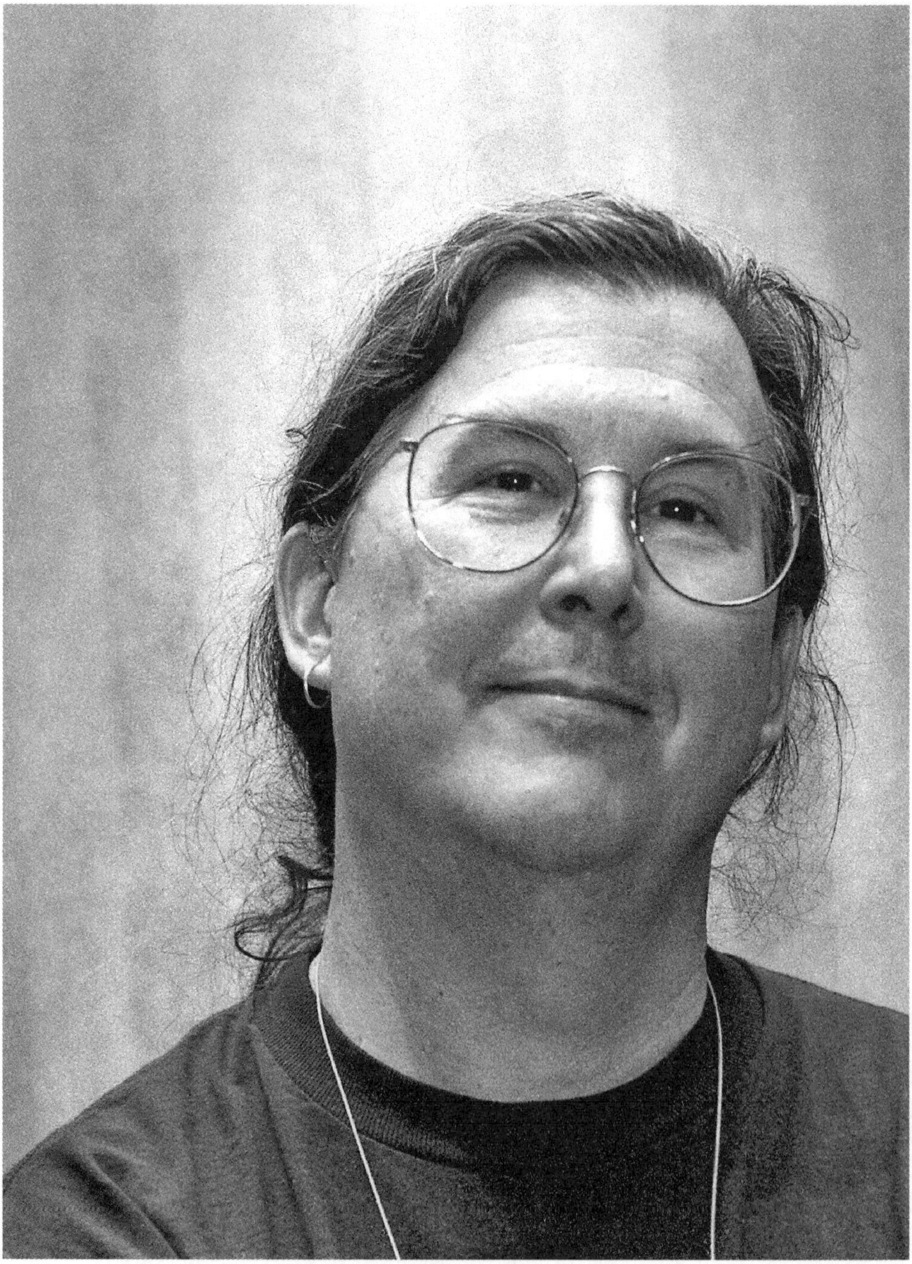

*Charles Vess*

## THE FANTASY AND FOLKLORE-FUELED ART OF CHARLES VESS

HAS BEEN A PART OF THE AMERICAN COMICS SCENE FOR OVER TWENTY-FIVE YEARS. THOUGH VESS BEGAN HIS CAREER AS AN ANIMATOR, HE SOON FOUND HIMSELF WORKING FOR SUCH PUBLICATIONS AS *HEAVY METAL* AND *NATIONAL LAMPOON*; AND, AFTER A DECADE OF WORKING ON VARIOUS COMICS, TEAMED WITH GAIMAN TO CREATE THE ONLY COMIC BOOK TO HAVE WON THE WORLD FANTASY AWARD [IN 1991] FOR BEST SHORT STORY – *SANDMAN* 19, "A MIDSUMMER NIGHT'S DREAM." VESS ALSO WORKED WITH GAIMAN ON THE FINAL *SANDMAN* ISSUE (75) "THE TEMPEST"; ON THE THIRD ISSUE OF THE *BOOKS OF MAGIC* MINI-SERIES; AND ON THE ORIGINAL ILLUSTRATED EDITION OF *STARDUST* [DC/VERTIGO, 1998], FOR WHICH HE PROVIDED 175 PAINTINGS.

ASIDE FROM HIS EISNER AWARD-WINNING COMIC-BOOK MINI-SERIES *ROSE*, MUCH OF VESS'S RECENT WORK HAS BEEN BOOK ILLUSTRATION. HE'S WORKED WITH FANTASY AUTHOR CHARLES DELINT ON *A CIRCLE OF CATS* AND *MEDICINE ROAD*, AND PROVIDED ART FOR THE *THE GREEN MAN: TALES FROM THE MYTHIC FOREST* ANTHOLOGY AND *THE FAERIE REEL*.

BUT THE ARTIST CONTINUES TO CHAMPION THE MEDIUM OF COMICS. HE SERVED AS GUEST EDITOR ON LAST YEAR'S SPECIAL COMICS ISSUE OF *LOCUS*, AND PROVIDES AN ANNUAL REVIEW OF COMICS AND GRAPHIC NOVELS FOR *THE YEAR'S BEST FANTASY AND HORROR*. HIS NEWEST BOOK IS *THE BOOK OF BALLADS*, COLLECTING, AND ADDING TO, HIS SELF-PUBLISHED COMIC-BOOK SERIES.

*What compels you to depict the organic in the field of fantasy illustration, where even the organic is often depicted as mechanical, as well as mechanically?*

[*Laughs.*] If I knew that I would know the meaning of the universe. It's something I've always been attracted to. In a glib sort of way, one of my explanations of the difference between science fiction and fantasy is that science fiction is art deco and fantasy is art nouveau. And I'm very attracted to the curvilinear, rhythmic forms of nature. It makes me happy to draw it, whereas I can struggle through drawing a building or drawing a spaceship or a robot. I don't derive any pleasure from it. And the more personal involvement and the more joy you've got in doing the drawing, the better it is. People can really see that in the work.

*So it just connects with you?*

It's just the way I am. There's some artists I know that are one or the other. There are some – very few – that are very versatile in both technological and natural stuff. One of the biggest joys of my life was when my career got to the point where I could turn down jobs that involve spaceships or robots.

*That was when you knew you'd made it?*

It was just like, "Oh, I like this…"

*You've recently returned to the medium that gave birth to your style. Most of your recent work has been book illustration.*

The book illustration allows me to spend more time on a single image. And to be able to really consider it, and put it against a wall and come back a couple of days later and go, "The head's not quite right." Which is not something you can really do when you're doing a comic. Comics are, other than animation, the most work that there is, but it offers the most freedom obviously.

*And the fulfillment that goes along with it?*

Well, the artistic freedom and the…it's such a low-tech thing that you can draw whatever you want and then publish it. And it doesn't cost you that much.

*It's a more democratic medium.*

Yes it is, but it also means that lots of crap gets published, but that gets in everything.

*What kicked off the recent surge in your book-illustration work?*

The starting point would be *Stardust*. Because it was enough of a project that it became a portfolio – you could show people and say, "This is what I can do." What really sold Viking was the big, super-duper limited edition portfolio I did of *Stardust*. I sent copies of that up to the editor and she showed it around to the art directors. They were all just sold on the work. I spent years trying to break into the children's book market, and you *could not* show an art director in that field any page that looked remotely like a comic book. Because they weren't looking at how you could draw, what you could paint, or anything. They just saw it as a comic book, and said, "That's not what we do, so we can't hire you." It's very difficult. Unless you have a good portfolio of work that's in the style that they're used to, it's hard to break over into it. The twelve years I lived in New York, every couple of years I'd go around to the children's book publishers. They would look at my work and say I was too sophisticated. Then I'd go around to the adult publishers, and they'd say I was too childlike. It went on and on and on. Finally you run into the right editor is all, someone who can look past the end of their nose and say, "You know, you could do that…" And Sharyn November's been a joy to work with. The children's books, the *Green Man* book, there will be a number of other things… It's really cool, and one of the things that goes on in the back of my mind is "This would make my mom happy." Because it's a book that will be in the bookstore. Every time I have anything published she's always said, "Well, son, is that going to be in the bookstore?" I can say, "Yeah. You can go right in there." It's kind of a kick to go in there and go to the young adult section – I've got a couple of covers in there and the *Green Man* anthology's in there – and say, "Here I am." [*Laughs.*] Every once in a while I've gone into a Barnes & Noble or a Borders or something and found a stack of them and just sort of looked around and sat there and signed them all and then stuck them back on the shelf and left. I did that once with *Stardust*, in San Diego. I did a drawing in it, and stuck it back on the shelf and left and thought, "That would be such a kick to come in and say, 'I think I'll buy this book,' and then say, 'Look, there's a real drawing here.'" I thought that'd be neat.

*Assuming, of course, it's someone who's smart enough to realize it's your work and not just–*

Yes, I hope so. I hope it's not just, "Oh, I'll have to rip this page out or white it out!"

*"I'm returning this book. Someone drew in it." It sounds like* Stardust *was a real turning point in your career.*

It was a big project. It was classy and a lot of people saw it.

*Both comics fans and book readers.*

Yes. It was published all over the place. I won a World Fantasy Award for the art in it, "Best Artist." So it was breaking down those barriers, slowly.

*You also won an Eisner Award for* Rose. *Like Neil, you have a large group of fans in both the prose-fiction and comics camps. There aren't many creators who have that situation.*

There's some, but it's that sort of crossover. There's so many niches and markets around that if you can exploit them you can really make a lot of money. I mean, I'm a commercial artist. I'm trying to make a living doing this. I don't want to make two-hundred-and-fifty dollars a month and a box of pencils – as my publisher once offered me for a project. No, I have a desire to live fairly comfortably, with a roof over my head. And I like to eat. I've starved enough. I've had plenty of years of that.

*How did you first come to work with Neil?*

At the San Diego Comic-Con, about the time that issue 4 or 5 of *Sandman* came out. I'd never met him. I saw a comment that he'd written in to *Amazing Heroes*, based on one of my drawings. He just came up and we started talking, and had a nice conversation about James Branch Cabell, who's one of my favorite writers. When he got ready to leave he said, "If you ever want to draw a *Sandman* let me know." Up until then he had been doing sort of modern horror, which is not anything I would ever want to draw in my life. So I thought, "Well, I'll never call him." A couple of months later, the African folk tale issue of *Sandman* [issue 9, "Tales in the Sand"] came out. It was a beautiful thing. I thought, "I could have drawn that." So I called him up. A couple of months later he said, "I've got an idea. Do you want to do *A Midsummer Night's Dream* again?"

I had illustrated the play, for Donning-Starblaze, the actual text. And Neil had come across that and he'd enjoyed it. He wanted to know if I wanted to try it again. I said, "Sure. That would be fun." He had already had the Shakespeare character in *Sandman* and it triggered something.

Art for *Stardust* magnet set [Graphitti Designs, 1999]: [clockwise] the Lilum, Tristran, Star. TM & © 2004 Neil Gaiman and Charles Vess.

*In* The Sandman Companion, *I think you remarked that the faerie folk you drew in "A Midsummer Night's Dream" [Issue 19] were influenced by fellow fantasy artists Brian Froud and Alan Lee.*

Well…they're influenced by Arthur Rackham, his faeries.

*Apparently some people complained when you and Neil won the World Fantasy Award for "A Midsummer Night's Dream." It was the first time the Best Short Story Award was given to an issue of a comic book.*

Some people were pissed off that a comic book would win a literary award. I didn't notice it that much actually. I didn't expect at all to win, and I was off playing ping pong or table tennis; then it won the World Fantasy Award, and it was really cool. At the awards ceremony, Neil said, "You know, we'll have to do the other Shakespeare play." I said, "Okay."

*Apparently he added, "Puts a little pressure on the next one." And that "next one," that "other Shakespeare play," was to be* The Tempest.

Yes.

*At that point did he begin discussing* The Tempest *as the basis for issue 75, the final issue of the series?*

Oh, it wasn't the end then. It was later on he realized it was really the last original play Shakespeare did, so it fittingly should be the last issue of *Sandman*. But that was also where he told me about *Stardust*, at that convention. We walked out into the cold desert air, drinking champagne, and he told me the story.

*I'd like to discuss* Stardust *again in a moment, but, for "The Tempest" – once again, I'm referring to* The Sandman Companion – *you used Anthony Burgess's Shakespeare as a reference. Why did you use this particular book?*

We were both doing research on Shakespeare, because we knew that "The Tempest" was going to be about Shakespeare, and not about the play. So we were both trying to get a hold on it. I had been in England, and Neil said, "Don't go to Stratford-on-Avon. It looks too different. I don't want you even thinking that." We both had a bunch of different biographies, most of them were from academic viewpoints that had no idea what the creative impulse could possibly be. And they were making these bizarre assumptions about why Shakespeare would have done something. We kept saying, "Because he felt like it? Because it was a good day?" They just didn't know what happened. Burgess is a writer, and he's creative, so he *did*. It was really a very nice biography, very interesting.

*In addition to the two issues based on Shakespeare's plays, you also contributed to an issue of* The Kindly Ones *[Chapter 6, issue 62]. How did that come about?*

The regular artist couldn't do the issue so they got someone else to do it, and then he couldn't do all of it. Neil came up with this idea – he'd been reading this folklore and he read this gypsy folk tale and he wanted to do it as eight pages. He said, "You'd be great!" Most people said, "Oh, it's just a throwaway, a little eight-page thing. Why is it in there?" I kept saying, "That's the entirety of *Sandman*, right there in eight pages. It's every theme – everything!" And it is. It's great.

*During* Sandman's *run, you also did an issue of Neil's original four-issue prestige-format* Books of Magic.

I did the third one ["The Land of Summer's Twilight"]. And the bizarre thing about that was they'd been through four artists before they got to me. I read the script and said, "Wasn't this written for me?" [*Laughs.*]

*Who were the other artists considered?*

There was Dave McKean, there was Kent Williams, there was Ted McKeever…

*McKeever would have been an odd choice. With his somewhat clanky, industrial style he was going to depict the land of Faerie?*

He was going to try to do the land of Faerie. Industrial faeries! There's Crank, there's Crude the oil faerie…[*Laughs.*]

*Getting back to* Stardust – *Neil's remarked that he wanted to write a Lord Dunsany-type story when he wrote it. Aside from Rackham, were there any other specific artists of Dunsany's era that influenced the look of the book?*

There's Edmund DuLac and John Bauer, a lot of different people.

Stardust *was in the same vein as your story in* The Kindly Ones *in that it featured heavily illustrated prose.*

The one thing that drives me crazy about the illustrated *Stardust* is that everyone says it's a comic book. I'm like, "What comic book is in there? There are no panels – it's an illustrated book." I kept saying, "This is so stupid." "The graphic novel adaptation of *Stardust*" – I kept saying, "It's *not* a graphic novel, it's an illustrated book." Just because they were put out by a comic-book publisher. It's like calling *The Dream Hunters* a graphic novel, and people do. You think, "No. It's a story that's illustrated."

*I suppose that's partly the fault of company marketing that attempts to sell it to only one particular market.*

But it's also the fault of the critics. Because it's coming from a comic-book company they just say, "Oh, it's a comic book." Nope.

*And so the review for* Dream Hunters *might wind up in the* Comics Buyer's Guide *instead of a literature review.*

Yes.

*How would you characterize your work with Neil?*

Working with Neil made me realize that the better the writer you work with, the better your drawing is going to be. The level of writing really dramatically went up with working with him. The better the source material you have, the better and more creative you will be.

*Have the two of you discussed working together again someday?*

We're talking about doing something. I have no idea what. We have too much fun working together to not work together, so we will.

*It sounds like the work you've done with Neil has, among other things, enabled you to construct a bridge to your recent book-illustration work. As a child, what did you respond to more strongly – children's books or comics?*

Oh, comics. What taught me the joy of reading was Carl Barks's *Uncle Scrooge* stories, and Edgar Rice Burroughs's *Tarzan*. I grew up with those and I didn't ever see any difference between the comic books and the comic strips and the *Conan the Barbarian* books that were then coming out and *The Lord of the Rings*, all that stuff. It just seemed to be one big stew pot that was exciting to think about.

*It was all just storytelling?*

Storytelling. I like it, and it really excites me. Whether it's panel to panel or just one image, I really like to get the viewer involved in images.

*Of your work to date, what gives the most pride?*

All of it.

*You don't want to single out any child for special attention?*

Not really. For the last couple of years I've just enjoyed everything I've done.

*So the last couple of years have been the most satisfying?*

There was a certain point, probably in the late '80s, where I realized I sort of need to grab fate by the throat and determine what I was going to do instead of waiting for people to come to me with projects. That sort of coincided with doing issue 19 of *Sandman*. Then I got this Spider-Man book [*Spirits of the Earth*]. Both of those came out within a couple of months of each other. They sort of put me on the map, retailer-wise. They realized people had bought this book, so then they bought other books. That's something that every artist and writer has to do. You've got to prove yourself.

# the FALSE KNIGHT on the ROAD

©95 · NEIL GAIMAN AND CHARLES VESS ·

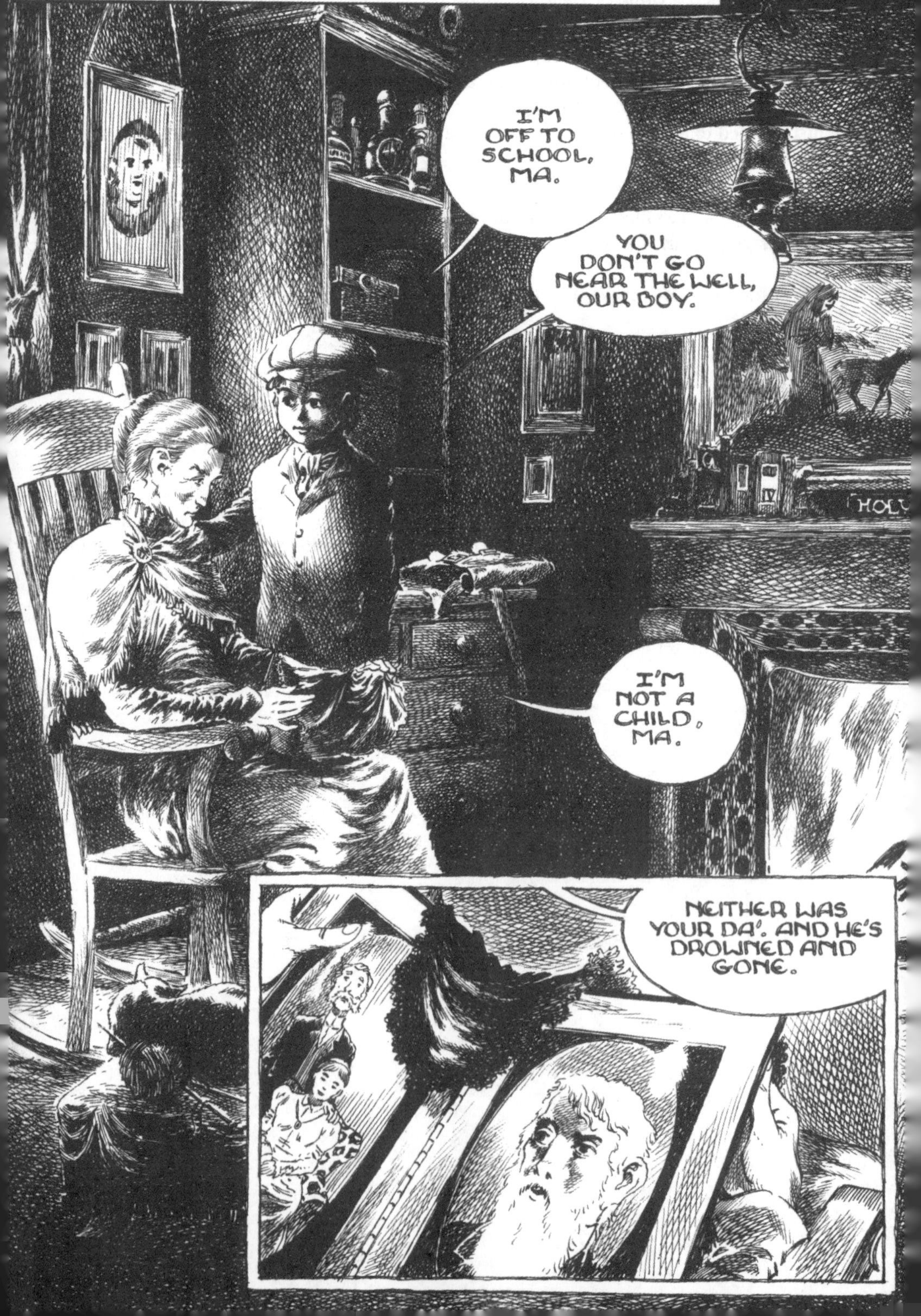

I'M OFF TO SCHOOL, MA.
YOU DON'T GO NEAR THE WELL, OUR BOY.
HOLY
I'M NOT A CHILD, MA.
NEITHER WAS YOUR DA'. AND HE'S DROWNED AND GONE.

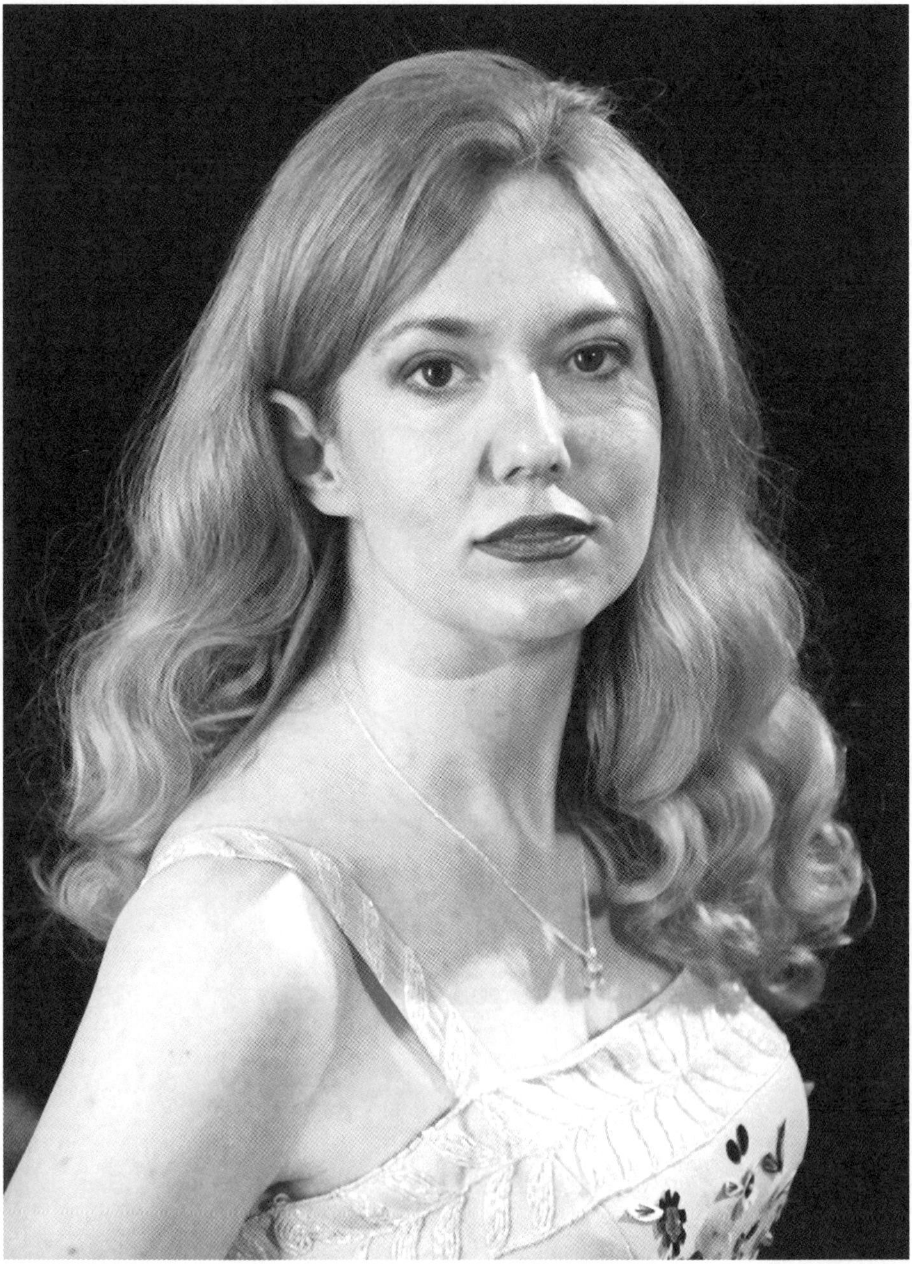

# COLLEEN DORAN, LIKE MANY *SANDMAN* ARTISTS, WAS AN

ESTABLISHED PROFESSIONAL BEFORE WORKING WITH GAIMAN. WHAT'S UNUSUAL ABOUT DORAN IS THAT SHE'D TURNED PROFESSIONAL AT THE AGE OF FIFTEEN, AND HAD CREATED HER ONGOING SCIENCE-FICTION/FANTASY COMIC-BOOK SERIES *A DISTANT SOIL* AT TWELVE.

DORAN'S EVER-CHANGING ILLUSTRATIVE STYLE ALSO SHINED ON COMICS LIKE *THE LEGION OF SUPER-HEROES*, *CLIVE BARKER'S HELLRAISER*, AND THE VERTIGO GRAPHIC NOVEL *ORBITER*, BUT *SANDMAN* FANS KNOW HER BEST AS THE ARTIST BEHIND "FAÇADE" [ISSUE 20]. THOUGH DORAN WAS TO ILLUSTRATE ONLY ONE OTHER *SANDMAN* ISSUE (34, CHAPTER 3 OF *A GAME OF YOU*), SHE WAS PRESENT DURING THE BOOK'S EARLY DAYS, AND HAS BEEN CALLED "PART OF THE *SANDMAN* FAMILY" BY GAIMAN.

DORAN HAS CONTINUED TO NOURISH HER LOVE OF FANTASY AND SCIENCE FICTION BY ILLUSTRATING *THE COMPLETE J.R.R. TOLKIEN SOURCEBOOK* AND DC'S *REIGN OF THE ZODIAC*. HER MOST RECENT WORK IS THE WARREN ELLIS-SCRIPTED *STEALTH TRIBES*.

*How did you come to work on "Façade"?*

I had won a government grant to study American popular culture, and I was with a group of cartoonists from around the world: Egypt, Czechoslovakia, the Philippines, Nigeria, Zimbabwe. One of the stops on the tour was DC Comics. "Well, I work here. This is no big deal to me." So I was off roaming the halls. I went into Karen Berger's office, and there was this good-looking guy in a black-leather jacket. Karen said, "Oh, this is Colleen Doran. Colleen, this is Neil Gaiman." I said, "Yeah, hi, how you doing?" and I walked out the door, and thought, "Wait a minute – *Sandman*!" *Sandman* had just started coming out, and Neil was only on issue 5 or something, and it was not doing well. However, I had seen the book and loved it. I went back in there and said, "*Sandman* is a great book! I love this book! You're Neil Gaiman!" He said [*impersonating Gaiman*], "Oh, Colleen, I'm so happy to meet you. I like *A Distant Soil*. I'd love to work with you on *Sandman*." I said, "Oh, man, I'd love to do that." They had just done that promotion with issue number 8 ["The Sound of Her Wings"], and it hadn't come out yet. They had advance copies. The book was struggling then.

*That was the first issue with Death.*

Yes, and it wasn't in the stores yet, and he gave me one – the limited edition, promotional thing. He signed it, and he put in his name, address, and phone number.

I am going to sell that puppy and make a million bucks! I still have it. Neil Gaiman's phone number! Eat your hearts out, girls!

Nobody knew who he was back then. I was really happy to get to be friends with him before he got to be "NEIL." It was great. His scripts were flawless. We spent a lot of time on the phone talking about how the story was going to be told, the body language. I remember he said he specifically wanted me to do this story. It was funny, because Mike Allred to this day claims, "Neil wrote that story for me. I didn't get the job, and it's your fault." He actually said that to my face. I was shocked. The first time I met him he said, "I've hated you for years." I said, "What the hell did I do to you? I don't even know who you are." He said, "Well, I was supposed to do that story, and I didn't get it." I said, "Tough weenie. Neil told me I was supposed to do that story, so too bad, so sad!" It never would have occurred to me to hold a grudge against someone because they got an assignment I wanted. Malcolm Jones did the most beautiful inks on that story – so, so gorgeous. Then, I was inked on another *Sandman* story by George Pratt and it was just a disaster.

*Chapter 3 of* A Game of You *[Issue 34]?*

Yes, it was horrible. I have not spoken to George Pratt since. One of his friends told me, "Well, George said, 'I don't care. Her work is no good. I'm going on vacation,' and he inked it in two days." I said, "I'm gonna break his fingers, if he ever comes near me." So every time he sees me, he flees! [*Laughs.*] I'll never forget it as long as I live. That book really hurt my reputation. After that issue came out, Harlan Ellison comes up to me and says – first words out his mouth, swear to God – [*impersonating Ellison*] "What the hell happened to you on that issue of *Sandman?*" I said, "Harlan, it ain't me. I swear to God. I can prove it, because I save all my pencils." For *years*, I was walking around with pencils for that book in my portfolio, so if anyone gave me shit, I would just rip them out and say, "This is what it was supposed to look like!" Even the art director at DC, Dick Giordano, came up to me and apologized for it. He'd been called in to pinch hit on the last pages of inks and he was very embarrassed, saying that he was told to keep the style consistent. He felt terrible about it because everyone thought it looked awful.

I don't really know what George Pratt was thinking when he inked that job because I only got a second-hand story about it. I don't care what went on in his head. Maybe he liked what he did, but I thought it was the worst ink job of my entire career, and I've had some bad ones. George is the most marvelous painter and I respect him. However, my pencils weren't enhanced by his inks. There was even some talk about having the inks re-done before DC collected the books in graphic novel format, but they didn't do it after all. Neil called to apologize for that.

Neil Gaiman is a prince. I just saw him about two weeks ago, and it was wonderful, because he is so happy. I don't think he was happy about seven or eight years ago.

*Why not?*

Well, we had a long talk. We're not going to get into all the particulars, but I will say we actually fell out of touch for a while. And he said, "I'm really sorry. I haven't been keeping in touch." I said, "Neil, the only thing I want is for you to be happy. You've moved on, you've gone into other places, you're doing other things and you've got new friends. Go right on ahead. Just live your life. You do not have to slow down for me, just go on." He looks great, he sounds great and he's just... One thing I can say is that he did have a bit of a complex because people were saying, "Well, you're not a real writer. You just write comic books."

*So you felt he had something to prove?*

He had something to prove, and he was very insecure. I can relate. Having that conversation with him was wonderful, because it would never have occurred to me that Neil Gaiman, this writer that everyone admires so much, would be insecure – *for two seconds*. It never occurred to me. It occurs to me that I would be insecure, because I'm insecure every minute of the day, but I couldn't believe that Neil was insecure, as if he lived on another plane of existence or something. Finding out that somebody – that I knew when he was nobody – I had built into some kind of uber-writer in my mind, forgetting that he's a human being just like everybody else, and that he had his own problems and his own concerns... I don't think I was as forgiving of him seven or eight years ago as I should have been. I thought he had attitude. But he told me, "I was just so upset that people weren't considering me a real writer. And now they can't say that."

*He's a* New York Times-*best-selling novelist.*

Yes. I remember fans really ripping him up. One was on the web writing about how arrogant Neil was for trying to be a real writer and how he should stick to comics. The fan was crowing because he had seen one of Neil's books on sale on the remainder table at a store, which is common for any author, whether Stephen King or John Grisham or Neil Gaiman. Remaindering doesn't mean that the book is a flop. I took the creep to task and all these fans went berserk, going off about how comic-book creators don't have any real talent, otherwise they wouldn't be doing comics, which is retarded, since almost every creator I know works outside of comics and does comics because they love them.

I wasn't as understanding as I should have been toward Neil. I'm so glad we had that conversation. We were all guest speakers at the American Library Association in Atlanta. Twenty-thousand librarians – these librarians paid this pre-conference fee to come and hear us speak about graphic novels. It was myself, Neil Gaiman, Art Spiegelman, and Jeff Smith. I was thinking, *"What am I doing here?* Why do they want me to speak in this august company?" I was nervous, but it went well. It was magnificent, the librarians were so positive. All of them were saying, "Graphic novels in libraries – this is the best thing that has happened in years. The graphic novels circulate better than any of our other books for young adults. We're so happy to have you here. It's the best pre-conference ever. You guys are great." We were all kind of walking around going, "No shit? Really? Us? Thanks!" [*Laughs.*] It was fantastic. I couldn't believe how well it went. It was the most enthusiastic audience. I got up there and said, "You know, when I was a kid, my teachers would take my comic books and throw them in the trash. They were certain they would rot my brain. And here I am speaking before all of you today." [*Laughs.*] The irony was obvious.

*Getting back to "Façade" – what were your thoughts when you first read Neil's script? It strikes me as a very dark tale for the sort of style you employed at that time. Your style back then could occasionally be somewhat ornate and fanciful. Neil remarked in* The Sandman Companion *that he felt you had a lot of potential but were being underused.*

I absolutely loved the script and was very excited to be working with Neil. I knew he was brilliantly talented and I wanted to work with him from the moment I

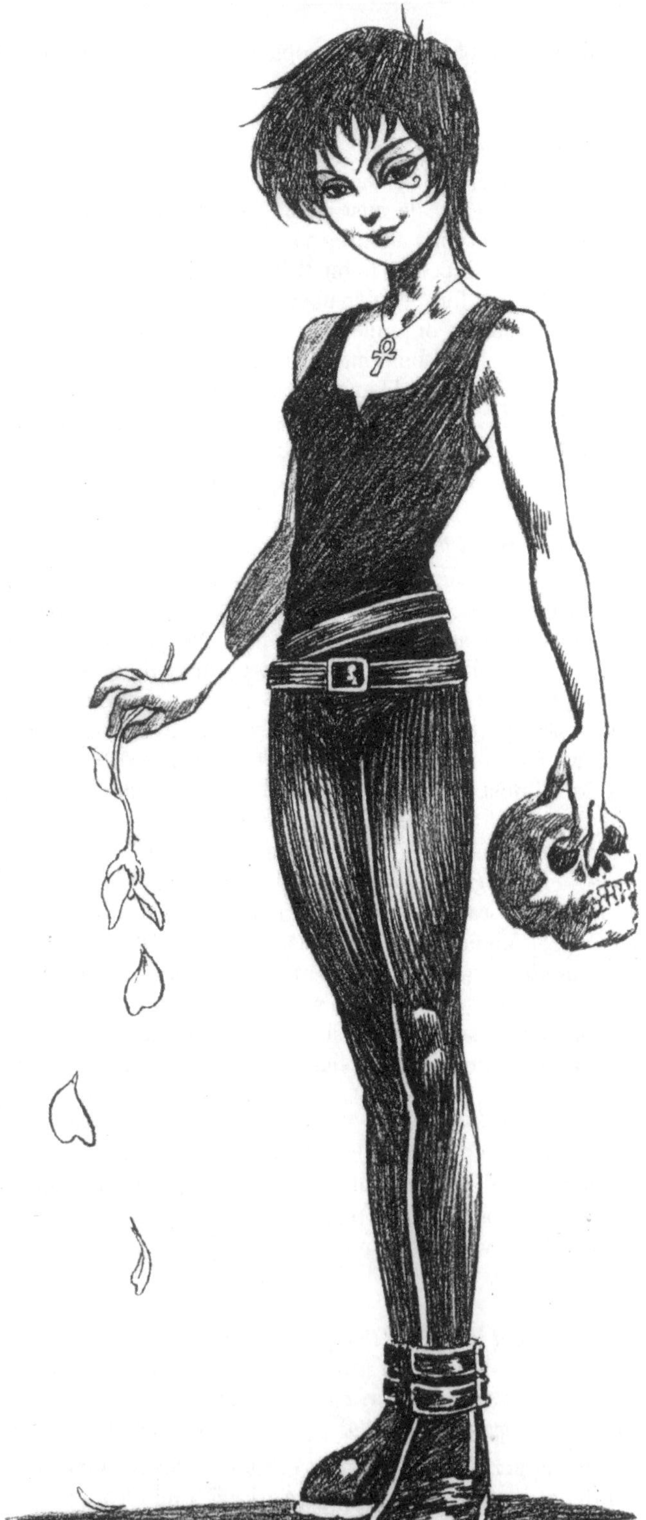

A "Death Doodle" by Colleen Doran. © 2004 Colleen Doran. Character TM & © 2004 DC Comics.

first read his work. I was excited about the prospect of being able to show some range in my own work as well. I had been typecast as a "girl" artist and people were often very dismissive of me and my work. To have an immensely gifted writer such as Neil tell me he thought I had talent and untapped potential was a real gift. The story was brilliant and very clever. I loved it and knew it was a special tale.

I also liked the theme of a woman trapped by the way she is seen by others. I think a lot of women have that experience, that despite their talents or the nature of their inner being, they are really just a walking façade and they wear the mask that makes the rest of the world comfortable with them.

*Were you disturbed at all by the story's suicide ending? Did you discuss it at any length with Neil?*

No, I wasn't disturbed in the least. It was completely in character. We discussed it at great length and even acted through certain scenes on the phone to get the body language correct.

Rainie died of lack of imagination. She couldn't conceive of a world in which she didn't conform, in which she didn't present a pleasant face. Here she was, an extraordinary being with talents that would make her immortal and give her opportunities many would kill to have. She could travel to the bottom of the Marianis trench, climb the highest mountain and get the world's most perfect view, and yet she couldn't deal with how people saw her. Her gift was wasted on her. There was nothing inside. So whatever she was outside was limited to the scope of her mind and that was a pretty narrow focus.

Lots of people are like that. Urania was just too dim to live long enough to appreciate what she had become. That may not have been all politically correct and empowering, but it was very true.

*The opening of "Façade" is interesting. How explicitly did Neil describe the degree to which Rainie would be seen in the first few pages?*

Very explicitly. His direction was quite specific. He was a very careful writer and knew precisely what he wanted.

*"Façade" may be the first issue of* Sandman *in which the title character is not present. But his sister Death plays a key role. Were you the envy of other artists because you had the chance to draw the popular breakout character of Death, whom few at that time had had the chance to draw?*

I don't know what other artists thought, but I sure as heck envied everyone who got to draw Sandman! I never really got a crack at the guy. Death had barely made an impact in comics when I got the script for "Façade," so it wasn't a big issue who got what characters. When I first met Neil, *Sandman* was on the verge of cancellation.

*Regarding, again, Chapter 3 of* A Game of You, *what made you decide to give Thessaly so much of your physical appearance?*

Neil told people that Thessaly looked like "Colleen with her makeup off." In other words, quite mousy. Also, a mouse that could roar, deceptively weak.

*When I spoke with Bryan Talbot, he remarked that he was brought in to pencil half of Chapter 5 [Issue 36] when you collapsed. Were you tremendously overworked at that time?*

Hunh? No way. That's not what happened. I was brought in to fill in for one issue, period. I wish to heck I had been hired to do the whole storyline, but wasn't.

It's possible that I was considered to be the original artist on the storyline. That may be what he was thinking. If I was, then this is the first I've heard of it. In 1992, I remember I got deathly ill with pneumonia and was sick for a good six months or more. My mother had to come live with me at that point. I may not have gotten the job in the first place for that reason. Everybody knew I was sick as a dog and every time I tried to get up and get back to work, I would relapse. I was working on *Shade* at the time and I am surprised Karen Berger ever hired me again because I couldn't make the deadline for anything. I was so sick.

I had been working on a *Legion of Super-heroes* tale and Curt Swan had to do about five pages of it. I couldn't even lift a pencil. Everyone thought I was a goner, but I recovered, obviously.

Sandman, *especially* A Game of You, *features some gruesome images, and you were given one of the more disturbing – Thessaly cutting George's face off and nailing it, along with his eyeballs, to a wall. How explicitly would Neil's script describe these scenes?*

Neil is always very specific. He is careful, highly detailed. He knows exactly what he wants. I just wish the final result had looked better. Or worse, depending on your point of view.

*You are known for being able to change your style to suit different projects, but is there anything that stays the same? What things do you always bring to the table with your art?*

I am solid on the body language. The acting of the characters is a vital, and largely ignored, element of the storytelling process in comics. I am quite conscious of how people move. I am sure I must look like a weirdo when I am out in public because I am watching everyone around me, studying. I am interested in the psychology of body language. I used to read all my father's forensic psychology books and I try to apply what I have read to the work as well.

I disliked acting because I was hampered by the way I looked. I am a little blonde woman and I got little blonde woman roles. That's nice if you're going to be an ingénue forever, but cartooning means no role is beyond me. It is exciting because I can be any character. I have to act, through my pencil, for every person in the book whether a brawny soldier or a little old lady. I think my way through every motion and expression, and I count myself successful when I have conveyed the information I want to convey without straying into caricature, when I have produced a natural-looking moment. I don't go in for hyperrealism, but I do want things to be emotionally real. I think I do this better than just about anyone. I don't think it is a skill most people in our business appreciate, but it is important to me.

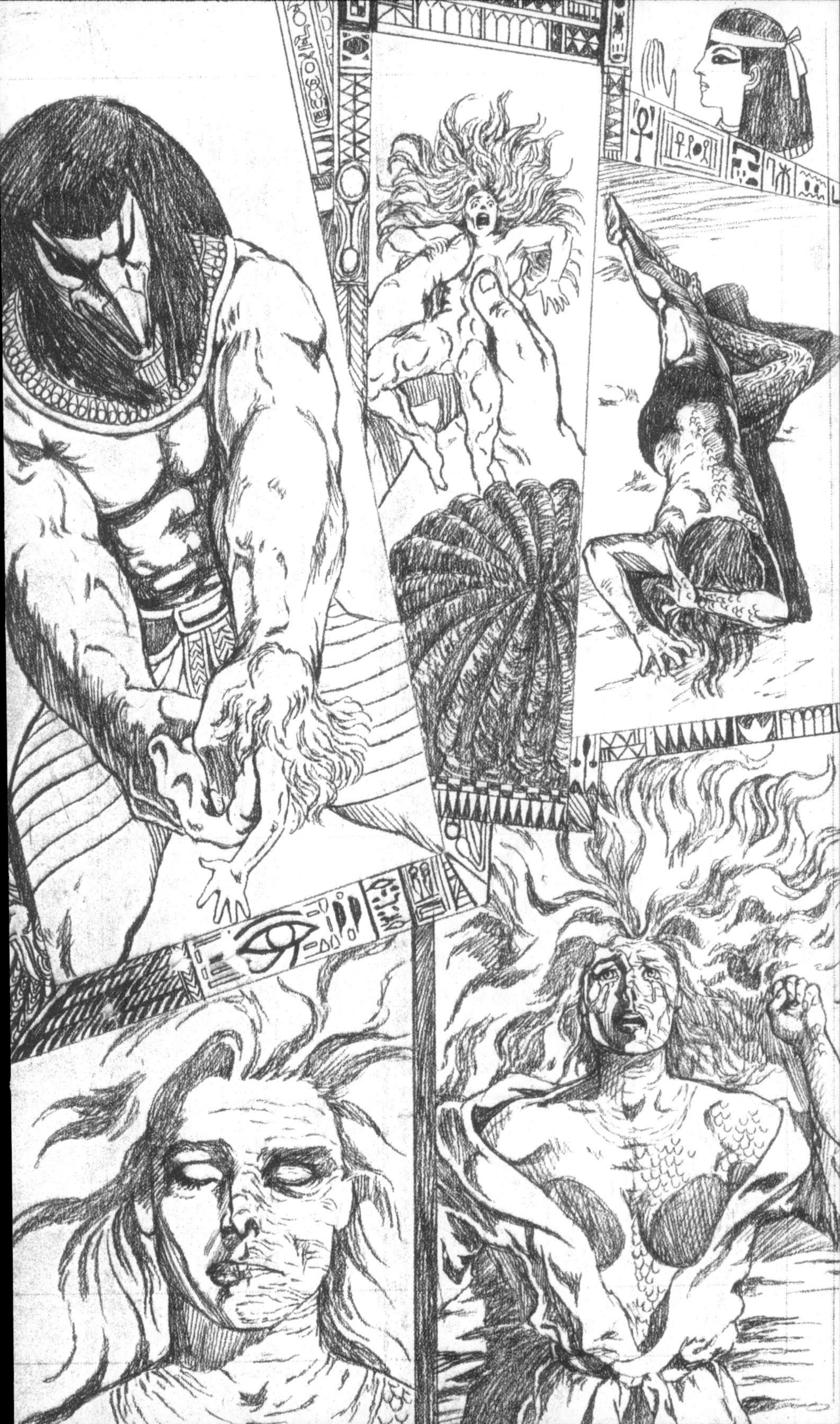

Colleen Doran's pencils for page 7 of *Sandman* 20, "Facade". © 2004 DC Comics.

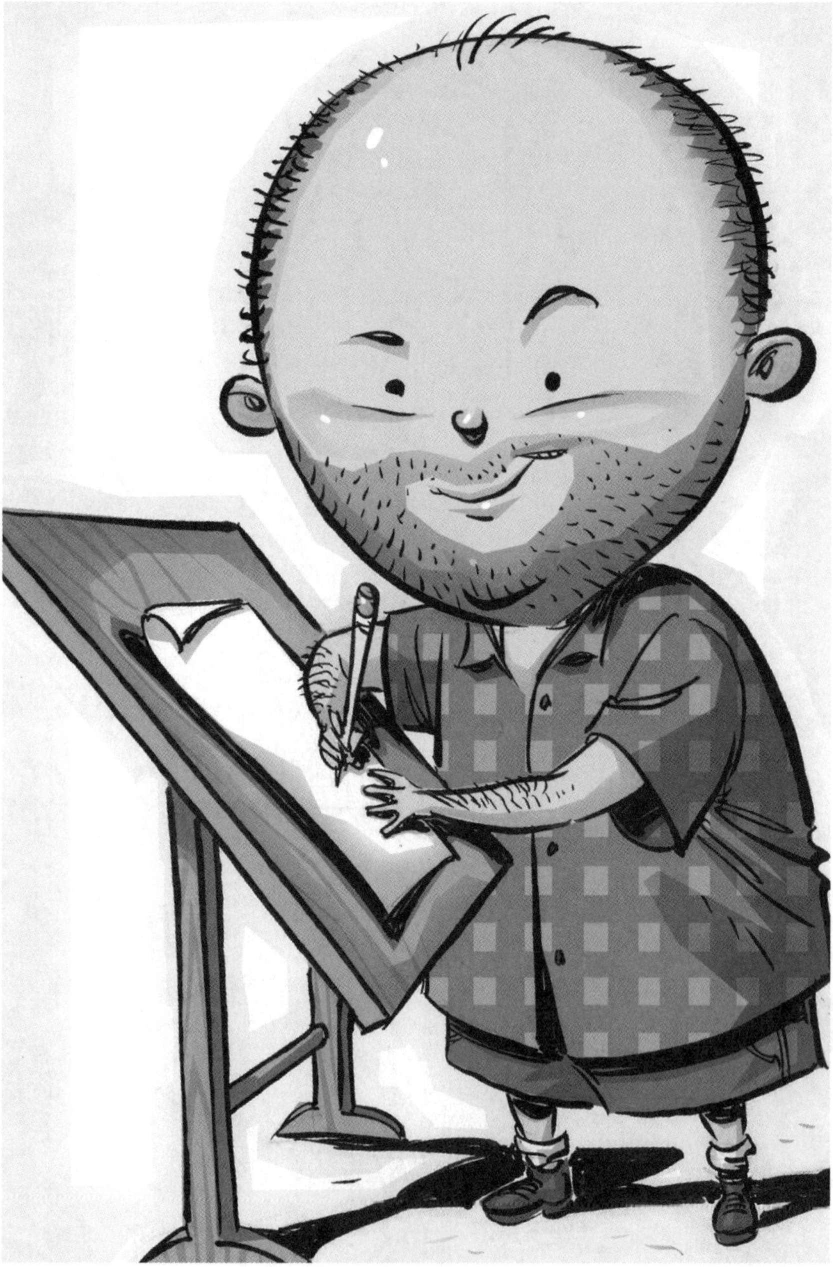

Self-portrait. © 2004 Shawn McManus.

*Shawn McManus*

# AS THE PRINCIPAL ILLUSTRATOR OF *A GAME OF YOU*,

SHAWN MCMANUS BROUGHT A RICH, CHILDREN'S-STORYBOOK-FLAVORED STYLE TO *THE SANDMAN* THAT SERVED AS A COUNTERPOINT TO A NON-"FAN FRIENDLY" STORYLINE ABOUT GENDER.

MCMANUS FIRST CAPTURED THE ATTENTION OF MANY COMICS READERS WHEN HE PROVIDED ART FOR TWO ISSUES OF ALAN MOORE'S *SWAMP THING*, INCLUDING THE *POGO* HOMAGE "POG" [IN ISSUE 32]. HE ALSO ILLUSTRATED *DOCTOR FATE*, *OMEGA MEN*, AND SEVERAL *SPIDER-MAN* TITLES BEFORE TAKING A BREAK FROM COMICS TO FOCUS ON ADVERTISING AND ILLUSTRATION WORK. BUT MCMANUS WAS BROUGHT BACK INTO THE FOLD TO WORK ON AN ISSUE OF *TOM STRONG'S TERRIFIC TALES* AND HIS *GAME OF YOU* CHARACTER THESSALY'S TWO VERTIGO MINI-SERIES.

THESE DAYS, MCMANUS SPENDS A GOOD DEAL OF TIME WITH BOOK-ILLUSTRATION WORK AND THEME-PARK DESIGN. THE FOLLOWING INTERVIEW IS UNIQUE IN THAT IT'S THE FIRST HE HAS GIVEN SINCE ART SCHOOL, IN 1978.

*Neil remarked in his introduction to the* Swamp Thing *collection,* Love and Death, *that "Pog," the second* Swamp Thing *story you did, was actually his favorite during Moore's run on the book. He said Moore knew your "lighter style would be ideal for the book, as indeed it was." How did you come to work with Moore?*

He asked Karen if I was available – it was all through Karen Berger – and I was. Alan told me that he actually wrote that story specifically for my cartoony style.

*What had you been doing prior to that?*

I think I did *Omega Men* for a year before that, and then the issue of *Swamp Thing*.

*Did you notice any subtle differences between Moore's approach to scripting and Neil's, between their methods of communicating with you?*

They're kind of similar, actually. They both knew what they wanted. As writers, they think very visually. They don't put too much in the story. They know the limits of what's going to go within the panels. Alan's script was very, very dense – for one panel, it might be three paragraphs. So you're looking at a fifty-page script for twenty-two pages. Neil's was a little less dense. Both obviously know what they're doing, they've been doing it for a long time. The best thing about it is that they write really visually, if that makes any sense. As an artist, I think it's really nice that they're not asking for too much. I don't know how much planning they do. I don't know if they do little thumbnails, or what the deal is. But it's really nice to work for those guys, to work on a script for either of them.

*I tend to think an artist would prefer a script that is not dense, not that detailed; that they might like to be given as much leeway as possible. But because those two, as you say, "think very visually," do you find them to be an exception?*

Yes, exactly. In fact, I actually would prefer to work on a plot, as opposed to full script. But with these guys – they did all the thinking. Everything was right up front, so it was a breeze to do.

*Did you find that because you didn't need to think about some of the placement of elements in the panel you could focus your energy on the actual illustration?*

Yes, yes. That's exactly it. It's really fun to do their scripts. It's kind of hard to explain unless you read one of their scripts, but they write so visually it's magic, man. I recently did an eight-pager for *Tom Strong* that Alan had written ["Blanket Shanty," issue 7 of *Tom Strong's Terrific Tales*]. The editor, Scott Dunbier, saw some of my children's book stuff, and he suggested sending some of that stuff to Alan. And Alan wrote a children's-book-style story around the illustrations that I did, for that style. I couldn't do the story justice. It sounds kind of weird, but it was so magical, reading this thing. I had these images in my head that were unbelievable. It was so much fun to do, visually. When I read the first page – and anybody who would read this thing would have a different image – it was awesome and beautiful. I did two *Swamp Thing*s, "The Burial" [issue 28] and "Pog," [but] I hadn't done anything with [Alan] since.

That was a whole different thing than what I'm used to doing. I do a lot of children's book stuff on my own, just to mess around with. And this was a little bit of that, so it really wasn't very comic booky at all. I tried to look a lot different. In a way, my stuff has changed, or I'm hoping it's changed. I've gotten a lot simpler since the early *Swamp Thing*s. I love the European artists, like Serge Clerc and Chaland, very cartoony, but very, very simple, and great storytelling, a lot of action in that stuff. Chaland is terrific, oh my God.

Incidentally, just as an aside, for some *Sandman* info, I actually was supposed to be the first artist on that book, way back… I forgot when it started, but Karen said, "Hey, I got this script from this guy," and she sent it to me and it was *Sandman*, with some sketches from Neil in there. I did a few little sketches on it, and she said, "Hey, you know what, this has a big long deadline, and what we really need – we want to get an artist for *Dr. Fate*, so why don't you do that one instead?" Because that one had a tighter deadline, I ended up doing *Dr. Fate*, when I was originally supposed to do *Sandman*.

*Sam Kieth was telling me about that. He said he wanted to work on* Doctor Fate *or* Swamp Thing, *but he was given* Sandman.

He would've been great on *Swamp Thing*. I don't know. There's a certain group of artists, and I think I was one of them, that really kind of levitated toward *Swamp Thing*, because when I heard they were going to do *Swamp Thing* again, I made a big pitch. I did a couple of sample pages and sent them up to Karen. Man, I wanted to do that so bad, and they gave it to Steve Bissette and John Totleben. I was kind of bummed out, but I couldn't have done the job they did. They got exactly the right artists for that. I kind of liked the Bernie Wrightson character, and they changed him a lot. It would've been fun to do, but those guys kicked my ass on *Swamp Thing*. I couldn't have done half the job those guys did.

*Well, you were uniquely suited to do "Pog."*

I'm glad they actually made the right choice with those guys, the deadlines were really tight. I loved that *Swamp Thing* book.

*Like Sam Kieth, you had a pretty strong Frazetta influence in your work at that time.*

Probably, yes. It was Frazetta and Wrightson, that whole kind of school that I've gotten away from.

*Were you influenced by book illustrators as well as by comic-book artists?*

Hmm…a little bit of both. I was a huge Wrightson fan. I was the biggest Wrightson fan on the planet. I tried copying his stuff just to kind of learn how to draw for a while. I'd hide all my bad drawing in shadows; although his drawing wasn't bad, he just did great shadows – along with Frazetta, Maxfield Parrish, Dean Cornwell, all those guys that everybody else was looking at. A little bit of everybody.

*I noticed you inked yourself on* Sandman. *You were one of the few artists to do so.*

I was probably unhappy with a lot of the inkers I had, so I just asked them if I could ink it myself. I think editors, or the ones I've dealt with, are happy if you can ink your own work, because it's one less person to deal with. It just depends on whether they like the style or not, but I've been pretty lucky, where they just said, "Go ahead and do it." Before that, I did *Dr. Fate* for two years, two years straight. I penciled and inked every issue except for one, which, for me, was pretty good.

*The one* Sandman *story you penciled prior to* A Game of You *was "Three Septembers and a January" [Issue 31].*

I loved that story. I don't remember the details, but it was about this guy in San Francisco who printed up his own money and everyone went along with the whole thing. On that particular one, Karen called me and said, "Are you available?" And luckily I was. That was my particular favorite, art-wise and story-wise, of that little run. It wasn't really part of the other arc I did, of *A Game of You*, but the way I think of it, it *was* part of that run. Because I did that and then jumped right into *A Game of You*. That was my favorite. It was a cool story about an eccentric guy, and it was really fun to draw.

*"Three Septembers and a January" was one of the first* Sandman *stories to prominently feature Delirium. How did Neil describe her to you?*

It was in the script. He described how she looked, what her attitude was – "She's very sleepy, almost in a drug state." I think Karen sent me some reference material, but Neil was very descriptive in his script, which was really helpful. I was going off his description and whoever had drawn her before me. I obviously wanted to make her the same character. Neil was also very descriptive about Despair. I drew her for a couple of panels. For an artist, all this stuff really helps.

*Your issues of* A Game of You *were some of the series' most eye-catching, with their rich, storybook-style art.*

Neil actually said that he chose me just for those specific cartoony characters – Wilkinson, the rat, and there were some others in there. It was so long ago I forget their names. It was fun to draw, but I think he had that in mind when he had me doing it, that kind of cartoony style.

*Sandman*'s such a well-written book. It was very intellectual, and it was something I might not have actually picked up myself. I kind of go for the more base comic book, like *The Rocketeer*, something I don't have to think too much about. But Neil's stuff… I'm glad I got into it. It's addicting. I'm glad I got into it because I started reading it once I got into it. The characters are great, the prose is great, the plot, everything. It was a lot of fun to do. One of my favorite artists that actually did the book was Marc Hempel.

*Karen Berger mentioned she felt both* A Game of You *and Marc's storyline,* The Kindly Ones, *were two of the standouts.* The Kindly Ones, *with Marc's expressionistic artwork, is quite impressive.*

It was awesome. It worked well with the story, and I'm a big fan of his stuff anyway. It's really, really simple, but I think there's a lot more behind it. I love looking at that stuff, it's so nice. And *Breathtaker*, when he did that…awesome. All his stuff is comprised of these weird shapes. He's so good, though. Simple, you know? The simplicity of it…

*Neil has also said that* A Game of You *might be his favorite storyline in the series.*

Oh, that's cool. I didn't know that. That's nice.

*He mentioned it in* The Sandman Companion. *He also mentioned that it demanded an artist who could draw "cute fantasy but also realistic horror, and mix them seamlessly."*

They couldn't find that guy, so they went to me. [*Laughs.*]

*Apparently, Neil wasn't happy with the way* A Game of You *was originally going, the way he was writing it. He suggested dropping it to Tom Peyer (*Sandman*'s assistant editor through issue 25), but then he saw some of the work you'd already done. Neil liked it and Peyer said, "No, we should keep going because this is good."*

Thank you, Tom – a debt of gratitude.

*You worked with Alisa Kwitney for the most part, since she was the assistant editor on* Sandman *by the time* A Game of You *saw print.*

Yes, and a lot with Karen. Karen's a pro. She's so awesome to work with. Unfortunately, I don't have a lot of interaction with her any more. The stuff I've been doing for Vertigo is through Shelly Bond, who I think learned a lot from Karen, and who is equally awesome. And Mariah Huehner, who's Shelly's assistant. She's cut from the same mold. I love working for those gals, they're so cool.

*One can see why Neil chose you, in part, for your ability to draw "realistic horror" –* A Game of You *has some of the more gruesome images in* Sandman.

There's that scene where the throat gets slit [Chapter 4, "Beginning to See the Light," issue 35, page 22].

*And that scene in Chapter 2 ("Lullabies of Broadway," issue 33), on page 15, Hazel's dream, in which her dead baby arises to attack a living one.*

Oh yes, that was pretty creepy, with all the teeth. I was just drawing what Neil had put down in the script. That was kind of creepy.

*But you were spared the scene in which Thessaly cuts George's face off his head. Colleen Doran got to draw that one [Chapter 3, "Bad Moon Rising," issue 34, page 12].*

Yes, she had the face tacked up to the wall. I got it afterwards. [*Laughs.*]

*What was it that brought Colleen on board for that issue? Did you need a chance to catch up?*

I was probably running late. I'm sure it was just a deadline issue. I'm sure I messed up at one point.

*Bryan Talbot came on board for Chapter 5 ("Over the Sea to Sky," issue 36), penciling half of the issue while you penciled the other half. Bryan was an interesting choice, since the two of you have such different styles.*

That was the split issue. It was a good idea, because it was such a contrast.

*Did Neil change the script to accommodate both of you?*

Probably not.

*The scenes in Barbie's dream world were in the same vein as* Alice In Wonderland *and* The Wizard Of Oz, *as well as Tolkien's work. Were you a big fan of that stuff as a kid?*

Not really. There was an Italian artist who had done *Pinocchio*. I bought a reprint of that book, and that's probably the first kids' book that I read, and I liked the illustrations. But I really didn't get into children's book illustration until I was a little older. When I was a kid, it was Dr. Seuss, and Maurice Sendak – great stuff. A few years ago, I discovered William Joyce and Chris Van Allsburg, some of those guys. *Jumanji* blew me away. It was so nice. Joyce and Van Allsburg are my favorites.

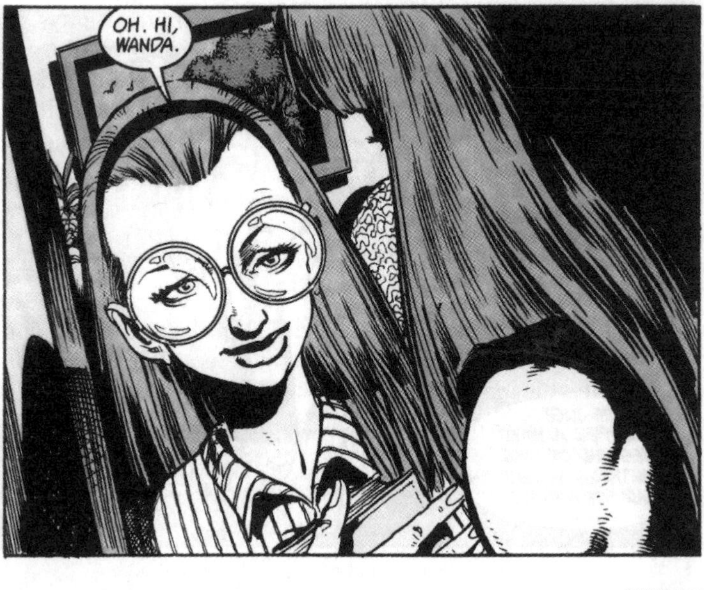
OH. HI, WANDA.

A Game of You *also featured realistic portrayals of lesbians and transvestitism, which one didn't typically find in mainstream comic books at that time. Were you at all familiar with that scene?*

What are you wearing right now? [*Laughs.*] For the two lesbians in that book, I think Neil had actually sent me this lesbian bondage book as a reference, to kind of get into the mood, and to see where they were coming from. It was a book of black-and-white photos, a little bit of nudity, but it was this punk-lesbian scene that was going on in Britain. He had sent it to Karen and Karen forwarded it to me.

*Did that influence the hairstyles, the look of the characters?*

A little bit. I wish I had gotten a little more out of it. His scripts were very descriptive – everything was in there – and he sent along that book for reference. I used a little bit of it, but I probably should've used more. I would use it now more than I did back then. I try to use a lot more reference now.

I've always been kind of lazy when it comes to using reference. I could've been a little more diligent in making things look a *little* more like they should have. A lot of the older stuff that I was doing, including *Sandman*, the anatomy...some of it was pretty bad. But I was doing the best I could and under the time constraints. So you do what you gotta do.

*It did look like there was growth in your work between* Swamp Thing *and* Dr. Fate, *and between* Dr. Fate *and* Sandman.

Oh, cool. Well, that's good. [*Laughs.*] *Dr. Fate* was inked for the most part with pens. When I did the *Sandman* stuff, I went mostly to brush, a little different look.

*To give your work a thicker, meatier look?*

Yes, just to try something a little different. The *Fate* stuff – I like that stuff a lot, but that was done with a lot of pens. It's a different look.

*These days, do you tend to favor the brush?*

I do. Looking at some of the European artists, a lot of those guys, it looks like, use nothing but brush. Actually, a lot of them use the pen also, but the guys I kind of lean toward are the ones that use a brush. I use a fake brush now. I don't know the brand name, but it's one of those brush-pens, those brush-markers. It has a tip like a brush, but plastic, and very flexible. I use those. I actually empty out the ink that's in there and put in some good ink. They're real easy to draw with and they give me a really nice line. I used these for the second *Thessaly* series.

*Thessaly was introduced in* A Game of You, *and you've illustrated both of her solo mini-series – do you have a particular fondness for her?*

Yes, she was probably my favorite, which led to the stuff I'm doing now. The stories have a lot of witchcraft, a lot of magic, a lot of monsters. It's fun stuff to draw. The more I draw her, the more attached I get to her. I think every issue looks a little bit better.

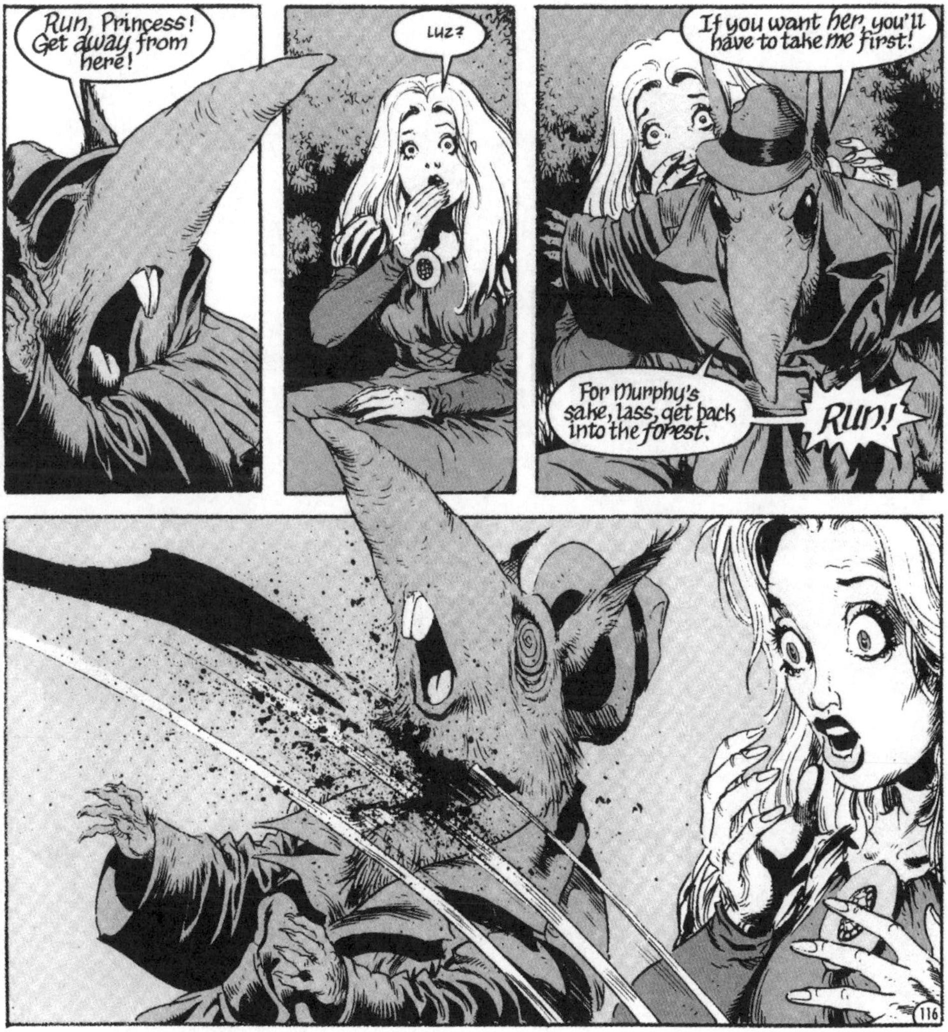
Run, Princess! Get away from here!
LUZ?
If you want her, you'll have to take me first!
For Murphy's sake, lass, get back into the forest.
RUN!
116

From page 22 of *Sandman* 35, Chapter 4 of *A Game of You*, "Beginning to See the Light" – "cute fantasy but also realistic horror." Pencils and inks by Shawn McManus. © 2004 DC Comics.
Previous Spread: Shawn McManus's Thessaly makes her first appearance; from page 7 of *Sandman* 32, Chapter 1 of *A Game of You*, "Slaughter on Fifth Avenue." Pencils and inks by McManus. © 2004 DC Comics.

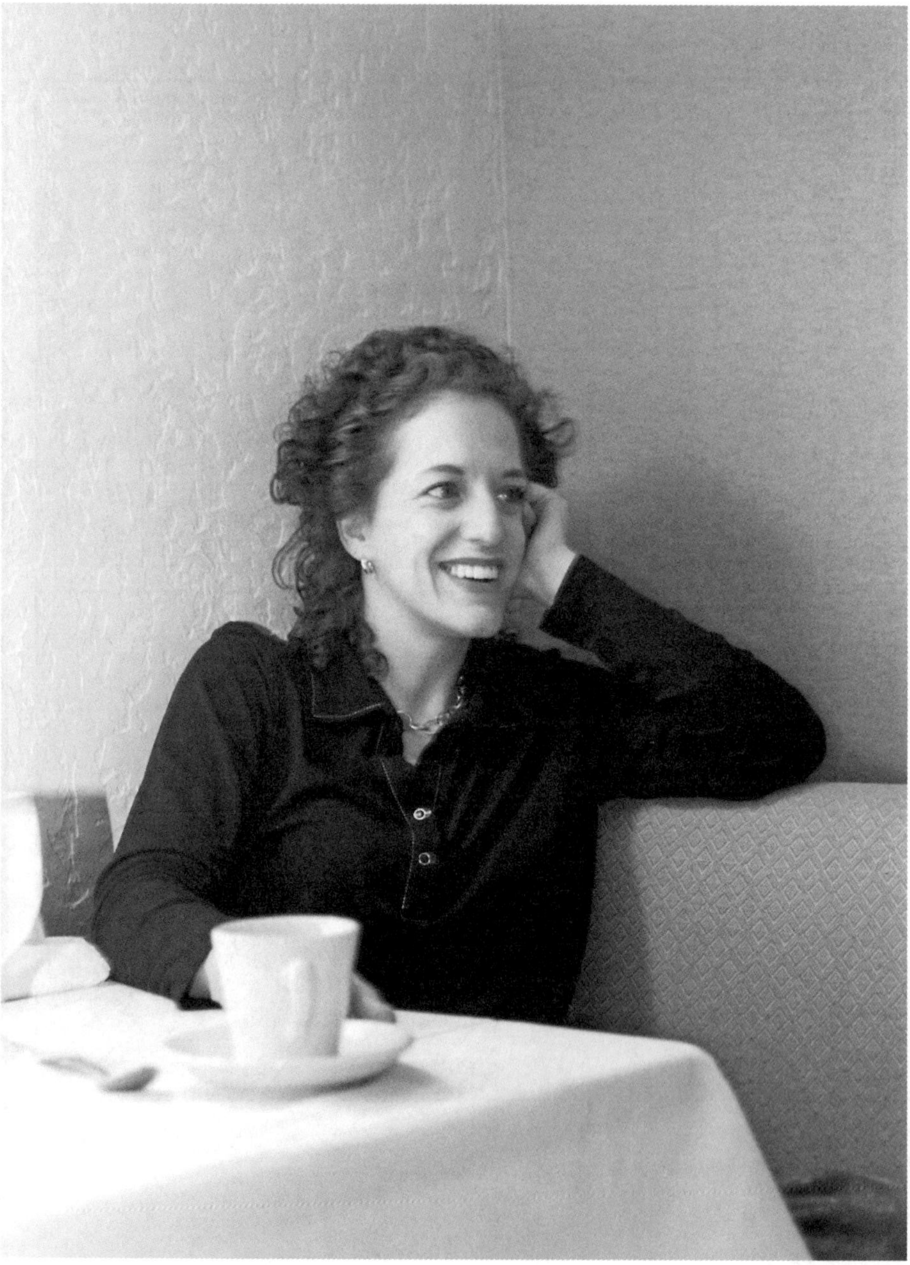

O

*Jill Thompson*

............................

# WHEN JILL THOMPSON MET WITH ME FOR THE FOLLOWING

INTERVIEW– AT THE 2002 PITTSBURGH COMIC-CON – HER ATTENTION WAS FIRST DRAWN TO THE PAGE OF SUNDAY FUNNIES I WAS READING. AFTER MAKING A "GAG ME" GESTURE AT THE SIGHT OF *CATHY*, THOMPSON POINTED TO LYNN JOHNSTON'S *FOR BETTER OR FOR WORSE*. "DO YOU EVER READ THIS?" SHE SAID. "THIS IS GOOD. THE CHARACTERS CHANGE. THEY GROW."

GROWTH IS SOMETHING THOMPSON KNOWS A THING OR TWO ABOUT. SINCE THE BEGINNING OF HER COMICS CAREER, ILLUSTRATING BILL WILLINGHAM'S *ELEMENTALS*, SHE HAS CONTINUALLY EVOLVED, TACKLING INCREASINGLY PERSONAL PROJECTS. MUCH TO HER FANS' DELIGHT, "PERSONAL," FOR THOMPSON, USUALLY TRANSLATES TO "FUN, CHARMING, AND LACKING IN PRETENSE." HER ART ON *BRIEF LIVES* MARKED SOMETHING OF A CAREER TURNING POINT – PRESENTING A CONFIDENT YOUNG ARTIST WITH A FRESH TAKE ON GAIMAN'S CHARACTERS, AND A LIVELY, EVOCATIVE STYLE.

THESE DAYS THOMPSON DEVOTES MUCH OF HER TIME TO HER OWN ALL-AGES *SCARY GODMOTHER*, AND TO PROJECTS LIKE THE MANGA-STYLE *SANDMAN*-INSPIRED *AT DEATH'S DOOR* AND THE UPCOMING *THE DEAD BOY DETECTIVES*.

............................

*Is it true that you first came to Neil's attention when you drew a nude sketch of Death?*

That's the lovely story he likes to tell, because it sounds much better than what I think the real story is. The way my editor at the time had told it, the assistant editor on *Wonder Woman* was a guy named Dan Thorsland, and he's worked at DC and Dark Horse, but he said they had been getting calls from Neil Gaiman, who had a *Sandman* story that he thought I should illustrate. I thought, "Oh my God, *Neil Gaiman!*" No one else had told me this before Dan. People had heard this before and no one had mentioned it to me, because I was under contract for *Wonder Woman*, and they wanted my contract to finish out and maybe I'd sign another one. But *Wonder Woman* really was not my thing; I did it and I look back at it and think, "This is really competent work." I probably couldn't draw like that any more, not necessarily the style, but that kind of...

*Subject matter?*

No, not subject matter, because I like super-heroes, but...I think I was really aping what I had seen before in it. I was really trying to live up to that, put some kind of [George] Pérezness in it, but I don't draw like that now. I've established my own style. I enjoyed working on *Wonder Woman*, but man, I *loved Sandman*. *Sandman* was definitely the kind of thing that I liked, and certainly like, to draw. It was much more up my alley. When I found out Neil wanted me to draw it, I said, "Oh God, I'll do it, but I've got all these issues of *Wonder Woman* to draw!" Dan said, "Let me work something out." So I got the call from Neil, saying he liked my work, and asking what I wanted to draw, and he would write a script that was feeling out the way that I worked and seeing what my strengths were. He would tailor the rest of his storytelling toward what I liked, which I thought was really considerate, and I guess he does that for all his artists – usually one issue to see how they mesh.

*That would have been the "Convergence" story ("The Parliament of Rooks," issue 40) you did before* Brief Lives?

Yes, the three stories that Cain and Abel and Eve tell. I was excited about that. Dan said Neil had seen my work on *Wonder Woman* and liked it and had been calling, and wanted me to do this *Brief Lives* story. But they had been telling him, "Well, no. She's under contract on *Wonder Woman*," so he kept putting it off. Finally, when he called Dan, Dan thought, "Gee, Neil Gaiman's calling about Jill – she'd probably want to hear about that." But Neil says, in *The Sandman Companion*, that he had seen this wonderful sketch I'd done of Death, in the nude. Not *me* in the nude, but Death was in the nude. And he liked it because he thought it was sweet and innocent and it wasn't salacious. I did it for this guy named Kim Metzger, who collects a lot of naked sketches, as well as sketches of other things – people made into snake-animals and things like that. (And I only mention this because Kim likes to be mentioned. He got mad when I talked around what he liked to get sketches of, so I always make a point of bringing up exactly the strange things that he's asked me to draw.) [*Laughs.*]

After I drew this nice pencil sketch, Neil was at the San Diego Comic Convention, and I was at the other end of the con, and Kim took it up to get an autograph and showed it to him, and Neil said [*impersonating Gaiman*], "What a lovely naked sketch of Death." Neil says that's the reason that he wanted me to draw *Sandman*, but I think if it was the *real* reason he wanted me to draw *Sandman*, there would have been a lot more Death in *Brief Lives*, don't you think? Death only appeared there a couple of times – it's all about Sandman and Delirium, so I think he's saying it for effect.

*It's not like Neil to spin a yarn.*

Nooooo. [*Laughs.*]

*When I interviewed Neil, he mentioned that, of all the* Sandman *artists, you were the most fun to work with.*

Really?

*Just from a personal point of view. He said you drew him "women who looked like women" and that you actually went to stay with him and his family. He said that at one point you were drawing at one end of the sofa, and he was writing several pages ahead at the other end. He said that was the only time that sort of thing happened on* Sandman.

Yes, *David Letterman* was on. At a certain point, I was only three pages behind him, for maybe the last three issues of that comic. And Neil's a good straight man, so I would make him laugh all the time. He'd just look at me sometimes and say, "You are so unusual." I don't know if it's the British humor/American humor thing, but he'd look at me and say, "I can't believe you said that." I liked to make him laugh.

*I read someone remarking that the dichotomy between you and Neil reminded them of Delirium and Dream.*

Oh, yes. We toured around a bit during that run. He was on his part of the Vertigo tour, and some comic-shop owners had me come out and we'd converge. That was the first time I saw the "Neil Gaiman Experience." You do a signing with Neil, and then you do your own signing and seven people show up, but five-hundred people were standing in line when you drove up. Literally! I'm not kidding. Some people drove from the last place he was, which was *San Francisco*. There were three girls who drove and slept in the parking lot to stand in line again and get Neil's autograph. This is totally true.

*Do you suppose he has more groupies than anyone else in comics?*

I guess so. Guys and girls both did it. It was amazing. I remember going out to eat and him being completely in black, with the sunglasses, walking down the hallway, and I'm looking at everything from a drawing or artistic standpoint. I'm wandering around touching things, my hair flying around, going "La la la." And it was probably very much like Dream and Delirium. He's just kind of going through everything and *quietly* noticing everything, and I'm very noisily noticing everything. But Delirium is not based on me in any way; she's based on Tori Amos. I used myself as a model for a lot of her body language, the way she sits or stands. I like things to look like real people are doing them as opposed to stiff poses. Maybe in that way, we are like Dream and Delirium. [*Laughs.*] I don't like green-mouse ice cream, though.

*Whenever I think of Delirium, I think of you.*

Thank you...I think.

*It's weird though, because I always thought you were much shorter.*

I'm taller than everybody I know, mostly. I usually feel very awkward and giant and freakish when I'm around other women, because I'm man-sized.

*No you're not, you're* super-model-*sized.*

Oh, God bless you! Hmmm...this *is* a good interview. I meet women who are five-two or five-four, I'm five-seven-and-a-half, and I like wearing high heels. So I feel gigantic all the time, which is okay. I wish I was six-feet tall, then I'd feel even better. I'd feel like a monster.

But yes, I went to Neil's house and met his kids. His son is "Michael" now, but he was "Mikey" then. I stayed there right before the Vertigo tour, and I remember Mikey had called and asked me if I would go roller-skating. His school had a roller-skating thing, but his [*with English accent*] mum and dad, neither of them liked roller-skating, and "You've got inline skates, Jill. Will you come and skate with me?" I said, "Well, I was supposed to go to this thing, but I could probably fly there first, stay for a couple of days, and then go. That would be okay." So I went skating with Mike.

A lot of times Mike would stand at one end of the hallway in his house, and I would stand at the other end of the hallway, and he'd come running at me, trying to knock me over. And he was like nine or ten. At a later visit, Mike is like seventeen,

DANNY - DARK PURPLE SKY ON PANEL FOUR. AND 5 as well - maybe midnite blue.

TITLE SANDMAN 48 24

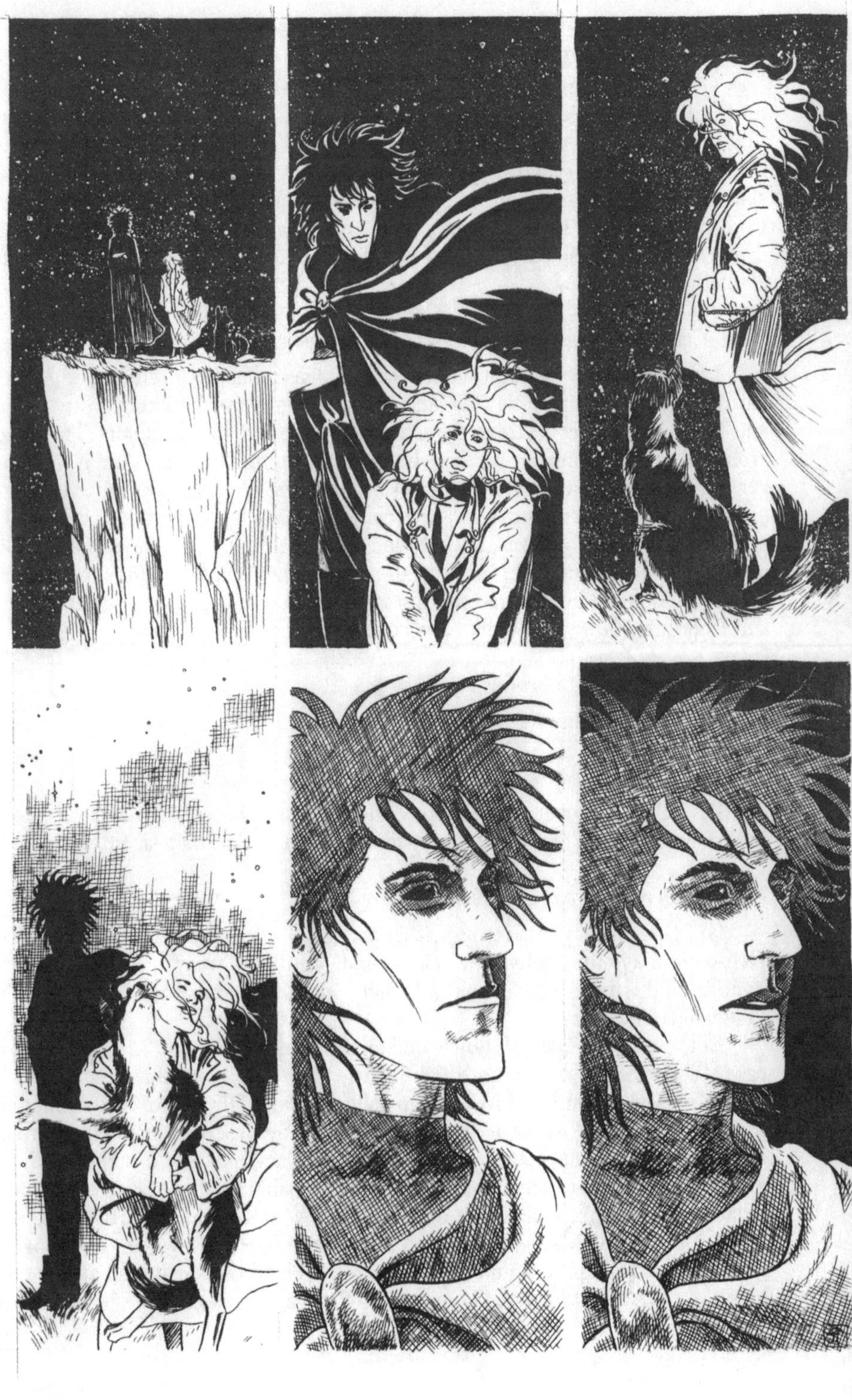

PAGE 24 OF *SANDMAN* 48, CHAPTER 8 OF *BRIEF LIVES*. PENCILS AND INKS BY JILL THOMPSON. © 2004 DC COMICS.

a big, handsome man with beautiful blue eyes, and he says [*with deep voice*], "Hello, Jill. How are you?" "*Aaargh!* I feel so old!" He's studious and smart, an amazingly intelligent young guy, and Neil says, "Mike, do you remember when Jill Thompson came to stay with us? And you would try to knock her over by running at her down the hallway? And she would let you believe you knocked her over because she would fall and flail on the floor when you hit her? And the third or fourth time she would just dig her heels in, so when you hit her you would bounce off her?" That's what I would do with the kids I would babysit. I would say [*claps hands*], "Come on," and they'd run at me and I'd fall over. Then the third time – by then they'd think they were going to do it – you'd ready yourself for it and – Boom! – they'd bounce off of you. [*Laughs.*]

I had a fun time. I liked working with Neil. I was very sad when I had to stop drawing *Sandman*. It was the perfect match, it was so effortless to draw that book. *There was never a problem.* There was never a time where you sat down at the table and thought, "I don't know how to draw this," because it was written for you. I have two pages that I kept from one scene at the very end of that arc, when Dream has to kill his son. Everything else is gone – anyone that wants *Sandman* pages is going to have to buy them off someone else, because it was ten years ago and I have no more *Sandman* pages except these two. One is the page where Abel is building himself a large, Rube Goldberg kind of contraption to sit on because it's raining and raining and Dream is so sad because his love has left him, and it's flooding the Dreaming [Chapter 2, issue 42, page 8]. It was very *Winnie-the-Pooh*esque; and that was when I knew that Neil and I completely meshed on this collaboration. He would sometimes suggest styles that things should be drawn in – references to, or an homage to, a certain illustrator; but when he wrote *this* scene there was no reference to anything, and all I could think of was *Winnie the Pooh*: "*And the rain, rain, rain came down, down, down, and the rain came down, down, down.*" And I thought, "I want to draw this in the style of the *Winnie the Pooh* illustrator, Ernest Shepard," so I looked at my *Winnie the Pooh* books and I started drawing in that style. Of course, I didn't ink it, so I don't know if it completely translated, but I mentioned to [inker] Vince Locke that this is what I was looking at and this is what I wanted it to look like. I would fax Neil Xeroxes of my pencils, and when Neil got these pages, he said that was exactly what he had been thinking of when he wrote that scene, and it was quite extraordinary that I picked it up without him mentioning it. I have that page and I've got the page where Dream has finished washing his hands after he has had to kill his son, and he's sitting in his chair in his white, white room, and he's weeping [Chapter 9, issue 49, page 20] because that's how I felt when I had to stop drawing *Sandman*. I remember drawing that thing – and I was sick as a dog – feeling horrible – saying, "I wish I could keep drawing this, it's the easiest (not "easiest" as in "there's no effort") and the best job I probably will ever have. It's fun, it's great, it's easy, and it makes a lot of royalties." [*Laughs.*] I remember begging him a couple of times, saying, "Please, please let me draw this. I'll draw it until it's over, and it will be on time every single month." He said, "I can't do it. I've promised arcs to other people." He has mentioned he wished he could have let me draw the rest of it.

It was so easy, and I would love to draw another one. That *Delirium* mini-series he's been promising me for *ten years now* [*laughs*], I would really like to collaborate with him on that. It would be interesting to see how we would work together now, with so much time and distance between working relationships. I work completely differently now. My style is different, but when I draw Sandman would it be the same? Would I fall back into that comfortable drawing style, like the way I draw Sandman at

PAGE 10/11 PANEL 1

I SEEM TO BE MOVING BACK INTO A READING AND PLOTTING KIND OF MOOD, WHICH HAS ITS UP POINTS AND ITS DOWN POINTS. THE UP POINTS ARE IT BEATS HELL OUT OF THE WATCH-A-LOT-OF-LATE-NIGHT-TV-AND-I-COULDN'T-COME-UP-WITH-A-STORY-TO-SAVE-MY-LIFE I'VE BEEN GOING THROUGH FOR THE LAST FEW MONTHS. ON THE DOWN SIDE, YOU CAN'T TYPE WHILE YOU'RE READING. AND IF I'M TALKING TOO MUCH I'M SORRY BUT I'VE STARTED READING A PILE OF LESTER BANGS AND YOU TAKE THE FLAVOUR OF WHAT YOU'RE NEXT TO IN THE FRIDGE, LIKE MILK. **NOTE TO MYSELF: HOW IS CAIN GOING TO KILL ABEL IN THIS STORY? I'D INCLINE TO POISON. OR THE FIRE.** OKAY. IT'S A DAY LATER, AND I'VE JUST FINISHED DRAWING THIS SEQUENCE OUT. IF THERE'S TROUBLE FIGURING IT OUT THEN I'LL THUMBNAIL IT FOR YOU. DOUBLE PAGE SPREAD. OKAY -- THE PANEL BORDER IS CAIN'S SILHOUETTE. THE SILHOUETTE IS FILLED WITH ROOKS. THE CAPTIONS ON THESE PAGES SHOULDN'T BE PLACED EXACTLY IN A PANEL, TODD. LET THEM LEAD YOU THROUGH WHAT YOU'RE READING, PARTLY IN ONE PANEL, PARTLY IN THE NEXT.

cap: "Rook: *Corvus frugilegus.* Also a word meaning to cheat or steal. Also a piece in chess.

cap: "Rooks are the most social of the *corvidae*. They build nests in rookeries (an obsolete name, incidentally, for a ghetto of thieves and whores), many hundreds of birds to a tree."

I suppose something vaguely like this
2
3
4
5
6

10
11

[TOP] EXCERPT FROM GAIMAN'S SCRIPT FOR *SANDMAN* 40, "THE PARLIAMENT OF ROOKS"; [MIDDLE] GAIMAN'S THUMBNAIL LAYOUTS FOR PAGES 10 AND 11; [BOTTOM] JILL THOMPSON'S THUMBNAILS FOR PAGES 10 AND 11. © 2004 DC COMICS.

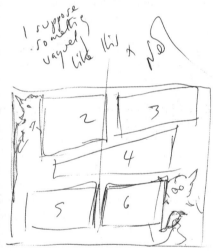

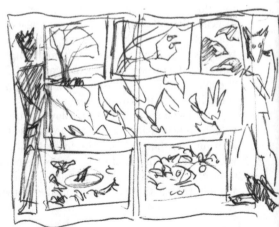

conventions? It's weird, you'd think that I'd draw him like Scary Godmother, because that's how I draw now. But when I draw Sandman, Sandman looks a certain way, and my arm just must naturally go back to that Sandman-drawing, and Death-drawing, where there's a little of the influence of Scary Godmother, but this is how Sandman looks to my arm. This is how it's supposed to happen.

*Were you ultimately satisfied with the inking on* Brief Lives, *with Vince Locke?*

Ultimately? No. Comfortably? Yes. And originally? Shocked, because at the time my pencils were very tight, and Vince is very loose. I love Vince's work, and I love that style, but there were instances during *Sandman* where I would ink things myself. I would ink entire pages, like that page I was just mentioning with Sandman crying. I inked three or four pages of that, because I wanted these certain scenes, because I wanted their faces to retain these little subtleties that no one has ever picked up on except me. There are exceptions: Al Gordon has inked my convention sketches and there was a slight nuance that other people would have inked over, but it remained. Terry Austin, too, on a pin-up. But I was a teenager then, so that was the hugest thrill. He was such a professional, he could make anybody look good; but the little tiny facial subtleties he totally kept. There were things that Vince wasn't getting completely, and being fussy and younger, I thought, "Oh my!" I didn't know how to get my point across. I was friends with Steve Rude, and he would do that all the time and then write critical comments in the borders like, "You have to learn how to draw a face," or "You're an artist. You must be an artist before you can be an inker," which I totally agree with, but I would never insult my inker knowing they were going to continue working with me while I was doing so. So sometimes I would just ink things and send them in. I never said, "I inked that. I should get paid for it." I wanted this certain scene to be all mine. It was selfish of me I suppose, but I thought Vince and I worked well together. We liked each other. We liked each other's work. We worked together when we were like, "What will we do with all these pages?" "Sell them, of course." And we'd say, "Well, what will we sell them for?" I'd say, "I don't know. Ask Neil, he'll know." And Neil would say to us, "Well, Mike Dringenberg says he gets *this* much money for them. So at the very least you should charge this much, because you [Jill]don't want to undersell him, and you [Vince] don't want to undersell her. And you should just have a price that you believe these pages are worth." Then Vince and I would discuss, and I'd get three quarters of the book back, and he'd get one quarter of it back, and we'd talk on the phone about stuff we wanted to keep for ourselves, which we have both probably sold by now, and then we'd trade back and forth to see what was nice. I liked working with Vince.

When you first start out penciling, you bring your pencil Xeroxes with you everywhere, because you want someone to see what *your work* looks like, because sometimes the inker is very well-suited to you, and sometimes they're not. I remember carrying Xeroxes of things with me all the time, and saying, "This is what it looked like before it was published." And people would say, "Wow, this is great!" because sometimes it didn't look at all like that when published. So the first thing you need to do is to find a collaborator who meshes well with you, or you learn how to ink. [*Laughs.*] Most people just learn how to ink, and they take the stuff and they do their own work. It saves time, too. I don't really pencil anything any more. What I used to pencil for Vince was completely finished drawings, shaded, all this stuff. Now, you can barely see what I put on the page, most of my drawing comes in the finishing stage. But I could never do that for someone else. If I had to pencil something for someone else, I'd have to do much more finished pencils, more than just some shorthand like "X" for black, because no one would know how to interpret what I was doing.

*Did you feel spoiled after working with Neil? In other words, did your expectations of other writers become greater than most could meet?*

I was very spoiled after working with Neil. His work was tailored toward my strengths. He delivers a good balance of exposition and explanation, so you always feel that it's a collaborative process. I've worked with other writers whose scripts were like reading instructions. You know, "This kind of shot with this and that on the walls," and all very technical. No room for interpretation. You know how you can read something and get a mental picture right away? Well this was the opposite of that. You were given such specific directions that you didn't get a picture in your head, you got a headache.

*How did you enjoy working with Grant Morrison on* The Invisibles?

I enjoyed working with Grant a lot. He wasn't as in touch as Neil was on a regular basis, but that's not his style. He says everything he wants in the script. When I worked on *Sandman*, I enjoyed the feedback. Grant was not into calling you up every week and chatting about what you'd drawn. But when you did see him, he'd let you know.

*It must be very satisfying to know that your most recent work [*Scary Godmother*] is your most highly regarded. That with all of your past success, your career is still on the rise. Are you comfortable with being a role model for young girls considering a career in comics? Do you have any advice for young people thinking of such a career?*

Role model? *Yeesh.* If I am, I hope I'm a good one. I try to put my best foot forward in my work. I love what I do and I don't take what I do for granted. I appreciate that I can make a living doing what I do best. Not everyone gets to do that.

My advice to someone trying to enter the comics field is to go to school, learn all you can. Learn the rules before you break them. Tell a good story. If you're an artist, you need that story to be understandable without any words. It should be a fifty-fifty blend of words and pictures. In my opinion. Be able to take criticism and act on it. That's hard to do. It sometimes hurts, but it will help you grow as an artist. Meet your deadlines and communicate with your editor. If the situation applies. It's like any other job, you have to put into it to get out of it or you won't grow.

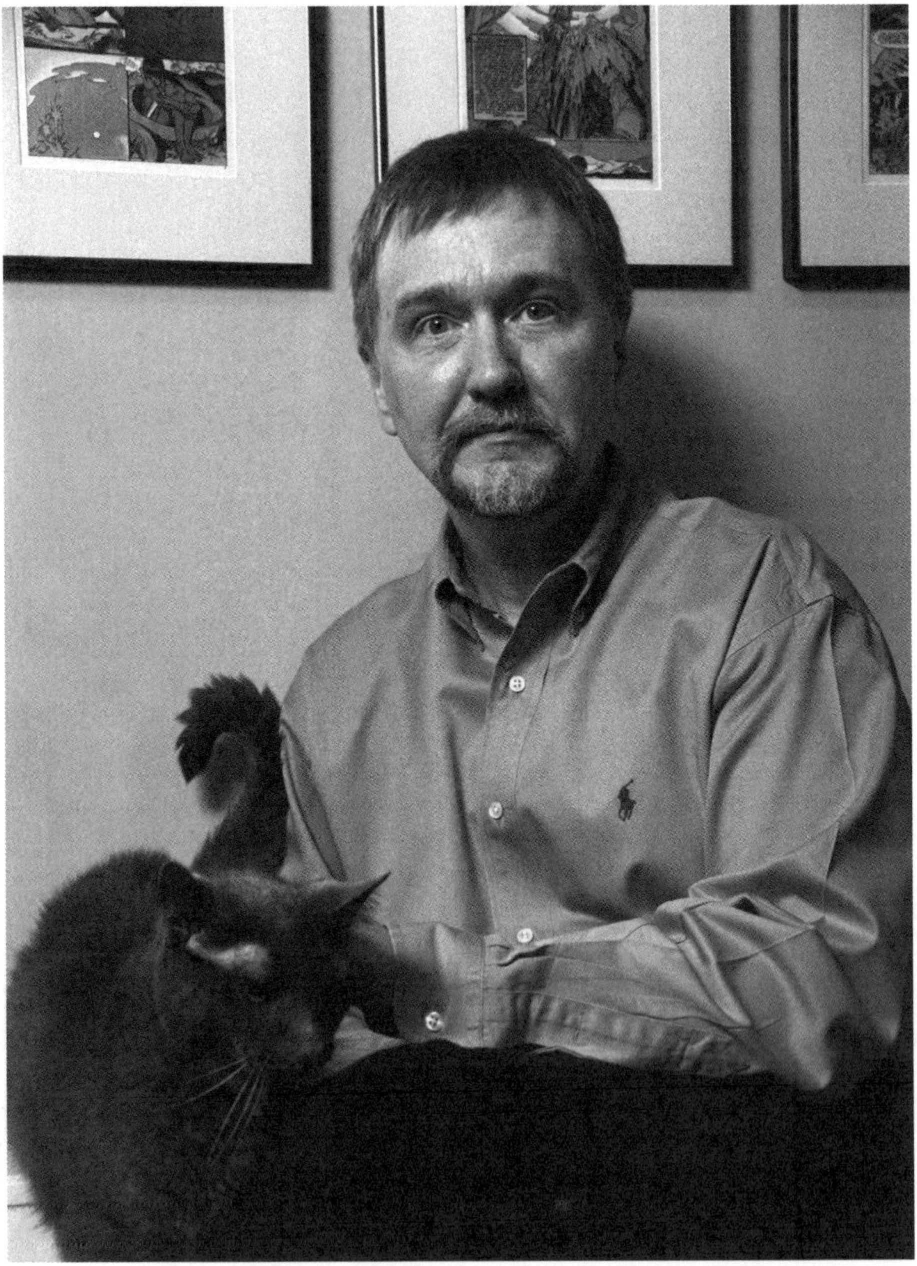

*P. Craig Russell*

## THE ELEGANT LINEWORK OF PHILLIP CRAIG RUSSELL

HAS GRACED MANY A COMIC-BOOK TALE OVER THE YEARS. SINCE HIS WORK FOR MARVEL COMICS IN THE EARLY '70S, RUSSELL HAS DEMONSTRATED HIS — AS WELL AS THE MEDIUM'S — RANGE IN TACKLING EVERYTHING FROM BATMAN AND MICHAEL MOORCOCK TO THE OPERA AND OSCAR WILDE. ALTHOUGH HE ILLUSTRATED ONLY ONE *SANDMAN* STORY [ISSUE 50, "RAMADAN"], HIS WORK PROVED SO POPULAR WITH BOTH CRITICS AND FANS THAT HE'S CONSIDERED ONE OF THE DEFINITIVE *SANDMAN* ARTISTS. HE WAS A GUEST, ALONGSIDE GAIMAN, ON NPR'S *TALK OF THE NATION* [9/18/03], ON WHICH HE DISCUSSED THEIR EISNER-WINNING *ENDLESS NIGHTS* COLLABORATION "DEATH IN VENICE," AND HE ILLUSTRATED THE AMERICAN LIBRARY ASSOCIATION'S *SANDMAN* POSTER. RUSSELL HAS ALSO ADAPTED SEVERAL OF GAIMAN'S SHORT STORIES TO COMICS — SCRIPTING "ONLY THE END OF THE WORLD AGAIN" FOR *OMNI DOUBLE FEATURE* AND PROVIDING FULL ART FOR *MURDER MYSTERIES* [DARK HORSE, 2002] AND "ONE LIFE, FURNISHED IN EARLY MOORCOCK" FOR *ELRIC* 0 [TOPPS, 1996].

WITH RECENT WORK LIKE ISSUE 50 OF DC/VERTIGO'S *LUCIFER* AND THE FOURTH VOLUME OF HIS OWN ONGOING *FAIRY TALES OF OSCAR WILDE*, RUSSELL CONTINUES TO EARN THE ADMIRATION OF HIS FELLOW ARTISTS AS HE MOVES CONFIDENTLY BETWEEN MAINSTREAM AND INDEPENDENT PROJECTS.

*You're in a position similar to Neil's in that you've been able to work on projects that stem from your own interests. How have you sustained this freedom for so long?*

Partly by not insisting on the highest rates in the world. That's one of the ways I've been able to find publishers, the smaller publishers. Not Marvel or DC, but companies that are interested in doing opera comics or the *Jungle Book* stories, the Oscar Wilde stories. I'm just not insisting that I get a *Batman* penciling and inking rate in order to do a project that I really love. Because I'm fairly certain, once I do it, there's a chance it's sticking around, of it having some longevity. I think that's part of the price you pay. If there's something you really want to do, then you make whatever compromise is needed. Of course, when it's really sweet is when it's something you really want to do – like *Sandman* 50 – and you get the high industry rates and it's still a project, I think, that has every bit as much validity as anything else. That's the best of both worlds when that happens.

*What led to your work on* Sandman *50 ("Ramadan")?*

Neil had seen illustrations I did for a book called *The Thief of Baghdad* – there were about a dozen single-page illustrations for a prose book, and it was all *Arabian Nights*, of course. So he had that in mind when he was writing this, and told me to do it just like I did in *Thief of Baghdad*, only moreso.

*"Ramadan" is interesting in that it remains the single most successful issue of the series. Certainly in terms of sales, but it's also well regarded by fans and critics.*

Well, I can only say that, for myself, it was the single best original script I've ever been handed in comics. It's a great story. It's one of those stories that ends – you think it ends – and then you turn the page and it ends again and you think it's finished and you turn the page and it ends another time. I mean it's a great piece of theater, it's a wonderfully structured story. And I think it was a good melding of the two of us together, and of course Neil says that, with certain stories, he writes them with an artist in mind – he knows their work, he knows what their strengths are, so he plays with that. I just think it was a good collaboration.

*Apparently you received a prose version of "Ramadan" from Neil and adapted it to comics. Is this true?*

Well, yes and no. I mean it was written as an original comic script, but I know that the way I like working best is to take the story... I think there are two separate things – there's the story being told and there's the telling of the story. I think they're separate things. The telling of the story is taking someone else's story that they just told you and retelling it. I'd known from inking an issue of *Sandman* [issue 24, Chapter 3 of *Season of Mists*] that he wrote a panel-by-panel script, [but] I think it plays to my strengths to just have the single words and to have to really think about it and then tell it. So I asked if he would do that for me, and he said that he would do it for the first half of the script, until Dream appears, and then he was going to do it tighter. So I sighed, and said, "Well, okay, you can't have everything." And that's what I did – I laid out the first half of the book, and once he saw that, and that his script was in safe hands, he said, "Okay," and then he wrote the rest of the book just as he did the first half, without a panel-by-panel description of it; just wrote every single word that he wanted in there, with a couple of stage directions. And then let me decide the panel breakdown – how many panels to use on a page, that sort of thing.

*But was the first half written as prose?*

No, no. He just simply wrote the first half [with] every single word, the dialogue and everything, but without a "panel this, panel that."

*So it was a very loose script?*

Almost as if it was a play, or just a short story that's a combination of prose and dialogue.

*And I assume you prefer working from a looser script, if you must work from one at all.*

In the adaptations, there tends to be two kinds: one that is pure dialogue – if you're doing a play or an opera, that's all words; there's no narrative prose, no descriptions. That, in its way, is a little easier, although on the other hand you have to come up with a lot more physical action to explain what's going on. You can't have the omniscient narrator telling you what your characters are thinking about. But I think it does go a little faster than having a real dense thicket of prose that you have to clear a path through and decide what goes in and what stays. And of course against that you play with how many pages you have to do it in. I did a couple of adaptations for *Classics Illustrated* – I did *The Scarlet Letter*, for Jill Thompson, and I did "The House of Usher," for Jay Geldhof. Now, "House of Usher" is like a fifteen-page story, and we had forty-four pages to do it in. *The Scarlet Letter*, dropping the intro, was a hundred-and-fifty-page story for which we had forty-four pages. So the latter was, obviously, the greater challenge. As a matter of fact, it probably worked better, because I think, on looking back on it, we had *too* much space to do "The House of Usher." And a few years ago, while I was on vacation, I took the story with me and laid it out again. I hadn't seen Jay's adaptation for about ten years, so I took it, redid it as a thirty-page story, and it's completely different from what I did ten years before. You would think you would come up with the same solutions, but not at all.

*By the time you worked on* Sandman *50, you were probably one of the more experienced artists Neil had worked with.*

That's probably why…I never thought of that before, but, Good Lord, yeah, I was probably the oldest *Sandman* artist ever. Thank you, I'm going home now! [*Laughs.*]

*I'm sorry.* [Laughs.] *Lovern Kindzierski, with whom you've frequently worked, was a guest colorist on "Ramadan"…*

I was real excited, working with Lovern, and I had to argue to get him into that position, because they had certain regular colorists that they'd use on the series. This was asking a big favor, to bring in somebody else who wasn't a regular on it. But we've worked together for ten years now (at that time, it was several years we'd been working together). And the color is so much a part of it. I don't think I'm a control freak, but I do like to talk to my collaborators, so I know we're all working on the same piece. You don't just drop blank pages into someone's lap and say, "Deal with this," and then walk away, and then complain about it six months later when it comes out.

*Since* Sandman *50, you've adapted Neil's published prose to comics. How does adapting Neil's short stories compare with working from his scripts?*

With scripts like *Sandman* 50 and the one I did for *Endless Nights* ["Death in Venice"], even though it's not written out panel by panel, it is a finished script and I am not editing anything – I'm using every single word. That's accepted going in. On the other stories [Neil] wrote as short stories – not as comic-book scripts – then I'm doing the adaptation. So I'm actually going in and crossing out lines, maybe describing something that the pictures are showing (and so we don't need the description). That's always a little bit tricky, because I'm used to adapting dead writers. They're not looking over your shoulder. I don't have to worry about them seeing it and saying, "What have you done to my story?" So that's a little dicey, but challenging, too. Because when you're taking one form and turning it into another, it has to work in that second form. So there are things you cut out, although I tend to err, at least in the beginning, on the side of leaving in too much. And then, once I get into finishing the drawing (and I letter it all out by hand, so I know how it looks on the page) then when I'm drawing it and I'm seeing it day after day, I start seeing lines, places I can prune and cut, and still get the same effect. So it's a balance between having enough meat on the page – because you want enough to read – but then there are times when you don't want much on there at all and you just want the pictures to flow. So it becomes a little balancing act, and the longer you can live with it, I think the better chance you have of finding that right balance.

*With your Eisner-winning story from* Endless Nights, *"Death in Venice," you went back to working from a script.*

Right, yes.

*What led to your involvement in that project?*

They actually called and asked. Neil wanted me to do Destiny – they were doing one for each of the seven characters. Because Destiny is in the long robes and all that, he wanted to see how I did long robes – like no one's ever seen me do long robes before. [*Laughs.*] So I said, "Yes." But Moebius was scheduled to do Death, and he had to drop out for personal reasons, so they asked me if I would do the Death story. Somebody else did Destiny [Frank Quitely].

*Were you familiar with Thomas Mann's original novel* Death in Venice?

I've read *Death in Venice* several times, years ago, and I've seen Visconti's film adaptation with the Mahler soundtrack, years ago. It's only occurred to me now that you asked the question that I should have watched it again to soak up the atmosphere and architecture. Dang!

*Getting back to your prose adaptations for a moment – did Neil have any input regarding your adaptations? Did you ever discuss the work with him?*

Not really. He faxed "One Life, Furnished in Early Moorcock" to me…

*So it was his desire to have you adapt that story?*

Well, I was working on *Stormbringer*, and he knew I was working on *Stormbringer*, and he had just written this Elric story, so he faxed it to me, just for my enjoyment, so I could read it. He'd just written it. But of course as soon as I read it, working on *Stormbringer* at the same time, it seemed just a natural to me to adapt. I think that was in the back of his mind all along. I thought it was my great brainstorm to do this, but I think there was a big hook he sent me, and I was the big fish that willingly bit at it. [*Laughs.*]

*How did you develop your clear-line style?*

I think that's sort of like your fingerprints, that's just who you are.

*You just tend to think that way?*

Yeah, I'm more linear than painterly. I like lines around things. Everything's sort of enclosed in its own special little space…

*The universe makes more sense to you that way?*

Yeah. [*Laughs.*] It's a way of ordering the universe. And there are a number of ways you can do that. You see people, in a sense, in the same style: very heavy and blocky, or you can do it very light and gracious. There's a whole range of ways of working within that style, but I think that's why as an inker I'd work better with, say, someone like Steve Ditko, when you want a clean, linear line. Because he finds the form, and does it simply.

*If I may go back to "Ramadan" for a moment – how did you decide on Dream's look for this story?*

Well, his physical appearance was already sort of established – the face and the hair. Neil suggested that as he was in an Arabian Nights he would be dressed appropriately. I was just looking for a design that would be visually striking. I think it's not a design that's particularly original. I mean Aubrey Beardsley and Will Clark worked in illustration at the turn of the century, playing with that sort of white, delicate pattern against a black background. I was doing a riff on that sort of thing.

*Did you intentionally create figures that were more cartoony, to contrast with the more realistic sets and environments?*

I was, at the time especially, going through a phase where I was moving away more from the photo-realism that I'd used before, and have since, a lot more often. I was working on *The Fairy Tales of Oscar Wilde* and making up most of that stuff out of my head. It's when it's appropriate for the story, and with that story – the *Arabian Nights* are very much a storybook – it made more sense to make the characters up out of my head. They had more of a fantasy feel, especially because, toward the end, it became a bit more realistic; and I wanted to contrast with the modern-day part.

*In recent years, you've combined some of the raw emotion of your early photo-realism work with the approach you employed at the time of "Ramadan." Has this been intentional?*

To me, style is two things at once. It's part conscious choice and part of who you are. I always try to find the right tone for a story and I'm always trying to make complexity simple. It can fool the viewer sometimes. Geoff Darrow looks to be enormously complex. If you look at, for example, his drawing of a supermarket aisle, the level of detail is amazing: every can on the shelf is carefully and individually drawn. But if you look closely you'll notice that every one of those cans is drawn very simply, not a wasted line. I'm also always trying to strike a balance between the use of establishment shots/backgrounds (which I used extensively early on to avoid anatomy) and long stretches where the story is conveyed entirely by the actions and interactions of the characters. *Sandman* 50, like my *Lucifer* 50, was one of those stories in which character and conversation played well against a constantly changing backdrop. The best of both worlds.

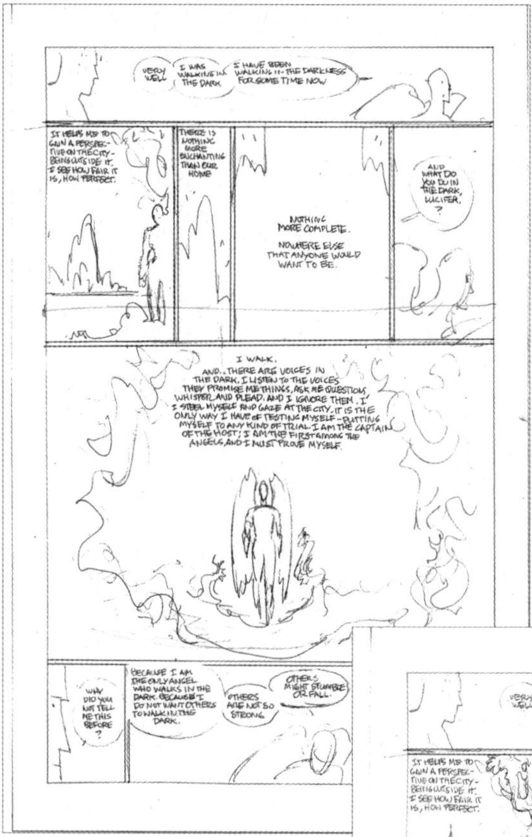
VERY WELL
I WAS WALKING IN THE DARK
I HAVE BEEN WALKING IN THE DARKNESS FOR SOME TIME NOW
IT HELPS ME TO GAIN A PERSPECTIVE ON THE CITY- BEING OUTSIDE IT. I SEE HOW FAIR IT IS, HOW PERFECT.
THERE IS NOTHING MORE ENCHANTING THAN OUR HOME
NOTHING MORE COMPLETE.
NOWHERE ELSE THAT ANYONE WOULD WANT TO BE.
AND WHAT DO YOU DO IN THE DARK, LUCIFER, ?
I WALK.
AND... THERE ARE VOICES IN THE DARK. I LISTEN TO THE VOICES. THEY PROMISE ME THINGS, ASK ME QUESTIONS, WHISPER AND PLEAD. AND I IGNORE THEM. I STEEL MYSELF AND GAZE AT THE CITY. IT IS THE ONLY WAY I HAVE OF TESTING MYSELF -PUTTING MYSELF TO ANY KIND OF TRIAL. I AM THE CAPTAIN OF THE HOST; I AM THE FIRST AMONG THE ANGELS, AND I MUST PROVE MYSELF.
WHY DID YOU NOT TELL ME THIS BEFORE ?
BECAUSE I AM THE ONLY ANGEL IN THE DARK. BECAUSE I DO NOT WANT OTHERS TO WALK IN THE DARK.
OTHERS ARE NOT SO STRONG
OTHERS MIGHT STUMBLE OR FALL.

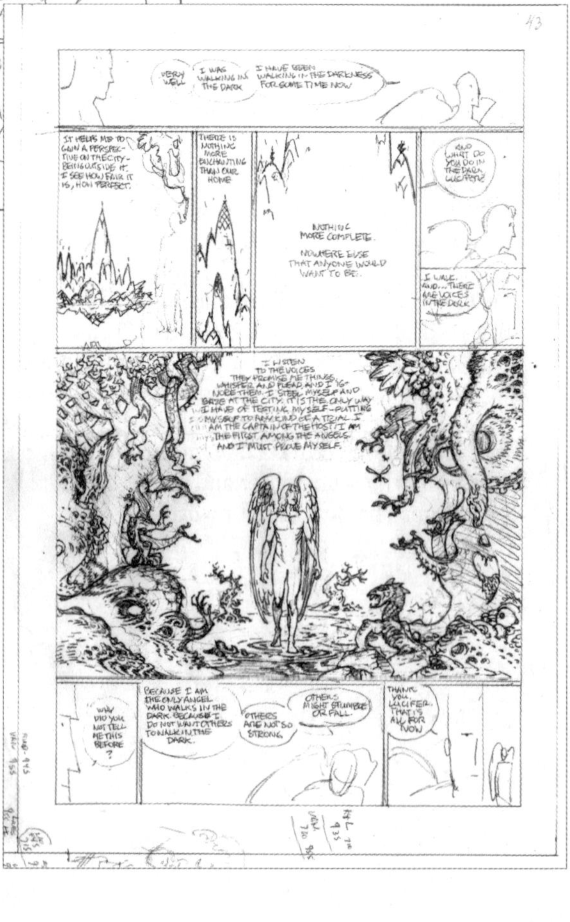
43
VERY WELL
I WAS WALKING IN THE DARK
I HAVE BEEN WALKING IN THE DARKNESS FOR SOME TIME NOW
IT HELPS ME TO GAIN A PERSPECTIVE ON THE CITY- BEING OUTSIDE IT. I SEE HOW FAIR IT IS, HOW PERFECT.
THERE IS NOTHING MORE ENCHANTING THAN OUR HOME
AND WHAT DO YOU DO IN THE DARK, LUCIFER?
NOTHING MORE COMPLETE.
NOWHERE ELSE THAT ANYONE WOULD WANT TO BE.
I WALK. AND... THERE ARE VOICES IN THE DARK
I LISTEN TO THE VOICES. THEY PROMISE ME THINGS, WHISPER AND PLEAD AND I IGNORE THEM. I STEEL MYSELF AND GAZE AT THE CITY. IT'S THE ONLY WAY I HAVE OF TESTING MYSELF-PUTTING MYSELF TO ANY KIND OF A TRIAL. I AM THE CAPTAIN OF THE HOST; I AM THE FIRST AMONG THE ANGELS. AND I MUST PROVE MYSELF.
WHY DID YOU NOT TELL ME THIS BEFORE ?
BECAUSE I AM THE ONLY ANGEL WHO WALKS IN THE DARK. BECAUSE I DO NOT WANT OTHERS TO WALK IN THE DARK.
OTHERS ARE NOT SO STRONG
OTHERS MIGHT STUMBLE OR FALL.
THANK YOU, LUCIFER. THAT IS ALL FOR NOW

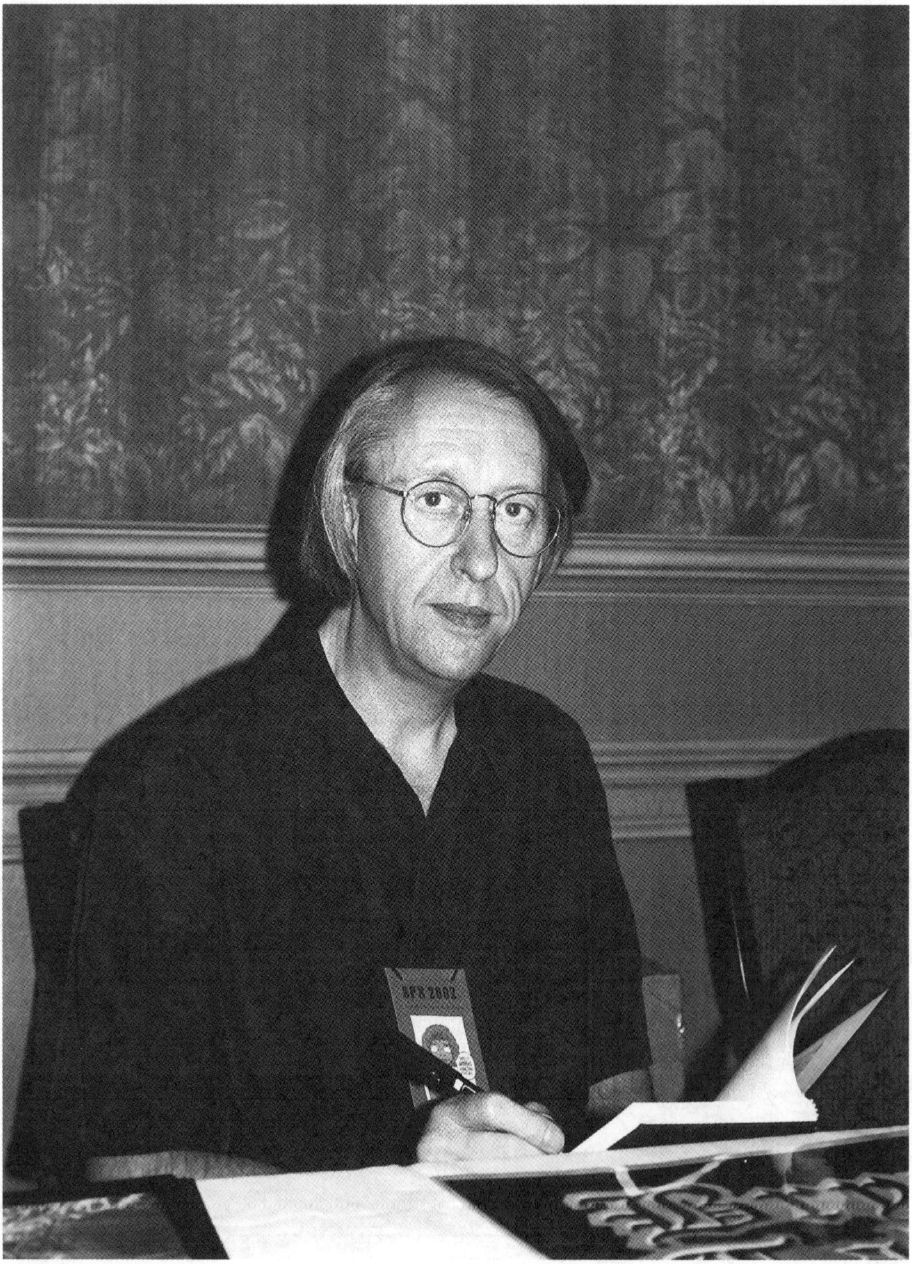
SPX 2002

PHOTO BY JOSEPH MCCABE

# HAD BRYAN TALBOT NEVER CREATED ANOTHER COMIC

AFTER HIS *ADVENTURES OF LUTHER ARKWRIGHT*, HIS PLACE IN COMICS HISTORY WOULD STILL BE SECURE. APPEARING AT A TIME (THE '70S) WHEN BRITISH COMICS – PARTICULARLY BRITISH FANTASY AND SCIENCE-FICTION COMICS – WERE AT THEIR NADIR, *ARKWRIGHT* IS CONSIDERED BY MANY TO BE THE FIRST BRITISH GRAPHIC NOVEL. BUT TALBOT ALSO CREATED BOOKS LIKE *THE TALE OF ONE BAD RAT* – A LYRICAL TALE OF THE AFTER-EFFECTS OF CHILD ABUSE AND THE VALUE OF FANTASY – AND A SECOND *ARKWRIGHT* SAGA, *HEART OF EMPIRE*, FURTHER CHALLENGING THE MEDIUM IN NEW AND EXCITING WAYS.

TALBOT'S WORK WITH GAIMAN, AS HE MENTIONS IN THE FOLLOWING INTERVIEW, BEGAN WITH SEVERAL SHORT PIECES THE TWO CREATED WHEN GAIMAN WAS STILL BASED IN ENGLAND. TALBOT WAS LATER RECRUITED TO ILLUSTRATE ISSUE 30 OF *SANDMAN* ("AUGUST"), THE SOLE *SANDMAN SPECIAL* ("THE SONG OF ORPHEUS"), AND THE FRAMING STORY TO *WORLDS' END*.

TALBOT IS AT PRESENT WORKING ON A NEW GRAPHIC NOVEL, *ALICE IN SUNDERLAND*. THE ARTIST DESCRIBES THIS WORK AS "A DREAM DOCUMENTARY."

*You've known Neil for quite some time, since the early '80s.*

Yeah, in the very early '80s. We actually first met in 1981 when he was introduced to me at a launch party in London for an underground comic. He was just writing magazine articles then; well before he started writing comics. About four years later, he interviewed me at a comic convention in Birmingham. By this point he was a journalist, working for a daily tabloid. I think he was gathering material for an article on comics. He was obviously into *Arkwright*, and we got on very well. He told me that he'd like to write comics and, even then, he had started becoming part of the comics scene, going to the conventions, hanging out with Alan Moore – so we all got to know Neil. Then this person (whose name I won't mention, a real bullshitter, with a long history of failed projects and extravagant claims that never materialized) announced that he was going to publish a high-prestige comic monthly. Come to think of it, his name wasn't his real name either. Anyway, this time, apparently, the comic was for real. He had wealthy backers, offices, the works, and it was going to happen. I think that Neil had already started writing scripts by now – one- or two-pagers for various magazines and alternative comics – and he was asked to contribute. Neil hadn't been around long enough to know that this guy spoke fluent bullshit. I think it was a back-

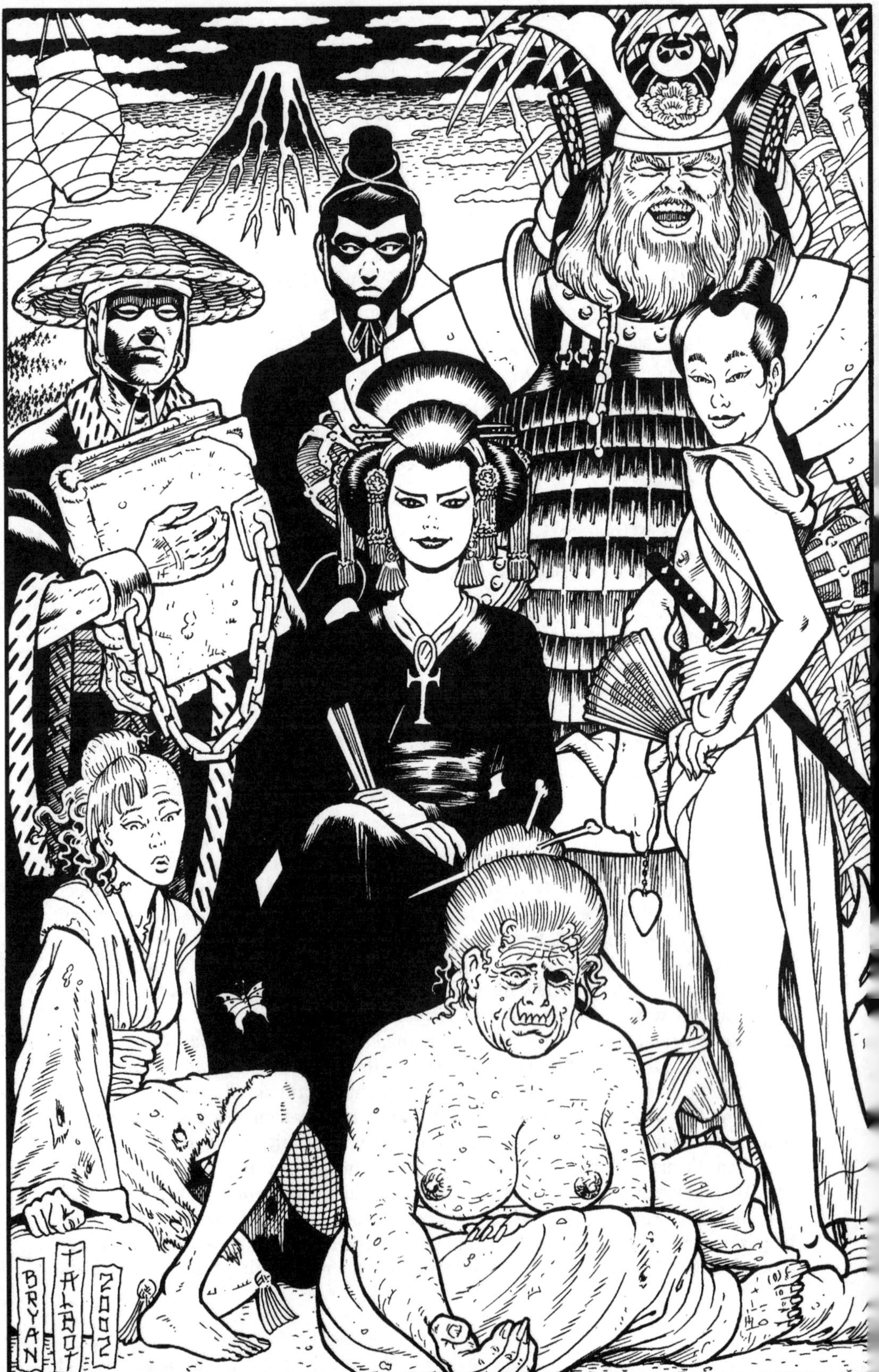
BRYAN
TALBOT
2002

end payment deal – no money up front. The publisher teamed Neil up with then fan-artist Dave McKean – and so a great partnership was born. They were developing a strip called *The Fox* – I remember seeing advance ads for it but no finished pages. I don't think they ever finished it because this guy didn't do anything, didn't pay them anything, then vanished. But, still, it got Neil and Dave McKean together. They then went on to do *Violent Cases* and Neil started submitting scripts to other comics, and pretty soon he was writing them professionally. DC were over here headhunting talent and Neil pitched them a revisionist version of *Black Orchid* with Dave as the artist and that was the start of their relationship with DC. I heard that, at the meeting, when Neil said he'd like to tackle Black Orchid, neither Dick Giordano nor Karen Berger could remember the original strip. Dick said "The Blackhawk Kid? Who's he?"

*Was "August" (*Sandman *30) the first project on which the two of you worked together professionally?*

Professionally, yes. But I'd done a couple of things with him, non-profit magazine things, such as the *AARGH! (Artists Against Rampant Government Homophobia)* book.

*This was Alan Moore's British anthology?*

Yes. Although Frank Miller had something in it and perhaps one or two other U.S. artists. Alan Moore published it [in 1988], under the Mad Love imprint that he'd created to self-publish *Big Numbers*. I did "From Homogenous to Honey" for it, a four-pager written by Neil.

Then we did an underground strip called "Sloth." It was published by Knockabout [in 1989], for *The Seven Deadly Sins* book. This was seven different writer-artist teams doing each of the different sins, and we got handed the most boring: sloth. So we did it as slothfully as possible. This proved to be its great strength – we were the only two contributors to the book who not only were guilty of our sin while working on the strip but also demonstrated the sin in the execution of it. We did the strip in a deliberate state of sheer slothfulness. Neil came up for three days before starting the script so we could discuss it. We used this time to lounge around, watch TV, sleep late and go to the pub a lot. It was sort of a Zen thing. We really discovered how to attain the plane of the irredeemably lazy and terminally slobbish.

*So you guys really practiced this, really refined your technique.*

Absolutely! And while I was drawing it, I'd sit at the drawing board, smoke a joint or two, stare at the paper for a while, start to draw and then stop after ten minutes or so to take time off, go and have a long relaxing bath or something.

And the script – the way Neil wrote it and the way I drew it – actually exhibited the sin right there on the page before your very eyes: it starts off with the first page completely finished and very clean, but, as you go on through the strip gets gradually less finished and progressively sloppier. The last page or two are just scribbled pencils and occasional pasted-up photocopies of Charlton Heston from *The 10 Commandments*.

*And this was intentional?*

Damn right. It was self-referential! The last page is half-finished but you can just about read it and get the punch line. And the page is photographed lying on the drawing board, with pens and brushes and stuff all over it, coffee rings on it, with a letter to Knockabout saying that we were sorry the strip was late but we've nearly finished and when do we get paid?

# An Honest Answer

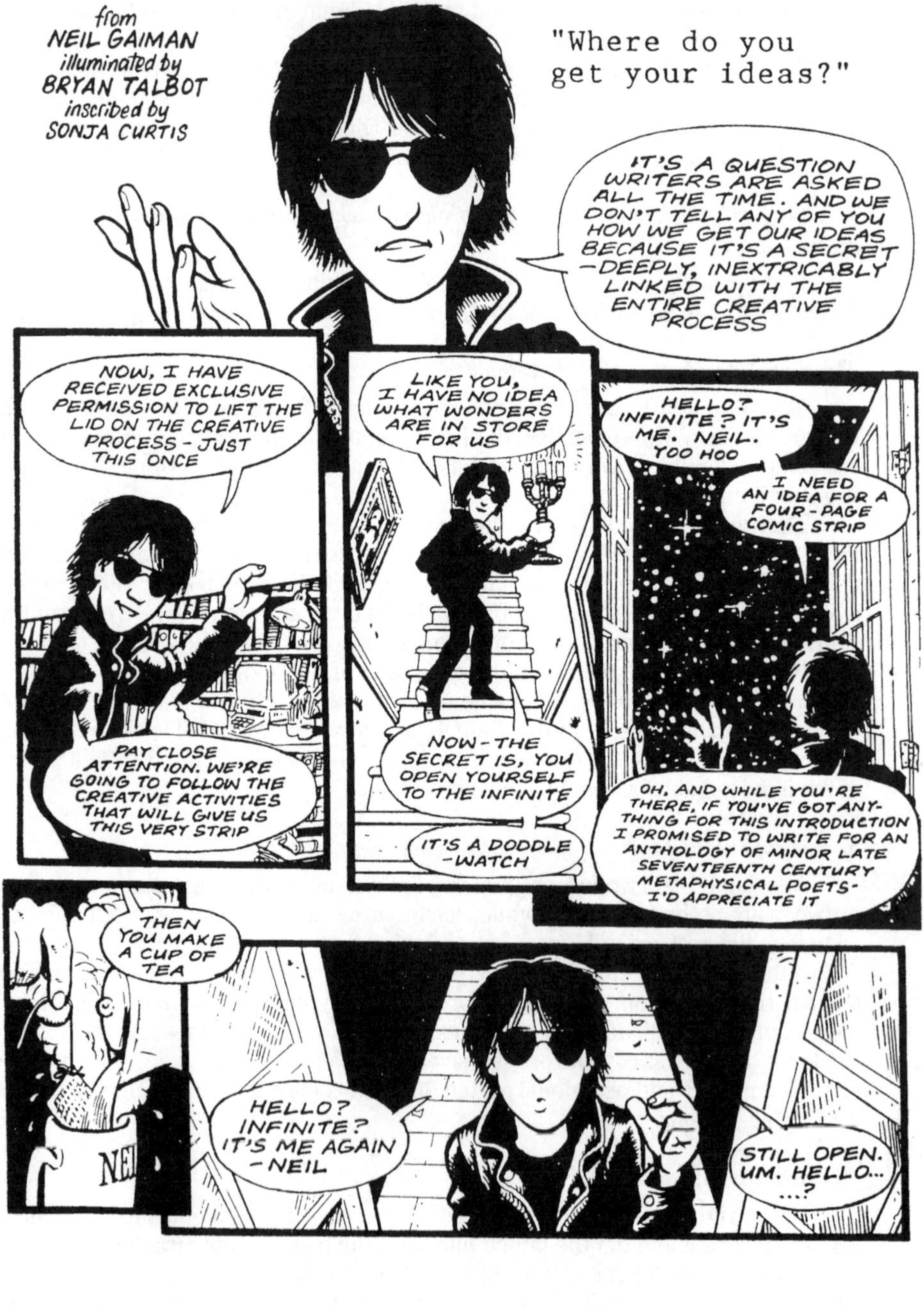
from NEIL GAIMAN illuminated by BRYAN TALBOT inscribed by SONJA CURTIS
"Where do you get your ideas?"
IT'S A QUESTION WRITERS ARE ASKED ALL THE TIME. AND WE DON'T TELL ANY OF YOU HOW WE GET OUR IDEAS BECAUSE IT'S A SECRET — DEEPLY, INEXTRICABLY LINKED WITH THE ENTIRE CREATIVE PROCESS
NOW, I HAVE RECEIVED EXCLUSIVE PERMISSION TO LIFT THE LID ON THE CREATIVE PROCESS - JUST THIS ONCE
PAY CLOSE ATTENTION. WE'RE GOING TO FOLLOW THE CREATIVE ACTIVITIES THAT WILL GIVE US THIS VERY STRIP
LIKE YOU, I HAVE NO IDEA WHAT WONDERS ARE IN STORE FOR US
NOW - THE SECRET IS, YOU OPEN YOURSELF TO THE INFINITE
IT'S A DODDLE -WATCH
HELLO? INFINITE? IT'S ME. NEIL. YOO HOO
I NEED AN IDEA FOR A FOUR-PAGE COMIC STRIP
OH, AND WHILE YOU'RE THERE, IF YOU'VE GOT ANYTHING FOR THIS INTRODUCTION I PROMISED TO WRITE FOR AN ANTHOLOGY OF MINOR LATE SEVENTEENTH CENTURY METAPHYSICAL POETS- I'D APPRECIATE IT
THEN YOU MAKE A CUP OF TEA
NEIL
HELLO? INFINITE? IT'S ME AGAIN -NEIL
STILL OPEN. UM. HELLO... ...?

Come to think of it, we *did* actually get paid for this strip, which means that "Sloth" was our first professional work together, not "August."

*Was this widely circulated?*

Yeah, published by Knockabout in the trade paperback *The Seven Deadly Sins*, which I think is now out of print. However, the seven-page strip "Sloth" is in *The Secret Files of Bryan Talbot* – a thirty-two-page collection of various, mainly underground, black-and-white strips from over the years, published by Knockabout a year or two ago. "Sloth" has also appeared in several other countries and, in fact, in the anthology *Alta Fedelta 2* in Italy, in February 2004.

*By the time you worked with Neil on* Sandman, *he had already been writing it for several years. I assume that because you had already worked together, Neil was able to jump past that starting period during which he discovered the strengths of an artist.*

I suppose so and, as with "Sloth," he came to visit first and talked it over. We were both big fans of *I, Claudius*, which was a big influence on the strip so I was well into the atmosphere that Neil wanted. After he sent me the script I sent him a few sketches, a few character sketches, and we were ready to go, though it did take me quite a while to do all the visual research. Everything in the strip – the costumes, furniture, buildings and so on – are as authentic as I could make them.

*What do you think led Neil to ask you to do that particular story? Which of your strengths was he drawn to?*

Neil says that he likes my work because I follow it to the letter. Many artists just do their own thing, but, if I'm working with writers, then as far as I'm concerned, it's their show, their vision and they are the director. I'm just the cameraman and my job is to visually tell that story as best as I can. Sometimes artists go their own way to such an extent that Neil even has to rewrite scripts so that the finished strip makes sense. But he also likes the fact that not only do I follow the script but I also elaborate it, adding extra stuff that fits in with his vision so that he gets more than he's asked for.

For example, in the *Worlds' End* story arc, for which I supplied all the framing sequences, some of the characters I'd drawn in early issues – extra, background characters not mentioned in the script – Neil wrote them into later episodes, so the artwork fed back into the story. When I work with Neil I always fax him pages as I do them, in little batches, so that he can see how the strip is developing.

I've been on the other side of this, of course, when I've written for other artists, and know how infuriating it can be to have an artist screw up something wonderful by not following directions and either re-conceiving scenes or simply drawing whatever's easiest and quickest.

*You also did a little work on* A Game of You. *And even though you only worked on one issue of that story, issue 36 [Chapter 5], you still had an opportunity to draw one of your trademark rats.*

Neil always puts a rat in the story somewhere when he's writing it for me, because for years I used to keep rats, of which he's met a few, and I also wrote and drew the graphic novel *The Tale of One Bad Rat*. For example we did a four-page strip called "An Honest Answer" when he was a guest at Eastercon, the big British science-fiction con, in about 1995. It was done for the con souvenir booklet and was a whimsical piece featuring himself talking to the reader about where he gets his ideas from. At one point in the strip, for no apparent reason, a rat walks across the table right in front of him [*Laughs.*] That was for me. "An Honest Answer" is also reprinted in *The Secret Files of Bryan Talbot.*

*And he put rats in the other* Sandman *stories you illustrated.*

That's right. There were a bunch of rats in "Orpheus" [*The Sandman Special*] and one in "August" that the emperor grabs and crushes in his hand. In *A Game of You* it's a rat sitting on a dustbin in the foreground of one panel. That was an interesting job, penciling those – sixteen, was it? – pages, half a book. I was called in right at the last minute. I got a phone call from DC telling me that Colleen Doran had collapsed from overwork and couldn't commit to all the book and asking me if I could pencil the shortfall in the next week and a half. I said, "Yeah, sure" and just dropped everything and did it. I think it was while I was in the middle of *The Tale of One Bad Rat.* I'm not sure whether the rat was already in the script or whether Neil stuck it in when he heard that I was drawing it. Another time I had to drop everything and work on *Sandman* was for the very last issue, "The Tempest." I did seven pages of pencils to help out Charlie Vess when the deadline became a bit scary. There's no rat in the bits I drew but there *is* a squirrel, which is basically a tree rat.

*Had you been following* Sandman *regularly when you were invited to illustrate "August"?*

Of course. It was *the* comic at the time. And I was in regular touch with Neil anyway.

*Having observed Neil's comics work from the start, how do you feel it's changed over the years?*

Well, he's obviously absorbed a lot of American culture. He's been all over America and has been living there for several years now, and that's fed into his writing. But, over the years, he's matured as a writer. The quality of his writing has consistently improved, almost from year to year. He couldn't have written *American Gods* ten years ago. He's really at the peak of his craft right now.

*You've been called the "Godfather of British Comics." Can you characterize British comics as opposed to American comics? Not just in terms of the industry, but also in terms of attitude.*

No, I can't generalize like that. Because when I think about American comics, super-hero comics obviously spring to mind – an American creation, an American genre – which you would think would need an American sensibility to write with any conviction. But when you look at all the British writers who are not only scripting them but scripting best-sellers, fan favorites, this is obviously not the case. And look at all the diversity right now, which is great – there's more and better comics being published now than at any other time, covering such wide ranges of interests. From Joe Sacco to Jeff Smith to Posy Simmons. And these stories – selling to a mainstream readership, not just to comic fans – along with the thriving small press, don't seem to have distinctly British or American differences, aside from the superficial ones of location, setting, local color. In Britain, there are creators who only want to do super-hero comics but also ones who want to do all sorts of comics, just like in the U.S. I don't think you can really point to distinct differences in approach. The biggest difference is in scale. The market for comics in the U.K. is minute, though slowly growing in the graphic novel sections of mainstream bookshops. There are only a tiny handful of comic books produced here, which is why most creators end up working for American companies.

As for "The Godfather of British Comics," can you remember who first said that because I don't know! It's probably because I was doing undergrounds and *Luther Arkwright* for a few years before most of the "Brit Pack," including Alan Moore, had started professionally, and am considered influential because they were reading my comics before they had stuff published themselves.

*I think I first came across the "Godfather" reference on Lambiek's online encyclopedia of comics artists. Going back to* Sandman *for a moment – you illustrated the only issue of the title that wasn't a part of the regular monthly series: the* Sandman *Special, "The Song of Orpheus."*

The style for that story came purely from its ancient Greek setting. So I could prepare for the book before I received his script, Neil discussed his ideas with me before he wrote it and he did a huge amount of research, considering that it was only a forty-eight-page story. I seem to remember that he read about five books on Orpheus – including a couple of hefty academic ones. We discussed Persephone quite a bit as we knew a strikingly beautiful woman named Persephone who would have been ideal as a basis for the character. As it turned out, I couldn't get hold of her to obtain her permission so I based her on the Pre-Raphaelite model Jane Morris instead. The only other character that was inspired by a real person was Destruction. This was Destruction's first-ever appearance and I did several sketches based on Neil's suggestion of the British actor Brian Blessed.

The closing sequence of "Orpheus" of the Baccantes tearing him to pieces was actually recolored by DC after the first version proved to be too hideously gory when colored naturalistically. That's why, in the published version, it appears in a dull blue monotone with all the splattered blood and wine slightly darker blue.

*Mark Buckingham inked most of your* Sandman *work, and Stan Woch inked "August." Did you prefer one's work to the other's?*

I hate to do this to Bucky, but for this issue I thought that Stan Woch was better. Mark was workmanlike, but...

*You liked the edginess Stan added to your work?*

Yeah, he strengthened it. Neil says that I'm my own best inker. It's because I change the pencils, improve the drawing when I ink. I like to complete the pencils for the whole issue (or, in the case of *Bad Rat* and *Heart of Empire*, the entire graphic novel) before I do the inks. Returning to the pencils I can see the weaknesses and change things, or add something new. Whereas, obviously, when an inker gets my pencils, he'll just go over the pencil lines instead of improving it, instead of changing anything drastically. That's his job. He won't think "Hmm, that hand's wrong – I'll just redraw it so it's perfect!" I wish! I think that Stan – because he has quite a nice sort of power in his inks – I think he compensated for any weakness.

*Have you and Neil spoken about doing any future work together?*

Briefly – well, you know his short stories that Dark Horse are publishing, reworked as comics by different people – P. Craig Russell's done one. He's asked me to do one of those, though it's going to be at least a year or two before I finish *Alice in Sunderland*, so I don't know whether it'll happen.

*Which story?*

"The Wedding Present." It was an easy choice because Neil based the house that the couple move to in the story on the house I used to have in Preston, Lancashire, and where he visited several times.

Do you remember in the very first issue of *Sandman* ["Sleep of the Just"] that the villain Burgess is said to have been born in Preston? That was written shortly after the first time Neil stayed.

*With your work on "August" and* Luther Arkwright, *could one assume you have an affinity for classical architecture?*

I do love medieval, more than classical architecture, but I only use whatever style the story requires. But, yeah, I wanted to give Augustus a classical feel, so I used a lot of horizontals and verticals in the picture compositions and some page-wide horizontal panels. Also I used a lot of white in the story, often having the characters standing on the pure white of the page. Augustus said that he found Rome in brick and left it clad in marble. Along with the costume and architecture, it gave the story a classical atmosphere.

*Do you tend to feel any more liberated when illustrating a fantasy story?*

Not in the writing as much as in the actual drawing, which takes a lot longer than the writing, twenty times as long. Well, the way I do it anyway – I take a lot of time over the composition of each page, the storytelling, the way the story flows. And my artwork is quite detailed, so it does takes a long time. I've never actually done a high fantasy story but definitely feel that if I was drawing a comic where I'd be creating the costumes, architecture, etcetera, without any regard for anything outside of the story, that it would be very liberating. Something like *Heart of Empire* even though it was fantasy under the surface, science fantasy, it required a helluva lot of research because it was mostly set in sort of a quasi-Elizabethan, quasi-Victorian milieu. So all the costumes and architecture and everything need painstaking research, even if I'm then going to adapt or change, exaggerate them in some way. Whereas a pure fantasy story – for example, *Bone* – needs no research. It's all very low-tech and self-contained and you can just make it up convincingly if you have the concept firm in your mind. All you need is a great story that's been thoroughly thought through.

*Are you as comfortable with a story set in the far future or distant past as you are with a contemporary project such as* The Tale of One Bad Rat? *Or do you find it depends on the level of detail you wish to bring to the particular story?*

No, it just depends what story I'm working on, what I've got an idea for. I do like historical stuff, but I'm happy with either. It all depends on the story. Still, ask me again if I ever get to do the fantasy tale that needs no research!

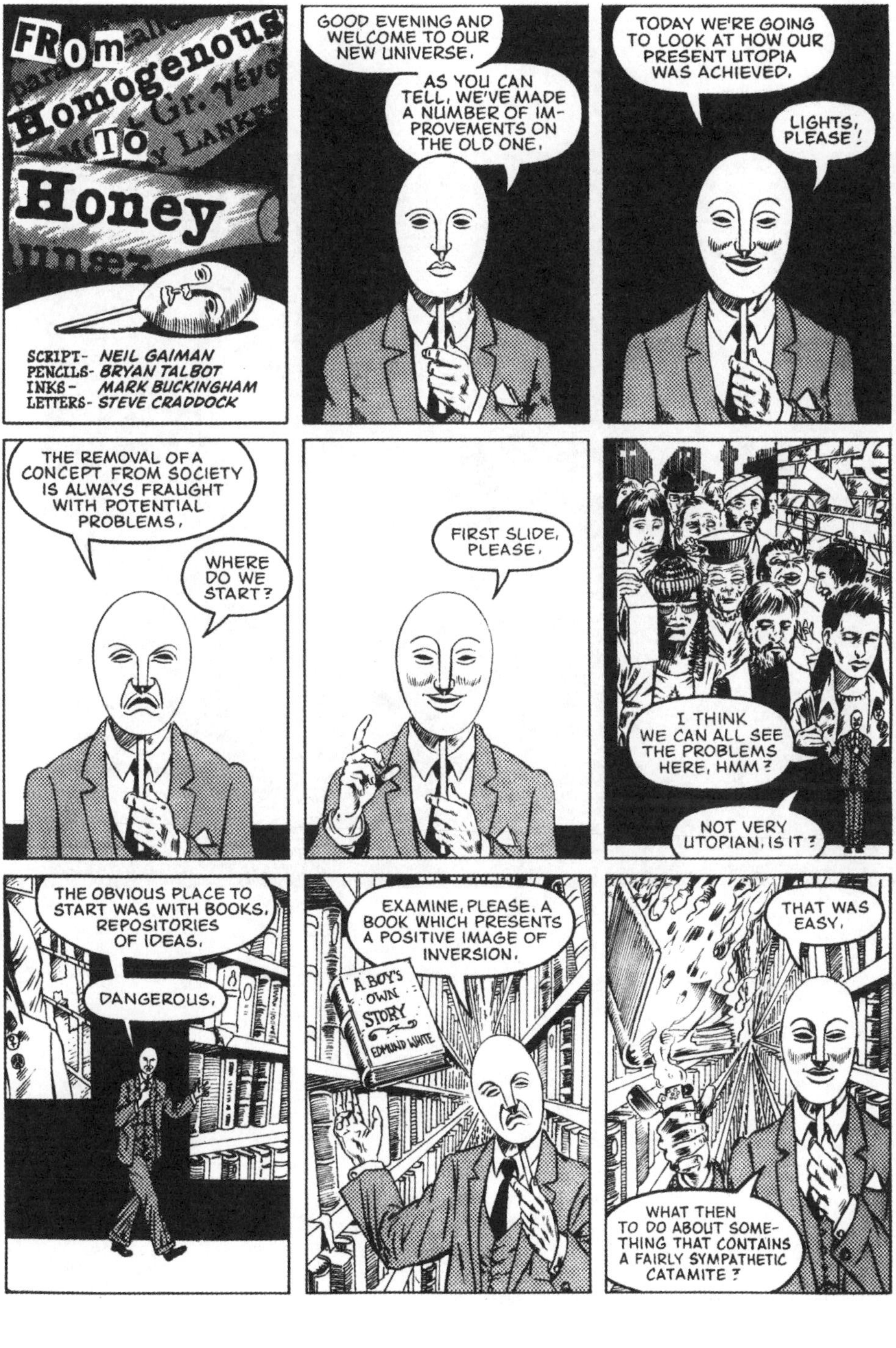
FROm Homogenous To Honey
SCRIPT- NEIL GAIMAN
PENCILS- BRYAN TALBOT
INKS- MARK BUCKINGHAM
LETTERS- STEVE CRADDOCK
GOOD EVENING AND WELCOME TO OUR NEW UNIVERSE.
AS YOU CAN TELL, WE'VE MADE A NUMBER OF IMPROVEMENTS ON THE OLD ONE.
TODAY WE'RE GOING TO LOOK AT HOW OUR PRESENT UTOPIA WAS ACHIEVED.
LIGHTS, PLEASE!
THE REMOVAL OF A CONCEPT FROM SOCIETY IS ALWAYS FRAUGHT WITH POTENTIAL PROBLEMS.
WHERE DO WE START?
FIRST SLIDE, PLEASE.
I THINK WE CAN ALL SEE THE PROBLEMS HERE, HMM?
NOT VERY UTOPIAN, IS IT?
THE OBVIOUS PLACE TO START WAS WITH BOOKS, REPOSITORIES OF IDEAS.
DANGEROUS.
EXAMINE, PLEASE, A BOOK WHICH PRESENTS A POSITIVE IMAGE OF INVERSION.
A BOY'S OWN STORY
EDMUND WHITE
THAT WAS EASY.
WHAT THEN TO DO ABOUT SOMETHING THAT CONTAINS A FAIRLY SYMPATHETIC CATAMITE?

PAGE 1 OF "FROM HOMOGENOUS TO HONEY", FROM *AARGH! (ARTISTS AGAINST RAMPANT GOVERNMENT HOMOPHOBIA)* [MAD LOVE, 1988]. PENCILS BY BRYAN TALBOT AND INKS BY MARK BUCKINGHAM.

*Marc Hempel*

## MARC HEMPEL'S WORK, WITH ITS INSPIRED WIT AND MINIMALISM
MAY INVITE COMPARISONS TO HARVEY KURTZMAN'S AND BERNARD KRIGSTEIN'S, BUT HIS PERSPECTIVE IS REFRESHINGLY DISTINCT.

AFTER CUTTING HIS COMICS CHOPS ON SUCH BOOKS AS COMICO'S *JONNY QUEST*, HEMPEL ESTABLISHED HIS UNIQUE BRAND OF HUMOR WITH *GREGORY*, A WELL-RECEIVED FOUR-VOLUME SERIES FROM DC'S PIRANHA PRESS ABOUT A MENTAL HOSPITAL'S SMALLEST INMATE AND HIS RAT FRIEND HERMAN VERMIN. DURING THIS PERIOD, HEMPEL ALSO ILLUSTRATED THE PRE-VERTIGO DC MINI-SERIES *BREATHTAKER*, A FAST-PACED THRILLER ABOUT A RELUCTANT SUCCUBUS. *BREATHTAKER* DEMONSTRATED HEMPEL'S FACILITY AT HANDLING DRAMA AS WELL AS HUMOR, AND WAS QUICKLY FOLLOWED BY HIS ELEVEN-ISSUE STINT ON *SANDMAN*, *THE KINDLY ONES*, THE BOOK'S CLIMACTIC STORYLINE, AND ONE OF ITS MOST VISUALLY REWARDING.

SINCE *THE KINDLY ONES*, HEMPEL HAS BECOME A PREMIER HUMORIST, WITH COMICS LIKE *TUG AND BUSTER* AND *NAKED BRAIN*. MOST RECENTLY, HE JOINED THE USUAL GANG OF IDIOTS AND BECAME THE REGULAR CARTOONIST OF *MAD* MAGAZINE'S "THE MAD SIDE OF..."

*Was* Breathtaker *the book that first drew Neil's attention to your work?*

Yes, Neil saw *Breathtaker* and he really loved it. That was the main reason that he wanted to do something with me. It ended up being *Sandman*. It was kind of a sequence of events: Neil had read *Breathtaker* and – later on, at a convention – Mark [Wheatley] mentioned to Neil that I was looking for work, and then I talked to Neil. Neil said, "I'd really like to work with you. I don't think it will be *Sandman*, but I'll have to keep you in mind for something." A couple of years later, further into the series, I get a call from Karen Berger and they want me to do *Sandman* – the last big story arc. And that was it. I guess it was partly also because Mike Mignola, who was the original choice, had other stuff going on. So it fell into my lap. Since then, Mike's said that I was probably the best person for the job, so that felt good.

*It is hard to picture another artist doing* The Kindly Ones, *after one sees your work on it.*

That's the way the universe is supposed to work!

*When I spoke with Neil he mentioned that he wanted you on that particular story arc because he wanted to reduce everything to shadows and shapes. He said he felt it worked better as a collection than a monthly comic. Since your style is so different, he felt that your work was distancing or jarring compared to the other monthly books a reader might pick up.*

See, it's not jarring to me because I live with it all the time. Other artists I look at are not that dissimilar in their approach, but I can see where it would be a little jarring. On the other hand, it can be jarring and appropriate at the same time. As far as it working better as a collection, I'll take Neil's word for it, because I haven't read it yet. [*Laughs.*] When I stop working on something, it's like, "I'll have to get around to reading this sometime and see if it really works or not." But I just opened up the book, knowing you were going to ask about it, and I started seeing all the little coloring errors and things I could have drawn better. [*Sighs.*] It's hard for me to look at and not see the mistakes. Then I come across some of the really nice pages and I think, "Ah! Maybe I did do a pretty good job after all. Pretty cool …"

*Neil has also said he paced the book slower at that point in the series, because he knew the storyline would be collected as a book. So he felt more comfortable proceeding at a leisurely pace than he did on earlier stories. That may have contributed to the effect he was talking about.*

Yeah. If he's writing it to be a book then I can see where it would work better in that format, as a collection of comic-book stories.

Sandman *had utilized the talents of some fairly lush illustrators up until this point – Charles Vess, Shawn McManus, etcetera. Since Neil had grown accustomed to scripting for these artists, did you ever find his ideas for the book's visuals differing from your own? Did he ever ask for more detail than you were comfortable providing?*

Well, Neil chose me for *The Kindly Ones* because my expressive drawing approach (especially as seen in *Breathtaker*) fit his vision for the story arc – so, no; there wasn't much in the way of conflicting artistic goals. While he did have a comment every now and then regarding my portrayal of a character or how I handled a scene, it was never related to "detail" or rendering. Storytelling detail was another matter altogether, and Neil and I discussed that quite a bit!

*What did the two of you discuss about the storytelling detail?*

In spite of the highly-detailed panel descriptions, I'd sometimes either have a question, or feel the need to change something for the sake of storytelling. Regarding the latter, Neil – who was always conveniently awake when I'd call at one in the morning – seemed to respect my visual and dramatic sense, and so usually went along with my changes. (As an example, it was my idea to give Rose Walker's "I hate love" line its own ultra-close-up panel [Chapter 9, issue 65, page 8].) Conversely, there were a few times when Neil wasn't satisfied with what I had come up with – but his suggested improvements always made for a more compelling panel or scene (that first large panel of Dream in Chapter 1 [issue 57, page 14] was a well-advised second take). At one time or another, pacing, lighting, "camera" angle, facial expression, background details and overall dramatic effect were discussed – and, thankfully, Neil and I were almost always on the same wavelength!

*Did Neil ever discuss doing a trial issue with you, prior to* The Kindly Ones? *He occasionally gave his* Sandman *artists a single issue to illustrate so he could see their strengths.*

No, actually. There was a few months gap between when I finished doing the fourth *Gregory* book and my start on *The Kindly Ones*. Mostly I was just waiting on the final script for number 57. But I didn't hear anything about doing a sample issue or anything like that. It was my understanding that it was supposed to just start right away. I did do some promotional pieces for advertising and for t-shirts; I think there was a trading card or two. Some of that was the earliest *Sandman* art I ever did, before I even drew a page of *The Kindly Ones*. So that was helpful in getting me in the mood. Actually, it surprised me that a lot of that stuff turned out pretty well. I guess I just rose to the occasion. [*Laughs.*]

*As the climactic story arc,* The Kindly Ones *featured characters from almost all of* Sandman*'s previous arcs. Had you followed* Sandman *up to that point? Had you familiarized yourself with all these characters?*

I did the best I could within the limited time frame. Mostly, I learned as I went – seat-of-the-pants type stuff. I had read some *Sandman* previously, but only maybe two or three issues (though including "A Midsummer Night's Dream" [issue 19]). It was great getting to draw everybody – but, frustratingly, once I felt I had a character nailed, I was off drawing somebody else after only a few pages!

*It's fitting that* The Kindly Ones *opens [in issue 57] with a couple of discussions between groups of women – the titular characters, of course, as well as Lyta Hall and her friend Carla – since one of your strengths is your ability to depict women. Female characters in comics are often depicted as being skinny, but yours are unconventionally so, as can be seen in* Breathtaker *and your* Futurotica *paintings. You're also not afraid to sometimes render women who are less than perfectly attractive.*

Ha! You said "*titu*lar"! I dunno – I seem to prefer women with thin builds...but I do have a range of appreciation. Curvy can be nice, and is fun to draw. This is just my preference – what I'm personally attracted to in a physical sense – and doesn't inherently apply to what I like to draw or find interesting. Heavy-set females [as in my] *Victim Victoria* have a nice, round shape, and are also fun to draw. It all depends on the concept/story/character. Both from a personal preference and artistic point of view, I prefer faces that are attractive, yet have a lot of character and convey personality. Classic beauty is often boring to me.

*Neil's script seems to employ a grid format for many of* The Kindly Ones *pages. Did he discuss this as a way to enhance the stained-glass feel of your work on the story?*

Neil suggested the six-panel-a-page grid as a way of establishing very evenly paced storytelling throughout the story arc – steady and cadence-like. I agreed to it, providing that things opened up in a big way as we neared the climax! Today (older and wiser), I might have suggested a different, more varied approach, though toward the same end.

*Chapter 7 [issue 63] features your take on Delirium. Her face seems decidedly un-Hempelesque. Did you use reference for her?*

Hmm..."un-Hempelesque," you say. Well, no specific reference was used – though I was keeping previous portrayals in mind, including Jill Thompson's. I'd have to say that, character-wise, Delirium was closest to my heart: a skinny, messed-up and confused chick with forlorn-looking dot eyes!

*You mentioned you felt your work improved as the story progressed. It certainly becomes more stylized. This is evident in such things as the look of Puck in Chapter 10 [Issue 66] versus his look earlier in* The Kindly Ones.

My work gets more stylized, more shape-oriented, as I become more relaxed and focused. Dream himself looks arguably better in the later issues.

*Your art also grows simpler as it matches the quickening pace of the story.*

Yes, I was more inspired toward the end; my drawing grew more passionate. It helped that I was able to ink my own work again [in Chapter 13, issue 69].

*Was there any specific design or style you turned to for inspiration for this story arc?*

I'd say probably not. Though, later on, while I was working on the last two or three issues of *The Kindly Ones*, I was definitely looking at Gustav Klimt. He was a member of the Viennese secessionist movement at the turn of the last century. His work is very sensual, and very shape-conscious. When I started looking at it again, it started opening up my brain to those possibilities, and I started pushing that angle more. In fact, there's one drawing of the Sandman's throne, where I actually rip off some of Klimt's little squiggly motifs. It might be in issue 69 [pages 3, 7, and 22].

*Who were your big career influences, initially?*

Initially, I would say my influences were Jay Ward and Chuck Jones. I loved the Hanna-Barbera stuff. I used to watch *Huckleberry Hound* all the time, *Colonel Bleep*, a lot of the old "future-primitive" early '60s animation. But when I got into comic books, it was Steve Ditko, Neal Adams, Bernie Wrightson.

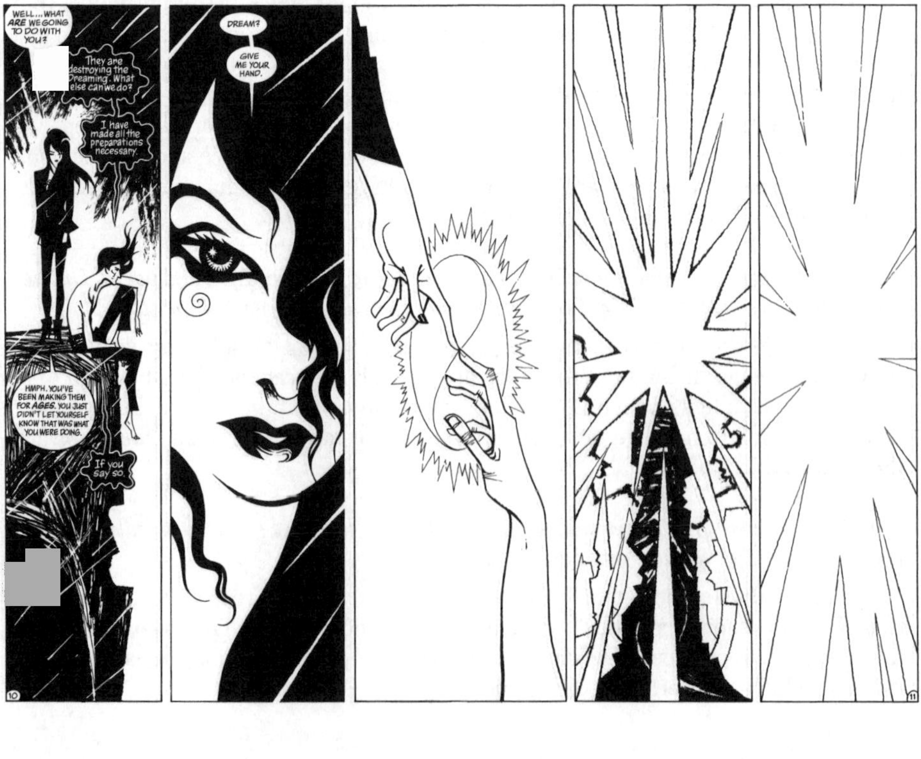
WELL... WHAT ARE WE GOING TO DO WITH YOU?
They are destroying the Dreaming. What else can we do?
I have made all the preparations necessary.
HMPH. YOU'VE BEEN MAKING THEM FOR AGES. YOU JUST DIDN'T LET YOURSELF KNOW THAT WAS WHAT YOU WERE DOING.
If you say so.
DREAM?
GIVE ME YOUR HAND.

*In its simplicity, your work has more of a European flair than that of many mainstream American comic artists. Do you have any influences among European artists?*

Back in the '70s, I'd say I was influenced by Moebius. I think I started drawing in the Moebius style, but still using a lot of black areas, which I've had a hard time pulling away from; it always looks too airy and empty if I don't put any blacks in there. Later on, I was appreciating Lorenzo Mattotti – I think he's Italian. He did *Fires* and *Murmur*. His stuff's just really great; he's probably one of my more recent influences. I don't think there are any other specifically European artists. I don't know...a lot of the guys who appeared in *Raw*. I can't name a lot of them off the top of my head, but *Raw* itself is a big influence, with Art Spiegelman. In fact, I was accepted in *Raw*! I was in *Raw* for about five minutes, until they pulled me out again.

*Why did they pull you out?*

Well, they had accepted a one-page cartoon I did, called "1947" – which I think has appeared in a couple of other places – for one of the last large-format issues. I think it might have been number 8. Then, several weeks later, they decided not to use me because they had changed the theme of the issue. I was really disappointed, because I wanted to be the first artist to appear both in *Marvel Fanfare* and in *Raw*, simultaneously. That would have been so cool.

*Getting back to* The Kindly Ones – *you did eleven issues in all, which is one of the longest runs of any artist on* Sandman. *But there were a few guest pencilers that came in the middle of that story arc.*

That was just a matter of DC needing to make their deadlines and get the books out. So it was a combination of fill-in artists, fill-in inkers, and the various "gallery" books that they put out at that time. It was basically because Neil was writing too slow and I was drawing too slow – a combination of both of those things. I was originally supposed to pencil and ink everything, back when it was going to be a five- to eight-issue series. It ended up being eleven issues.

*You did eleven, and there were two issues (62 and 64), Chapters 6 and 7, with fill-in artists.*

So, thirteen.

*How happy were you with the inking? You inked yourself a couple of times, but you also had D'Israeli for four issues and Richard Case for another four.*

Richard was our first choice, but I think he was on another project, so he wasn't available the first time around. D'Israeli, as he's professionally known – I forgot his real name [Matt Brooker]; he lives in England – was recommended by Vertigo. Either Karen or Shelly [Bond] was recommending him and sent me a few of his books. I liked him enough to give him a try. It worked out pretty well. His inking was a little shaky in the first one he did, but then he got quite a bit better. Oddly enough – I've talked with him on the phone a couple of times – he doesn't even use India ink. He uses liquid acrylic. Evidently they can't get good quality ink over there or something. It's good enough, though; it's black and shiny and I have no problem with it. But then, later on, when Richard Case was available we just had to give him a try, and I liked his stuff as well. It worked out pretty nicely. He and I are pretty good friends at this point, but I don't see him that often these days.

*Richard Case's work was –*

Very compatible, yeah. Not identical to my approach, but it fit. Of course, my inking's the best! You can write that down if you want. Put it on the record. [*Laughs.*] I just like inking my own stuff. I would have been really happy if I had been able to ink everything, but it just didn't work out that way. And I could have done the covers, but I don't think that Dave McKean would have been too happy about that.

*Richard Case tries really hard to become you in pages 13-18 of Chapter 12 [Issue 68]. He gives it a good shot, but he can't seem to break everything down the way you do, as is evident in his depiction of the Faerie maiden Nuala.*

I don't know if he was trying to deliberately ape my style, but I thought Rich did a good job. It's a tough position to be in – plunked down in the middle of a story like that. Oh, well…if I had been a bit faster in the penciling department, Rich wouldn't have had to draw those few pages on his own!

*Daniel Vozzo named you as one of the few* Sandman *artists keen on getting involved in the coloring. Did you find your approach to coloring differed much from Danny's?*

My approach to coloring is probably different than Danny's (as would be expected) – but he seemed very open to my suggestions, and followed my more meticulous notes to the letter. This I very much appreciated, though I'm sure it was a bit of a nuisance for him. At any rate, every stage of comics production is important, and should serve the storytelling. It's impossible to draw a (metaphorical) line and say, "Well, it's just the coloring," or whatever. It's all integral.

*Do you have a favorite scene or moment in* The Kindly Ones? *Neil's remarked that he's fond of the scene in which Lyta goes mad, and you moved the setting back and forth from a sort of myth landscape to a modern city.*

I have to flip through this collection while I'm talking to you, because I've forgotten a lot of this. I liked issue 69 the best, the climax. It has a nice two-page spread with the close-up of Death and the touching of the fingers in a Michelangelo kind of way [pages 10-11]. By that time my art just really pulled together, and I was able to ink that issue as well. As far as specific sequences…I'm looking through the book…anything from the last couple of issues.

I was really on my game, as they say. Yeah, before that point it's more hit-and-miss, but I can't say there's one specific place.

*Issue 69, the final issue of* The Kindly Ones, *is certainly the most Hempelesque, with you inking yourself. And the final conversation between Dream and Death really stands out. Death, in particular, has rarely looked as lovely as she does in the panel you mentioned, the close-up on page 10, right before your "Michelangelo moment." It's somewhat difficult to believe this is the same artist behind the zaniness of* Gregory.

I'm nothing if not versatile! I love doing darker, dramatic work as well as humor. I'm a man of many moods. I'm also a Gemini, which might explain a lot! By the way, I decided to redraw that Death close-up from scratch, as my first attempt was a tad stilted. I knew it had to be a killer shot, so I took another stab at it, and happily nailed it with take two. The final art has a paste-up, but it was worth it!

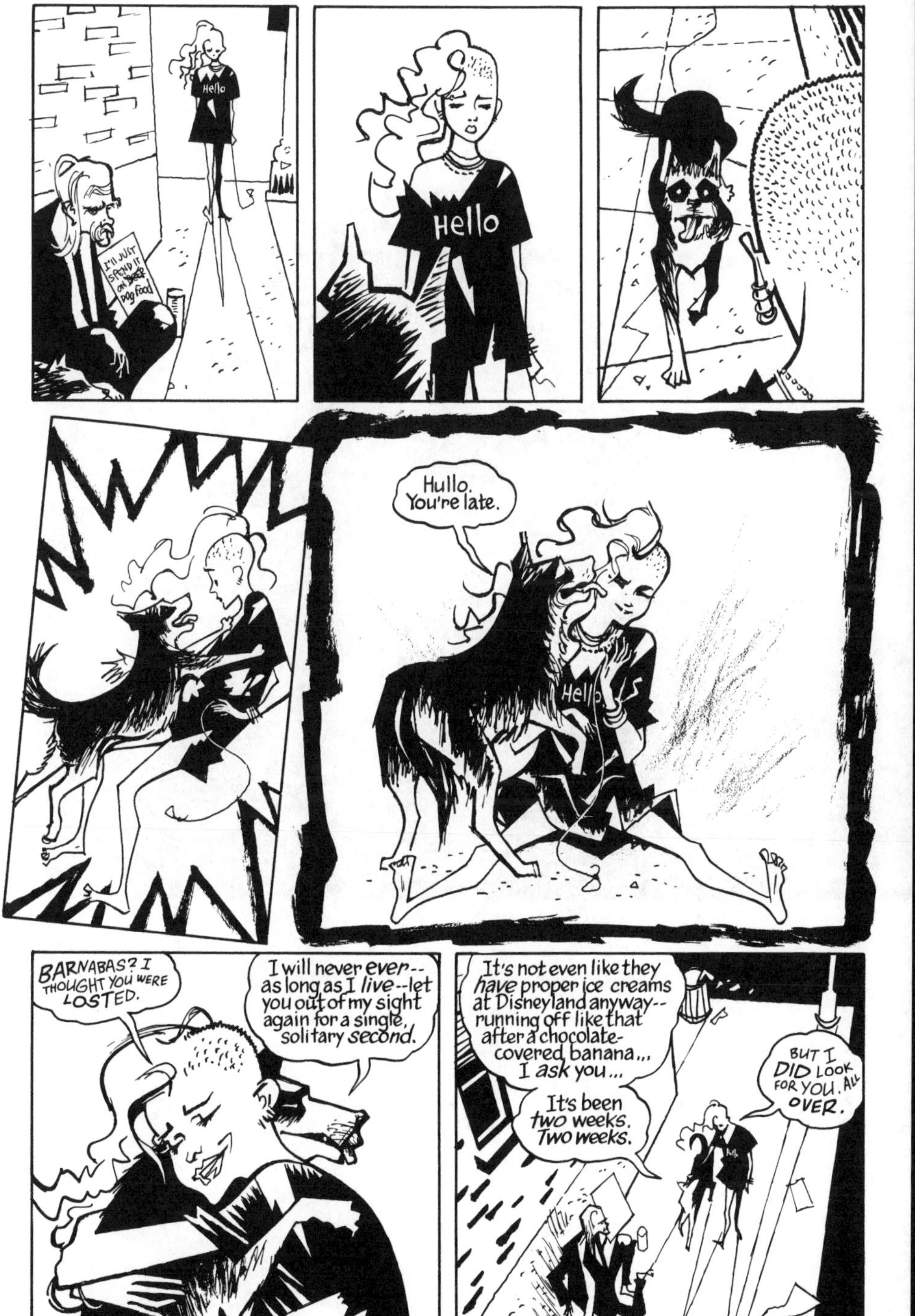
Hello
I'll just spend it on ~~beer~~ dog food
Hello
Hullo. You're late.
Hello
BARNABAS? I THOUGHT YOU WERE LOSTED.
I will never *ever*-- as long as I *live*--let you out of my sight again for a single, solitary *second*.
It's not even like they *have* proper ice creams at Disneyland anyway-- running off like that after a chocolate-covered banana... I *ask* you...
It's been *two weeks. Two weeks.*
BUT I DID LOOK FOR YOU. ALL OVER.
14

Delirium and Barnabus, page 14 of *Sandman* 69, Chapter 13 of *The Kindly Ones*. Pencils and inks by Marc Hempel. © 2004 DC Comics.
Previous Spread: "The Michelangelo Moment," pages 10 and 11 of *Sandman* 69, *The Kindly Ones*, Chapter 13. Pencils and inks by Marc Hempel. © 2004 DC Comics.

## Michael Zulli

THOUGH MICHAEL ZULLI HAD MADE HIS *SANDMAN* DEBUT SEVERAL YEARS EARLIER, WITH ISSUE 13 ("MEN OF GOOD FORTUNE"), IT WAS WITH *THE WAKE* THAT THE BOOK'S READERS WERE TREATED TO THE FULL POWER OF HIS DETAILED COMIC-ART RENDERINGS.

ZULLI'S PROFESSIONAL COMICS CAREER BEGAN IN 1986, WITH *PUMA BLUES*. HE LATER PARTIALLY ILLUSTRATED THE INFAMOUS *SWAMP THING* 88 (WHICH FEATURED THE TITLE CHARACTER MEETING JESUS CHRIST), BEFORE DC REFUSED TO PUBLISH IT, AND THEN JOINED GAIMAN ON *SANDMAN*. ZULLI HAS WORKED OFTEN WITH GAIMAN OVER THE YEARS — ON THEIR UNCOMPLETED *SWEENEY TODD: THE DEMON BARBER OF FLEET STREET* FOR THE LATE HORROR ANTHOLOGY *TABOO*; ON THE DESIRE SHORT ("HOW THEY MET THEMSELVES") IN *VERTIGO: WINTER'S EDGE* 3; AND, ALONG WITH ALICE COOPER, ON THE THREE-ISSUE LIMITED COMIC SERIES INSPIRED BY COOPER'S ALBUM *THE LAST TEMPTATION*.

ZULLI'S POST-*SANDMAN* WORK INCLUDES A NUMBER OF VERTIGO TITLES AND ILLUSTRATIONS FOR J. MICHAEL STRACZYNSKI'S NOVELLA *DELICATE CREATURES*. HE RECENTLY ADAPTED SEVERAL GAIMAN SHORT STORIES TO COMICS — TWO IN *NIGHT CREATURES*, AND A THIRD, "THE FACTS IN THE CASE OF THE DEPARTURE OF MS. FINCH" (FROM A TALE IN THE BRITISH EDITION OF *SMOKE AND MIRRORS*), FOR A FOLLOW-UP VOLUME, BOTH TO BE PUBLISHED BY DARK HORSE.

---

*What comics work had you been doing, besides* Puma Blues, *prior to* Sandman?

At that time, I know that I had set a personal goal to experiment with the medium as much as I could, to be able to find different ways of expressing myself in it. I don't have a background in comics, and *Puma* was basically me growing up in public with my trousers around my ankles, desperately trying to figure out how *this* was done, what happens if you do *this*. After a while, when I felt like I started to get the hang of it, my natural curiosity asserted itself, and I started wanting to play with the form, to see what I could do with it. I remember doing small, short stories. Luckily, a friend of mine, Steve Bissette – and John Totleben – had just started up *Taboo* around that time. And I started doing short stories, each one with a specific idea in mind on how to push the medium around. I did a short story that I wrote and drew called "Mercy," where I took whatever text was in the story and double-burned it underneath the actual drawing. Much like a billboard, or advertising in a lot of ways – where you read and perceive image simultaneously, without consciously reading words out like you would in a novel, or even a comic panel or a balloon. I had this strange idea that I wanted to be able to break down the barrier between the balloon and the page. It was less than successful, but all of them, those little things, were interesting experiments. That's where I was, as far as I can remember, at the time when Neil and I first met. I was on a panel in San Diego, on religion and comics. This was just after *Swamp Thing* 88 had broken out all over the place. That was basically "Swamp Thing meets Christ in the Garden of Gethsemane." It was, compared to many things that go on today, absolutely innocuous. It really was. It was ridiculously reverential.

*You worked with Neil on a serialized adaptation of* Sweeney Todd: The Demon Barber of Fleet Street *for* Taboo*, but only a small portion of the work saw print before* Taboo *folded. Did the two of you try taking the project to other publishers?*

*Sweeney* was always meant to be in *Taboo*, the great attraction being the ability to vary page counts as the story moved us. When that option disappeared we felt it was only fitting to retire the project until such time as it became possible to continue in the original spirit. It's just that it hasn't happened yet; though believe me, we are both aware of its unfinished status. What the future holds for it, I honestly can't say. The time and place is lost in which *Sweeney* was born. The circumstances surrounding its genesis are as important as the thing itself. They were rare and remarkable times. I fear we'll not see a flowering of so much diversity and creativity in this "industry" (which is the operative word here) again. But as Fats Waller once said, "One never knows, do one?"

*The recurring* Sandman *character you penciled, Hob Gadling...*

Oh, he's my man, Hob. I get no credit for Hob, you know? Everyone else gets credit for creating all this stuff. [*Laughs.*] But Hob and me, we go way back. Oh, yes. I love the guy.

*You based him on Jethro Tull's Ian Anderson.*

Yes, I did. Neil was looking for more of a Bob Hoskins sort of type, but I just saw Ian Anderson in him, somehow. I wanted to get some of that old Scottish, raw-boned kind of feel to it. Early on in his career, they used a lot of those medieval motifs. Hob was a redhead, he showed up with a beard first, and it just struck me – Ian Anderson when he was in mid-level Tull. At one point, I very much loved the music.

*You drew three issues featuring the character, including his, and your,* Sandman *debut: "Men of Good Fortune" [issue 13]. You mentioned that you first met Neil in San Diego on a panel. Was that when he first discussed this story with you?*

I think, for the way that actually happened, you probably have to ask Neil. Because, honestly, I had so much going on at the time I'm not sure how I got to issue 13. I know we talked a lot. I remember Shelly [Bond] calling me for the first time. I remember talking to [inker] Steve Parkhouse. The actual production of the book is pretty much a blank. I have memories of pages of it going missing at the office. (There are still eight pages of that that disappeared somewhere. I was, for many years, on a very diligent quest to find them. I kept an eye out at shows, and I had people watching art dealers for that.) But as for sitting down and actually drawing the book... I do remember drawing the last page, strangely enough. I remember drawing the page with the handkerchief – the invention of the handkerchief. I still have a couple of the books that Neil sent me for reference that I've neglected over the years to return, which is horrible of me, of course. Several of them were destroyed by one of my bull terriers, which was a real shame because I could've used them at the time. But I can't remember actually sitting down and drawing the thing. I was probably so terrified I was in a fugue state the whole time.

*The second Hob Gadling story, "Hob's Leviathan" [issue 53], included one of the few double-page spreads found in* Sandman *– the sea serpent spread.*

Oh, yes. God, I wish I had had another page to do it. I wanted it to open out to another page. I would've loved to have had more time. They never give you enough time to really work these out. The one thing Neil was *adamant* on was that the thing was absolutely, beyond-comprehension *huge*. [*Laughs.*] I remember that distinctly. That was a trip. I remember getting copies of the inks back in – Dick Giordano did those. I'm grateful for him stepping up and actually trying to deal with it; because, like I said before, I'm not easy to ink.

*Giordano was an interesting choice.*

He *does* have a bit of an illustrative background, from working with Neal Adams, that sort of thing. In a lot of ways, it was a fairly inspired choice at the time. Again, there were a lot of people that just couldn't deal with it. So I have a very limited amount of choices that would do it any kind of justice whatsoever. They needed Dick to do it because, well, he was faster than I am. I'm not the fastest inker in the world. I *can* pencil very, very fast if I have to. But inking… I'm just not a fast or facile inker. It takes me real effort to translate my own pages into ink, to a point where I'm satisfied. In an effort to keep to some sort of reasonable schedule, they generally called in inkers for me back then.

*You also penciled Hob's final* Sandman *appearance, in the* The Wake's *epilogue ("Sunday Mourning," issue 73), the Renaissance fair issue. Were you at all a fan of Renaissance fairs?*

Let's put it this way: I got on a plane, flew out to Neil's place, got thrown into a car and driven across the damn state. It was ninety-eight degrees out, and the humidity was also ninety-eight. In fact, it probably resembled Cambodia on some level. I got taken out into the middle of nowhere, where all these people were dressed up in all this stuff, drinking mead ale and saying "thees" and "thous" and "thithers." After about four or five hours of that, I'd had just about all the Renaissance fair that I could ever handle again. Everybody deserves to see one at least once. If you do it twice, I personally think that you need to seek professional assistance. [*Laughs.*] Once was quite sufficient for me, thank you. But I have to admit that a lot of the old buildings and things that were in the fairgrounds, I was enchanted with. Yes, I did enjoy a lot of that. There were some real bodices rocking around there that were rather interesting, too, but we'll leave that for another time, all right?

*One can really see a strong difference between "Men of Good Fortune," inked by Steve Parkhouse, and your later full-art job on* The Wake.

[*Laughs.*] Steve told me once, "One thing I've learned is never try to ink on a painter because painters don't draw like draftsmen, they draw like painters, which is an entirely different approach to drawing." It's a pain to try to ink me. I wouldn't wish it on anybody, to tell you the truth.

*How close were your original pencils on "Men of Good Fortune" to what we later saw of your full art on* The Wake?

*The Wake* was an entirely different beast. I was just talking about this earlier today with Mike Carey up at DC. *The Wake* was penciled very conservatively. A lot of people have this sort of idea that that's what my pencils look like before they're inked. That is not the case. That was a very separate approach that I used in the making of that book. But, to this day, every now and then when I look at it, it bothers me. Because at the time, it was difficult enough to get the powers that be there to allow that technique to actually happen, to be published, even though I'd done it before. I'd figured out how to do it well before. I had to play it very, very conservatively, so I *approached* it very conservatively. I penciled it, in many ways, the way I would've inked it. That's why it has, very much, sort of an inked feel to it in a lot of ways: because I approached it that way on purpose. I purposely overlooked a lot of the ability of the pencil to render suggestiveness, rather than explicitness, which is the grace of a pencil – its ability to have the line remain ambiguous. It has a mystery to it that calls the viewer into a sort of strange relationship with it. You have to fill in and invest emotionally into it, a lot more than, say, the pen and ink, which is, of course, the definition of the word "graphic" – it is explained for you. There's no getting around an ink line. It's goddamn there! [*Laughs.*] It starts here, and it ends here, and it gets a little thicker in the middle, maybe, or it gets a little fuzzy along the edges. But it's black and it's white and that's it.

*One occasion on which you inked yourself, but with a different end result, was another book you did with Neil –* The Last Temptation. *There is an ambiguity to your line on that book, a certain wispiness.*

A lot of that had to do with the fact that I did it all on Duo-shade paper, paper invested with two separate mechanical patterns. You actually paint on a fluid that develops the patterns into black line for the purposes of reproduction. That gave it a lot of the ambience, the gray scale that a pencil would have probably imparted on it. It softened the ink down, and gave it a roundness that it wouldn't have had otherwise. It became less harsh. I prefer using [Duo-shade paper] rather than mechanical press-on tones. I like the immediacy of it. I just enjoy working with Duo-shade a lot, probably because of the very fact that it does tend to blend pen and ink, and imparts a pencil-like quality to it.

*But you didn't want to use that on* The Wake?

No. If I remember correctly, I think Neil suggested that I use the finished pencil on that because he had seen the work I had done with adapting a short story of Ramsey Campbell's, called "Again," that was published in *Taboo* [issue 5]. It was all done in pencil. That harkens back to what I was doing around the time of "Men of Good Fortune." That was one of my experiments: If you're drawing so well in pencil, why bother inking the damn thing? That was just one of the questions I asked myself while I was sort of learning my chops. I thought, "Well, how do you do that? How would it look? What are the problems involved?" So I set myself the task of doing it. I think that's one of the reasons why Neil suggested that I actually do that. Also, he's

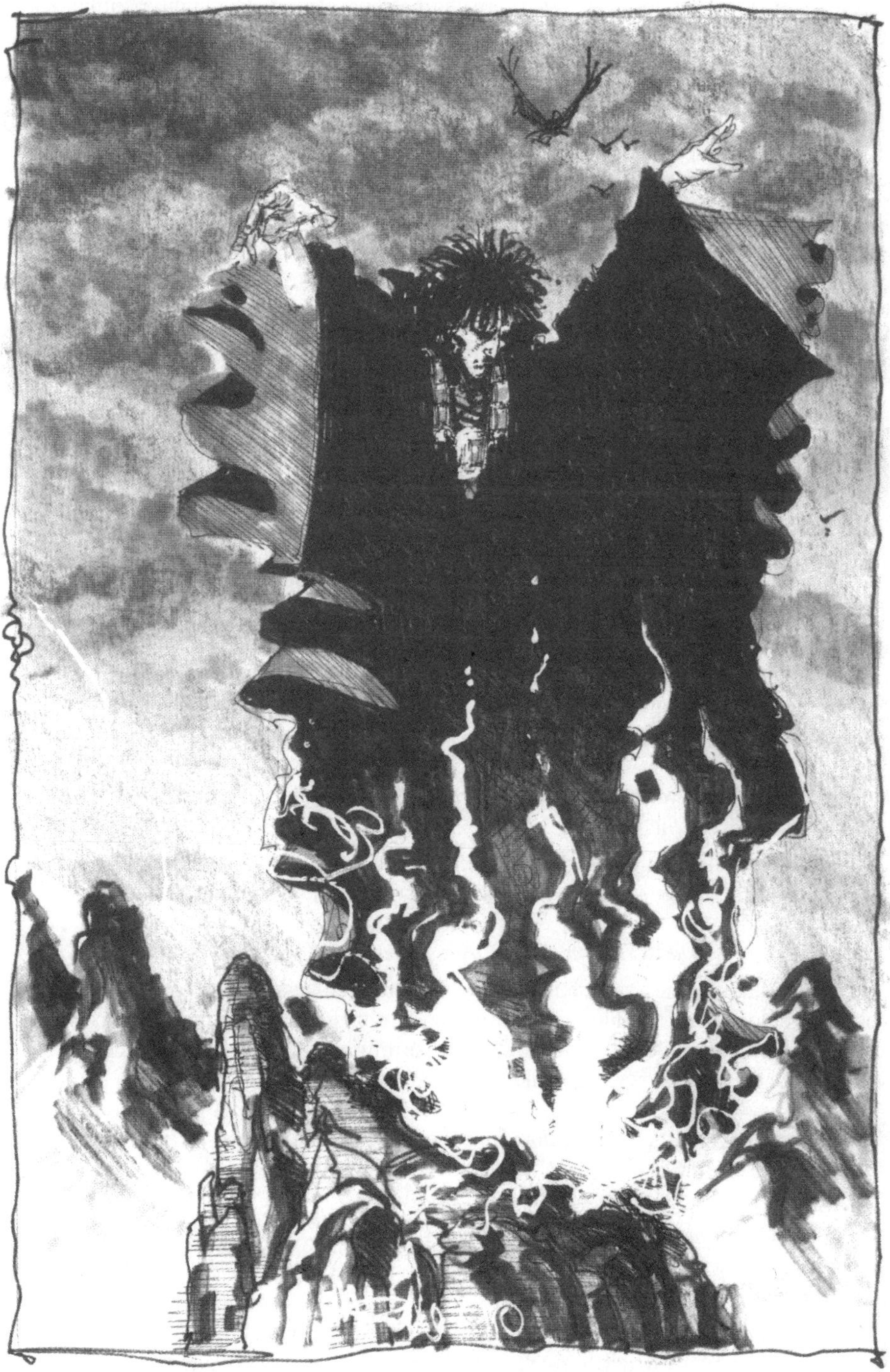

Sketch of the Sandman by Michael Zulli, from *The Sketchbook Series Number Three: Noodles, Sketchbook Stuff, Random Drawings, and Telephone Squiggles*

always been a fan of how I pencil. I pencil like a painter, and it is not like the sort of stuff you'd see splashed about in *Wizard*, or something on how to pencil a comic. I draw much differently than that. I think Neil's always been a fan of that, and he's always felt that anybody who inks me has always sort of lost some of that ambiguity that we spoke about. Actually, I find in *his* work that softness around the edges, if you know what I mean. It's always fascinated me about his work, too.

*There is a tone that remains flexible throughout his writing.*

He's very painterly with his words. They're full of suggestion and innuendo. The pencil is also like that, is very good at that. I think that's one of the reasons why he suggested it in the first place. I was thrilled, of course. I'm all for any way, shape or form of taking the medium and bending it as far as possible, trying new things, making it look different, expanding its range. That just gives one more tool to the artists of the future to express themselves with. So I'm all for it.

*Another reason Neil's said he chose you for* The Wake *was the sheer contrast between your style and the minimalism of Marc Hempel on the previous story,* The Kindly Ones.

You have no idea how many times, reading *The Kindly Ones*, I would call him up and say, "Why couldn't you let me do this? [*Laughs.*] *I want to do this one, too.*" There were a thousand pages in there, and I swear, I just said, "Oh God, if I'd got my hands on that... Oh, jeez, if I could only have been able to do this one..." Yes, it really got to me. [*Laughs.*] I really loved the story and the way it was done. Marc's work was amazing, totally amazing. But there were times when I was saying, "Oh God, if I could've gotten onto that, I could've made him do *this*, or done *this*." I redrew the whole thing in my head as I was reading it.

*You've mentioned before your love of symbolism, and that surfaces in* The Wake *in such elements as the colors of the flowers.*

That was basically all mine. I don't think you'll find a spot in any of Neil's scripts that says "...and the barge is decked with blue roses." That was me.

*How did Neil describe Daniel's – the Sandman's successor's – character to you?*

"Like Sandman if he was sixteen." Less hardened, less experienced – what Morpheus would have been like as a young man, at sixteen. Not quite fully grown, still a bit of a boy, but old enough to have some authority, some weight. I think I just remember him specifically saying, "Like Sandman, when he was sixteen."

*If I may go back to* The Last Temptation *for a moment – how did your participation in that project come about?*

The original guy that was going to do it didn't want to. There are a few sequences in there that I'm still pretty proud of, to tell you the truth.

*It's a surprisingly elegant little mini-series.*

Neil's just one of those damn good writers, you know what I mean? When you don't have a script [with which] you're called upon to essentially transform a sow's ear into a silk purse – it's already a silk purse – the sky's the limit. It takes a hell of a load off your back. I find working with Neil to be just about as easy as basically falling off my own feet. It's no problem. Neil has a deep, abiding love of language and uses it really, really well.

*Were you a fan of Alice Cooper's music?*

When I was younger, no. [*Laughs.*] Quite honestly, no. I developed an appreciation of what he does. I *immersed* myself in Alice Cooper for months. It was all I listened to. I went out and bought tons of old CDs, albums, and tapes; I listened to them in the car, and drove my ex completely out of her mind. I watched Alice Cooper videos all day long. I was *literally* living and breathing Alice for months. I did come out of it with an appreciation of what he does. I may not be the biggest fan in the world, but he is a consummate professional. He's very, very good at what he does, and a hell of a nice guy, too. But it was a tough story to draw, it really was. It was one of the toughest things I ever had to do with Neil.

*Why is that?*

I don't know. It might be because I was dealing with an actual person. Doing a licensed thing, I didn't expect it to be quite as intense as that, but…Alice has people that have to be kept happy. That watch out for him, and watch out how he's shown, how he's seen, and what his image is like. I hesitate to use the word "handlers," because that's not the case; but some people watch out for him and they have to be kept happy. They were occasionally a bit finicky. In the long run, it did improve the project in a number of ways, but it was constricting in several other ways. That may be where my earlier statement came from, a reflection of that.

*What kind of look did you wish to create for that book?*

I think a part of me was trying, believe it or not, to capture some of the feel that Wes Craven used on the very first *Nightmare On Elm Street*, which was, physically, probably the best looking of the bunch. It had the most ambiance. I think I was trying to get some of that in there, if I can remember correctly. I was calling on my own particular experience and exposure to horror movies. I'm good friends with Steve Bissette, I was basically growing up with *Creature Features*. I was trying to get some of that in there, adapt some of that feel to it.

*Neil obviously thinks highly of your work. He's brought you in to work on a number of different projects. You've recently been adapting his short stories for Dark Horse ["Daughter of Owls" and "The Price," in* Night Creatures*]. Did he provide you with scripts for those comics?*

Oh no, he didn't give me any scripts at all. I'm adapting it myself, and then he's going back over it and scripting over my adaptation. We work very, very fluid. I'm not one of those people that needs a whole lot of direction. As a matter of fact, the more directions you give me, the more likely I am to become miserable and start getting fussy. I play well with myself, but not too well with others. [*Laughs.*] So I can be pretty much trusted to be left alone in the house while the parents go out to have dinner somewhere. I'm not likely to stick my fingers into light sockets. Neil doesn't really need to give me a whole lot of direction. Over the years, we've more or less come out with a way of working that is…*malleable*, for lack of a better word. Sometimes it's very specific, but most of the time, it's sort of a middle path between leaving me entirely on my own and over-directing me. He knows me well enough to know that over-direction won't get the best out of me. If I have room to be able to think and to apply myself to any given particular situation that's being written about, I will do my best to enhance it as far as I can go; hopefully, to some degree of success. The work is the thing and as soon as I'm done with it, I can either go back and do it again to try to make it better, or I can just do what, I guess, you're supposed to do when you're a professional – say, "Okay, that's it. It's a wrap. That's a piece of time and space. There you go." Sue me. [*Laughs.*]

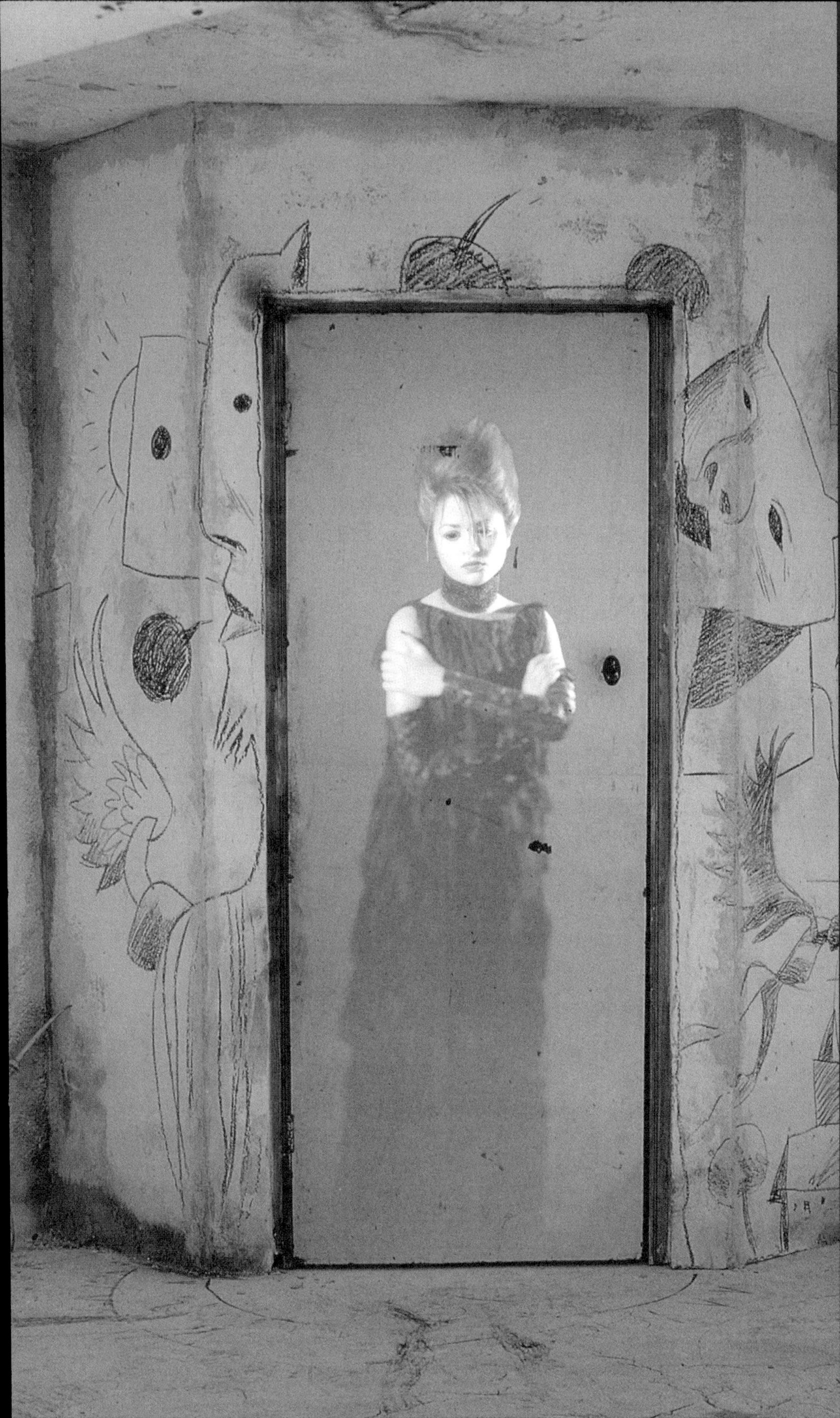

Lost in a Dave McKean world... Promotional art by McKean for *MirrorMask*. TM & © 2004 Sony Pictures and Jim Henson Films.

(A) Cover of *Violent Cases* [Titan/Escape, 1987]. Art by Dave McKean. © 2004 Neil Gaiman and Dave McKean.

(B) Cover of *Signal to Noise* [VG Graphics and Dark Horse, 1992]. Art by Dave McKean. © 2004 Neil Gaiman and Dave McKean.

(C) Cover of *The Tragical Comedy or Comical Tragedy of Mr. Punch* [DC/Vertigo, 1994]. Art by Dave McKean. © 2004 Neil Gaiman and Dave McKean.

(D) Cover of *The Day I Swapped My Dad for Two Goldfish* [White Wolf/Borealis, 1997]. Art by Dave McKean. © 2004 Neil Gaiman and Dave McKean.

(E) Variation on a theme… Cover of *This Desert Life* [Geffen Records, 1999]. "I really like the guy, Adam, who's the [Counting Crows'] leader," says Dave McKean, "but I could not shift him on the cover – he was completely married to that. He wanted exactly that color and texture and composition. All I did was reshoot the collar and tie and do a different bowler hat." Art direction by Bill Merryfield, Dave McKean, & Adam Duritz. Illustrated by Dave McKean. © 2004 Dave McKean. All rights reserved.

(F) Cover of *The Wolves in the Walls* [Harper Collins, 2003]. Art by Dave McKean. © 2004 Neil Gaiman and Dave McKean.

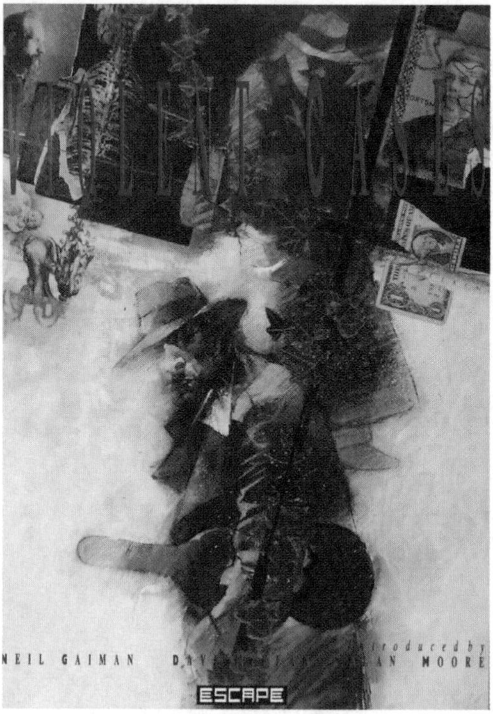
NEIL GAIMAN
ESCAPE

-A-

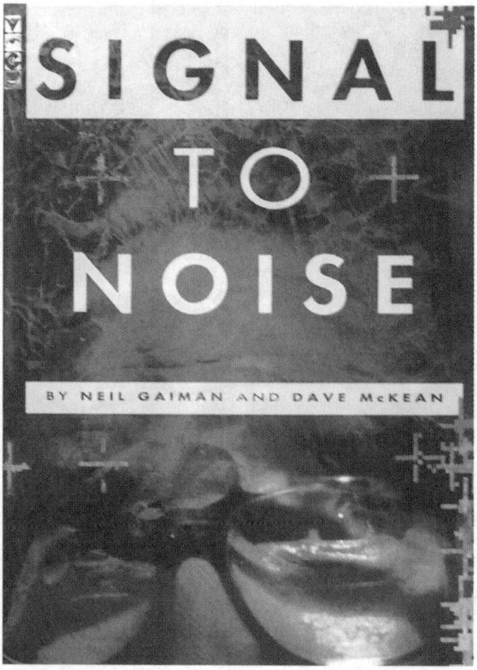
SIGNAL
TO
NOISE
BY NEIL GAIMAN AND DAVE McKEAN

-B-

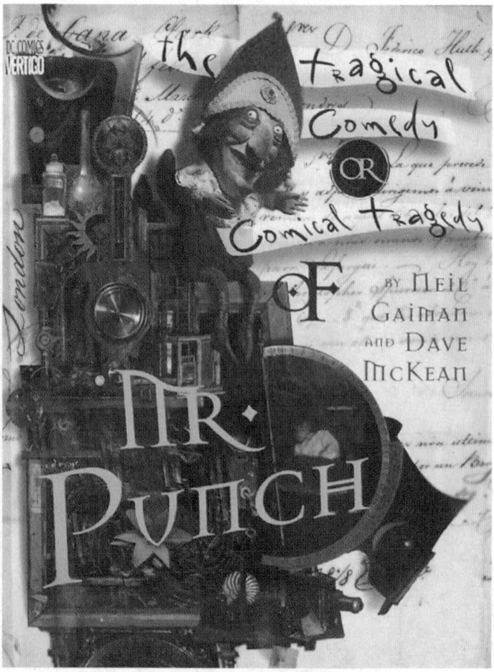
DC COMICS
VERTIGO
the tragical Comedy
OR
Comical tragedy
OF
BY NEIL GAIMAN AND DAVE McKEAN
MR. PUNCH

-C-

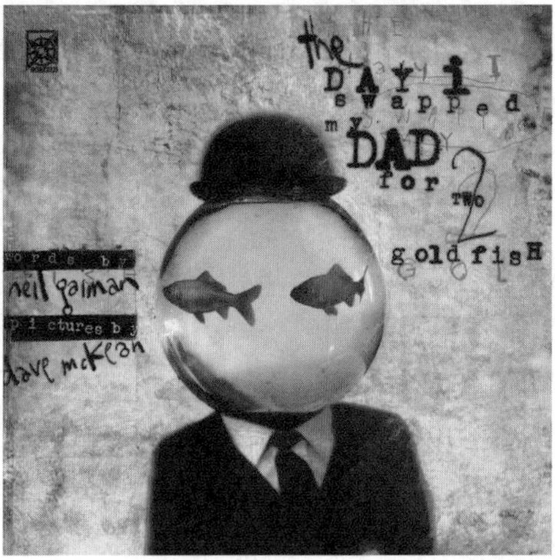
the DAY i swapped my DAD for TWO 2 goldfish
words by
neil gaiman
pictures by
dave mcKean

-D-

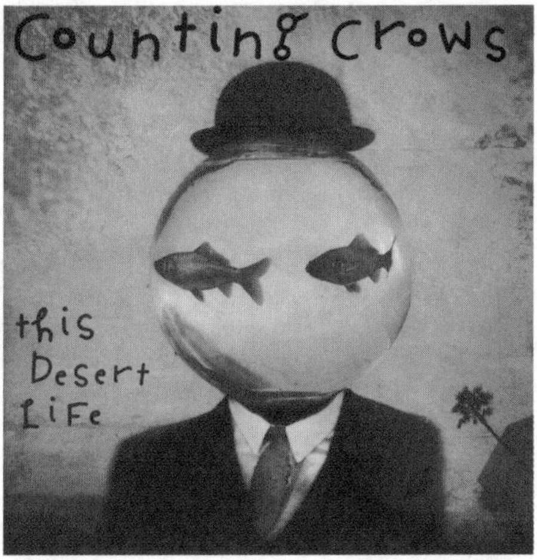
Counting Crows
this Desert Life

-E-

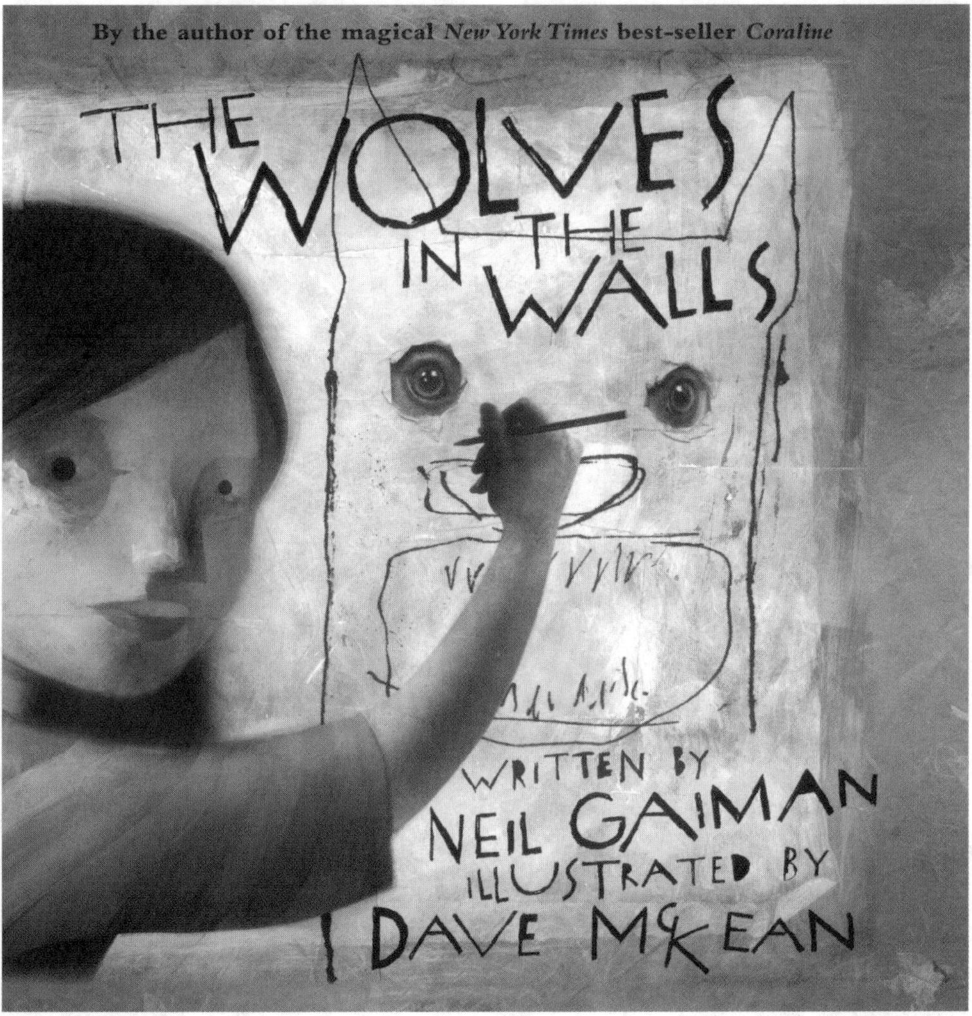
By the author of the magical *New York Times* best-seller *Coraline*
THE WOLVES IN THE WALLS
WRITTEN BY
NEIL GAIMAN
ILLUSTRATED BY
DAVE McKEAN

-F-

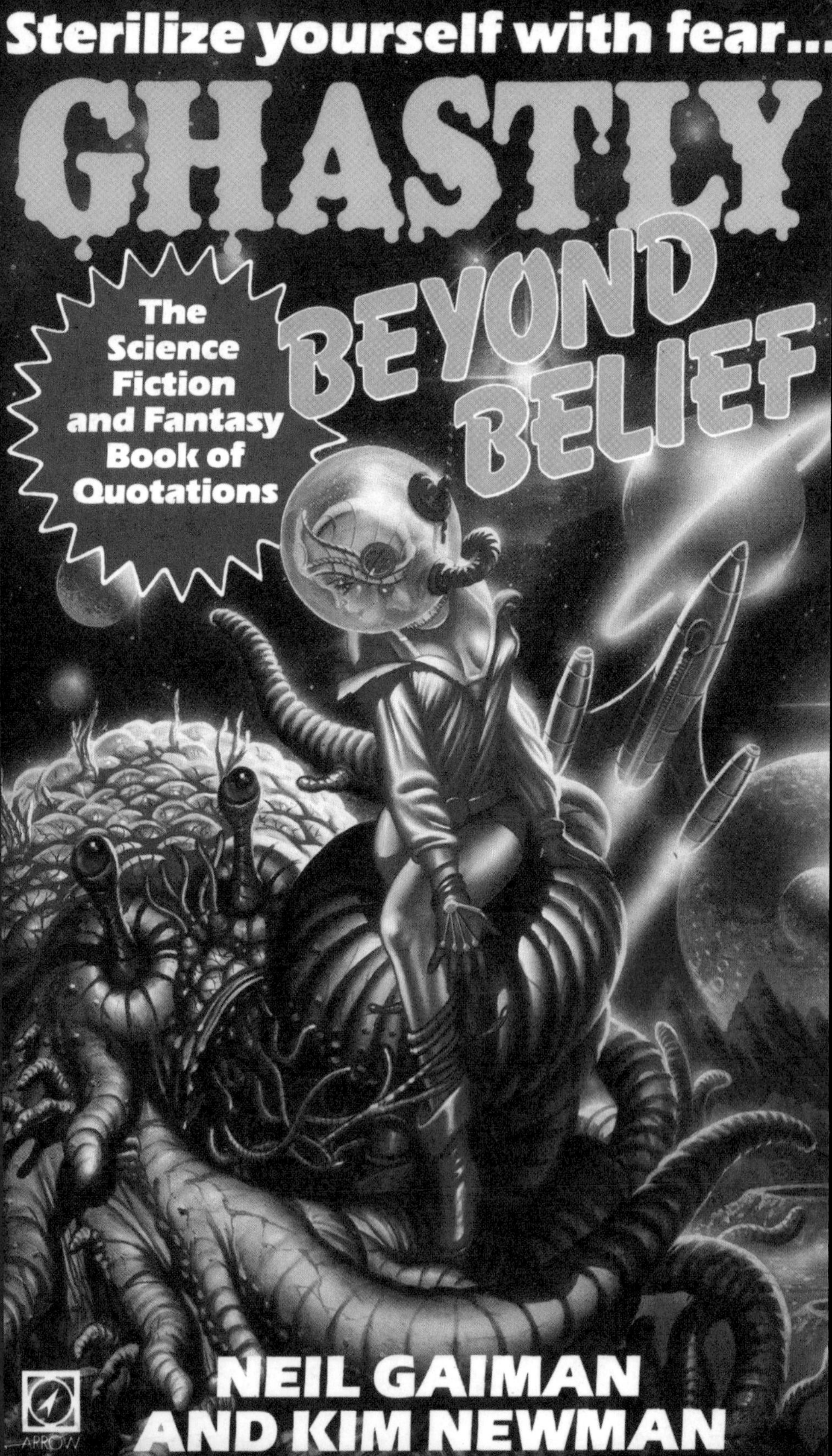
Sterilize yourself with fear...
GHASTLY
BEYOND BELIEF
The Science Fiction and Fantasy Book of Quotations
NEIL GAIMAN AND KIM NEWMAN
ARROW

Cover of *Ghastly Beyond Belief: The Science Fiction and Fantasy Book of Quotations* [Arrow, 1985]. Designed by Neil Gaiman and Kim Newman (illustrator uncredited). © 2004 Arrow Books.
Cover of *Now We Are Sick: An Anthology of Nasty Verse* [DreamHaven Books, 1994], trade paperback edition. Art by Gahan Wilson. © 2004 Gahan Wilson.

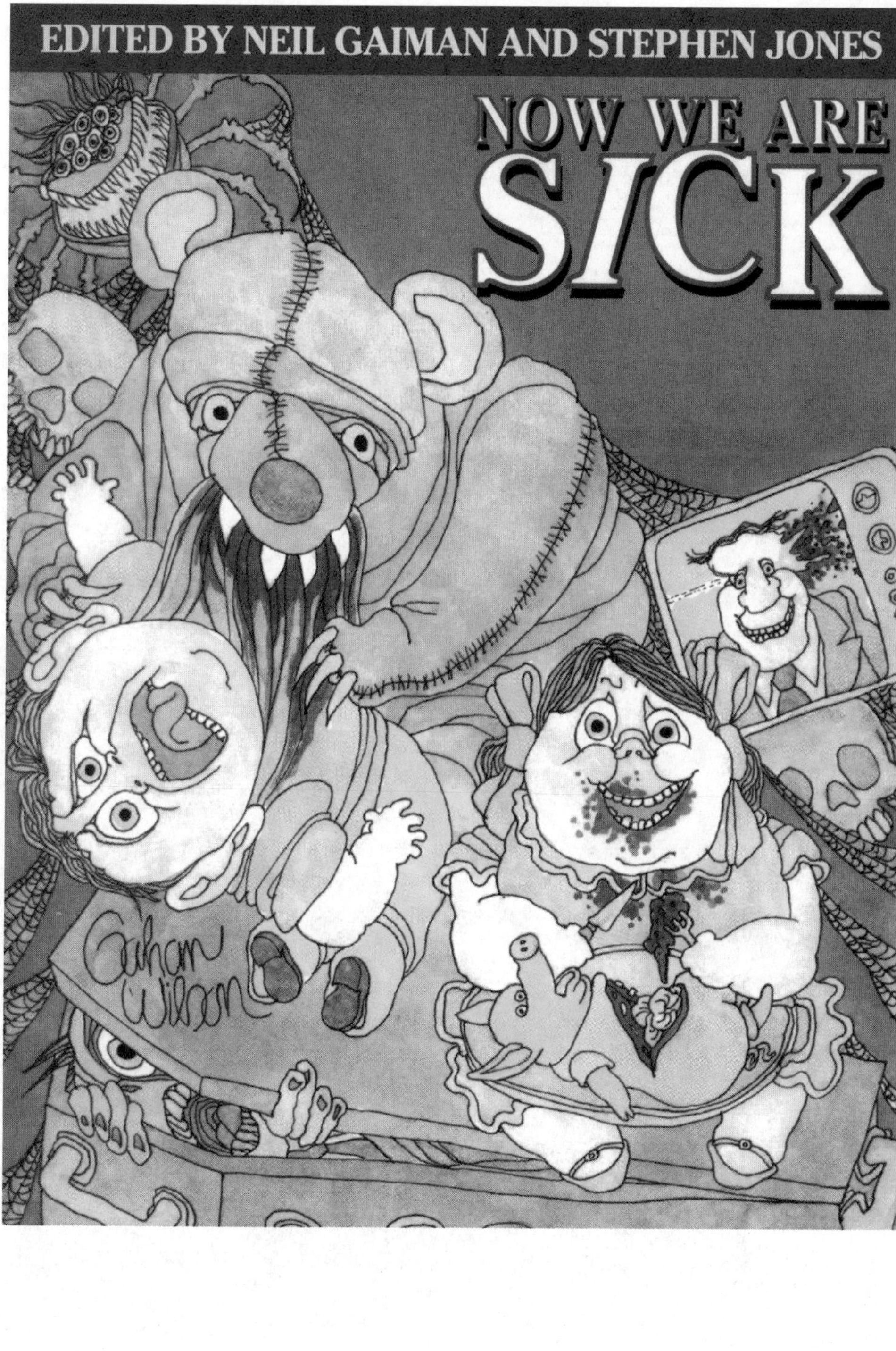
EDITED BY NEIL GAIMAN AND STEPHEN JONES
NOW WE ARE
SICK
Gahan Wilson

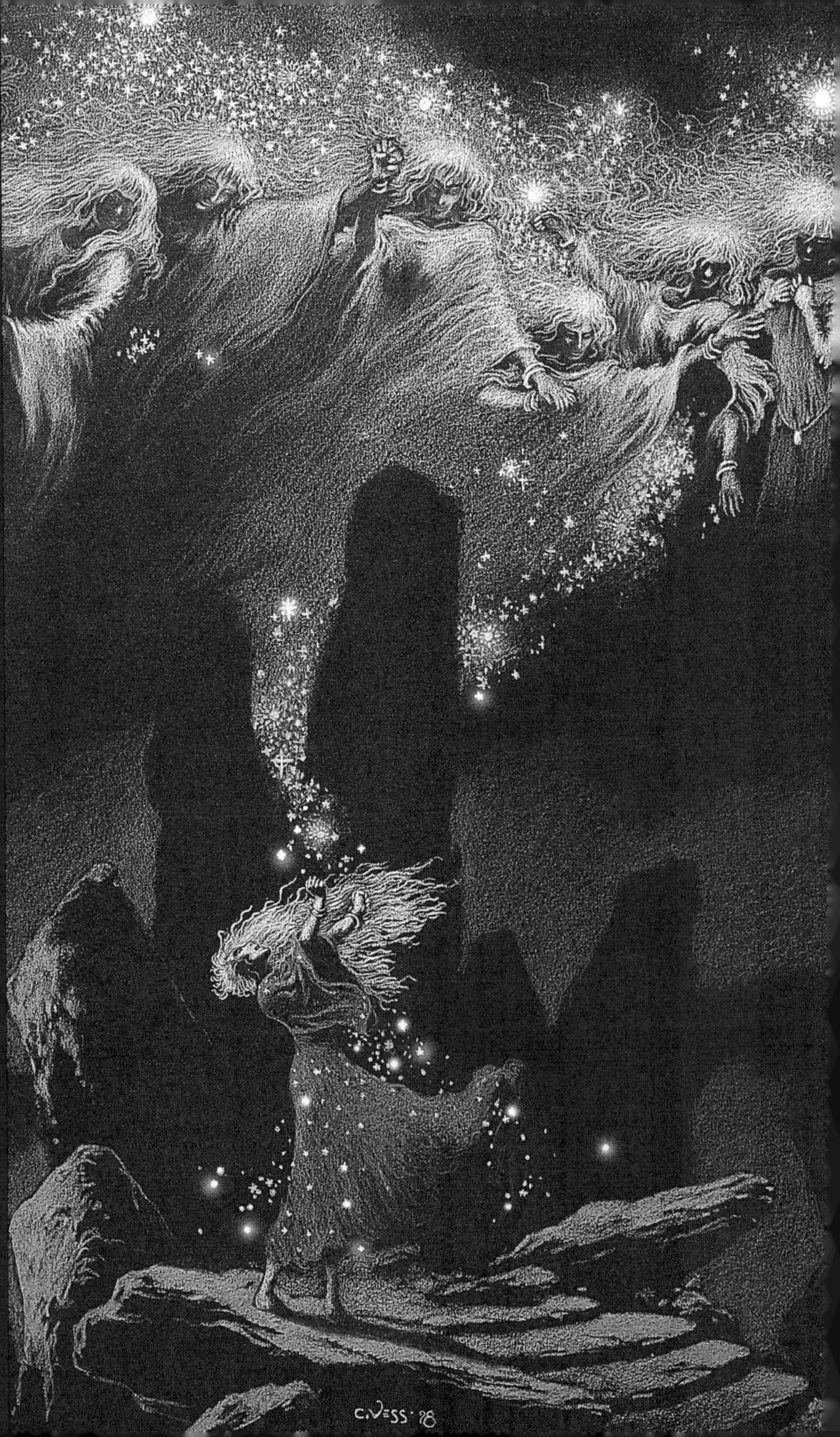

The final image of *Neil Gaiman and Charles Vess's Stardust* [DC/Vertigo Comics, 1997], "The Slow Dance of the Infinite Stars." Art by Charless Vess. TM & © Neil Gaiman and Charless Vess.
The Dreaming, from *Who's Who in the DC Universe* 15. Art by Mike Dringenberg and colors by Tom McGraw. © 2004 DC Comics.

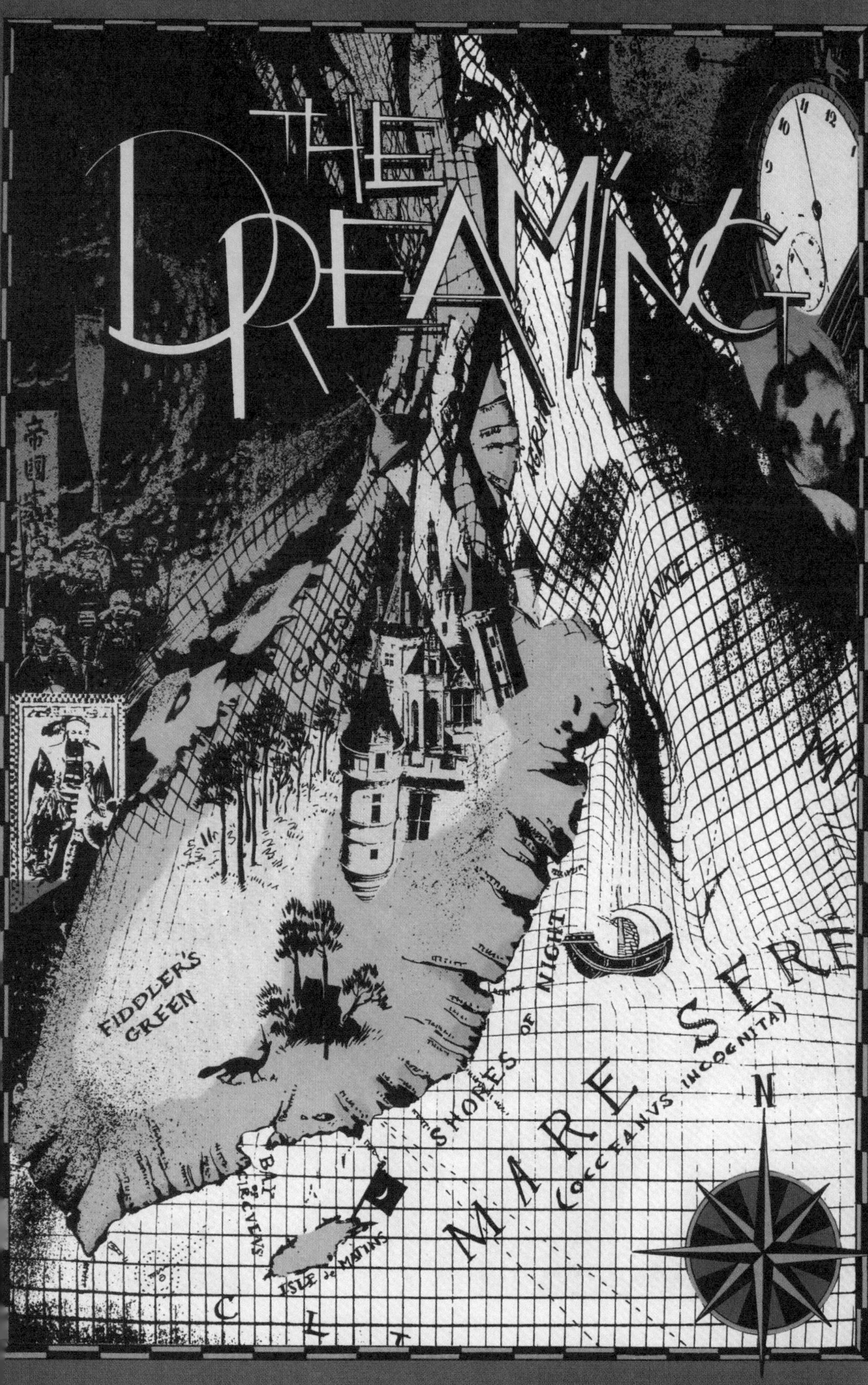

THE DREAMING
FIDDLER'S GREEN
SHORES OF NIGHT
MARE SERE
(OCCEANVS INCOGNITA)
ISLE de MATINS
N

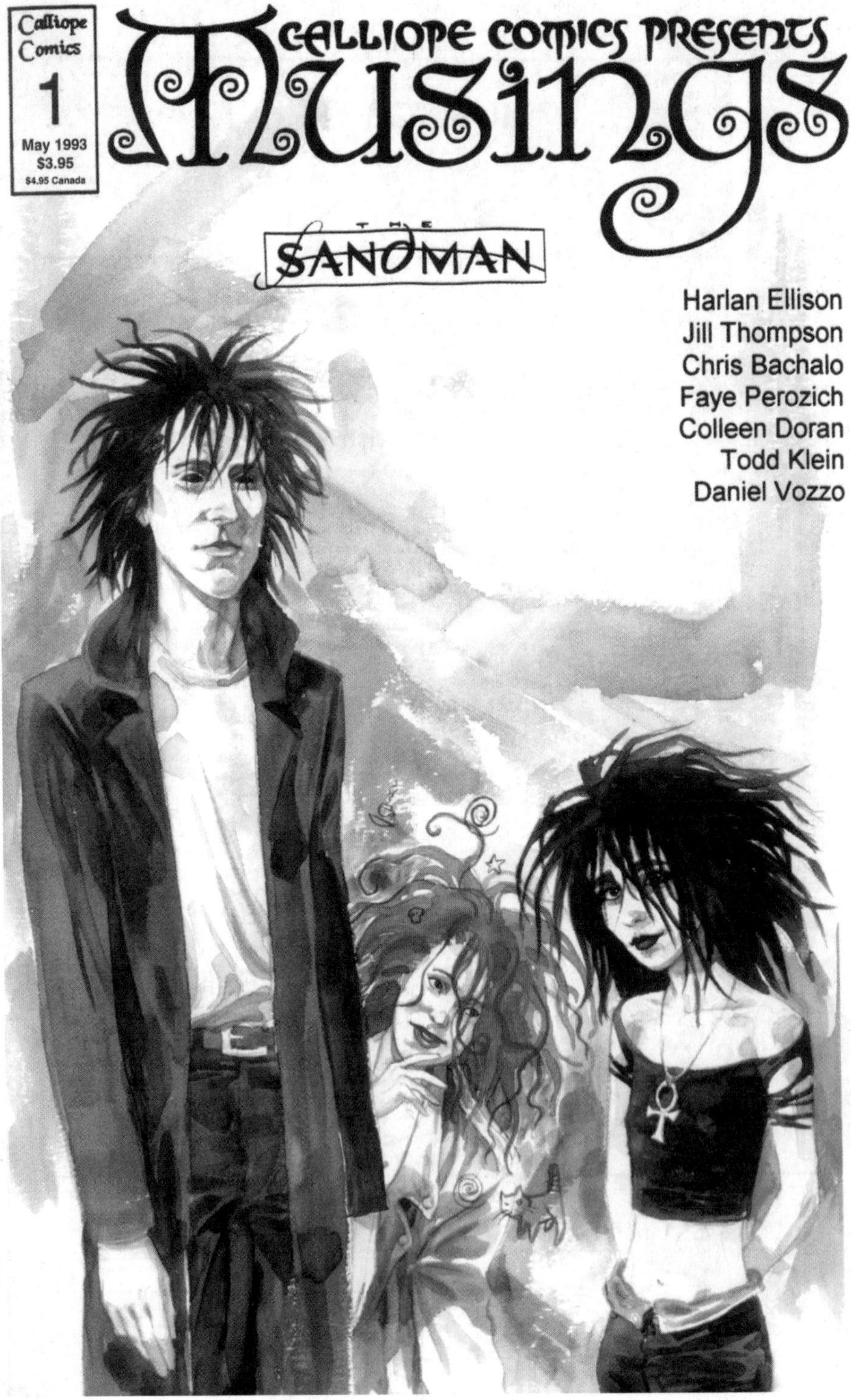
Calliope Comics
1
May 1993
$3.95
$4.95 Canada
Calliope Comics Presents
Musings
The Sandman
Harlan Ellison
Jill Thompson
Chris Bachalo
Faye Perozich
Colleen Doran
Todd Klein
Daniel Vozzo

"Ill Met by Moonlight, Proud Titania" [The Donning Company, 1988]. "One of thirty black-and-white and color illustrations done for a new edition of the William Shakespeare play *A Midsummer Night's Dream*," says Charles Vess. "Neil saw this edition and then asked me if I would like to reinterpret the play as part of his *Sandman* series." © 2004 Charles Vess.

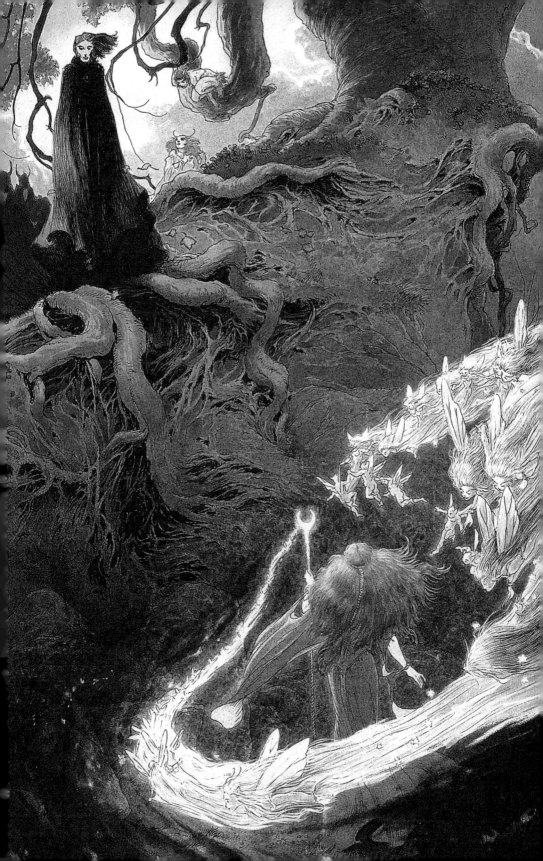

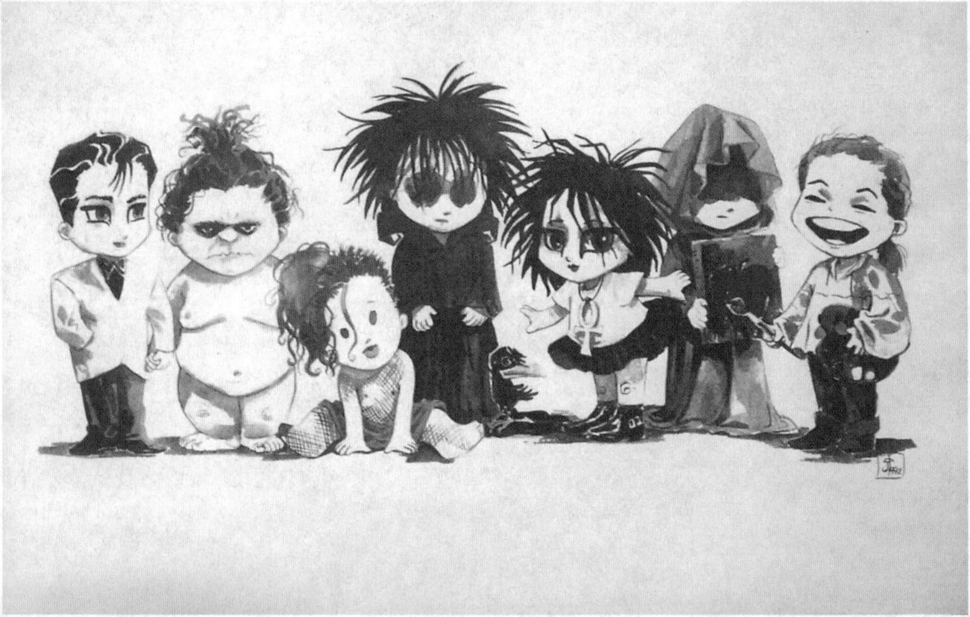

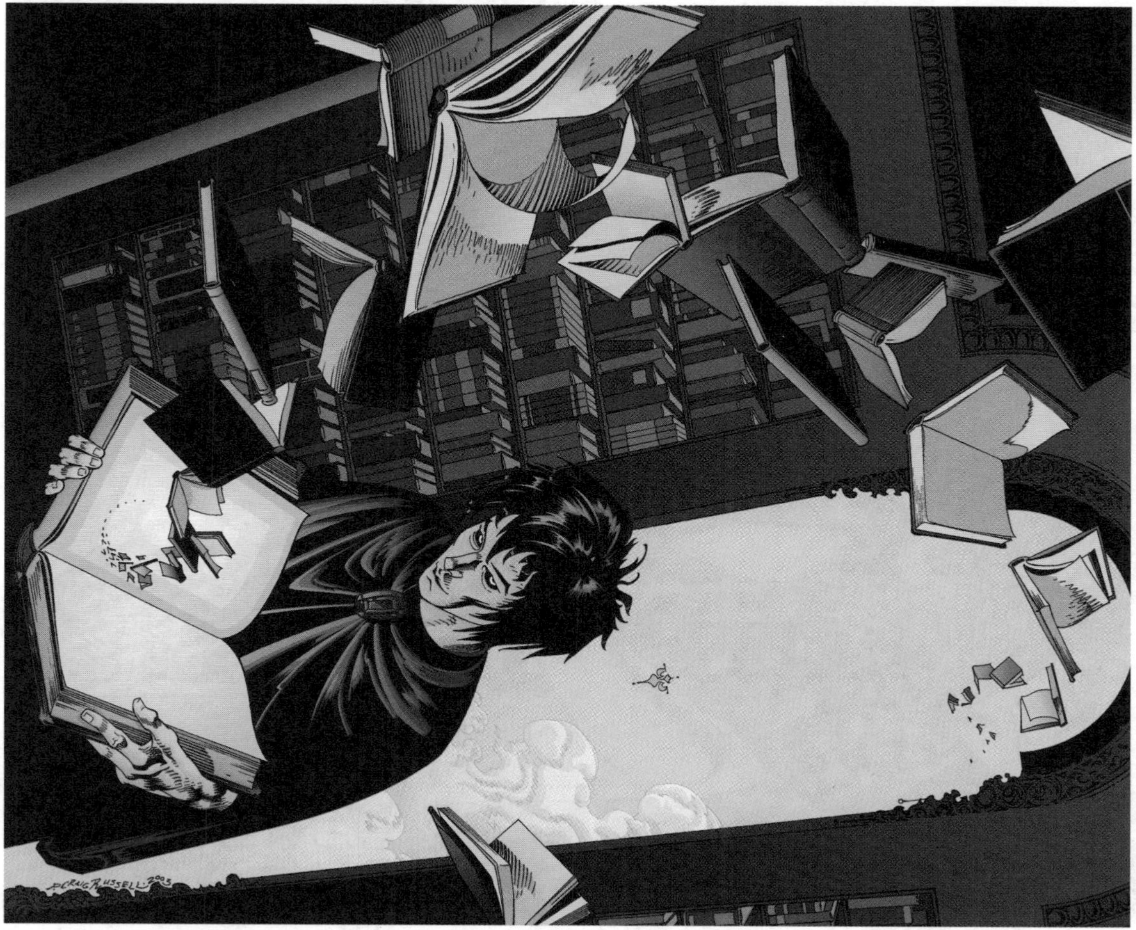

The first color image of the Little Endless, published in *The Little Endless Storybook* [DC/Vertigo, 2001]. Art by Jill Thompson. © 2004 DC Comics.
Illustration for the American Library Association *Sandman* poster. Art by P. Craig Russell and colors by Lovern Kindzierski. © 2004 DC Comics.

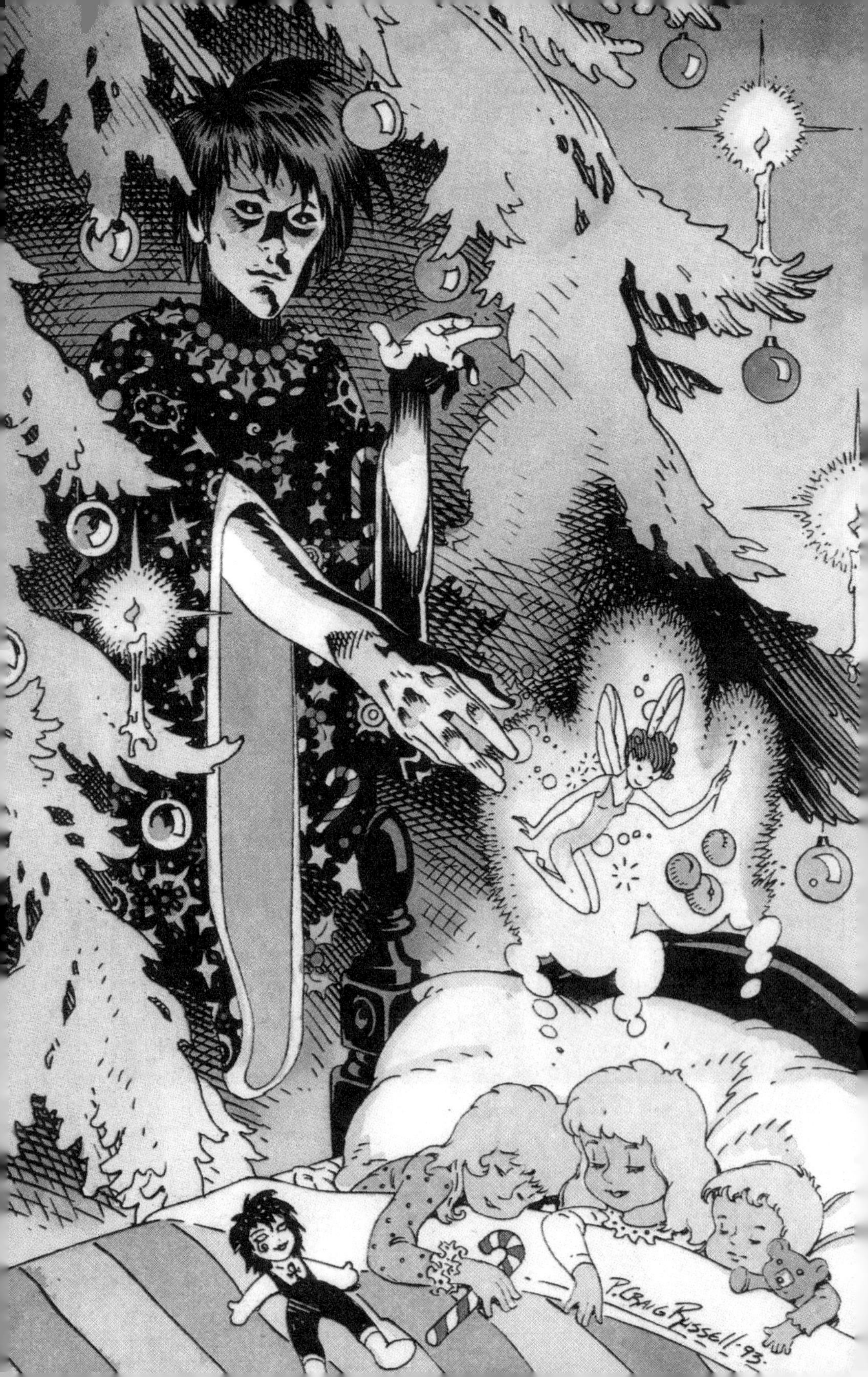
P. CRAIG RUSSELL · 93

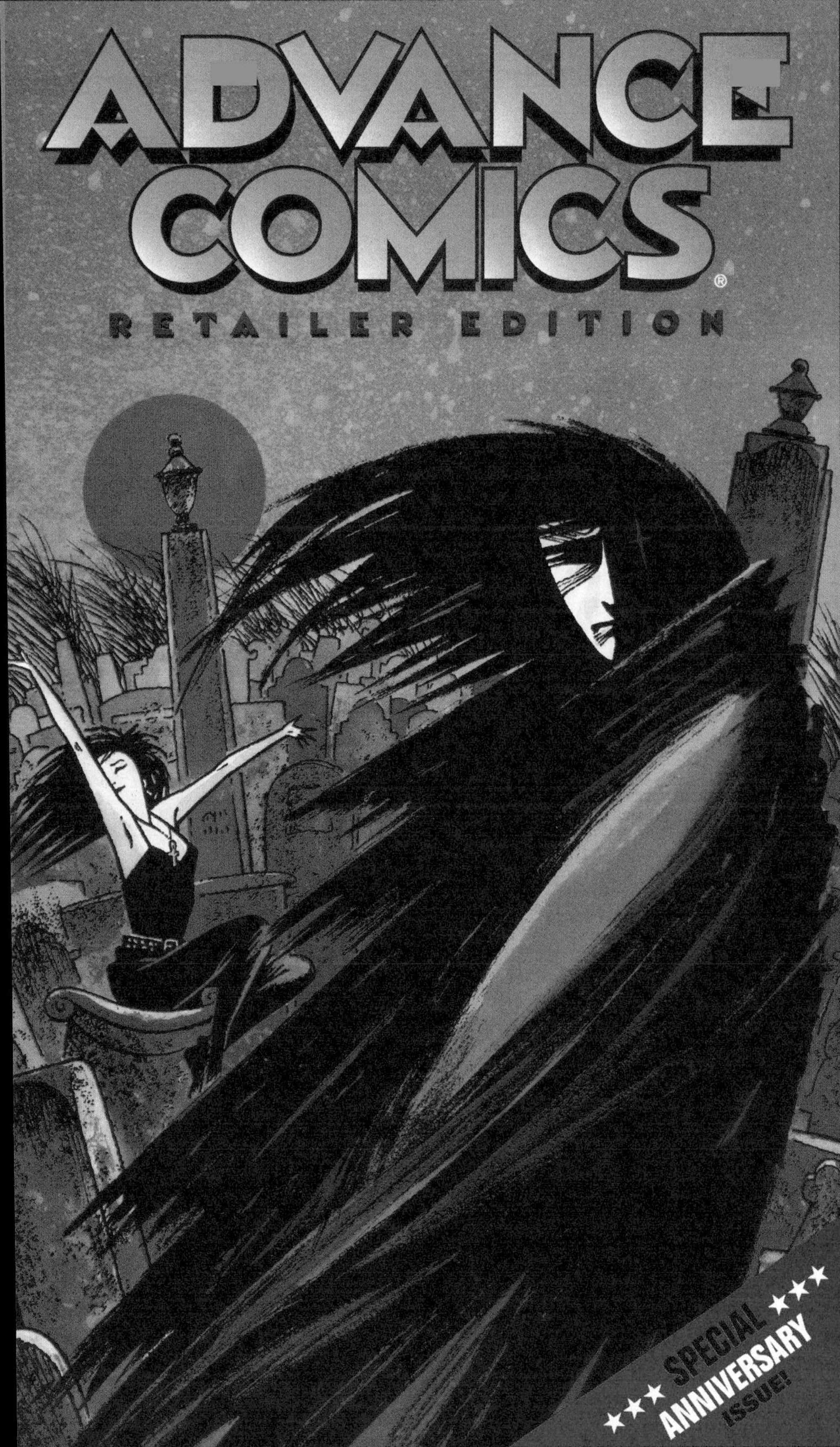
ADVANCE
COMICS®
RETAILER EDITION
★★★ SPECIAL ANNIVERSARY ISSUE! ★★★

The 1993 *Sandman* Christmas promotional postcard. Art by P. Craig Russell. © 2004 DC Comics.
Cover of *Advance Comics* 6. Art by Marc Hempel. © 2004 DC Comics.

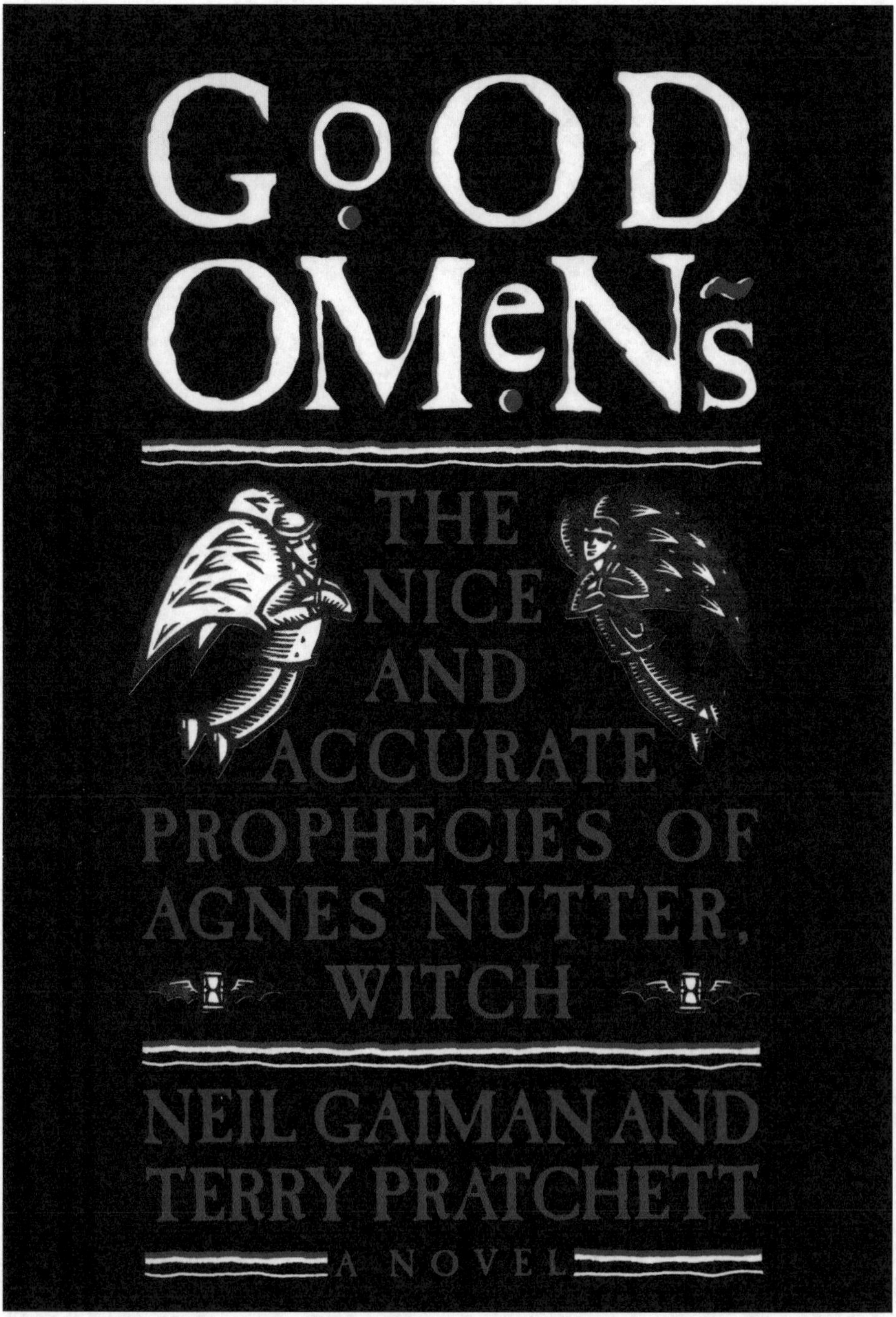
GOOD OMENS
THE NICE AND ACCURATE PROPHECIES OF AGNES NUTTER, WITCH
NEIL GAIMAN AND TERRY PRATCHETT
A NOVEL

Cover of the U.S. edition of *Good Omens* [Workman, 1990]. Designed by Charles Kreloff and illustrated by David Frampton. © 2004 Workman.
Cover of *A Walking Tour of the Shambles* [American Fantasy, 2002]. Art by Gahan Wilson. © 2004 Gahan Wilson.

# A WALKING TOUR OF THE SHAMBLES

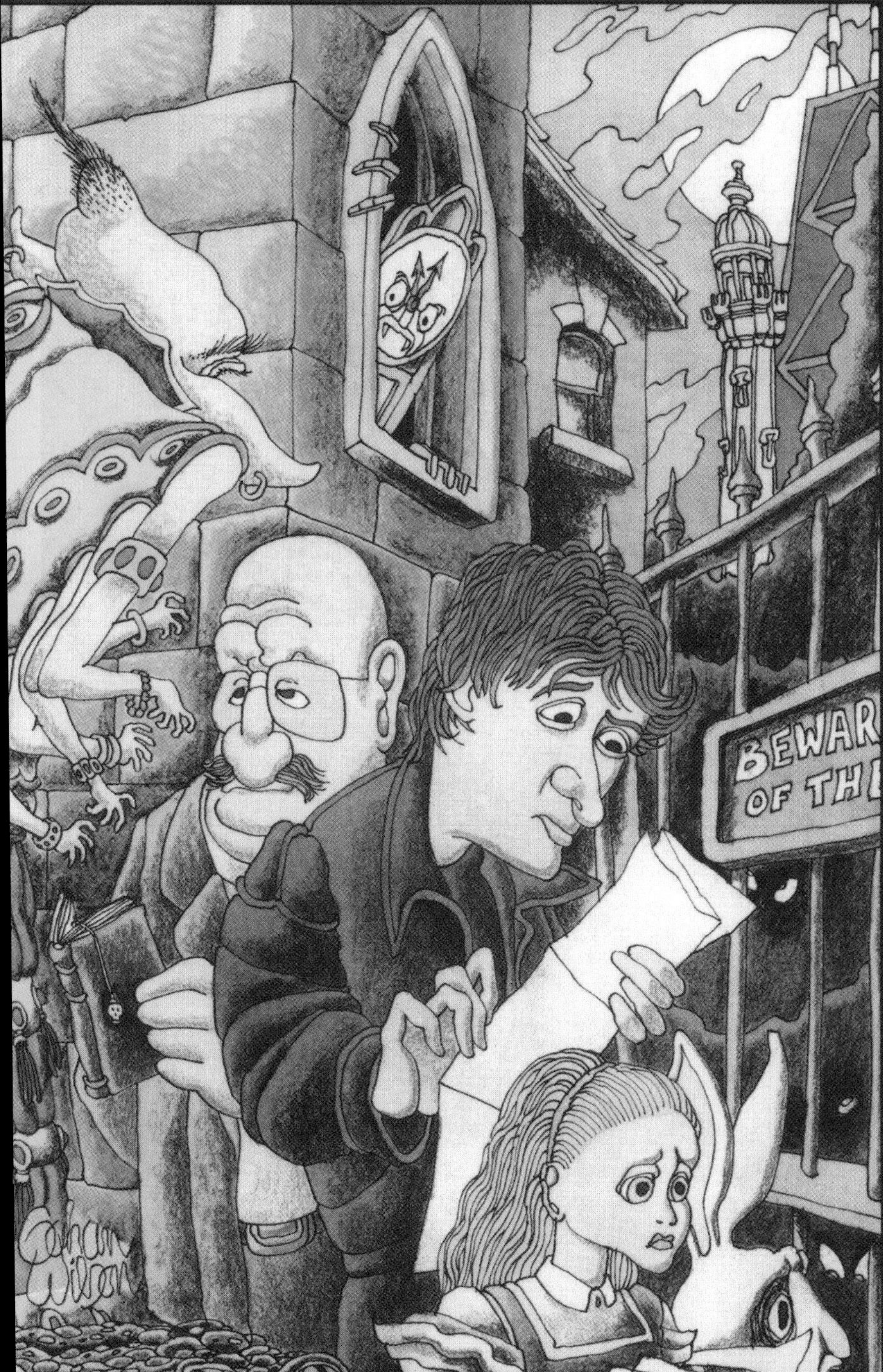
BEWAR
OF TH

GENE WOLFE & NEIL GAIMAN

LITTLE WALKS FOR SIGHTSEERS # 16

16

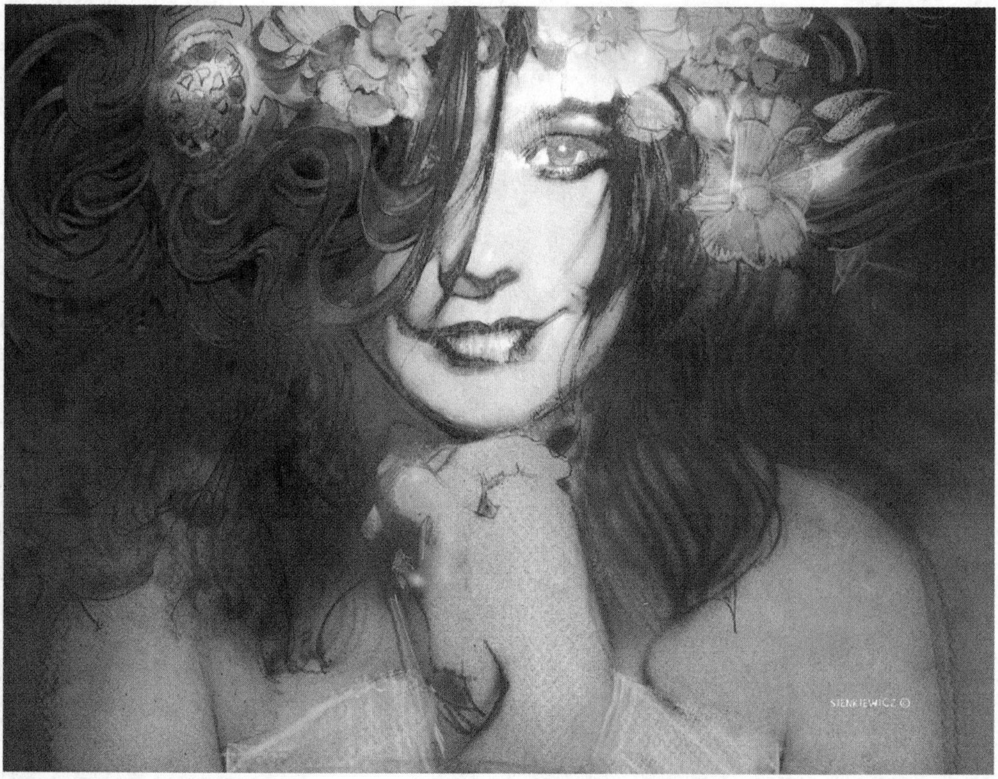
STENKIEWICZ ©

Portrait of Tori Amos, by Bill Sienkiewicz, for the cover of the *2005 Tori Amos RAINN (Rape, Abuse, and Incest National Network) Calendar*. Sienkiewicz also illustrated "Going Inside," featuring the Amos-inspired Delirium, for Gaiman's *Endless Nights*. Courtesy of Ken Meyer, Jr. © 2004 Bill Sienkiewicz.

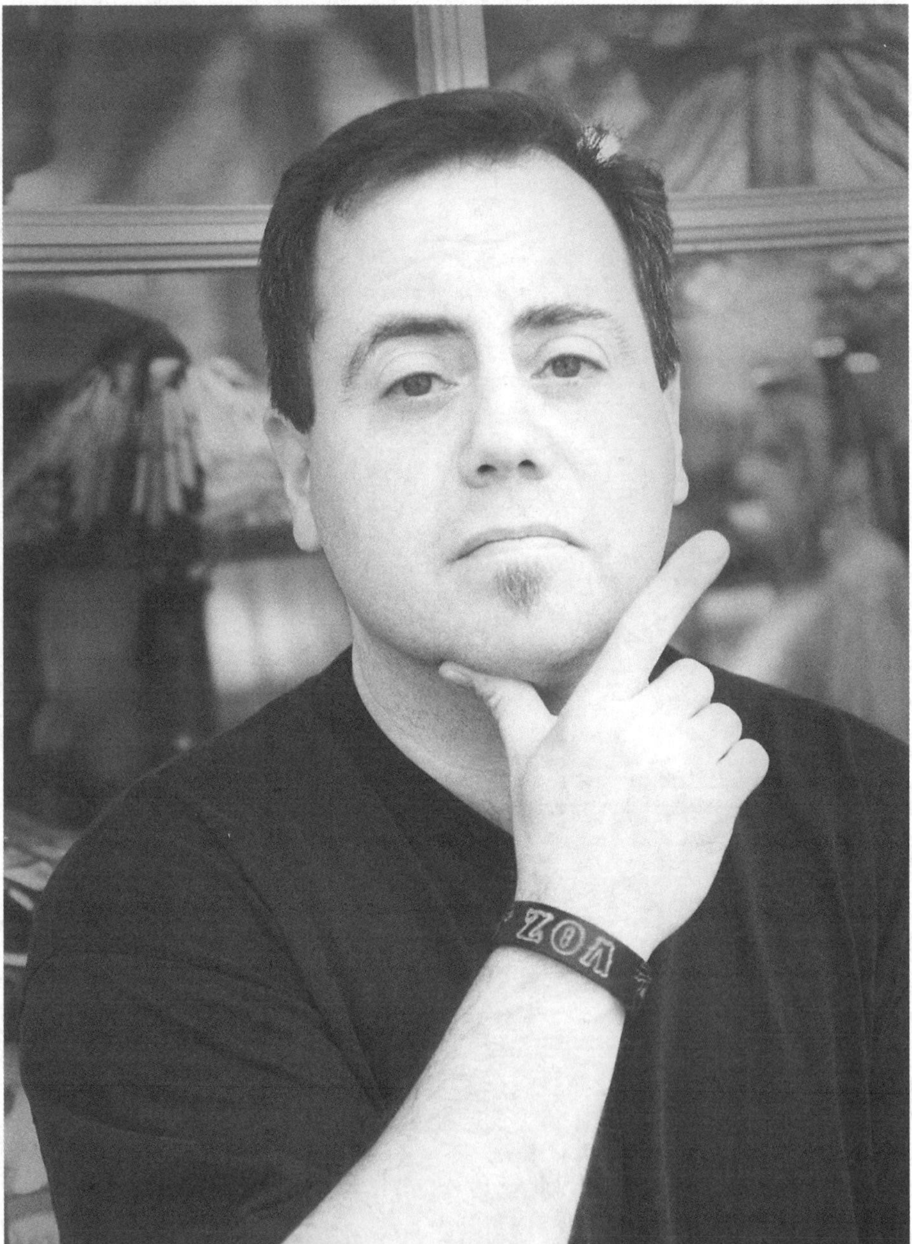
VOZ

*Daniel Vozzo*

## DANIEL VOZZO CREDITS GAIMAN FOR PROVIDING HIM WITH

A COMIC BOOK THAT NOT ONLY ALLOWED HIM TO DEMONSTRATE HIS SKILLS AS A COLORIST, BUT THAT LED TO A WIFE AND FAMILY AS WELL. (VOZZO'S WIFE, STEPHANIE, WAS A LONGTIME COMICS FAN WHO FIRST BECAME INTERESTED IN MEETING VOZZO UPON LEARNING HE COLORED *SANDMAN*. "LONG ENOUGH AGO," GAIMAN POINTS OUT IN HIS ONLINE JOURNAL, "THAT THEY HAVE A [TWELVE]-YEAR OLD DAUGHTER.")

VOZZO CAME TO COMICS FROM A PUNK-ROCK BACKGROUND, BY WAY OF PUBLISHING. HE HAD ONLY WORKED AS A COLORIST FOR A SHORT TIME WHEN HE WAS BROUGHT IN TO COLOR ISSUE 23 OF *SANDMAN* [CHAPTER 2 OF *SEASON OF MISTS*]. HE STAYED TO COLOR, WITH ONLY A COUPLE OF EXCEPTIONS, THE REST OF THE BOOK'S RUN, AS WELL AS SUCH VERTIGO TITLES AS *THE INVISIBLES*, *LUCIFER*, AND *FABLES*.

"WHEN THE VERTIGO LINE AT DC BECAME ESTABLISHED, IT OPENED UP A NEW DOOR AND IT JUST KEPT ME BUSY," SAYS VOZZO. "I STILL PLAY MUSIC PART-TIME, BUT IT'S VERY PART-TIME." WHILE CONTINUING WITH HIS REGULAR COLORING ASSIGNMENTS, VOZZO PURSUES YET ANOTHER ARTISTIC PASSION – ACTING.

*Will Eisner once explained his thoughts on the use of color in comics. He said the presence of color on his pencils was like that of a full-piece orchestra playing behind a concert soloist. Do you find many pencilers share this viewpoint? Do many tend to feel drowned out by color? Or do most feel comfortable with it?*

Since I've worked on DC/Vertigo books for quite a while now, I have been fortunate enough to work with many different artists and writers. I've gotten different feedback from many of them. For the most part, I believe that artists, pencilers, and inkers, feel that the color *can* enhance their work, helping it along. But it's just like everything else: it depends on how it's approached. If it's over the top, the color can take away from the penciled work, or it can add to it, depending on how it's applied. I think that, most artists like having their work colored. Although there are some that may feel that the coloring only takes away from their work. So I have to be really careful when I work with somebody who might feel this way. I don't take it personally, but I tend to try to ease their mind, and say, "Look, I see each piece of art as individual, whatever the style. I try to apply color for whatever the art calls for, that's how I try to approach the book." For example, there was the last storyline in *Sandman*, *The Wake*, drawn by Michael Zulli. The art was all done in pencils, it was not inked at all. And Michael was comfortable with me as a colorist because I'd worked closely with him before, spending detailed discussions with him by phone; but he needed someone to use a lighter palette than the norm. Unfortunately, I wasn't doing the color separations at that time, I was just doing color guides for the books. They used my guides, having a separator apply the colors. But, on my guides, I made sure that I used a lighter palette and tried not to take away from any of the fine pencils. His artwork is very textured, and you don't want to lose any of the fine lines. So I purposefully went lighter and he was happy with it. I personally felt that it may have printed a little darker than I had hoped, but he seemed happy with it.

I try to work closely with the artists and the writers to make them feel as comfortable as possible with me. I would try to let the writers know that as a colorist, I read the scripts before I even start working on the book. I like to hear it directly from them if there is anything that they're leaning toward, as far as what they're trying to convey. And I'm usually in contact with the artist by e-mail or phone, especially if it's an artist that I've never worked with before. I'll say, "I've seen your work colored up before. Is there anything you would like me to steer away from?" And they'll be honest with me. They'll say, "I like your work, but just avoid doing this or that." For the most part, the penciler is not too concerned that there is coloring applied to their artwork; but, moreso, whether it's a *capable* colorist doing the work. I think, at this point, *most* artists are comfortable with having their work colored.

*You had the opportunity to work with quite a number of artists on* Sandman, *for which you were brought on board with issue 23, the second chapter of* Season of Mists.

At that point, it was going on two years that the book had been published. And it had already become popular by then. It was exciting because I personally liked the book. It was one of the books that I enjoyed reading, not because I had to, but because I wanted to. I enjoyed the writing, as well as the artwork. The first time I met Neil Gaiman, he mentioned to me that he had spoken to Karen Berger about wanting me to color the *Sandman* books. At the time, I believe I was coloring *Doom Patrol* and *Shade, the Changing Man* for the Vertigo line. When Neil mentioned my name, I was a little bit surprised because I had not been coloring for all that long. I was just starting to color and I had a lot to learn – I still do. So it was surprising to me that he even brought my name up. Within two months of meeting Neil, I got a phone call from Karen Berger saying, "Would you like to jump on board with *Sandman*?" I was thrilled! I was a little nervous, being that it was such a popular book. But at the same time, it was exciting to work on a book that I actually loved to read. It was great to join the *Sandman* team.

Steve Oliff, one of my favorite colorists at that time, was already doing his own computer separations, and had colored a couple of the previous issues before I came on board. At that time, especially with me doing color guides and not separations, it was a tough act to follow. But I was told that, as happy as they were with Steve, it just didn't fit in with his scheduling. So I just went with it. I guess they liked my work because, with the exception of issues 50 ["Ramadan"] and 74 ["Exiles," which artist Jon Muth colored], I worked all the way up until the last issue, which was 75 ["The Tempest"], as well as coloring *The Sandman Special*.

There was an interesting story with issue 51 ["A Tale of Two Cities"]. When issue 50 came about, they had mentioned that P. Craig Russell, who was doing the pencils, had always, at that point, used his friend, Lovern Kindzierski, to do colors and seps on his issues. They had asked me if I would mind that Lovern Kindzierski would step in. I said, "No, not at all." But then when I saw how gorgeous the book looked – because Lovern, like Steve Oliff, had been doing his own separations as well as doing a really nice job on the coloring – I was a little worried about jumping back on board with issue 51. At that point, I was not doing my own separations. In my opinion, they weren't the sharpest separations. There was a lot about the color separations on issues 23 through 49 that I had worked on that I wasn't happy with. I mentioned that I hoped to get a different separator on *The Sandman*, because I was thinking about leaving the book. That's when Karen Berger said, "We wouldn't want you to leave the book. I'll get back to you on this." Within a couple of days, she called me back and said, "We have a new separator." I was a lot happier with issues 51 through 75, because the separations improved, and that made the coloring look a whole lot better.

*Neil seems to get involved with a number of different parts of a comic's production. What kind of working relationship does he have with you as a colorist?*

We have a very good relationship. Neil was one of the first writers I had ever worked with, to whom I had mentioned, "Hey, I read the scripts, so if there are any color notations, or any specifics that you want, a certain mood to come across, mention it in the script, because I will read it and abide by it." He was happy to hear that. After a while, when I became a regular on *The Sandman*, there would actually be suggestions directed toward me in the script, which helped. And I like to do that, if I have the chance, with every writer. I wasn't there for the very beginning, but I was on board pretty early on for Neil's comic-book career, so we got to speak on the phone a lot and go over things. And even when things started getting reprinted in trade editions, there were a few things that Neil had asked to have re-done, as far as coloring changes. He asked me to recolor a few things. He actually would love to have a lot more recolored as far as the first couple of storylines. In fact, if you read some of the reprinted trade editions, I think the credits state, "Selected recoloring by Daniel Vozzo."

Working with Neil is great. Anything they ask me to do of his, I know right off the bat I'm going to love it, as far as the writing goes. That always helps. You get to enjoy the book that you're working on. We still keep in contact, not as often as I'd like, but we're trying to do some recoloring on some of the old issues, since they're constantly being reprinted in hardcover editions. Hopefully, in the future, we'll be able to get that done. Because these books, I know, are going to be around for a long time.

*Before becoming a colorist, you were part of a band that opened for the Clash and the Ramones. Neil, of course, was also in a punk band, in the '70s. Did you find the two of you shared a similar sensibility?*

I would like to think so. At first, I didn't know much about his background and he didn't know much about mine. Maybe that's why we clicked and hit it off. I was fortunate enough to open for many of the original punkers. I'm giving my age away, although I am *younger* than most of those original punkers. [*Laughs.*] My band was younger. We were fortunate enough to open for a lot of them in the States. Neil was a lot closer, being in England, to these bands when they first came about. We were supposed to open one show for the Clash. This was during the Clash's last tour, actually, and when you open for the Clash, it's a scary thing because you know the people are there to see the Clash and not the opening act. But it turned out that not only did the audience take to us, but the Clash themselves liked us. So they ended up taking us on tour for a few more shows with them. That was a dream come true because, at that point, I wasn't even involved in the comic-book industry yet. My main focus was music then, and I got to play with the guys that I looked up to and idolized. From there, we started doing shows with bands like Billy Idol, Public Image Limited (which Johnny Lydon from the Sex Pistols formed), the Ramones, and bands like that. It was just a great run for a couple of years. It was really good. And then, of course, I found out that Neil had played in a band. It's always good to find out someone you know has the same interests, and the same likes. I think that helps and it does come across in your work sometimes. That's one of the reasons why we work well together.

*It's perhaps ironic from a coloring standpoint that* Sandman's *main, recurring cast of characters, the Endless, are, for the most part, presented in black and white. But the stories themselves call for a large palette.*

With *The Sandman*, Neil has these stories taking place in different time periods and different locations. You have to try for a different feel within each storyline. If the characters are in Hell, you're going to use a lot of hot and bright colors. If the scene is set in Renaissance days however, you try and go with that, and make little changes here and there. It's not so difficult to work around. The characters are mostly black and white, so you just work with it, and you hope you're applying the colors that work best with the rest of the setting. You go more with the feel of the book than anything when it comes to *Sandman*. I think that's the best approach. I don't know how well I've hit on that, but that's what I try to do.

*In that sense, does it allow you more room for self-expression than other titles?*

Yes, I guess it would. It also depends on the artwork, how simplistic it's drawn. There are other titles that I've worked on where the story takes place in modern-day time. Sometimes I'd work on a title and I'd feel limited in what I can do. But when you're working on something like *Sandman* – don't forget it's a fantasy book – when you're working on a fantasy book you can get away with more. It frees you up a little bit.

*Even if Neil's scripts are tighter than those of other writers?*

Yes. Neil is a team player. I think he enjoys not having to take on the responsibility of everything himself. He likes everyone to share their input with him. He's a team player that doesn't mind you picking up the ball and running with it. If he doesn't agree with or like something, he'll let you know it, which is fine. And then you change it because he is the man. [*Laughs.*] You want to make him, or any writer, artist or penciler happy. As far as I'm concerned, I want to make everyone happy with the books I work on, and that includes the readers. I want the people that I'm working with to say, "Hey, you really did a nice job and hopefully we'll work together again." You hope to please everybody.

*How involved did* Sandman's *artists get with the book's coloring? Did they add many notes to Neil's scripts?*

Every storyline had a different artist, a different penciler, and different inkers. A couple of artists, not many, but there were a couple, had more to say about it than others did. I had no problem with it. The greatest thing about working on *Sandman* is not just the fact that I'm working with Neil, but that I also got to work with a lot of artists. There were a few of them… Marc Hempel, for example, worked *very* closely with me on the issues for *The Kindly Ones*. I was literally on the phone with him for every issue. That's just the way Marc is, that's how he works. He was used to a lot of his work being done in black and white. And for his artwork that was in color – I could be wrong – but I think maybe in the past he had done the coloring himself, or had someone working very closely with him. I could tell he was a little bit worried, so we were on the phone all the time discussing his concerns. I love Marc as a person as well as an artist. I think he's hysterical, he's a real funny guy. I really enjoyed working with him. It took a little more time, being on the phone with him for so long, though [*laughs*], but I had no problem with that. So, there are artists who tend to have more to say about it than others; Marc being one of them. I think those issues came out well, because of Marc's input.

*As far as some of* The Sandman*'s recurring features went, did you find Delirium to be the biggest challenge, with her multi-colored word balloons?*

I did, only because of the fact that I was not doing my own color separations at the time, and I had to do color guides by hand with watercolors. That was a little bit of a hassle. I tend to think that if I was separating it on my own, it might have looked a little different, for whatever reasons. It wasn't too difficult to do. It was just one of the reasons why I wished I was separating my own stuff on the computer, because of things like Delirium's balloons, as well as her hair. The time she showed up with multi-colored hair – you want it to look just right. Sometimes it did, and sometimes it didn't.

*How would Neil or Todd Klein describe Delirium's word balloons to you?*

Someone must have mentioned to put the color in. I don't recall. But I do remember Neil being specific about her eye colors being different – one blue eye, one green eye. I think, looking back, if I were to recolor those issues, I would probably knock the lettering itself out in color, and do a lighter gradient of colors for the word balloons themselves. That's just a little change I would make. I would have to go over that with Neil, of course. [*Laughs.*]

*Do you have an issue or storyline that you particularly enjoyed working on?*

As far as *Sandman* goes, I really enjoyed the *Worlds' End* storyline. I think part of it was I had just gotten a new separator for my color guide work, and it just looked a lot neater. The colors matched my color guides more. Not just that, I enjoyed the story and the artwork a lot. We had a few different artists on that: Mike Allred, Dick Giordano, Bryan Talbot, and Michael Zulli…just some of my favorite artists all wrapped up in that one storyline. As far as other stuff goes, I always enjoy working on something that has Neil's characters in it, even if he didn't write it, like Bill Willingham's *Thessaly*. That was a limited series that I enjoyed very much. And I really love *Fables*, one of the current titles I'm working on now, which is also written by Bill Willingham. The writing to me is fantastic, as it was in *Sandman*. Even though I'm doing the coloring, I enjoy the writing, and it makes it much more fun to work on the book.

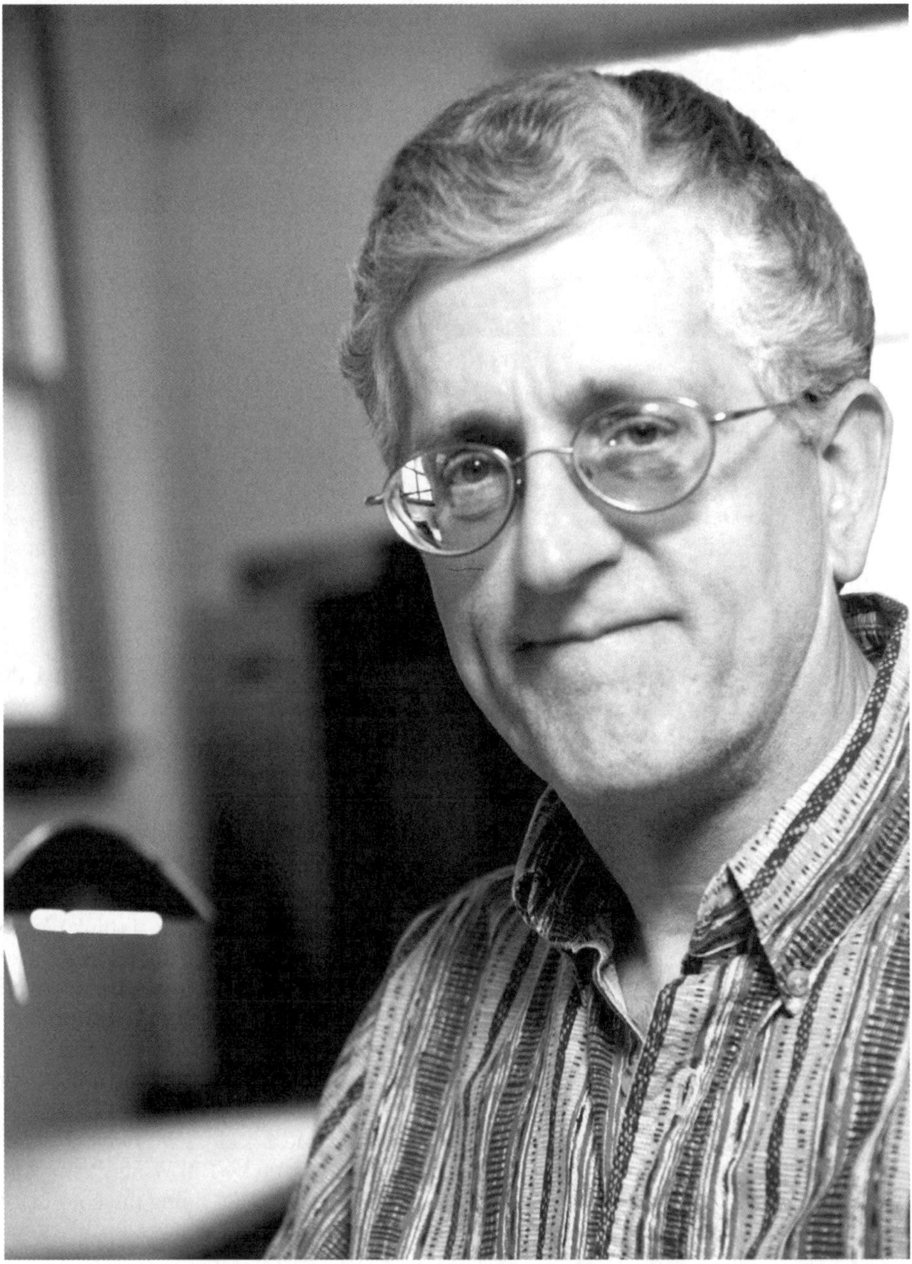

*Todd Klein*

## TODD KLEIN LETTERED ALMOST EVERY ISSUE OF *SANDMAN*

– AS WELL AS *BLACK ORCHID*, *BOOKS OF MAGIC*, BOTH *DEATH* MINI-SERIES, *ENDLESS NIGHTS*, AND *1602*. NO INDIVIDUAL (WITH THE POSSIBLE EXCEPTION OF DAVE MCKEAN) HAS WORKED WITH GAIMAN ON SO MANY COMIC BOOKS.

KLEIN BEGAN HIS CAREER DOING ILLUSTRATIONS FOR SCIENCE-FICTION, FANTASY, AND COMICS FANZINES, BEFORE JOINING THE DC PRODUCTION STAFF IN 1977, WHERE HE WORKED FOR TEN YEARS BEFORE GOING FREELANCE FULL-TIME. ALTHOUGH HE'S HELD VARIOUS POSITIONS OF COMICS PRODUCTION – INKING, COLORING, AND, IN THE CASE OF *OMEGA MEN*, WRITING – THE VAST MAJORITY OF HIS WORK HAS BEEN LETTERING, FOR WHICH HE HAS RECEIVED, TO DATE, ELEVEN EISNER AWARDS, MORE THAN ANY OTHER *SANDMAN* COLLABORATOR.

IN ADDITION TO HIS WORK WITH GAIMAN, KLEIN HAS LETTERED NUMEROUS OTHER BOOKS; INCLUDING ALAN MOORE'S AMERICA'S BEST COMICS LINE, FOR WHICH HE PROVIDED COVER DESIGNS AND CONTINUED HAND-LETTERING *TOM STRONG* AND *PROMETHEA* LONG AFTER MOST MAINSTREAM COMICS HAD SWITCHED TO COMPUTER LETTERING. KLEIN CURRENTLY LETTERS APPROXIMATELY SEVEN MONTHLY COMIC BOOKS.

*As a letterer, you must have derived a certain amount of satisfaction from working on a set of characters – Sandman's Endless – who are so strongly identified by the lettering of their speech. This seems to be somewhat unique in recent comics.*

It's something that's gradually developed over the years. You can certainly find precedence. If you look at the comic strips... *Pogo* is a great example – and that came out in the '50s – of using different styles for different characters. *The Spirit* is another one that used that technique pretty often, not as much as *Pogo*. In comics, the first time I really remember noticing it was on the original *Swamp Thing*, which was lettered by Gaspar Saladino in the early '70s, and he had a very distinctive style for *Swamp Thing*. It's gradually developed since then. You have to be careful not to overdo it – first of all, because it becomes hard to read if there's too many different styles. And also, it isn't really called for. You don't want to do it for the sake of doing it. There has to be a good reason.

When Neil and I started working on *Sandman*, he was gradually coming up with these requests to do different styles. I thought, the way it was written, it worked well, and I was happy to do that. It wasn't until we hit *Season of Mists* that it really started becoming quite elaborate, where he was bringing in all these different gods and characters from other mythologies, and wanted each of them to have a different style. That's where we looked at the situation and said, "Do we really want to do this?" And we decided "Well, let's do it as long as it makes sense and as long as it doesn't interfere with the reading of the story." I think, over the years of *Sandman*, I counted close to fifty different styles that we used altogether. I think *Season of Mists* had the most in any one storyline, but there were other stories that had quite a few also. And then, of course, once you've established something for a character, you have to go back to it every time that character reappears. This can be a problem sometimes, because there were cases where Neil would write a character with a note saying, "Let's do something exotic, like curlicues." I would say, "Well, that's fine, but how often are we going to see this character, because it's going to take me a lot of time and I don't want to spend an extra hour per page. Is this going to be a regular character?" And he would say, "Oh, don't worry, this is just a one-time appearance." Of course, two issues later, the character would be back. [*Laughs.*] So at times, it was kind of a problem, but we got through it all and it worked out well. And there were other cases where we needed a particular historical reference, like the Shakespeare issue, the final issue [issue 75, "The Tempest"]; where I did a lot of research to get something that would be an approximation of what Shakespeare's handwriting might have looked like. You do have to keep it appropriate, but sometimes little things like that can really add to the storyline, I think, as far as the style or the font used.

*How much input does Neil give, as far as the different lettering styles go? In the case of Desire's speech, I believe it was your decision to use an art nouveau poster style.*

That was the character design, and the art to me suggested art nouveau. But I had to do something I could letter consistently without too much difficulty. Real art nouveau lettering is not designed to be hand lettered, so I had to come up with some kind of a compromise that would work. I don't really know where that came from particularly. It just looked right. It was one of those things where it looked right to me and I showed it to Neil and he was happy with it. For the most part, he would just give me general ideas of what he wanted. He would specify a style and just say, "Let's do something like this," or "Here's a direction to go in," more than specifying exactly what he wanted.

*Some of the other lettering styles for the Endless included Destiny's, whose speech was rendered in italics, and Destruction's heavy lettering, with heavy black border.*

That was just meant to give the impression that he spoke loudly, and to differentiate him from the others a little bit. In the *Season of Mists* storyline, where all the Endless were first talking to each other consistently [the Prologue, issue 21], I just felt it made more sense to do something a little different with each of them, so that when they had crowd scenes you didn't get them easily confused. It was just a technique to make it easier to tell one apart from the other.

*The lettering of Delirium's speech in* Endless Nights – *in Dream's story ["The Heart of a Star"], in which she was still actually Delight – although it changes, as it usually does, in size and shape, featured a lesser degree of wobbling and slant.*

That was something Neil suggested. He wanted it to be not as full-blown in its effect. So I tried to come up with something that was half-way between normal lettering and the full-blown Delirium style for Delight. And I showed samples to Neil. I think I had a couple of different ideas about it, and he picked the one he liked the best. Delirium is one character whose normal style I can't do on the computer, and a lot of those stories were done on the computer. For the Delirium story ["Going Inside"], I actually did her lettering by hand, and then scanned it and combined it with the other computer-lettered stuff. So it all worked together, but it took a lot more time than usual because of that.

*The first unique lettering style to surface in* Sandman *was Dream's. Was it your idea to have the white lettering on the black background?*

No, actually I was against that. That was a production effect. I lettered it normally and a negative copy was made in DC's production department, and pasted on top. I did letter it with a heavier pen because I knew they were going to do that, so I thought that would give it a better chance of reproducing. But I still felt that with the variation in reproduction and with the variation in the darkness of the letters the way they were copied, I felt it would be hard to read in places, and it was, actually. But Karen really liked that idea and she really wanted to go with it, so they did it. Of course, now I can do it myself on the computer and get a more consistent look, because I can control how wide the letters are. Before, when they were making photographic copies, it depended upon the exposure. If they overexposed it, the letters were too thin. If they underexposed it, they were too wide and kind of ran together. If you look through the collections, you'll see cases of that.

*One of the most interesting lettering styles you developed was for Mathew, the raven, with the lines of the letters overlapping and creating the image of scattered sticks.*

Exactly. That's what I was going for – you drop a bunch of pick-up sticks on the ground and it spells out some letters. That's the effect I was going for. And Mathew's a raven, who has a kind of rough, scratchy voice, so that was a part of it. Also, I just felt it gave it an untidy look that matched his character, an untidy approach to life, I think.

*What was Neil's input in this case? Did he say something like, "Have him speak in a scratchy manner"?*

I couldn't say for sure, but that's probably what happened. I don't remember exactly what Neil asked for, but I know he asked for something. One thing that he did ask for – on "A Dream of a Thousand Cats" [issue 18], he wanted to come up with a concept where we wouldn't have the animals actually speaking. So we came up with a combination of a thought balloon and a speech balloon, so it would have some aspects of both. We used that in a few other places as well. That was Neil's concept.

*One of the other specific styles you came up with was for Barnabus, the dog.*

Yes, his upper and lower-case style, I just thought, fit his personality for some reason. It's kind of a rounded, maybe slightly childish style that I thought worked for him. He has a typical dog character that suggested that to me. [*Laughs.*]

*How much input do you have in the coloring behind the lettering?*

I think, in a few cases, if I had something specific in mind, I would write a note on the edge of the page for the colorist, and hopefully they saw it and paid attention to it. Sometimes they didn't, but, nowadays, if I'm lettering on the computer, I actually color the lettering myself. Sometimes they change it if they don't like it, but at least there's something there that I had in mind. For instance, for Delirium, all the lettering in *Endless Nights* I colored myself, though of course in the original series it was done by Danny Vozzo.

*You lettered every one of the* Sandman *stories with three minor exceptions: two issues of* The Doll's House *[11 and 12] and Kevin Nowlan's eight-pager in* Vertigo Jam *1. Any particular reason for skipping these?*

Well, I missed some time on those two *Doll House* stories because I was getting married and on my honeymoon. However, I had lettered about half of the first of those issues, and then they had John Costanza re-do what I had done to make it consistent, which I understood. But little bits of my lettering are in there, like the title and some of the captions. That's why that happened. And the other one – Kevin Nowlan is a fine letterer and I think he really just prefers to do his own lettering and I have no problem with that. I think he's great.

*Neil has called you "possibly the best letterer in the business." What, in your opinion, constitutes good lettering?*

I think lettering should enhance the story, and not distract from the reading of the story. So anything that I can do to help the story, make it better, is what I try to do. If that involves just being very bland and quiet and staying out of the way, then that's what I'll do. And if I can find a place to enhance the story by being more noticeable, by coming up with a style or something emphatic that really stands out, then I'll do that. But it all has to go back to telling the story best.

*How does one become a letterer? What led you to this vocation?*

I always liked comics, first of all. I had gone to art school for two years, and then I had been doing some non-art jobs. And then I decided that I really wanted to try to get into comics. So, I put together a portfolio of samples, and I came to New York, and I had two appointments – one was at Marvel, and one was at DC. The Marvel appointment was a job opening for an art director, and I wasn't really qualified for that, so that was a no-brainer. They just said "No," basically. The DC appointment was to show samples to the art director, Vince Colletta. He basically said I didn't have what it took to be a comics artist at that point, but there were some mechanicals that I had done (which is kind of a technical term for layouts, putting things together on a page) for an air-conditioning company that I was working for at the time. He thought DC's production manager might be interested in seeing that. So he brought me in to see Jack Adler. who was the production manager at the time. I showed him my samples and he said, "Well, I think what you're doing here shows some promise, and I have an opening for two weeks coming up, where one of my people are going to be away. I could use some extra help – would you like to come in for two weeks?" I said, "Sure." I took my vacation from my other job and did that for two weeks. At the end of that time, the person I had been filling in for decided to leave, so they offered me the job as a staff production person, full-time, which I took.

Now, one of the jobs at that time in production was doing lettering corrections, and fixing other people's mistakes on covers and story pages. And also on staff was John Workman, who was a letterer at the time. He kind of got me started with lettering and showed me some basic techniques. Then, in studying the work in-hand, I picked up more things as I went along. Eventually, in a couple months, I was able to get some freelance work. But that was a part-time job, doing it in the evenings. There were a number of jobs that could've resulted from production work – a number of colorists were there; there were people doing inking and other kinds of artwork on occasion – but the lettering just appealed to me the most, of all the jobs available. That was how I got into the lettering end of it. I was always interested in lettering anyway. I had a grandfather who was a sign painter, who had got me started with some basic alphabets and showed me some things. I was also very interested in Tolkien's alphabets in *The Lord of the Rings*, and I used to imitate those and kind of make up my own alphabets from that. Those are some things I was interested in previously, which led me in that direction.

*You've worked extensively with both Neil and Alan Moore – how does their approach differ in terms of their involvement with the lettering?*

Alan is very much open to any ideas or suggestions by anybody he works with. He has a very definite idea of what he has in mind; and he gives you lots of information in the script – sometimes more than anybody could possibly process. [*Laughs.*] But he always adds, as a coda to anything that he writes, "Please, if you think of something better, or if you think of a different way to do it that works for you, just go with it." He wants you to contribute your creative ideas. Now, I think Neil pretty much learned comics writing from studying Alan's work. Neil was also a lot like that. In the early days on *Sandman*, Neil and I would talk on the phone or occasionally correspond by mail. He would ask me if I had lettering style ideas to contribute, or if I had any thoughts on what was going on, things like that. It was very helpful for me to have that chance to interact with him, and listen to my input. A lot of times, I didn't have a whole lot to add because what he was doing was, I thought, just fine. And what he was asking for went right along with what I had in mind to begin with. Neil, more than any other writer I've worked with, writes the kind of stories I'd write if I could. Still, it was nice to have that interaction and talk about the process with him. Alan and I don't really talk about the work that much, unless there's something he wants that I don't understand, or can't do. He throws out all these ideas and lets you come up with whatever you think works, and he's usually happy with whatever you decide. I can't recall a case where Alan just outright objected to or rejected anything that I did, whereas with Neil, he wants to see what you're doing and usually has an opinion on it. We're mostly in sync, but once in a while, he'll ask for changes or suggest a different direction.

*Outside of Neil's stuff, what has been your most ambitious project? Would* Promethea *be up there?*

Yes, *Promethea* is probably right up there with *Sandman*. They're both very challenging and offer lots of things for me to sink my teeth into creatively. I don't know if you saw the issue with the two-page spread that was all lettering in *Promethea*. (I think it was issue 23.) That took me about two weeks to do – the entire spread is all lettering; it's all different languages, all different styles. It's like a graduate course in hand-lettering, essentially. [*Laughs.*] I had to do the research myself, to find all the translations, and characters, and styles. But it was a lot of fun, too.

*Do you ever ask if your page rate could be bumped up a little bit for jobs like that?* [*Laughs.*]

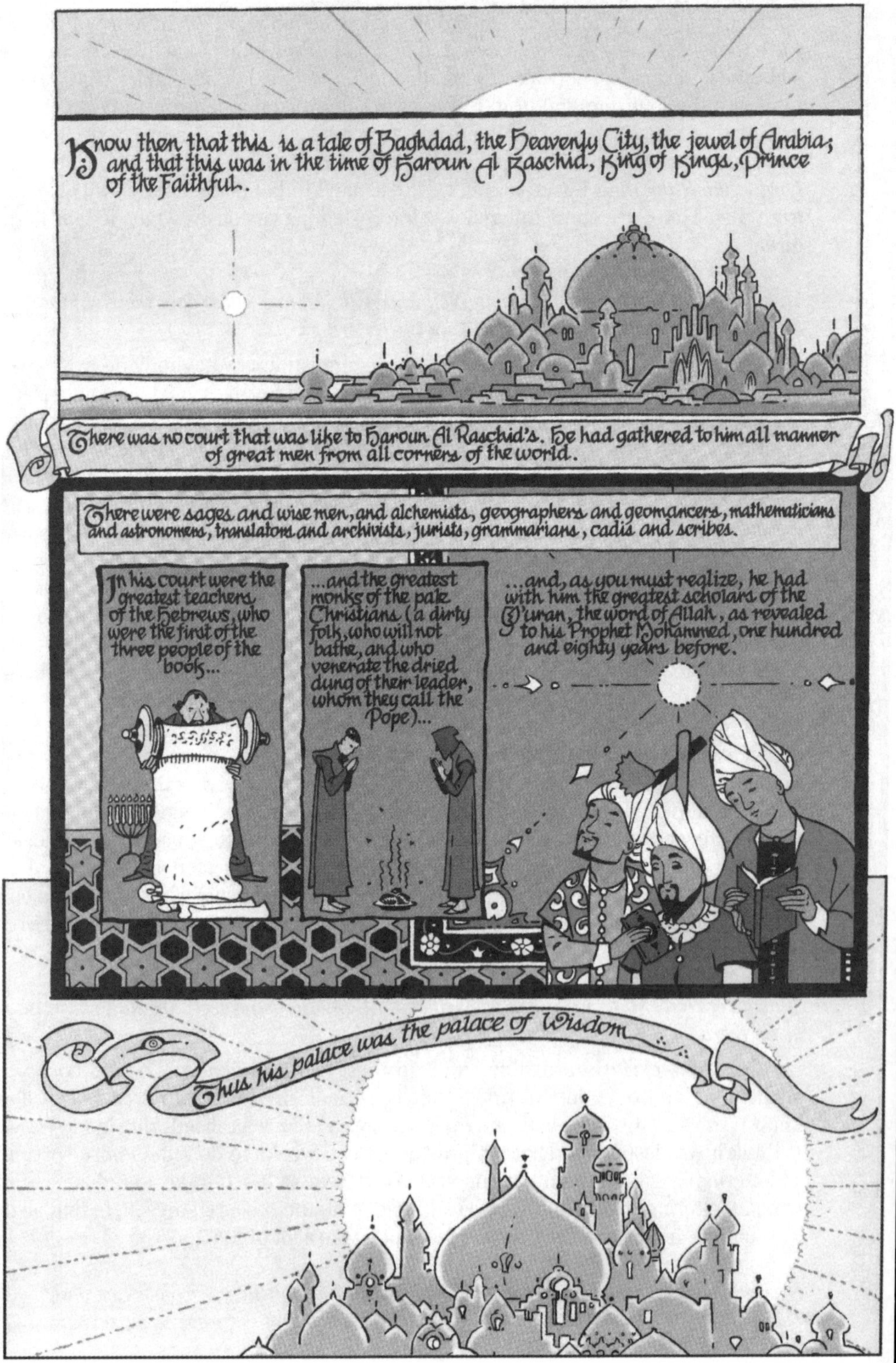
Know then that this is a tale of Baghdad, the Heavenly City, the jewel of Arabia; and that this was in the time of Haroun Al Raschid, King of Kings, Prince of the Faithful.
There was no court that was like to Haroun Al Raschid's. He had gathered to him all manner of great men from all corners of the world.
There were sages and wise men, and alchemists, geographers and geomancers, mathematicians and astronomers, translators and archivists, jurists, grammarians, cadis and scribes.
In his court were the greatest teachers of the Hebrews, who were the first of the three people of the book...
...and the greatest monks of the pale Christians (a dirty folk, who will not bathe, and who venerate the dried dung of their leader, whom they call the Pope)...
...and, as you must realize, he had with him the greatest scholars of the Q'uran, the word of Allah, as revealed to his Prophet Mohammed, one hundred and eighty years before.
Thus his palace was the palace of Wisdom

Todd Klein's lettering takes center stage... Page 2 of *Sandman* 50, "Ramadan." Pencils and inks by P. Craig Russell. © 2004 DC Comics.

It tends to even out in the long run. *Sandman*, in some cases, took me a lot longer than the average job, but then I would get another job that was very easy, and that would even it out. With Alan's work, *Promethea* is the most challenging, but then some of his other work was fairly easy, so it all evens out in the long run. I think the only time I ever got an extra rate was on *Sandman* 50 ["Ramadan"], and that wasn't my idea. That was Karen's idea because it was done with a calligraphic style that did take me quite a bit longer than usual. And when she saw it she thought I deserved some extra money for that.

*Was that the most challenging* Sandman *story for you?*

I'd say the final Shakespeare issue was the most challenging. Issue 50 was really a lot of fun, since Craig Russell had essentially laid out all the lettering for me. I knew exactly where everything was going to go. In fact, I was working over inked pages in some cases, where he had actually inked in the balloon borders. But he had penciled in all of the lettering first, so I knew exactly how to fit it in. As far as the style, once I came up with the idea, it was fairly straightforward to do it, just a matter of being consistent. The idea was to do something that looked kind of exotic, and slightly oriental. I don't know where it came from, but it just came to me, and once I had it I went with it.

*It seems that out of all the individuals who work on a monthly book the letterer and the colorist usually receive the least amount of attention. Do you ever get frustrated with this situation?*

No. I think that, from going to conventions and talking to people, I've decided that maybe ten percent of the people who read comics actually pay attention to who does what, and would know anything about who the letterer and various other people on the book are. That's not so bad, really. I think it's probably true in many other areas as well – if you go to a movie, how many sound designers' names do you know? Or set decorators'? I've always felt that the people whose attention I appreciated the most were the people I worked with. As long as they were appreciative of what I did, and paid attention to it, I was well compensated, as long as I was being paid as well. I have gotten quite a bit of attention over the years myself, I think, probably more than I deserve. I do get my name on the cover of the Alan Moore books I letter, and I have gotten cover credits on a few other projects over the years, and I've won lots of awards. I really can't complain. It's kind of nice in a way to walk around San Diego and say hello to an occasional fan, rather than being mobbed like Neil gets mobbed when he goes to a convention. It's kind of a double-edged sword there. [*Laughs.*] If you want the attention, you have to be ready to deal with it.

OTHER FANCIES

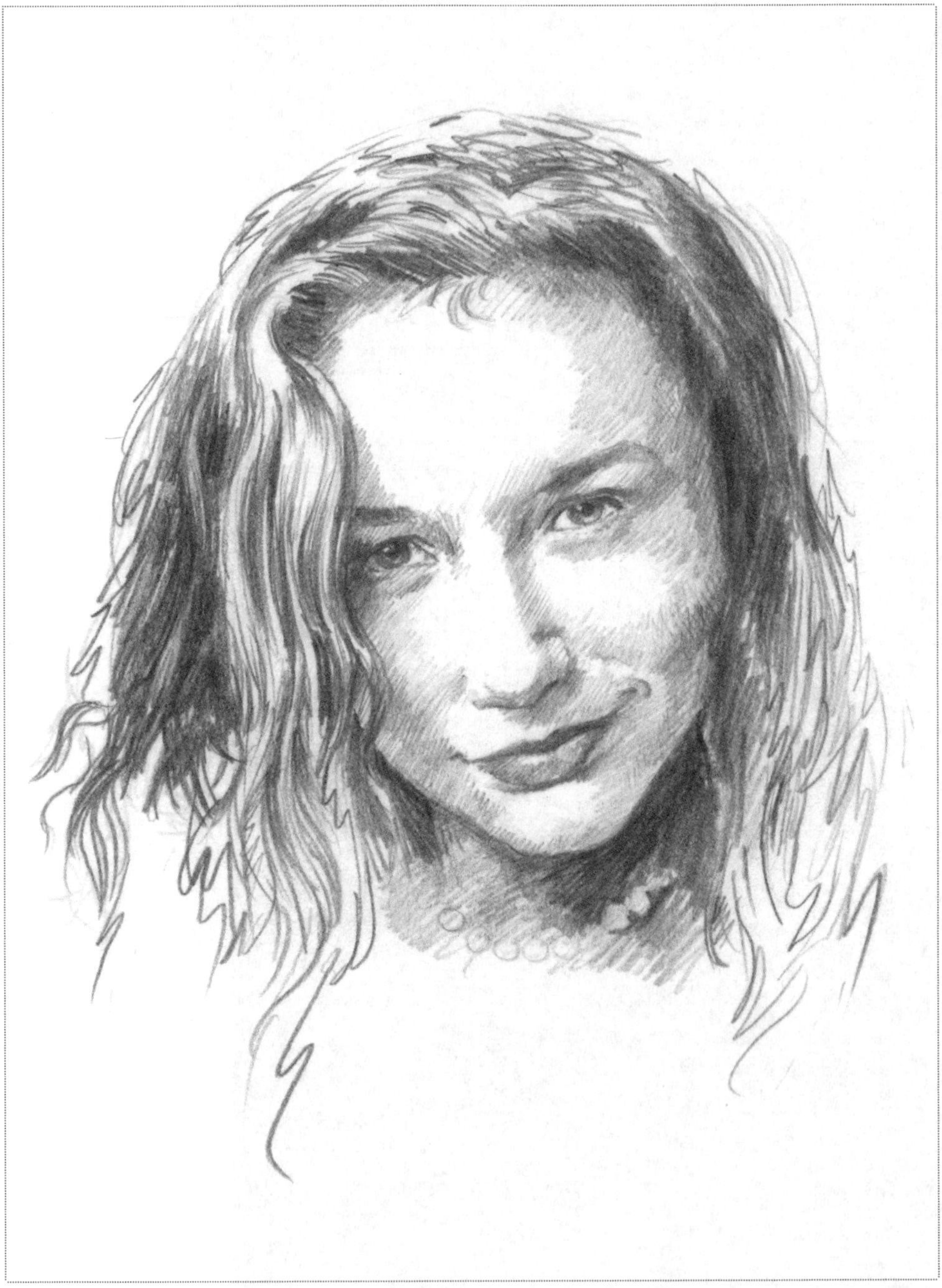

*Tori Amos*

---

# AS A MULTI-PLATINUM RECORDING ARTIST, TORI AMOS
IS ONE OF THE FEW INDIVIDUALS INTERVIEWED FOR THIS BOOK FOR WHOM THE GENERAL
READER MAY REQUIRE NO INTRODUCTION.

ALTHOUGH SHE HAILS FROM NORTH CAROLINA, AMOS FIRST MADE HER MARK IN THE
U.K. (WHERE SHE BRIEFLY RESIDED IN THE EARLY '90S) WITH HER BREAKTHROUGH
ALBUM, 1991'S LITTLE EARTHQUAKES. ONE OF THE ALBUM'S SONGS, "TEAR IN
YOUR HAND," CONTAINED A LINE ANNOUNCING TO THE WORLD, AND GAIMAN HIMSELF,
AMOS'S FONDNESS FOR THE WRITER'S WORK.

LITTLE EARTHQUAKES (RELEASED IN THE U.S. THE FOLLOWING YEAR BY ATLANTIC
RECORDS) WAS FOLLOWED BY 1994'S UNDER THE PINK, 1996'S BOYS FOR PELE,
AND 1998'S FROM THE CHOIRGIRL HOTEL; EACH A HIT AND EACH WITH ITS OWN
TRIBUTE TO GAIMAN, WHOM AMOS HAD BEFRIENDED SINCE LITTLE EARTHQUAKES.
THOUGH THEY'D CONTINUED TO TRADE "WINKS" AT EACH OTHER IN THEIR WORK, IT
WAS NOT UNTIL 2001'S STRANGE LITTLE GIRLS [ATLANTIC], THAT THE TWO, IN A
SENSE, COLLABORATED – WITH GAIMAN ASSISTING IN THE ALBUM'S DEVELOPMENT,
AND PROVIDING DESCRIPTIONS (IN ITS CD BOOKLET) AND SHORT PROSE PIECES (IN THE
ACCOMPANYING TOUR BOOK) FOR EACH OF THE "GIRLS" FEATURED IN ITS SONGS.

ON HER MOST RECENT ALBUM, 2002'S SCARLET'S WALK, AMOS EXPLORED AMERICA
THE SAME YEAR GAIMAN TOOK A SIMILAR JOURNEY WITH HIS NOVEL AMERICAN GODS.

---

*You and Neil have traded "winks" at each other for some time now, starting with your
line (from "Tear in Your Hand"), "If you need me, me and Neil'll be hangin' out with
the Dream King." Yet at the time you wrote this line, you had not yet met Neil. What
was it about his writing that first earned your admiration? Is it different from that
which you enjoy in his recent work?*

Because Neil's work is steeped in mythology it pulled me in immediately, being a
mythology buff myself. After we met and realized that, very simply, we held a spiritual
brother and sister archetype, he would pop in and see me in the oddest places. I would
get sent stories to read even in the down under of Down Under. He would find me
somewhere in Australia – I can't even pronounce its name. My spiritual brother would
send me stories. I would pop in and see him just to have a coffee and wave to Odin
and Freya before jumping on a plane to make a concert. Because our background,

our training, comes from studying archetypes and mythology, our whole relationship is about reading between the lines and pushing each other to be great. Good is not good enough.

*Neil wrote stories for each of the characters in the songs from* Strange Little Girls. *And these stories were featured in the [*Strange Days *2001 Tour Book]. I assume the photos of each character came before Neil's stories, but did you and Neil discuss these characters at length before he wrote these tales? How closely did Neil's interpretations of these characters match yours?*

Neil came to see Tash when she was just a couple months old. Mark, Neil, Tash and I sat in the beach house as the winds were howling outside and began building the foundation of what became *Strange Little Girls.* That I had men involved from the beginning as my think tank was imperative for this concept to work. You see, crawling behind men's eyes and finding out what made them say what they say, think what they think, judge how they judge, and discover how they feel about women, was my fascination. But I could not invade them so I pulled together a team of men who let me interview them, find out the male muses that most represented how they felt and then I chose to become the anima; the female essence in the male songs. Neil, Mark, Marcel and Johnny were right there challenging me all the way. Because Neil was a core part of my think tank, he was right there when I went to the next level which became developing the visual characters. The late, great Kevyn Aucoin, was a major part of the visual development of these women. Karen Binns, who I've worked with since the beginning, was there developing the women with me – coming from a woman's point of view, how they would appear. Then of course, Neil wrote the stories after hearing my perception with my team.

*Do you have a particular favorite of Neil's stories for* Strange Little Girls? *Does it match your favorite of the girls?*

Death is my favorite. The woman that sings "Time," we saw her as Death. When we created the persona of Death and I stepped into her she was the most calm of all the girls. I truly loved being Death. I felt extremely relaxed and more complete than any of the other women.

*One of your b-sides, "Sister Named Desire," refers to Desire, Delirium's older sibling. And Neil has said that he, in part, based Delirium on you (though he wrote, in his introduction to your* Pink Tour Book, *that you have "a little delirium, a lot of delight"). Were you consciously writing part of this song from Delirium's perspective? The line "Got a sister named Desire... Teach me about them old worlds big brother" – is this "big brother" Dream? Or is it Destruction, Delirium's other older brother?*

I'm obviously not going to commit to that because that would take away so much from so many who need to be able to choose. I was aware that Delirium/Delight had a sister named Desire so when I wrote this was I writing as Tori or as Delirium? A bit of both.

*You seem to share Neil's outsider perspective of America. Your* Scarlet's Walk *was released not long after Neil's novel* American Gods, *and both of these works feature an individual's journey across America's heartland and a self-discovery of sorts. And Neil wrote a story inspired by* Scarlet's Walk *("Pages from a Journal Found in a Shoebox*

*Left in a Greyhound Bus Somewhere Between Tulsa, Oklahoma, and Louisville, Kentucky"), which was featured in the album's tour book. In what way did you and Neil influence each other while writing these works? You both, in a sense, began your careers in London – what other parallels exist in your evolution as storytellers?*

Well, I think we both are quite clear on the fact that if you don't know the ancient myths then you don't really have a wealth of character development to pull from. All the great storytellers knew their myths like children know their ABC's. That it isn't taught in the schools makes me wonder why they don't want the masses to know these myths. The reason is there is great power in these stories. There is almost a map on how to develop your spiritual self. By understanding your spiritual archetype you can step into the one that you relate to and you can begin to understand the consequences of their actions. There seems to be universal law built into these myths. The Christian law is also integrated – all the religions, all the cultures. This is something Neil knows like the back of his hand. If there is something I don't know I call him up and vice versa.

*You've thanked "the Faeries" in your album credits, and Neil has remarked, again in his introduction to your* Pink Tour Book, *that there's "fairy blood" in you. Are there fantasy writers other than Neil whose work you enjoy?*

If you really go back to historical references, to the Ring Lords, the church, about a thousand years ago, basically changed the stories that came down from the Tuatha de Danann, diminishing the great cultures into miniaturized versions of themselves. So when I speak of the fairy faith, I'm referring to some of those powerful beings that are in Irish and Welsh mythology and so on.

*Your own music has evolved in various ways since the days of* Little Earthquakes. *I assume your tastes have also changed – what is it about Neil's work that continues to hold your interest?*

I think Neil is always striving as a writer to excavate the human psyche in the masses and in himself, in men as well as women and, more recently, in children (with his children's books). He makes magic carpet rides tied together with words that take us to worlds we would never go to – Neil's worlds. He is channeling them from old storytellers that sat around fires thousands of years ago. They are whispering in his ear and he is listening.

Alice Cooper as the Showman, from page 15 of *The Last Temptation*, Book Two. Art by Michael Zulli.
*The Last Temptation* © 2004 Nightmare, Inc. and Neil Gaiman. Illustration © 2004 Michael Zulli.

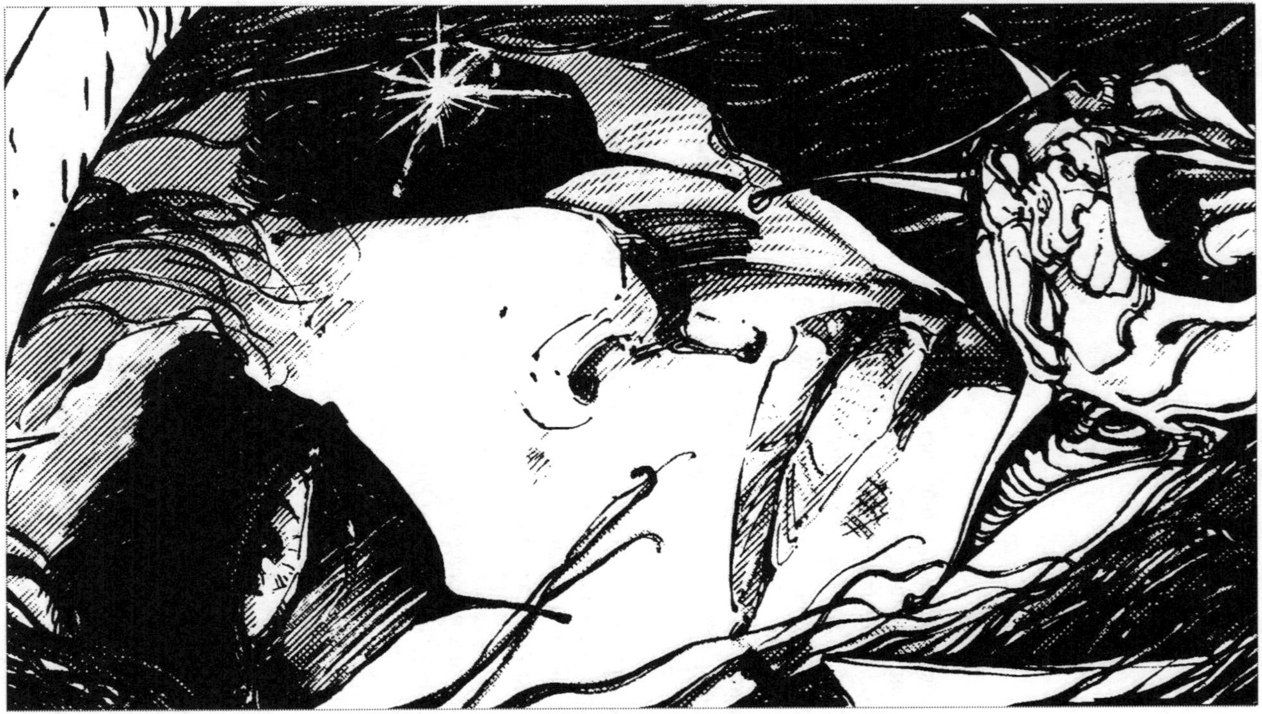

*Alice Cooper*

---

# A TRUE ROCK 'N' ROLL ICON, ALICE COOPER BEGAN HIS CAREER

AS VINCENT FURNIER IN THE ARIZONA-BASED ALICE COOPER BAND. AFTER MOVING TO DETROIT, THE BAND ENJOYED SUCCESS WITH A STRING OF HIT ALBUMS – AND TEEN ANTHEMS LIKE "I'M EIGHTEEN" AND "SCHOOL'S OUT" – BEFORE SPLITTING UP IN 1974. COOPER, HIS NAME NOW LEGALLY CHANGED, CONTINUED AS A SOLO ARTIST, CRAFTING CLASSIC ALBUMS LIKE *WELCOME TO MY NIGHTMARE*.

COOPER IS A LIFELONG FAN OF THE HORROR GENRE, WHICH HE USED TO PIONEER THE MEDIUM OF SHOCK ROCK (BLAZING A TRAIL LATER FOLLOWED BY SUCH ARTISTS AS KISS, THE SEX PISTOLS, AND MARILYN MANSON). AND IT WAS GAIMAN'S USE OF THE MACABRE THAT PROMPTED COOPER'S INVITATION TO COLLABORATE ON HIS 1994 ALBUM *THE LAST TEMPTATION* [EPIC RECORDS], FOR WHICH GAIMAN CO-DEVELOPED A STORYLINE AND SCRIPTED A THREE-ISSUE COMIC-BOOK SERIES. (ORIGINALLY PUBLISHED BY MARVEL AS PART OF THEIR LATE MARVEL MUSIC LINE, IT WAS COLLECTED IN 1995 AS *THE COMPLEAT ALICE THE LAST TEMPTATION*, AND IS CURRENTLY AVAILABLE IN A DARK HORSE EDITION.)

AFTER MORE THAN TWENTY-FIVE ALBUMS, AND A CAREER SPANNING FIVE DECADES, COOPER CONTINUES TO RECORD AND TOUR. HIS LATEST ALBUM IS *THE EYES OF ALICE COOPER*.

---

*How did* The Last Temptation *develop? What informed your conception of it?*

I wanted to make a point on a story. I think every story ends up with at least one point, one thing to take with you. And on this one, it was sort of... I wanted to use a device that was a little bit like *Something Wicked This Way Comes*, and also kind of connect that in with the temptation of Christ. It was sort of like a kid that was being tempted with everything. He was going to be given everything. All he had to do was join the circus. Which was sort of a parallel to "Just buy in to everything that the world has to sell you." And so any kid would. A chance to be in the circus, a chance to get away from your old life – "This is going to really be exciting." Except for the fact that everything around him is decaying. Everything in the circus is decaying. And in the end, the kid doesn't buy into it. It just drives the Showman crazy because he can't understand why the kid wouldn't buy in. So it's sort of celebrating the fact that the kid made the right choice.

When I explained that to Neil, I think that we were both pretty much thinking the same thing. Then it was just a matter of letting Neil go with the details. Musically, as soon as we started talking – I think sometimes in talking with somebody, another writer, you're picking up song ideas. I was writing songs while we were talking, at least titles and ideas for songs. But they all work together. I can't tell you if it's the chicken or the egg...it's one of those things where an idea starts up and everything starts being written from there.

The Last Temptation *featured the character of Stephen, who was introduced in your earlier album* Welcome to My Nightmare. *Is it safe to assume this character is somewhat autobiographical?*

I use Stephen as an everyboy. Stephen is every kid. Stephen is sort of my code word for "This could happen to you or anybody." So Stephen is just that little boy inside everybody. And we all have gone through these experiences. In the *Nightmare* show, Stephen was any little kid who's ever had a nightmare. I never really was specific about that. I'm Stephen sometimes, you're Stephen sometimes – everybody. Whoever relates to that nightmare, or whoever relates to that situation is going to be Stephen. This little kid of course was Stephen. He was the "every little kid."

*[In his foreword to the collected* The Last Temptation*] Neil remarked that, when he got a call from Bob Pfeifer at Epic Records inviting him to participate, he was told you were a fan of his work. How did you first discover Neil's work?*

Like anybody else. I think that one of the first ways that I was introduced to him was the fact that my son collects *Star Wars*. We had been collecting for about ten years. So every time you buy a *Star Wars* character, you're either in a comic-book house or you're at a sci-fi convention. I kept seeing Neil's name pop up. I finally picked up a couple of the comic books, and that's really when Bob Pfeifer came in and said, "I know this guy named Neil Gaiman," and I said, "Oh yeah, I know who he is."

And, of course, Neil kind of invented his own lifestyle there with the whole being-up-all-night-and-sleeping-all-day – he's got that vampire mentality. But a very funny guy. We can sit and talk and connect on a lot of different levels. I think we have a similar sense of humor. So I always find something funny in the macabre myself. If I can't find something humorous in it, then it's probably something I don't want to know about.

*Neil also mentioned in that foreword that you know "more about bad Italian horror movies than anyone who doesn't write books about them for a living."*

*[Laughs.]* I became a bit of a horror/sci-fi aficionado. Because I think, for one thing, I am very low-tech. A pad of yellow paper and a pen is about as high-tech as I go. Everybody I work with is on Pro Tools. I'm the only one I know who just walks in with a pad of paper and a pen. To me, I just get better ideas that way. I get lost in the buttons a lot of times. I think Neil's a little bit like that, too. I think he would rather have a pad and a pen than a whole studio full of gadgets.

*Neil wrote that you both agreed that, for a teenager, reality is the most terrifying thing of all. And he wrote that while you liked some of his ideas, you weren't "as keen on others." Were there any of his ideas that you didn't feel quite worked for the project?*

No. I was very, very happy with the project. I think he just went through the lyrics a lot and understood the lyrics. Being a writer, and him being a writer, we work in words more than anything else. So I would write a song, call him up and tell him what the song was about, and then he would take it from there, and then exaggerate it from there. The great thing about the collaboration was the fact that I *totally* let Neil Gaiman be Neil Gaiman. And he lets Alice Cooper be Alice Cooper. When I gave him the lyrics, and gave him the songs, and gave him this and that, and then the idea – I could walk away and not talk to him for a month, knowing that it's in good hands. If he would've come back and it would've been a totally distorted story, I would've said, "This isn't what we were going for." But as soon as I got it, I said, "Oh yeah." If anybody on this planet got the idea, it was him. He embellished on it in places where I wouldn't have, that I appreciated, which is great. I think that he didn't come in from the left wing–and I'm not necessarily right wing – but the whole idea on this thing was, "Does morality win?" And, in this case, maybe morality not winning would have sold more copies, but morality winning, to me, was the point.

*Originally you asked Neil for a short story. At what point in the project's evolution did you realize you wanted a comic as well?*

I think we were all kind of thinking, "Wouldn't it be great if...?" I try to write all my material so that it can be a movie, a comic. I'm very, very story oriented. When I write songs, very rarely do I write a song that's just kind of an ambiguous bunch of lyrics that make you go, "Oh, well, that's an idea..." I always try to develop characters. That's why I like working in concepts. "A nightmare – okay, we need characters for this nightmare. Who is this guy? Why is he this?" To me, character-driven stories are really important. That's just the way I write. I think when you hear an Alice Cooper song, you should be picturing these people. It's very much like writing short stories. Almost every one of my songs is just a short story, and then all those short stories should add up into one big story. I think that's what comics are like, too.

*How did you like [Michael Zulli's] artwork in the comic?*

The artwork was incredible. In fact, I was just yesterday in the Beverly Center mall here, and I happened to walk into a store. This place called Traffic. And this guy goes running back, and brings out the three-set version, with all three comic books in one. He just happened to have it there. [*Laughs.*] And I signed it, and everything like that, the whole thing. It's just amazing to me how many people that are comic-book collectors, after the fact, went out and bought the comic books. I looked at the artwork – I hadn't seen it in a long time – and I said, "It's really good." I've always admired guys that can do that. I was an artist when I was a kid, in high school and college – that was my major – and I never was good enough to be a comic-book artist. I always really liked comic-book artists, because I thought they were *really* good artists.

*This wasn't your first foray into comics. Back in 1979, Marvel Comics published an Alice Cooper comic book [Marvel Premiere 50, "Tales From the Inside"] based on your album* From The Inside. *How satisfied were you with that book? How involved were you with it?*

Well, first of all, if you're in this business, and you've done just about everything, and you've gotten pretty much all the awards, you start figuring, "What's left?" Being a Marvel comic hero? That's like having a *Pez dispenser.* I always tell people the great thing about being a Marvel comic character is that you get great abs. They draw you with great abs and good shoulders. They really give you good features and everything like that, so I was very impressed with myself. [*Laughs.*] It's great that Stan Lee was another guy that sort of got the concept, and had fun with it.

I always created Alice Cooper to be a character you could have fun with. He's an American icon – and not me, the *character* is. The character's an American icon, and he's also like Zorro, or Dr. Jekyll and Mr. Hyde. Those are characters that anybody can write about. I've always said that twenty years from now, there's no reason why somebody shouldn't pick up the Alice costume and become Alice Cooper – because he's an American character – [and] do their own version of Alice Cooper.

*That's sort of a unique concept in [contemporary] music.*

Yeah. I've always looked at it... I want Alice to be owned by the public. I don't really want to own Alice. I would like Alice to be part of the American texture, and sort of always be rock's resident villain. I think, after thirty-five years now, or thirty-some years, he gets that title.

*Neil compared him to Dracula, Freddie, and Jason.*

Yeah. Well, if you go into Spencer's Gifts now... Rob Zombie and I are good friends – and Ozzy of course. I said, "The funny thing is, you know, we're the new werewolves and Dracula and Frankenstein." I said, "That's who we are. We are those to this generation – or to our generation – we are the monsters. To the point where we have our own action figures." [*Laughs.*] Do you know how funny it is to have an action figure? It's pretty funny to go into a store and to see an action doll of yourself. Because when I'm not on stage or not on tour, I really disassociate with Alice. I don't really connect with Alice that much. When I'm on tour, I'm immersed in it so I'm always Alice. When I'm off tour, I kind of forget about Alice a little bit. So I'll walk into a store and, all of the sudden, I'll see all this Alice stuff. I'm just like a consumer, like anybody else, I go, "Oh, that's pretty cool. Wow, that's neat."

I like the idea that, to me, if I were just a kid... I developed Alice to be my favorite rock star. And if he ever is not my favorite rock star, there's something wrong. If I could hypnotize myself...if somebody would hypnotize me, and then show me all these rock stars and say, "Show me your favorite," I think I'd pick Alice every time. He's there for my enjoyment, too.

*Do you feel that* The Last Temptation *album marked a slight turning point in your music?*

It was a little sophisticated for the audience. I admit that. But, again, my audience was getting a little bit older. I think the kids didn't really connect with it. And the kids are always looking for their own identity anyway, so they're going to connect with Kurt Cobain more than they will with Alice Cooper. Even though they are going to have to deal with Alice Cooper long after Kurt Cobain, because Alice is still going to be here. At one point, they're going to have to deal with Alice Cooper because he's just not going to go away. And there's too much back catalogue for them to ever ignore him later on. So I just kind of let the generations go by and go by, and then pretty soon they all get around to Alice Cooper.

I try not to write down to the audience. I would rather write up to them, and have the audience have to struggle a little bit to get the story, or at least take them some place and not sort of back down to them. I could write teen angst ballads all day, but I like the idea of them having to struggle with the fact that...like on *Brutal Planet* and

*Dragon Town*, of going, "Wait a minute. If there is a hell, how do I stand?" That's a question that I can't answer for them. Nobody can answer it, but it's a *really* disturbing question. That's my job, to give them that disturbing question, not *"Hey, let's go get laid."* Everybody's going to tell them that. I'm going about it a little differently. I'm trying to hit them with things that are – and I think Neil is one of the people that gets that – sometimes you've got to give the opposite view. You would expect me to be going, "Hey, just go do what you want to do," and Alice is going, "No, what if you're responsible? Then you're in trouble!" [*Laughs.*]

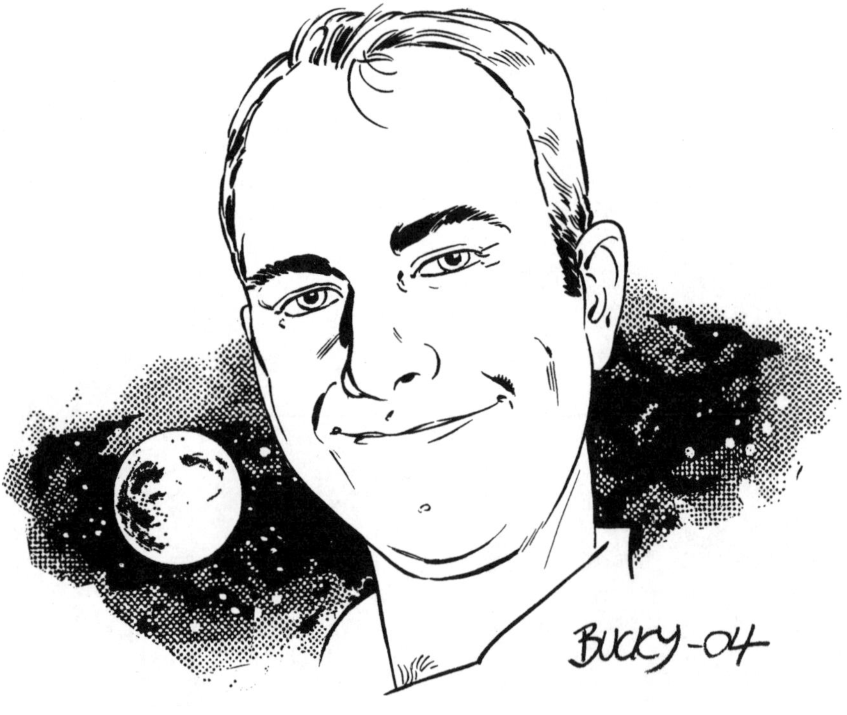
BUCKY-04

SELF-PORTRAIT. © 2004 MARK BUCKINGHAM.

*Mark Buckingham*

# MARK BUCKINGHAM HAS BEEN LINKED TO GAIMAN SINCE

HE BEGAN HIS CAREER – MOST SIGNIFICANTLY AS THE PENCILER OF *MIRACLEMAN* DURING GAIMAN'S EIGHT-ISSUE RUN ON THE COMIC IN THE EARLY '90S. (THE TWO STILL SHARE ONE-THIRD OF *MIRACLEMAN*'S OWNERSHIP.) BUCKINGHAM ALSO INKED *SANDMAN* (*THE SANDMAN SPECIAL* –"THE SONG OF ORPHEUS" – AND *WORLDS' END*) AND THE TWO DEATH MINI-SERIES, *THE HIGH COST OF LIVING* AND *THE TIME OF YOUR LIFE*, BEFORE TAKING OVER THE PENCILING CHORES FROM CHRIS BACHALO ON ISSUE 3 OF THE LATTER SERIES.

BUCKINGHAM CONTINUED TO INK BACHALO'S PENCILS ON THE MARVEL TITLES *GHOST RIDER 2099* AND *GENERATION X*, AND SERVED AS PENCILER ON *MORTIGAN GOTH: IMMORTALIS* (FOR MARVEL U.K.), *DOCTOR STRANGE: SORCERER SUPREME*, *STAR TREK UNLIMITED*, AND *PETER PARKER: SPIDER-MAN*. HIS MOST RECENT WORK HAS FOUND HIM, ONCE AGAIN, AT VERTIGO, DRAWING THE EISNER AWARD-WINNING *FABLES*.

*When you began working on* Miracleman, *you were given fluid deadlines, an opportunity to work with a writer you knew well, and a chance to explore a variety of penciling styles, because of the stories that Neil wanted to tell. It's interesting that the title of your* Miracleman *storyline was* The Golden Age, *because this strikes me as an ideal situation for a young artist.*

Yes, it certainly was. Neil and I had met in January of '87. We'd gotten to know each other through the Society of Strip Illustration, which we both had joined that year. As associate members, initially, because we were both so new to comics and had nothing in print to show for ourselves at that point. I was fascinated by the things he was starting to do with Dave McKean, with *Violent Cases* and some work that he'd been preparing for a comic that never appeared called *Borderline*. I was aware of what Neil was up to and was very interested in what was going on.

Neil and I actually did start to do some work together by the middle of '87, because he was one part of a three-way writing team with Eugene Byrne and Kim Newman, writing comedy material for a satire magazine called *The Truth*. At the same time that they were writing quite a few articles and features for that, I'd got myself selected as one of the main artists to produce artwork for that magazine on the strength of a strip I'd done for a charity comic called *Strip-Aid*. It was just a one-page silly little strip about a man inflating a condom over his head until it burst. But the point was that the style of the strip was right – it was open and light and simple and fun, and it was just what the editor of this particular magazine had been looking for. Not being one to miss out on an opportunity to start my comics career off, I took as many jobs as I could on this particular publication, illustrating articles. I had a one-page strip about pub conversations; I had a newspaper-style strip called "Haemorrhoid's Rabbit" (it was a very daft thing); and I also was doing cover artwork and other bits and pieces. Amongst the things I was doing was illustrating these features that Neil was writing, so that gave us a working relationship very early on in both our careers.

I showed this strip I'd drawn to the same guys, Don and Lionel, who produced the *Strip-Aid* charity comic, for this magazine they produced called *Heartbreak Hotel*. I did a four-page strip for that called "The Wild Side of Life" and I showed it to Neil. It must have been at the Christmas party of the Society of Strip Illustration. Neil took a look at this and said, "Well, this is really lovely." I'd done a lot of humor stuff prior to that, [and] I'd lost confidence, a little, in myself as an illustrator of action-adventure stuff. I thought, "Well, I'm really more of a cartoonist deep down, so maybe that's the way I should go."

But *Heartbreak Hotel* was taking four-page strips, so it was an opportunity for me to do something that was more in that sort of super-heroic vein. It basically involved this robot-girl, love-slave character getting lost and turning up in the middle of this swamp, and being taken in by this old tramp. It was a strange little story, but what was nice about it was there was a quality to the drawing in terms of the lightness and the delicacy of the female character, and the little Tinkerbell effect was very *Miracleman*esque – in contrast with a lot of the darker turns and the moods and the realism of the stuff that was going on around her.

Neil saw this four-page strip, and said, "Well, this is really lovely. This is actually the sort of thing I'm looking for for *Miracleman*." I didn't even realize at that point that he'd been talking with Alan [Moore]. Then he explained to me that Alan had basically wanted to pass the mantle of writing *Miracleman* onto him. And he was looking for an artist to work with, and would I consider doing *Miracleman*. I was a kid who was still on my degree course with very little experience in comics. Suddenly, I had somebody offer me one of the comic characters that I loved most in the world, and something that had been very crucial in keeping me interested in comics. The whole of the Warrior line of comics – with *V For Vendetta* and *Miracleman, Bojeffries Saga, Father Shandor, The Spiral Path* – all these things that were happening were really good-quality British strips written by the best writers and drawn by talented artists. It was a really good time. I felt the weight of that lineage certainly weighing on me with Neil saying, "How about doing *Miracleman*?" He explained that he'd been working on it with Dave [McKean], which I knew from the meetings that we'd had previously. He said, "Obviously, as a writer, I can produce far more material than someone like Dave's got time to paint." Because of the amount of effort and time that Dave was putting into his work at that point, especially with doing covers and things as well, for *Hellblazer* and stuff like that. There was a limit to how much he could do. So Neil knew he was going to need to start finding other artists to work with.

I was really shocked that he asked me, but it was a wonderful surprise. It took a year before we actually were able to start work on *Miracleman* because of negotiations over contracts and stuff, and making sure the exchange of Alan's share of *Miracleman* to be handed over to Neil and I for supposed safe keeping – but that didn't quite work out. [*Laughs.*] In the mean time, Neil had also started developing *Sandman* at that point, and he and Karen [Berger] were looking for working artists for that. So he put my name forward and showed some of this material, and some other bits and pieces I'd been doing, to Karen. She liked it, and she thought I was ready to be an inker at DC, but not a penciler at that stage. Also, because I was a little bit concerned about how well I was going to be able to cope with trying to do professional comics work and trying to get through my degree (because I promised my parents I would get my qualification and see that course through), I actually shied away from pursuing that *Sandman* job any further at that point; and then immediately had this blind panic that I had given up an important opportunity to start my career moving. At which point, Neil came back to me in late January and said, "Well, I've been talking with Richard Piers Rayner, and he's taking over as the artist on *Hellblazer*. Perhaps you could maybe try and get in as the inker on that." We arranged a meeting for Richard and I to meet at the subsequent Society of Strip Illustration meeting. That was good, and we got on very well, and I thought, "Well, this seems like a good idea." Richard promised to send me some pages so I could do some samples for Karen. I did a few, but unfortunately they were pieces from a project that Rich had been self-publishing, rather than the actual pages of *Hellblazer*. I didn't do as good a job on the initial batch of samples as I really would have liked. And it showed. I was in too much of a hurry, I was sort of desperate to get some stuff in. I sent this stuff to Karen and didn't really get any response, and I was a bit concerned. I phoned her up, and she said, "Your work's not really quite what we were looking for." I thought, "Here goes my career, heading down now from the high point of talking with Neil back in January. Things aren't looking quite so good." But Neil encouraged me to not be downhearted by this and to try doing another set of samples, and get them in quick and maybe try and "razzle-dazzle her," as Neil says. So I did. I got back to Richard, and Richard actually now had some penciled pages of *Hellblazer*, because he had started work on the comic proper, so he sent me a couple pages from the first issue. I sat down and spent hours, absolute hours, trying to be as precise and delicate and careful with the quality of the rendering, really practicing my brushstrokes. I did some really high-quality samples to get those in. (By the way, I know I'm going on about my past, but it's all relevant to getting back to *Miracleman* at some point.) And it worked. I showed these new samples to Dave and to Neil, and they both thought they did look really good and gave me a lot of encouragement. I sent them in to Karen. But what I didn't realize was that Neil and Dave both actually phoned Karen themselves, independently, and said that they'd seen these new samples and thought they were very good, and thought it would be a really good idea if she gave me the job. [*Laughs.*] Karen phoned me up and she said, "You know, you have some very influential friends." And gave me the job!

Neil basically has been my savior throughout my life. [*Laughs.*] I don't know if I'd ever have achieved any of the things I have without his friendship, and…almost this sort of fatherly figure looking over me and just making sure everything's okay. Because the next thing he did was recommend me to Mark Waid for penciling and inking (a full-art job) the Poison Ivy *Secret Origins* issue [36, "Pavane"] which was really good fun. I thoroughly enjoyed that, my first chance to draw Batman. Neil wrote that. It's one of those rarities that's never been reprinted anywhere. When they did the *Midnight Tales* collection for Neil, all the Vertigo stuff, the things that were missing from that period – the early part of Neil's writing career at DC that nobody's seen – were the secret origin of Poison Ivy and a Riddler story that he did, for *Secret Origins* [*Secret Origins Special* number 1, "When is a Door"] as well; and, I think, one other thing. Of course, it was [in] that period when he did the *Action Comics* final issue [642], when it was the weekly anthology for a little while. And that one, more recently, got its second wind as *The Legend of the Green Flame*, a prestige book. Again, Neil recommended me for that. [*Laughs.*] One of the first things Neil did on that book was to recommend me to pencil one of the segments. He was trying really hard at that point to get me as much experience in professional comics as he possibly could, knowing that once everything was sorted out with *Miracleman* contracts, he would want me to be in a position from which I could tackle *Miracleman*, a position of confidence, having spent a year working properly in comics.

It was good. The Poison Ivy thing went very well. Richard, unfortunately, for personal reasons, had to leave *Hellblazer* after about seven issues, so that gave me a chance to take over as penciler, which meant that I had five more issues of a comic under my belt as the artist as well. It was nice to be from the other side of the fence, to be just penciling, and to be working with someone like Alfredo Alcala, who gave you a good sense of the difference and demands of the industry, and seeing how your stuff can change so much in relation to the people that you work with. I was learning a lot at that point, as well as sort of doing little strips and bits and pieces of my own, and developing different approaches and seeing what I was capable of. And all of that was part of this process that I was going through with Neil, of preparing myself for *Miracleman*. And just being aware of the fact that we were going to be doing these tales of the people who inhabited Miracleman's world, rather than diving straight into a major story arc involving the cast as the readers knew it. Because we knew a direct comparison with Alan would be a really bad idea. [*Laughs.*] We needed to tell a very different type of story in order to make the book ours.

Right from the outset, Neil and I talked a lot about the fact that we wanted to do these stories from the viewpoint of the people whose lives we were following. And to try and create art styles that were individual to each of those characters. That was a real joy, because it meant that I had an excuse after each story to try a different art style and to develop my career further and see what happened. Your initial comments about how it was an appropriate title because it was a "golden age" for me with my career is totally true, because it was like having a sketchbook in public. I really was having this opportunity to experiment and to try new things, and just to see how much versatility I could drag out of comics. *Miracleman* was never an ordinary super-hero comic, but it was nice to have an opportunity – especially in that period in the early '90s, when there was so much exciting experimental work going on in comics – to really see how far we could push things within the super-hero envelope. Yes, it was wonderful. A lot of the ideas for what we did were coming from Neil as much as from me. Neil was very much into grid layouts at that point, and quite often stories would start with a structure, and the art style would fall into it a bit later on. It was a very interesting time, and a fascinating way to work.

*Would Neil do thumbnail grid layouts himself?*

No, not really. Neil and I used to get together, I'd go and stay with him in Nutley. We used to spend time together at Neil's home, and I'd stay over for a night or two, and we'd go for long walks, and sit and watch *Addams Family* videos, and drink Drambuie, and stay up until four in the morning. And just… *figure stuff out*, talk about the type of stories we were going to tell and the structure of the whole three-part, eighteen-issue epic we were planning to unfold. It was wonderful. I've always loved best working with people that I truly feel I can collaborate with – we can get inside each other's minds, understand each other's working methods, try and draw on each other's strengths. And, if possible, really have a friendship with someone you understand and you're

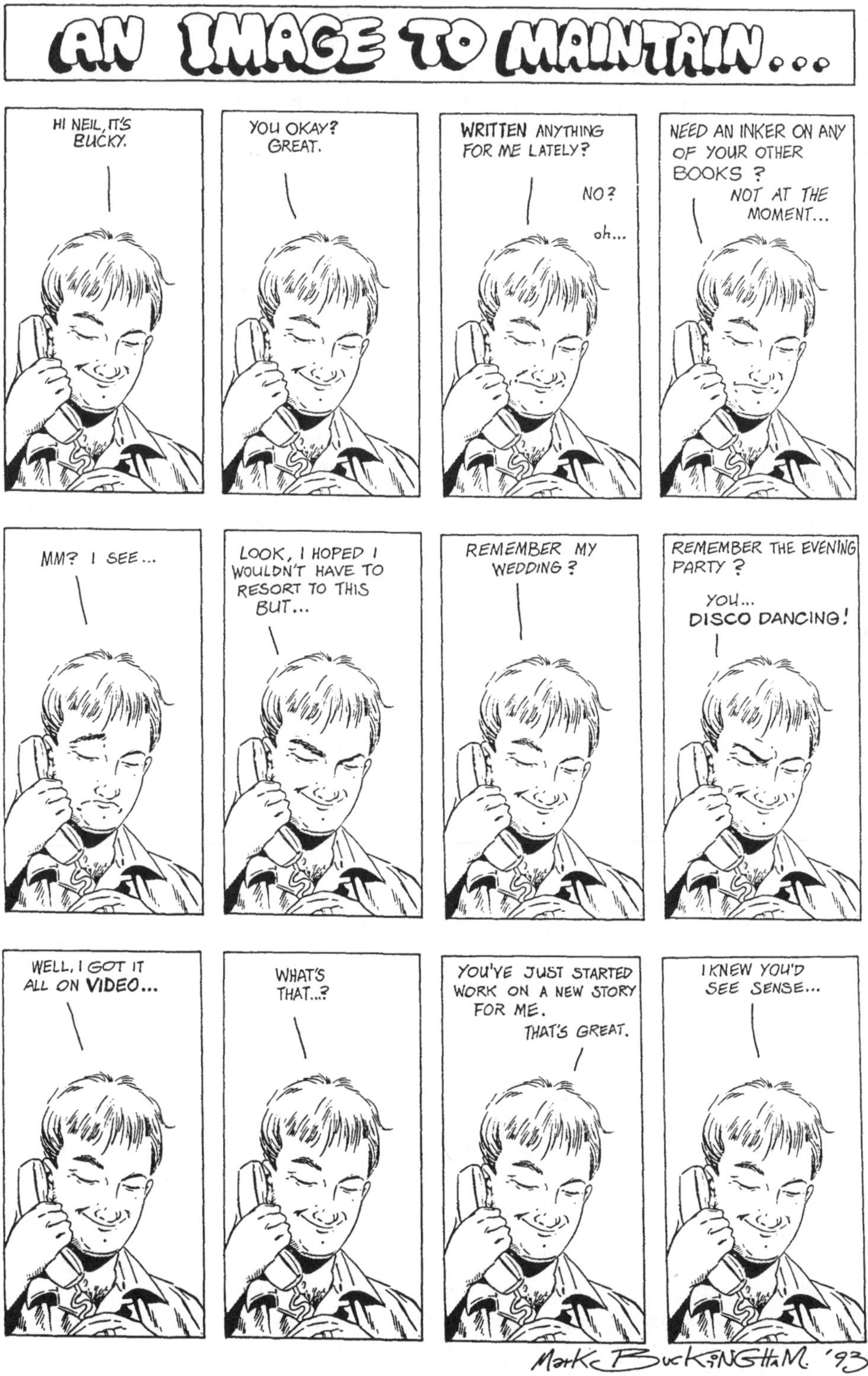
AN IMAGE TO MAINTAIN...
HI NEIL, IT'S BUCKY.
YOU OKAY? GREAT.
WRITTEN ANYTHING FOR ME LATELY?
NO?
oh...
NEED AN INKER ON ANY OF YOUR OTHER BOOKS?
NOT AT THE MOMENT...
MM? I SEE...
LOOK, I HOPED I WOULDN'T HAVE TO RESORT TO THIS BUT...
REMEMBER MY WEDDING?
REMEMBER THE EVENING PARTY?
YOU... DISCO DANCING!
WELL, I GOT IT ALL ON VIDEO...
WHAT'S THAT...?
YOU'VE JUST STARTED WORK ON A NEW STORY FOR ME.
THAT'S GREAT.
I KNEW YOU'D SEE SENSE...
MARK BUCKINGHAM '93

"An Image to Maintain..." from *Guest of Honor – Neil Gaiman* [Moondog's Inc., 1993], published for the Chicago Comicon. Script, pencils, and inks by Mark Buckingham.

comfortable with. You really feel that you can make each other try different things and push each other, and it's a *fun and exciting* experience.

Working with Neil always has been an experience like that. It's always been a joy. It's always been like playtime. [*Laughs.*] And I know it sounds dumb, because it's always a job, and sometimes it's really hard work, but...*it's not hard work*. It's a *challenge*, but it's always such an exciting experience that it doesn't *hurt*. That's really how I sum it all up. *Miracleman* was just...a dream project. It was a character that I'd always wanted to draw. It was a book that I'd always admired. The fact that I'd always envisioned myself doing it in a style not too dissimilar from something between Garry Leach and Alan Davis's stuff, with a little bit of the fluidity and the delicacy of the Totleben stuff... I had in my mind a thing that I wanted to do with *Miracleman*, but what I ended up doing with Neil was completely different. It was like, "Okay, throw everything else out. Let's just see what a Mark Buckingham comic would really look like, if you forget everything else that's ever happened and just be yourself." That's really what *Miracleman* was about.

The strange thing is I've spent most of my career since then trying to get back [*laughs*] to that magical point, because it's so easy when you get more and more established in this business and you follow other people on books, or you're working on characters with forty years of continuity, say Spider-Man, where you're weighed down by people's expectations. And you know that people have certain favorite versions of a character, and you're trying to synthesize elements of that in order to produce something that will satisfy as many people as possible. In the process, you may produce an excellent piece of work, but it's not necessarily true to you. This is the battle that I've had for years – finding the balance between me and the audience. It's interesting... But certainly *Miracleman* will always remain that testing ground where I really felt that I was being true to myself.

How long was I just talking for? A half an hour? I'm sorry. How many questions have you got? [*Laughs.*]

*Well, not too many now. [*Laughs.*] It doesn't seem like there's very much controversy in your relationship with Neil.*

That's true. I can't imagine ever falling out with Neil. I can't imagine how anybody *could* fall out with Neil, for the simple reason that Neil is the most honest and genuine person in this bloody business anyway. He always remembers his friends. He always remembers his *fans*, to a degree that I find surprising. The number of times I hear him talking about people he's met at conventions and reminding them of the last time he saw them as much as them recognizing him... The rapport he has with people – he's so friendly, so genuine, so honest, and he's so open. If you are a friend of Neil's, you really are his friend, and he really *does* care, and he really does look out for people, and he doesn't forget you. He's a man who now lives in another country, and he has all these other things going on in his life with the books, and with the writing for movies, and directing and everything else. But when I'm with Neil again, I'm back to being with the same guy that I knew sixteen years ago, and it's as comfortable as if he were still Neil the journalist-who's-trying-to-break-into-comics. The only difference is that he's usually got a hundred-million people rushing around him trying to ask him to do different things. But he always has time for people, and that's important, and I hope he never loses that. But, certainly, I can't imagine anybody ever falling out with Neil. [*Laughs.*] The only people who don't like Neil are the people who have basically hurt him along the way. If you pick a fight with Neil, then that's different. If you're a major comic publisher that happens to own something that Neil and I want back, then beware. [*Laughs.*] But as far as anybody else goes, he's the nicest guy on the planet.

*When you stopped penciling* Miracleman, *you had completed artwork through the first half of the third* Silver Age *(the storyline that followed* The Golden Age*) issue.*

Yes. 23 ["The Secret Origin of Young Miracleman"] and 24 ["When Titans Clash!"], the first two parts of the *Silver Age*, saw print. 25 ["Trapped in a World He Never Made"] was written, drawn, lettered, and the only thing that wasn't done on that was Matt [Brooker]'s ("D'Israeli" is his pen name) coloring. Which is a shame, because I would've loved to have seen Matt's coloring. But then, of course, if he had, he, too, like I, wouldn't have been paid for that last issue. [*Laughs.*] So I would rather he didn't have the hole in his bank balance for that particular piece of work. But 25 was done, bar the coloring. As far as 26 goes, Neil had written the first eight pages, and I did the layouts for the first three or four of those, at which point, we realized that Eclipse was gone, and we had to stop.

A lot of the delays we had on *Miracleman* were partly to do with us and the fact that we were busy, or I was trying too hard to develop new ideas and new styles; and Neil was getting busier and busier. But, also, a primary part of it was the fact that Eclipse got slower at paying, and we found ourselves in a situation where we would finish an issue, wait for the money to come in, and then start the next one. [*Laughs.*] That did build some extra waiting time into the work as well.

*After* Miracleman, *you worked with Neil on* Death: The High Cost of Living, *inking Chris Bachalo. One can see a similarity in your work from that period to Chris's.*

Certainly, I absorbed a lot from him. I mean, partly it was the practicalities of it, because he was very much an artist in demand, in the ascendant; and I saw the benefit in being able to work very closely with Chris and to be able to continue projects in his absence, in a style very close to his. And so you'd see a lot at that period in time. The other thing you've got to bear in mind is that I wanted to do more work as an artist in my own right. But, outside of *Miracleman*, I was primarily known as an inker and that was a struggle for me, because it meant that once *Miracleman* had gone, I had limited outlets in which to really continue to be the kind of artist that I wanted to be. So, as time went on, without being able to really develop that side of me further – because all my time was taken up with inking other people – I really did lose my own personality as an artist at that point. I knew I wanted to draw again, but it was difficult with Vertigo because they valued me so much as an inker. It was very easy for me to just keep taking inking jobs and not to push the penciling side of what I wanted to do. So when Chris made the leap from *Shade* and *Death* over to Marvel to do *Generation X* and *Ghost Rider 2099*, I went with him.

And when we came to *Death*, the second series [*The Time of Your Life*], when Chris left halfway through, it was almost like, well, the only opportunity was for me to draw it, really, because I don't think anybody else could have pulled off quite such a good mimic job at that particular point in time, to make it such a consistent read that you weren't so obviously aware there had been an art change. Obviously, your keen comic fans can spot the differences, but I tried very hard to keep the rhythm and the flow and the structure exact. And, stylistically, it was as close to Chris as I could possibly get. I probably would've been closer still if I'd have inked it myself, but obviously that wasn't practical with a limited amount of time on a project like that. We

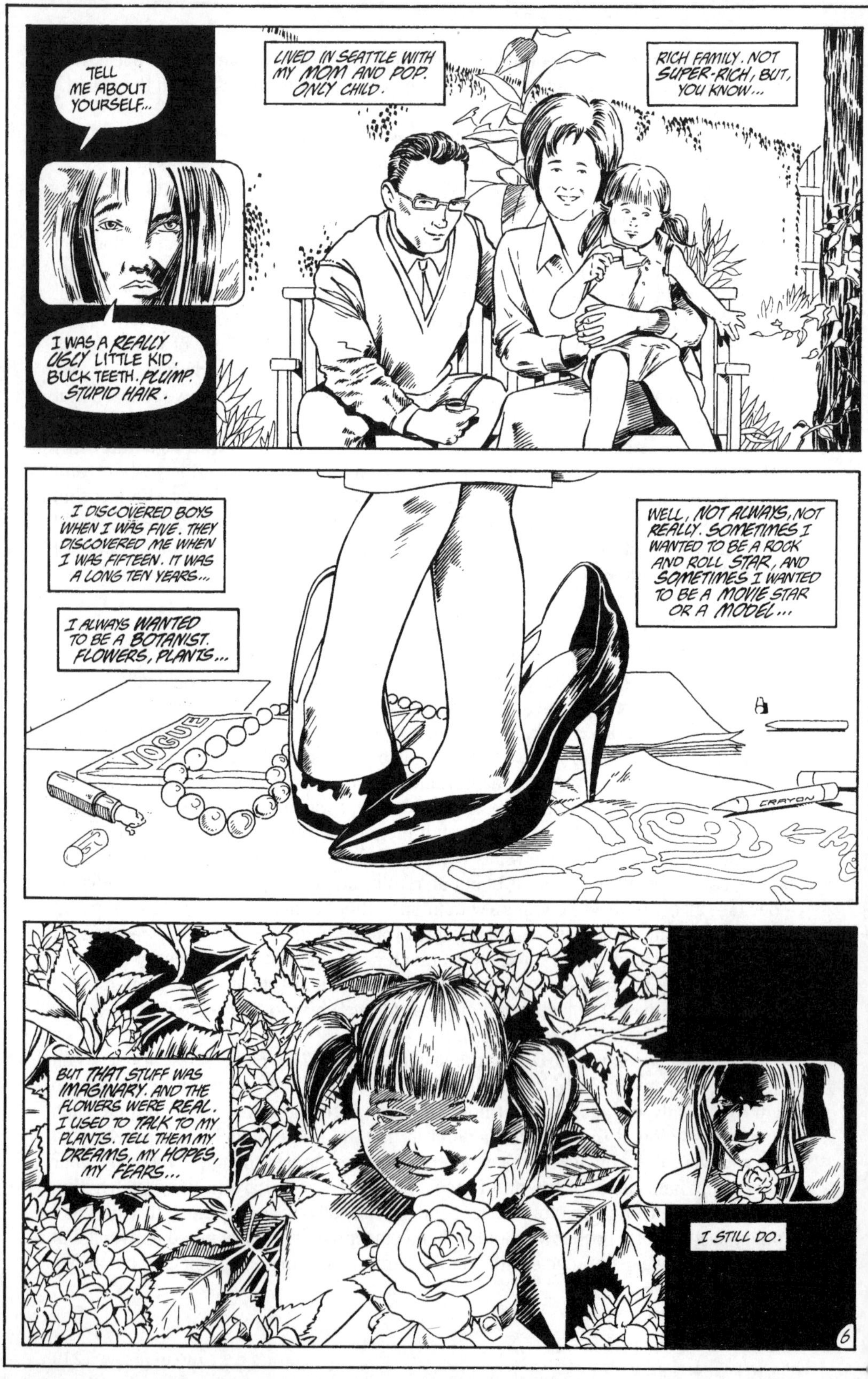
TELL ME ABOUT YOURSELF...
I WAS A REALLY UGLY LITTLE KID. BUCK TEETH. PLUMP. STUPID HAIR.
LIVED IN SEATTLE WITH MY MOM AND POP. ONLY CHILD.
RICH FAMILY. NOT SUPER-RICH, BUT, YOU KNOW...
I DISCOVERED BOYS WHEN I WAS FIVE. THEY DISCOVERED ME WHEN I WAS FIFTEEN. IT WAS A LONG TEN YEARS...
I ALWAYS WANTED TO BE A BOTANIST. FLOWERS, PLANTS...
WELL, NOT ALWAYS, NOT REALLY. SOMETIMES I WANTED TO BE A ROCK AND ROLL STAR, AND SOMETIMES I WANTED TO BE A MOVIE STAR OR A MODEL...
VOGUE
CRAYON
BUT THAT STUFF WAS IMAGINARY. AND THE FLOWERS WERE REAL. I USED TO TALK TO MY PLANTS. TELL THEM MY DREAMS, MY HOPES, MY FEARS...
I STILL DO.
6

brought Mark Pennington in, who did a fabulous job and kept it very close to what Chris and I had done in the first half. Creatively, that was a very satisfying moment. It worked. It was a struggle, but we got there.

A lot of people were very appreciative of my efforts at that particular point in time, and quite amazed by how well I was able to keep the consistency with Chris's stuff. The problem was, at that point, to try to be more of an artist in my own right. Because then I started to get more offers for work on the back of what I had achieved with *Death*. But it was me getting lost again in this Bachaloesque style, and more and more people wanting me to kind of "do the Chris thing for us." It was a struggle. It took me a long time to try and water those influences back down again and try to bring different elements in. A lot of the time, what tended to happen was, rather than me finding myself, what I tended to do was just bring in a lot of other people's comic influences again. So there would be a burst of Kelley Jones or a bit of Mignola or there'd be a bit of Kirby. The last big one was the kind of Kirbyesque thing that hit me in the early part of *Fables*, and the latter part of my *Spider-Man* run. It was very important to me to try and get back to basics, and to concentrate a lot more on what I was doing in panels, rather than elaborate panel structure. It was very much just me trying to get back to a purity of comic form. But, having done that, what was really nice was it made me realize all the things that were missing that were part of my style and my personality that I lost along the way.

The real changing point was when I did that little two-page strip with Neil ["True Things"] at the beginning of 2003, in tribute to Alan Moore for the TwoMorrows book [*The Extraordinary Works of Alan Moore*]. Because it was a two-page strip that Neil had written and that I was going to draw, and it had no relationship to anything else that I ever had to do or ever had done, it meant that I could be totally myself. What happened was that I dragged back into my work all those things that I'd been doing way back when I last worked with Neil. So there were elements from the humor strips that I'd been doing in *The Truth*, there was me using textures and tones again that I hadn't done in years, there was some quite realistic work in some of the ways I was handling Alan's figure. And it was the contrast of those things with quirky little design elements and the cartoon figures, and the playfulness of panels shaped like teacups and things like that, and the dancing milk bottles and stuff like that. It was just me getting back to being myself, and really surrounding myself with work that I was doing in the first three or four years of my career; where there was a purity of vision and there was the confidence of youth that said "I can do this better than anybody else." The fact that I couldn't is beside the point, but what was important was I believed in myself then. And I believed that what I could do was unique and special and different, and it was coming purely from me. It wasn't weighed down by all the fears of how I'd be compared to other artists or the weight of continuity or the weight of expectation. It was just me trying to rediscover what it was that made me work as an artist. And I have to thank Neil for that, because once again, he picked the perfect moment to come in and save me, artistically. [*Laughs.*] Because, after that, I then went onto the *Storybook Love* story arc in *Fables*, and I took all the elements that I'd been developing just in that two-page strip. I spent a week on that two-page strip, but the amount of work I did around it was really important. It was the thinking time that I allowed myself when I was doing that that really made the difference.

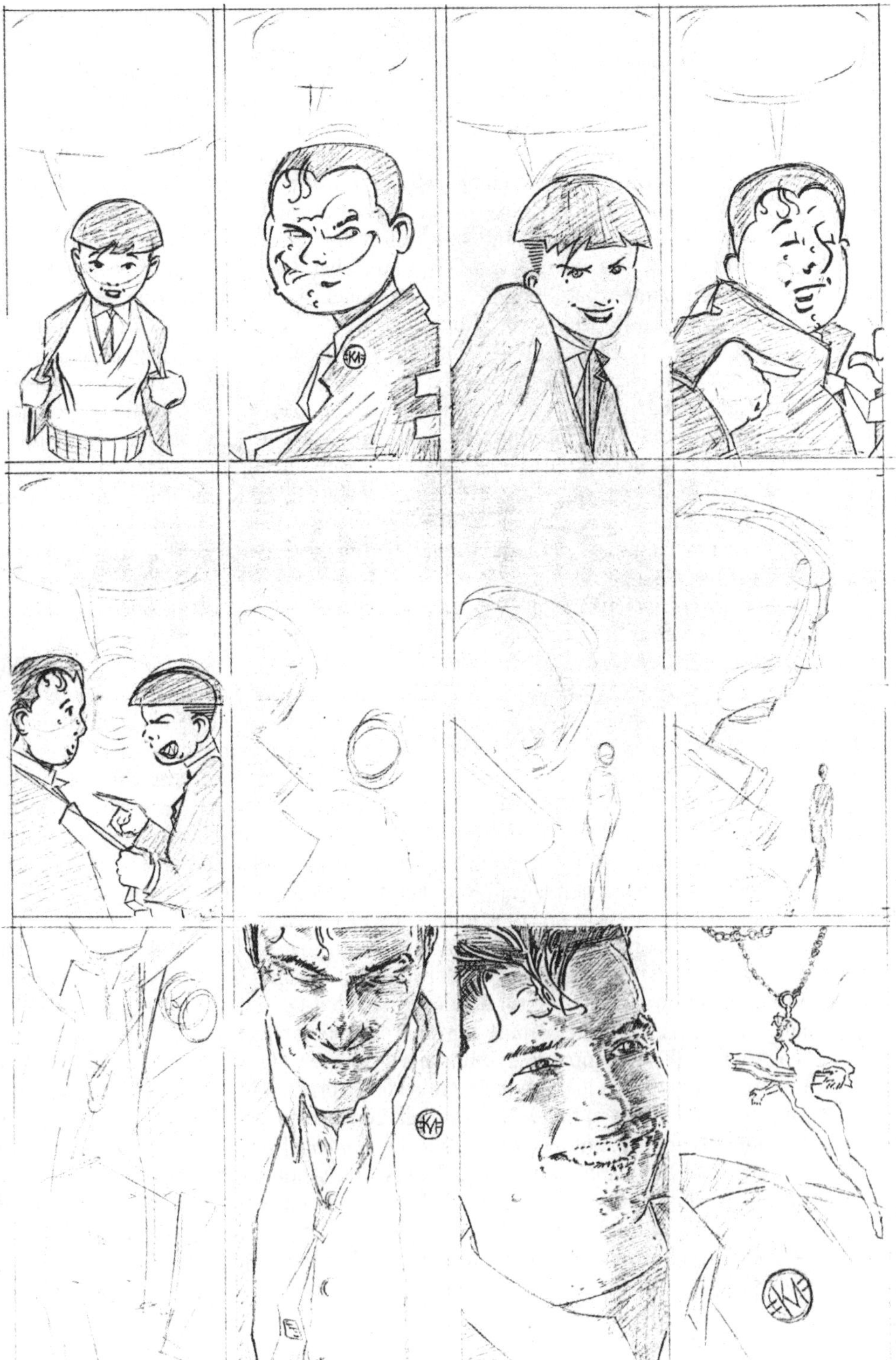

Mark Buckingham's pencilled and inked versions of page 8 of "Trends," from *Miracleman* 18. © 2004 Neil Gaiman and Mark Buckingham.

Previous Spread: The origin of Poison Ivy (Buckingham's first "full-art job" for DC), from page 6 of *Secret Origins* 36, "Pavane." Pencils and inks by Mark Buckingham. © 2004 DC Comics.

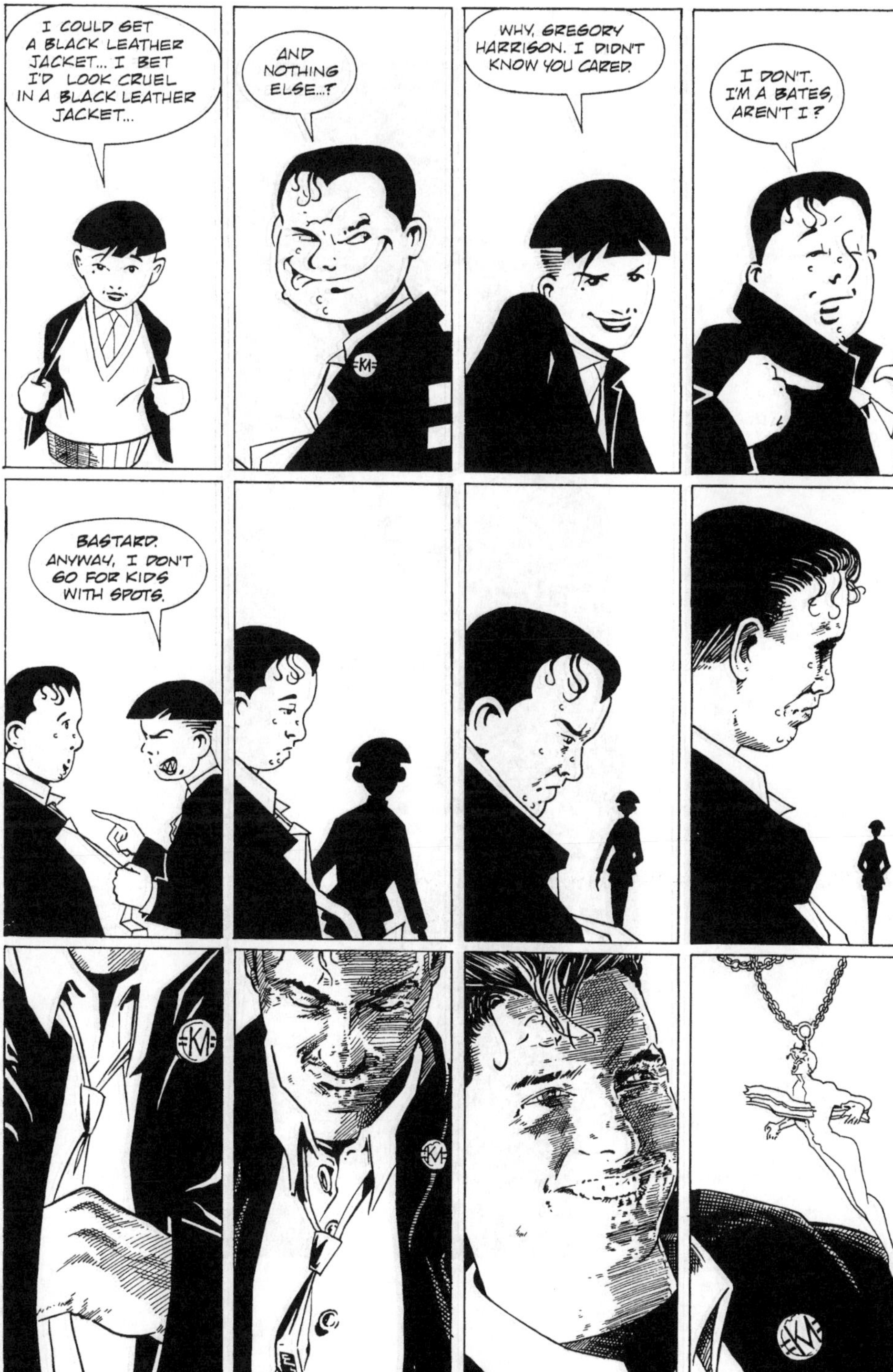
I COULD GET A BLACK LEATHER JACKET... I BET I'D LOOK CRUEL IN A BLACK LEATHER JACKET...
AND NOTHING ELSE...?
WHY, GREGORY HARRISON. I DIDN'T KNOW YOU CARED.
I DON'T. I'M A BATES, AREN'T I?
BASTARD. ANYWAY, I DON'T GO FOR KIDS WITH SPOTS.

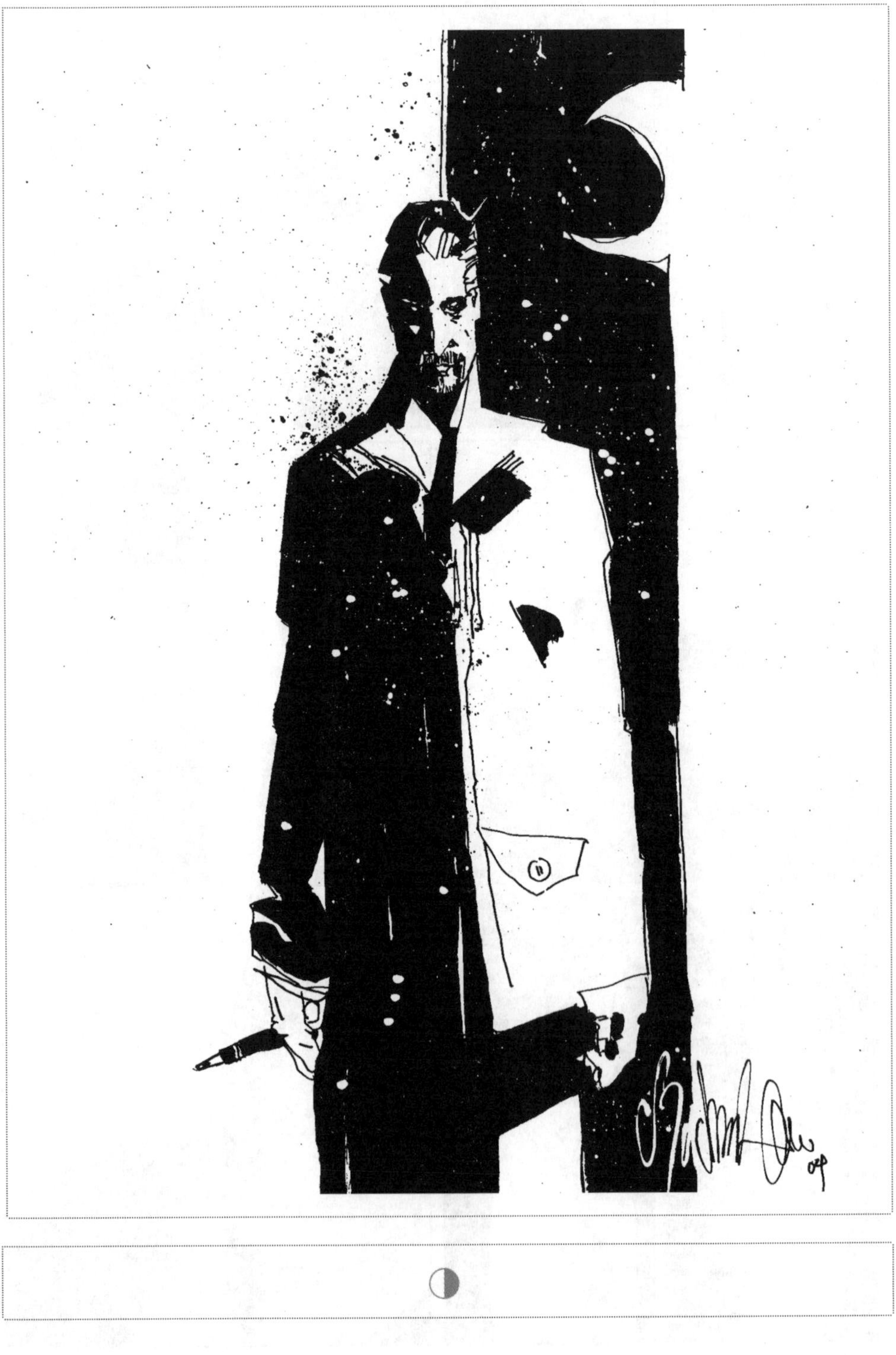

Self-portrait. © 2004 Chris Bachalo.

# CHRIS BACHALO CHANNELED HIS FONDNESS FOR DRAWING

A MORE SUBTLE FEMALE FORM THAN THAT TYPICALLY FOUND IN MAINSTREAM COMICS INTO HIS PENCILS FOR THE FIRST DEATH MINI-SERIES, *DEATH: THE HIGH COST OF LIVING*.

BACHALO HAD MADE HIS PROFESSIONAL COMICS DEBUT SEVERAL YEARS EARLIER ON ANOTHER GAIMAN COMIC, *SANDMAN* 12 ("PLAYING HOUSE"), WHILE WAITING TO BEGIN HIS FIRST REGULAR ASSIGNMENT, *SHADE, THE CHANGING MAN*. AFTER HIS RUN ON *SHADE*, BACHALO TEAMED WITH INKER MARK BUCKINGHAM ON NOT ONLY *THE HIGH COST OF LIVING*, BUT ALSO *GENERATION X*, *GHOST RIDER 2099*, AND THE FIRST TWO ISSUES OF *DEATH: THE TIME OF YOUR LIFE*. BACHALO LATER REUNITED WITH GAIMAN WHEN HE ILLUSTRATED THE FIRST ISSUE OF *THE CHILDREN'S CRUSADE* – THE FIRST AND, TO DATE, ONLY VERTIGO ANNUAL CROSSOVER – AND WITH DEATH AS WELL ON A SHORT PIECE, "THE WHEEL," FOR DC'S *9-11: VOLUME 2* BENEFIT ANTHOLOGY.

IN RECENT YEARS, BACHALO HAS ILLUSTRATED SUCH BOOKS AS MARVEL'S *UNCANNY X-MEN*, *ULTIMATE WAR*, AND *CAPTAIN AMERICA*. HE HAS ALSO CREATED HIS OWN SERIES, *STEAMPUNK*, WITH WRITER JOE KELLY, FOR DC'S CLIFFHANGER IMPRINT.

*Your first professional comics work – or at least your first work to see print – was in* Sandman *12. Since* Sandman *already had generated some momentum at this point, it must have been an intimidating first assignment.*

By the time *Sandman* reached issue 10 it was picking up a lot of steam. It was getting very popular with a readership in comics as readers were beginning to embrace the mature titles that DC was publishing. I was a huge fan of the book and it was very exciting. At that point, because of its success, Karen [Berger] was developing new properties and attracting new talents, especially from England. She was working on a new property with Pete Milligan. They were going to take a look at an old series, the Steve Ditko title *Shade, the Changing Man*. At about this time, I had just graduated from university and I was looking for work. I'd sent samples of my work to DC that caught their interest. They thought that I had a nice take and that I had a grasp for storytelling. As history reflects, I managed to work my way onto *Shade*, but it wasn't ready yet, as Peter was still writing the first issue.

I know Mike Dringenberg worked very slowly and they needed a fill-in artist for issue 12 of *Sandman*; so, while I was waiting around for *Shade*, they said, "Do you want to give this a try?" I said, "Sure. That'd be great." Again, I was a huge fan of *Sandman* and the opportunity to work on that book was great. I recall it was August of 1989. There were a couple different layers of pressure applied during this time. Number 1 was that I hadn't drawn many comics, only a few. If you added up everything I did, I think I had maybe half-a-dozen twenty-two-page comics that I did with my friends in school. And, number 2, none of them were done in a month. So, there was this pressure of working with this huge publisher like DC Comics, and working with this great new comic that I absolutely loved and the reality of having to draw it in a month. I thought, "This is great." I recall the experience of drawing that particular issue being miserable, because I was still living in my parents' house and my studio was in my room and I had a lousy drawing table. It was August, so it was very hot, and we didn't have any air conditioning in the house, so my hand was sticky with perspiration and was sticking to the paper. [*Laughs.*] And I had broken a finger on my drawing hand – my pinky finger. Halfway through the issue, I got stuck conceptually. I recall the whole experience as being miserable. I was very unhappy with the work.

I think my saving grace on that particular book was Malcolm Jones, who turned my miserable pencils into something that was beautiful. I owe him a lot, and I was very sad that he passed away the way he did. I thought he was a really talented person. On the back of one of the original art boards – I don't know if he was bored or something, but he drew this amazing picture of Sandman in pencil. He really should've been drawing the book more than me, because I thought he could draw better than me. [*Laughs.*] I thought, "Wow. He has a really good take on this character. What am I drawing this for?" He was a really talented person. I'm not sure what was going on in his life where he felt compelled to do what he did. That's very sad. But I owe him a debt of gratitude because I thought he did an amazing job over me on that particular book, and I really needed it. In the end, I think it worked out well, and everyone seemed pretty happy.

*How familiar were you with the Jack Kirby Sandman you drew in your debut story, "Playing House"?*

I had no idea who that was. [*Laughs.*] I really didn't.

*So much of what Neil was referencing in that issue was new to you?*

It was brand new. [*Laughs.*] They sent me reference on the character. That's really all I knew about him. I concede that I don't know a lot about pre-1974 comics history. That's when I started collecting, in the mid-'70s – *Werewolf by Night*, things like that. I don't know a heck of a lot before that. I know a little bit about the Silver Age, but going back to the '50s and '40s, I know very little about the books.

*Just how tight were your pencils for* Sandman *12?*

I think I would describe them as being uncertain. I was very new at what I was doing, and, because of that, I had a lot of uncertainty about how to approach it. I wouldn't say "loose" because I've seen guys do loose work, and my work wasn't that loose. Everything was on the paper, but it was a little more…"feathery." A lot of scribbly-linework stuff. It definitely wasn't confident. There was room for interpretation. I think Malcolm took it upon himself to add a lot of linework, which I thought was really good and gave it some depth. That's a comment that I make to people who show me their portfolio and they're uncertain about parts of their work.

You can notice that, because the line quality fades or they put a lot of scratchy marks on the page. I'll make that comment to them, "Here, you're not confident." Maybe it's in rendering a certain muscle or something – they hint at what they want to put down, because it's kind of there, but it kind of isn't. That was what was happening with me. I asked Richard Bruning, who was in charge of hiring new talent at the time "Why did you pick me?" Because I didn't think, in general, that I drew very well. He said, "I think you have a good grasp on telling the story. That's solid. That was the big reason why your artwork attracted us to you." At the time, Neil was writing fairly tight scripts, with each panel broken down with direction. So all I really had to do was put down what he was telling me to do. If there was an easy part, that was it.

*One thing that had evolved by the time of* Death: The High Cost of Living *was your ability to draw attractive female characters.*

I owe it to Dave Stevens. [*Laughs.*] I thought John Buscema drew brilliant women. I was in love with Belit (Conan's girlfriend around issue 100; she dies in issue 100 – it was tragic) as a kid, when I was growing up. She was just the greatest. [*Laughs.*] I thought he drew the best women. They were so pretty, and yet were very simple.

*How did Neil describe the way he wanted Death to look in her debut mini-series,* Death: The High Cost of Living?

I don't really recall specifics. I just recall that she was to be young, sixteen, and obviously gothic.

*Did you already have an idea of how you wanted her to look?*

No! That was a real challenge for me because it was the first time that I had to take a character, especially a character that was emerging as someone who was going to be very popular. With *Sandman* 8 ["The Sound of Her Wings"], there had been a lot of talk about her, a lot of buzz. I thought, "Wow, this is an exciting new character. It's a very interesting take on Death." I felt an immense amount of pressure. I was putting a lot of pressure on myself, on what take I was going to present. Obviously, Mike Dringenberg had a take on her. I figured I could emulate that, or I could take it upon myself to create the version that I wanted to see, the one that I thought she should be. Neil always encourages that: "Go for it. Do what you want. I trust you. Do what you think is best." I debated with myself for a while, and in the end I thought (it's really the only rule of thumb I use today in regards to any established character that I take on) to create a version that I liked, and that I was comfortable with. That's what I did with her.

*You used your niece as a model – is that right?*

I actually brought her over one day, dressed her up like the character, and took a few pictures. The most specific image that resulted from that was the *Death Gallery* image – the big double-page image of her sitting on the floor [pages 1 – 2]. That's directly pulled from one of the photographs. She was game, so she gave it a try.

*Your version of Death looks a little younger than Mike's version.*

Yes. Because, like I said, she was sixteen years old, so I tried to keep in mind somebody who was that age. Death is a neat character because she's wise, and I think that's why a lot of people are attracted to her. And she's happy. She's the most popular character in the Vertigo universe because she's happy. Most of the other characters in the Vertigo universe tend to be miserable. They're anti-heroes, and Death is not. She's still dark – dresses in black, white skin, lurks in the shadows a little bit – but the thing is she's happy, she's wise, and she knows a lot of stuff. For me, that's what was very attractive about her character, because she always appears to know what's going on and what's going to happen. I think people take comfort in that, like moths to a flame…without the incineration.

*Some people point out the spin on the traditional Grim Reaper persona. But she's also appealing because she refutes the theory that ignorance is bliss. Here is Death, who is extremely wise and intelligent, but is happy with that awareness. When one encounters insightful characters in modern fiction, they're often jaded and miserable.*

This is a huge issue, you could probably talk about it for hours [*laughs*], but I guess it depends, ultimately, on the person's personal make up and their experience. Some become jaded, others embrace it, see it for what it is, and are positive about it. I think that's the way she is. She knows a lot. She's a wise person and that's the way life is – bad things happen, good things happen. It just is. There are no big ups and downs with her, which makes her – and Neil commented on this once – a very difficult character to write, because she, ultimately, has no conflicts. Her character has no conflict. And if you don't have conflict, you don't have a story, or at least an interesting one, which is why I think Death stories aren't about Death. They're about other people. That's why *High Cost of Living* worked really well, and maybe *Time of Your Life* didn't work so well, because she was more important in *The High Cost of Living*. It was her day, so it was more about her, whereas *Time of Your Life* was about other people. Obviously, *High Cost of Living* was a lot more successful. I get very few comments on *Time of Your Life*. There are two things that people recognize me for – it'll probably be my legacy – *Death: The High Cost of Living* and *Generation X*.

*Neil described your collaboration with inker Mark Buckingham on* High Cost of Living *[In* The Comics Interview Super Special: Sandman*] as something that "doesn't actually look like Chris and it doesn't look like Mark Buckingham. I'm not sure who it actually does look like; it's sort of like a punk Brian Bolland or something."*

Yes, that's fair. At the time, I was thrilled to have Mark as an inker. He was really good. I had known him from his work on *Miracleman* and I was really curious, somewhat puzzled, about the idea that he would want to ink someone else. I remember being in the DC offices when we were talking about the project. The subject of inker came up, and Mark Buckingham. "Why would he want to ink something like this? He's an artist himself." They said, "No, he'd like to do it." I was thrilled. The idea of having a person of his quality inking my work was like being in Nirvana. He was a positive member of the team. His influence showed through. He did a good job and he did make me look better.

*Neil also remarked in that* Comics Interview Super Special *that his only real regret was not having "48 pages per issue," for that first mini-series. Do you recall Neil trying to compress some of his scripting into fewer pages?*

Yes. I always get that feeling with him. He has a lot to say [and] doesn't always have the room to say it. I'm with him. The more pages the better. When I read a script, I try to break it down in beats. When it's with Neil [*laughs*], there's just always wonderful little beats and little moments in between dialogue. I think, "Oh, this bit would be so great to put in there," or "What's the character doing while he's talking? Can I put it in?"

Comics are obviously a written medium and they're a visual medium. I like comics, because it's a true mix of the two. The most successful comics are ones that are visually interesting and well written. I don't think that happens very often. With Neil, you obviously have someone who's a tremendous storyteller. It's my job to come in and try to support that wonderful story that he's telling. I put a lot of pressure on myself to tell the best story that I can, to make it as visually interesting as possible. Going back to the space issue, the more space I can have the better. With that story, and *Time Of Your Life*, there wasn't a lot of room to express the visual part of the story. Sometimes it was very difficult to put everything down that I wanted to put down, as there was a lot going on, a lot of people talking and sharing ideas. I felt that if we had two more issues in that story, that would've been fantastic.

*Despite that,* High Cost of Living *does seem to have a looser, more improvisational feel than much of* Sandman. *Did you get that impression, having worked on both titles?*

After working on *Sandman* with Neil, he gave me more room to improvise. He put in the directions but he didn't put in so many page breaks. He said, "You break them up. I trust you to tell a good story." He made basic suggestions as to where each page break would be, and I took it from there. I look at my job as being similar to that of a director, in which I have a script and it's my job to interpret the script to the best of my ability and to dress it up, and tell a story using pictures. I said, "That's amazing that you would give me that responsibility," so I took it very seriously. I hope in the end he was happy with it. I think he was. People that read the book [were]. Having that room was tremendous, and I do think it added a little bit to the pacing of the story, and maybe it added, like you said, to the spontaneity, and made it a little more open.

*You left the second* Death *mini-series,* The Time of Your Life, *after two issues. What was the reason for your departure?*

I was working on *Generation X* at the time. It was doing really well, creatively and financially. But, before I'd left to go and do that, I promised Karen that I would do another *Death* series if it came up. I was about a year into *Generation X* when the new *Death* series came up. So I said to her, "All right, I'll commit *this* much time to do the series."

At the beginning, it was very exciting because I wanted to do a better job, because I wasn't one-hundred percent happy with *High Cost of Living*. I told Marvel, "I want to do this. I'm going to be gone four or five months." We were all set to go...

I think, at that point, Neil was receiving a lot of opportunities and he was probably taking a lot of stuff on. I don't believe that the *Death* series was a priority with him, so what was happening was that I was getting one to two pages a week to draw. Four months went by, and we had an issue done. I thought, "Oh no, this is a disaster!" I actually ended up waiting six months. I had Marvel waiting for me. It started costing a lot of money – I was making a lot more money working on *Generation X*. At six months, I said, "You know what? I can't do this." In hindsight, it probably would've

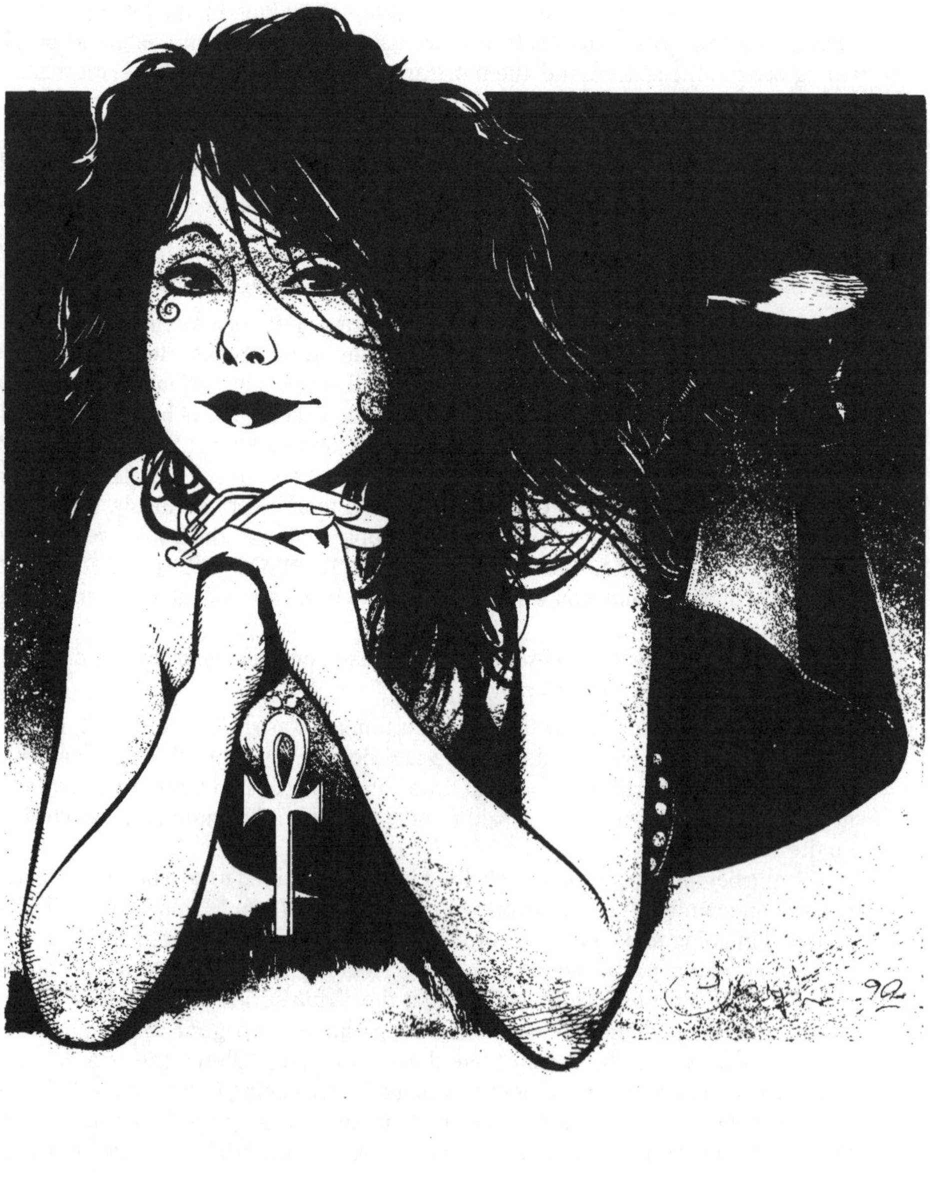

DEATH, FROM THE COVER OF *COMICS INTERVIEW* 116. PENCILS AND INKS BY CHRIS BACHALO. CHARACTER TM & © 2004 DC COMICS.
NEXT SPREAD: SEXTON MEETS DEATH, PAGE 16 OF *DEATH: THE HIGH COST OF LIVING* 1. PENCILS BY CHRIS BACHALO AND INKS BY MARK BUCKINGHAM. © 2004 DC COMICS.

been better for me to have gone to Vertigo and told Karen, "When it's done, let me know, and at that point I'll make time for it." Usually, Neil's been pretty reliable. He's a little bit on the slow side with scripts, but not that slow. I'm not sure what was going on, but I had to go back to *Gen X*. I had to leave. It wasn't a great time, no one was really happy about it. [*Laughs.*] It was pretty miserable. I was really miserable, and I hated doing that. But I had to think of the big picture.

*What did you think of Mark Buckingham's impersonation of your style on the remainder of* The Time of Your Life?

I thought it was a great impersonation. I looked at it and thought, "Wow. That's kind of spooky." But it was right on, right down to the layouts. Everything was pretty much right on. It was a little eerie seeing somebody mimic my work as well as he did.

*He told me it was strange for him, too, because, after that, he was sort of identified with that style.*

Yes. He used that style for a little while. I think he's gone away from that, which I think is good for him. On his own, he does a really good job. Going back to *Miracleman*, that was really good stuff that he'd done. He should draw like that.

*Not to keep harping on Death, but how familiar were you with the Goth culture? For example, was Death's top hat in* The High Cost of Living *your idea?*

Yes…I think that was me. I can't be one-hundred percent sure of that. I was only vaguely familiar with the Goth sub-culture. I grew up in suburbia, Orange County. [*Laughs.*] There's no color, no culture here. If you took bleach to a community, that was the community I grew up in. I didn't see a person of ethnicity, really, until high school.

That's how white it is out here – cookie-cutter houses all stacked nice in a row. The idea of the gothic movement? I vaguely knew what the gothic movement was, maybe through music. But I really wasn't into that kind of music. I knew very little about it, but I did a little research and found out that it was very black, with white skin, things like that. I burned a lot of candles, attended séances. [*Laughs.*] I did a little research on and off, but at the same time, as an artist I try not to do too much research to a point where I'm too influenced by something else. I want to have my interpretation of what the movement is about, or the look, or the scene or the style. I want to sample it but I don't want to engorge myself on anything. Obviously, if you're writing a biography or doing a period piece, it's very important, because you want to communicate authenticity. But when it comes to something like this, that's modern, I want to look into it – I want to see how they dress, a little bit of the culture, their beliefs, values, whatever – but then I want to react, to create something new. That's where you take a bit of a risk, because you may be rejected, or at the same time, you might be embraced – "Wow, this is a little different. This is kind of neat. I like what you did with it." I think that's been the case, especially with that series. I've really not heard a negative comment about it.

*In* The Sandman Companion *Neil mentioned the Goth girl fashion of wearing a top hat seems to have started with Death's top hat in* The High Cost of Living.

Yes. It just seemed appropriate somehow. In *Time Of Your Life*, I drew the umbrella. I found that it was brilliant the way Neil made the umbrella important in the story. I like props, and Death really doesn't have a prop. An easy prop is a cigarette. If you're drawing Constantine, he has a cigarette. Even if they're standing, talking with somebody, or eating, having a drink – you have something to work with as far as the character and their gestures are concerned. They're doing something. Adding to her ensemble with the hat and the jacket... They're practical elements, but I think they're in keeping with the integrity of the character, which was always very important. Because you don't want to introduce something and have people ask, "Why would she have that object?" You don't want to distract the reader with something unnecessary or out of character.

*And Death's elements went with the fetishy mindset of the sixteen-year-old Goth girl.*

Another thing that it does is – when you see those accessories, you associate them with that book, which is why, in *Time of Your Life*, she doesn't have those items. There's the umbrella – so that's her prop in that series. If I did another one, I'd probably come up with something else that would lend importance to that series, that moment in time.

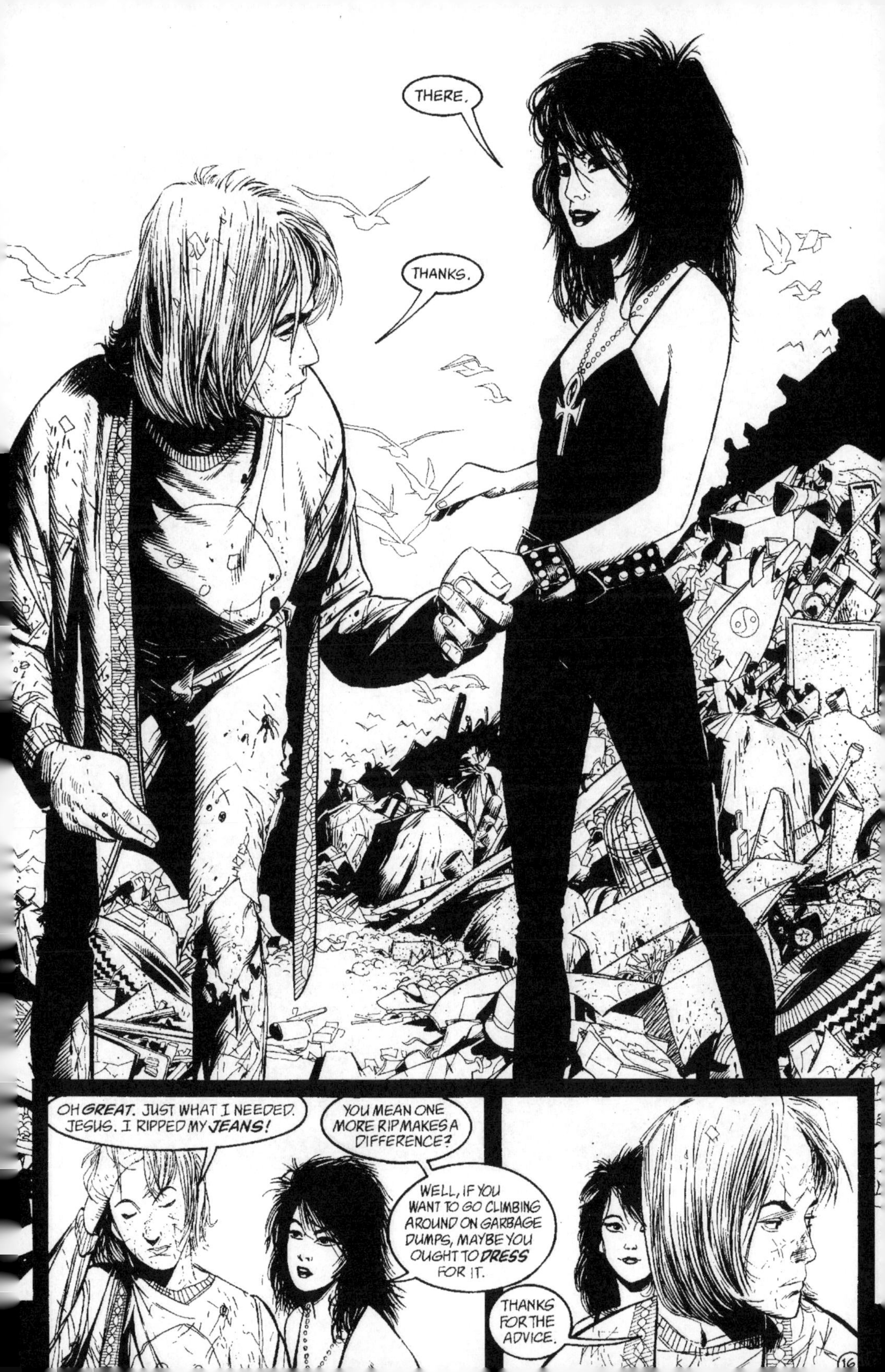
THERE.
THANKS.
OH GREAT. JUST WHAT I NEEDED. JESUS. I RIPPED MY JEANS!
YOU MEAN ONE MORE RIP MAKES A DIFFERENCE?
WELL, IF YOU WANT TO GO CLIMBING AROUND ON GARBAGE DUMPS, MAYBE YOU OUGHT TO DRESS FOR IT.
THANKS FOR THE ADVICE.

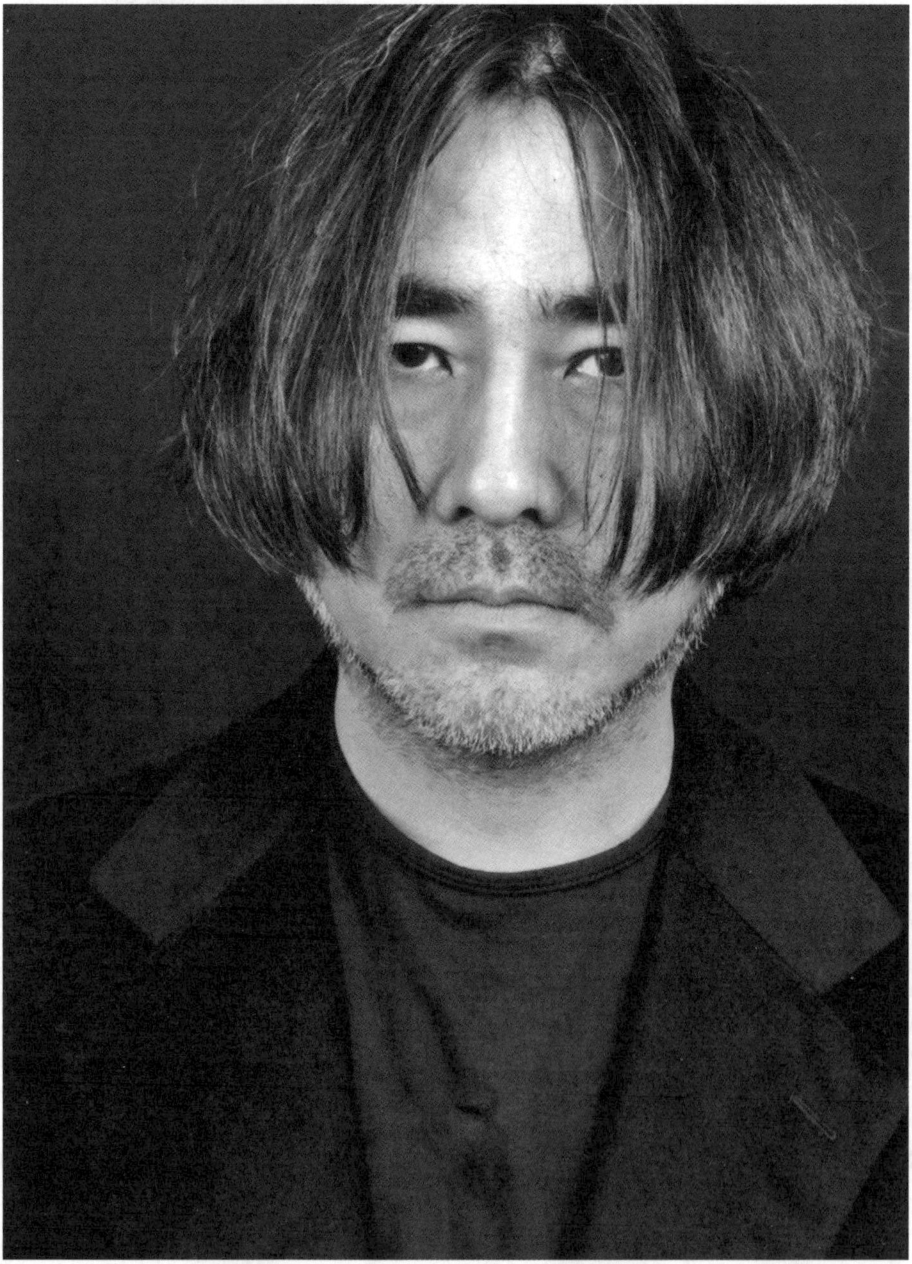

PHOTO BY NITIN VADUKUL, COURTESY OF YOSHI SEGOSHI. © 2004 NITIN VADUKUL.

# THE ETHEREAL ILLUSTRATIONS OF YOSHITAKA AMANO

DANCED ALONGSIDE GAIMAN'S WORDS IN THE FIRST EXTENDED PIECE OF SANDMAN PROSE FICTION, *THE DREAM HUNTERS* [DC/VERTIGO, 1999].

RAISED AT THE FOOT OF MOUNT FUJI, AMANO BEGAN HIS CAREER AT THE AGE OF FIFTEEN, WHEN HE PRESENTED HIS ARTWORK TO THE JAPANESE ANIMATION STUDIO TATSUNOKO PRODUCTIONS. AFTER ONLY A YEAR OF TRAINING, AMANO DESIGNED CHARACTERS FOR SUCH CARTOONS AS *GATCHAMAN* (KNOWN AS *BATTLE OF THE PLANETS* IN THE U.S.) AND *CASHAAN: ROBOT HUNTER.* EVER THE RESTLESS ARTIST, AMANO RETIRED FROM TATSUNOKO AT THIRTY AND BEGAN HIS CAREER AS A FREELANCER. TWO YEARS LATER (IN 1984) AMANO RELEASED *MATEN* (*EVIL UNIVERSE*), HIS FIRST COLLECTION OF PAINTINGS.

AMANO HAS COLLABORATED WITH NUMEROUS WRITERS THROUGHOUT THE YEARS, ILLUSTRATING – AMONG MANY OTHER BOOKS – *VAMPIRE HUNTER D.* HE HAS ALSO PROVIDED CONCEPT ART FOR SUCH VIDEO GAMES AS THE ORIGINAL *FINAL FANTASY,* AND CRAFTED HIS OWN MULTI-MEDIA PROJECTS, SUCH AS *HERO.* FOLLOWING THE SUCCESS OF *THE DREAM HUNTERS,* AMANO PROVIDED ILLUSTRATIONS FOR MARVEL COMICS' *ELEKTRA AND WOLVERINE: THE REDEEMER.* AND 2003 SAW THE U.S. RELEASE OF *THE COMPLETE PRINTS OF YOSHITAKA AMANO,* REPRINTING HUNDREDS OF THE ARTIST'S ILLUSTRATIONS.

THE FOLLOWING INTERVIEW FINDS AMANO ILLUSTRATING GAIMAN'S SHORT STORY "THE RETURN OF THE THIN WHITE DUKE," FOR ISSUE 30 OF *V* MAGAZINE.

(Amano's words are translated from the Japanese by Mr. Yoshi Segoshi.)

The Dream Hunters *is a unique* Sandman *tale in that it is an illustrated prose story. Had Neil discussed with you the possibility of doing it as a comic, or was it always intended to be an illustrated story?*

That was originally my suggestion and DC Comics agreed to go along. I can't really do comics. It requires a different mindset. Also, for me, Neil has always been a novelist, not a comics writer.

*Had you read any of Neil's work before working on* The Dream Hunters? *If so, what was your impression of it?*

No. I couldn't get hold of any of his work translated in Japanese, and I'm not good with English.

*How familiar were you with the Japanese folk tale Neil used as the basis for* The Dream Hunters? *Is it the sort of folk tale most Japanese citizens are familiar with?*

The stories of fox and badger tricking humans are very popular among Japanese folk tales, and we are familiar with them since our childhood. Also, there is a whole variety of stories about dreams emerging into reality or vice versa. Those stories are deeply rooted in Japanese culture. I often feel the dreams are more attractive than reality, and can't stop the urge of making it into a picture.

*In* The Dream Hunters, *the range of your illustration is impressive. Your paintings move from the expressionistic to the abstract. Do you always try to explore this range, or did* The Dream Hunters *help evoke it more strongly because of its imagery?*

I think it happened that way because I was pretty much inspired by Neil's story. I never intentionally tried to combine different styles.

*You've mentioned before that your favorite illustration was featured on page 59 of the book. You've said that you drew this as a mental landscape, an image that had no connection to the story. Do you often try to insert such images into your books?*

I have a tendency to draw more pictures than are actually required when I'm interested with a project, some of them are often not directly related to the story. The picture you are talking about is the one I drew as the heroine's mental landscape. Neil's writing is so imaginary that I get millions of pictures in between the lines.

*Was there a specific type or movement of Japanese folk art that inspired your work on* The Dream Hunters? *Did you refer to the work of any particular artists?*

I was very much conscious about Japanese tradition when working on *The Dream Hunters* (after all, the story takes place in old Japan) but not any particular artist or style.

*You've described the most challenging thing about* The Dream Hunters *to be determining how deeply to pursue the historical events in the story, because Neil was knowledgeable about the historical setting. Do you typically prefer to stay away from historical research for your images?*

Usually, I don't place much trust in historical accuracy. We can't go back in history and see it by our own eyes, can we? For example, there are so many different styles in armors and we can't exactly place them in historical order or what belongs to whom. By imagining myself as one living in that era and letting my imagination run, I can have more vivid, livelier results.

*How was* The Dream Hunters *received by your fans in Japan? Do you feel the Japanese are very accepting of a western writer rewriting a Japanese myth?*

We still see monks and Inari (a small temple that worship fox) in our daily life in Japan. Whether it was written by a Japanese or a Westerner, the subject and the materials are a familiar one, and Neil had a very good grip on them, so I think Japanese readers didn't feel any sense of incongruity. I certainly didn't!

*Manga is enjoying a huge growth in popularity here in the U.S. right now. How do you feel American comics are typically perceived in Japan? Do you find your opinion of American comics is similar to that of most Japanese?*

I think most Japanese familiarize themselves with American comics through movies these days. You know, *Superman, Batman, Spider-Man,* etcetera, etcetera. Younger generations encounter them on the movie screen first, especially in Japan. For my generation, they were part of our daily life. It was a big part of the American Dream package, and we admired it. I myself had a big influence from American comics and Pop Art.

*What interested you in the book you did for Marvel Comics,* Elektra and Wolverine? *How did it compare with your experience illustrating* The Dream Hunters?

*Elektra/Wolverine* takes place in contemporary New York City and that was stimulating for me. I was in New York City at the time! I worked on it as if to make a motion picture instead of making an illustrated book.

*You've described your early animation on* Gatchaman *(known in America as* Battle of the Planets *or* G-Force*) as representing your adolescence. What is it about that work in particular that prompts this reaction?*

I was a character designer at Tatsunoko Production at the time. Gatchaman was the most popular character I created and the name, Gatchaman, always brings back the memories of my younger days.

*At the time you decided to leave animation for freelance work, was your decision considered unusual? Would this move be any more common in today's Japan?*

I think it was an unusual move at that time. I designed anime characters at Tatsunoko, but the final drawings are done by animators and my own drawings never got out of the studio. I wanted to try my possibilities as an illustrator/painter. At the time, the boundaries between different media were more strict than they are today; but in my mind, I didn't pay much attention to the difference in media, even then.

*What elements contribute to the fluidity of your work? Is your style, in part, a result of your frustration with the limits of animation design?*

I don't feel any frustration with anime any more. In my mind, images are always flowing, changing, moving, as if they are alive. You can see your own past, present, and future in one drawing.

*There's an unusual eroticism present in your work that recalls Gustav Klimt. To what degree were you influenced by Klimt?*

I was very much influenced not only by Klimt but also by Arthur Rackham, Munch, pre-Raphaels, etcetera, etcetera. I remember that I was attracted to Klimt by the oriental element of his works.

*You began creating work in New York City in 1997, and you've described it as your "fantasy city," a place where you can "dream freely, without constrictions of the known." What is it about New York that inspired you?*

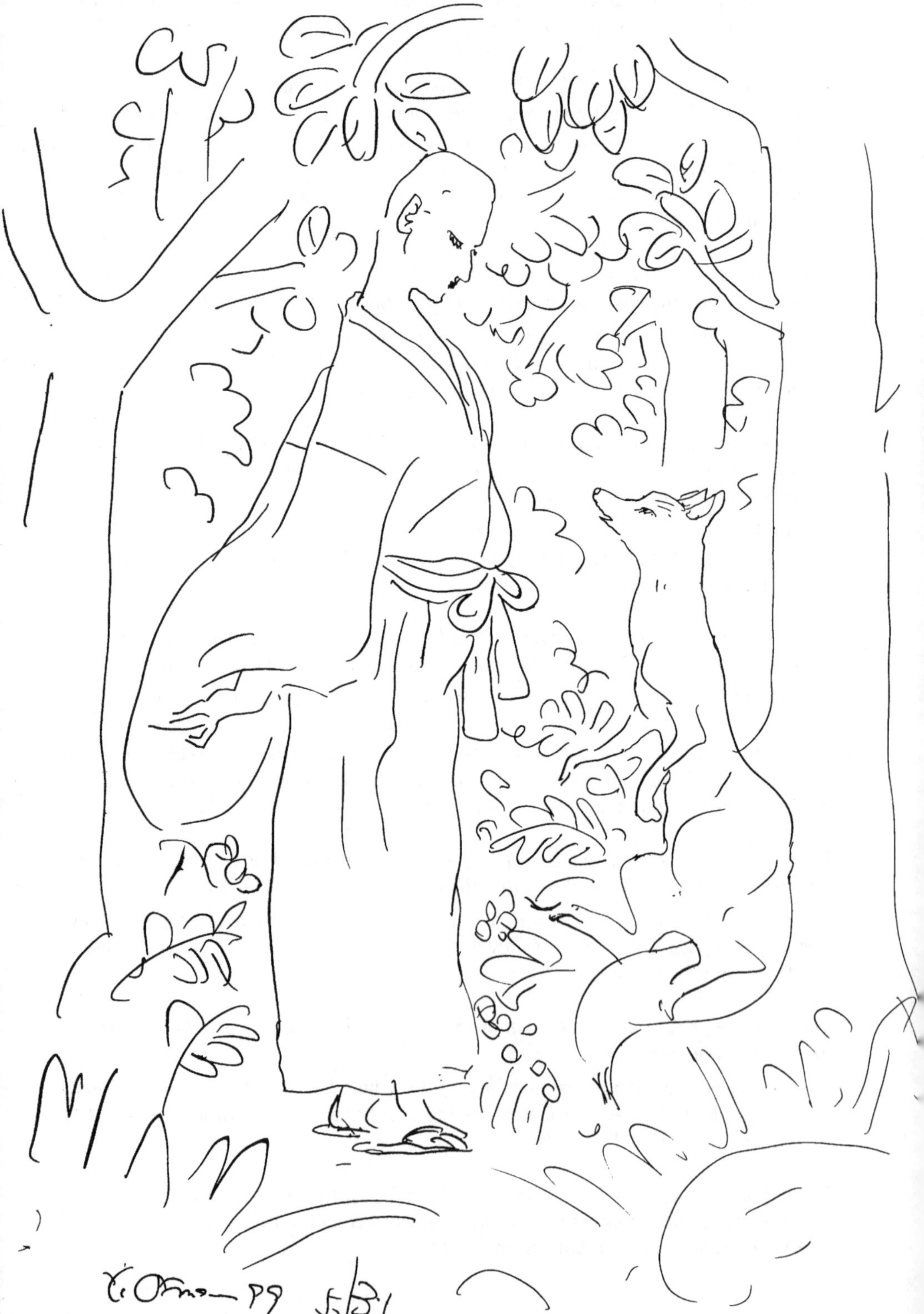

If it was one-hundred years ago, it must've been Paris, the cultural center of the world, you know. I felt it's New York City now. I wanted to place myself in it, see and feel it directly with my own eyes and skin. Yes, we can have a lot of information, doesn't matter where you are, but for me, actually being there makes a whole difference. I wanted to see talented people directly. Typically, Neil Gaiman!

*You've remarked, regarding your initial move to freelance work, "Once your life is too stable, your creativity dies." Was this also the reasoning behind your temporary move to New York in 1999?*

Yes, that's part of it. But now that I've spent many hours in New York City, I'm looking for the next one.

*Do you find you have a large, loyal group of Japanese fans who will follow your work on many different projects, from video games, like* Final Fantasy, *to books, like* Genji?

I think I do. Many of my fans seem to follow whatever I do in different media.

*You seem to find inspiration from many different sources, spaghetti westerns for* Vampire Hunter D, *operas for* Hero. *Is there any medium or artistic movement that you don't care for?*

I can't say I don't like any particular style or artistic movement. There are those I don't care much about, but that's not to say I don't like them. Every style, movement, medium has a reason why it's there, and I appreciate the variety and diversity of them all.

*In the afterword to* The Dream Hunters, *Neil remarks that you love comics but do not draw them. Why is this? Have you attempted to draw comics?*

Well, actually, I did try comics once (*Aman Saga*)! I enjoyed doing it, but at the same time, I realized that it's not really for me. I tend to be too particular in the details of each picture, and you can't work that way in doing comics. It's the balance between each picture and the storytelling and, as I said before, it requires a different mindset.

*Like Neil, you work comfortably in a wide range of media. Is there one you prefer?*

My job and interest is in creating images. In that sense, I'm doing the same thing whether it becomes a computer game or an illustrated book as an end product. Creating images and putting it down on a sheet of paper is what interests me since when I was a child. That's my root and that's what I still do.

*In addition to your work with Neil, you've also produced images inspired by the work of western writers such as Gene Wolfe and Michael Moorcock (particularly the* Elric *books). Who are your favorite western writers?*

I love Moorcock! He never works with stereotype, and the setting of the environments and characters are fantastic.

*What do you think attracts Japanese writers to your work? Do you think this is different from that which attracts American writers?*

I'm not a writer so I can't speak for them, but I don't think it's any different whether he's Japanese or American. I read the story just as any reader would and draw whatever images the story inspires in my head. I don't think I'm special as a reader. I'm a straightforward guy!

*In the afterword to* The Dream Hunters, *you commented that this collaboration was the first greeting between you and Neil, in a relationship that will build and take many forms in the future. Have the two of you discussed any other specific projects?*

I'm currently working on a project with Neil. It's a new concept on a fashion magazine. Instead of usual photos of models wearing nice clothes, we'll make it into an illustrated story. Actually, I have to finish my drawing by tonight and send it to Neil, otherwise everybody's gonna kill me!

*Dave McKean, one of Neil's most frequent collaborators, told me that he considers art to be a defining of the language. How do you view your work? Do you feel it has redefined some of the visual references in the media you've explored?*

I hope my work contributed to the richness and the diversity of what we have today, but redefined the reference? I don't know, it sounds a bit too strong a word for the works I've done. I just hope my images give readers something unique and far reaching, instead of limiting their imagination to one stereotype.

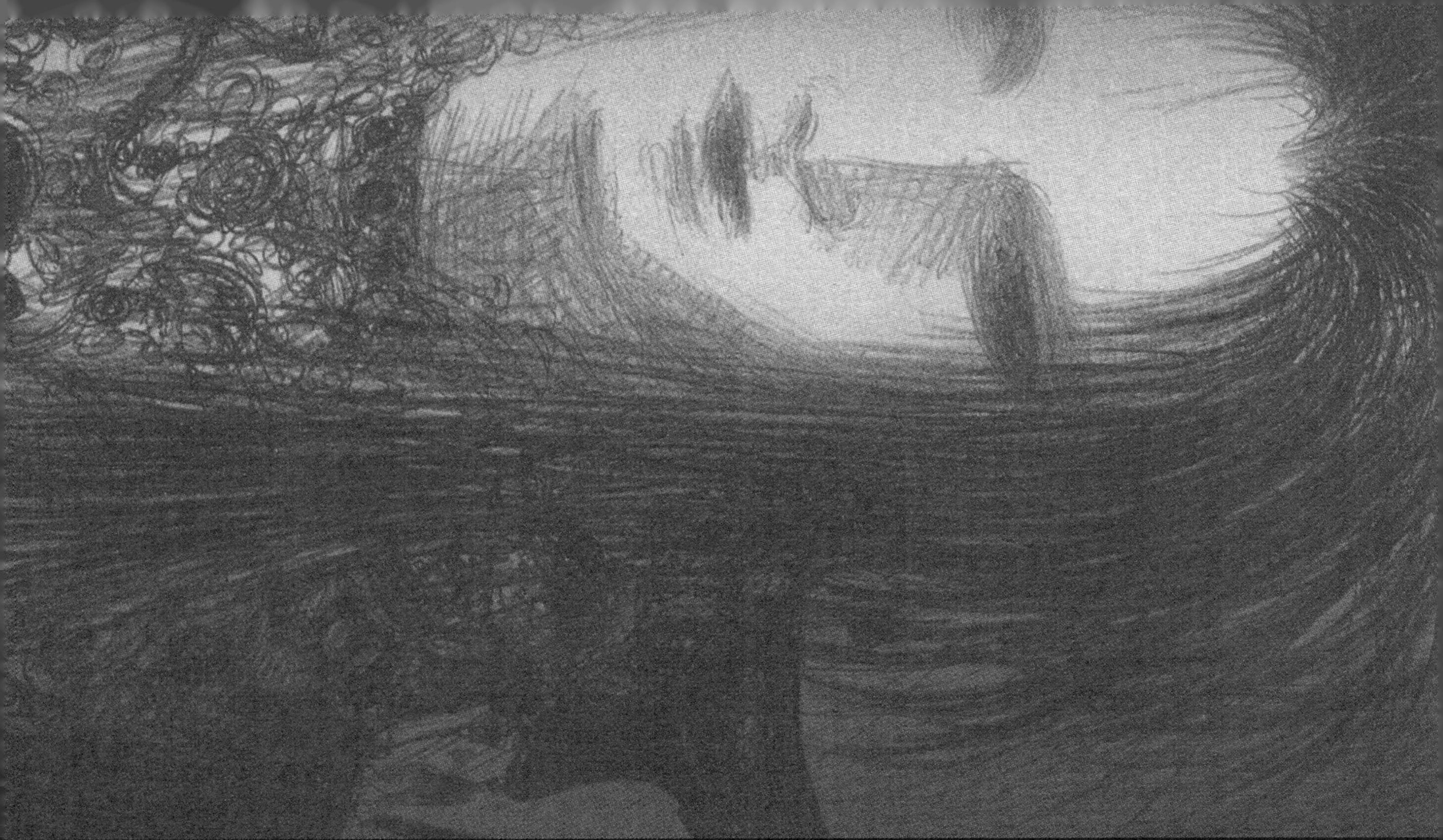

Yoshitaka Amano's Sandman, from page 152 of *Amano: The Complete Prints of Yoshitaka Amano* [HarperCollins, 2003]. Characters TM & © 2004 DC Comics.
Previous Spread: Sketch for *The Dream Hunters* by Yoshitaka Amano. Characters TM & © 2004 DC Comics.

*Andy Kubert*

----

# AS THE YOUNGEST SON OF LEGENDARY COMIC-BOOK ARTIST

JOE KUBERT, ANDY KUBERT MAY FEEL A CERTAIN PRESSURE TO UPHOLD THE FAMILY NAME. BUT IF HE'S AT ALL BURDENED BY THIS, HE SHOWS NO SIGN OF IT.

HIS ATTITUDE IS UNDERSTANDABLE. SINCE THE EARLY '90S WHEN HE TOOK OVER THE PENCILING CHORES ON *X-MEN* FROM JIM LEE, KUBERT HAS BEEN A FAVORITE OF MARVEL COMICS FANS. HE'S SERVED AS PENCILER ON SEVERAL OF THE COMPANY'S HIGH-PROFILE TITLES, INCLUDING *CAPTAIN AMERICA*, *ORIGIN*, AND, MOST RECENTLY, GAIMAN'S UNIQUE TAKE ON THE MARVEL UNIVERSE, *1602*.

IN ADDITION TO HIS WORK AT MARVEL, KUBERT CONTINUES TO WORK IN WHAT HE CALLS "THE FAMILY BUSINESS" – TEACHING AT THE JOE KUBERT SCHOOL OF CARTOON AND GRAPHIC ART IN DOVER, NEW JERSEY, FROM WHICH HE GRADUATED IN 1984 ALONGSIDE HIS BROTHER ADAM.

----

*With* Origin *and, now,* 1602, *you seem to have carved out your own little comics sub-genre – historical super-hero fiction. How did you get involved with* 1602?

[Marvel editor-in-chief] Joe Quesada had asked me to do both of these projects. Maybe he figured I could handle it, which was very nice. I saw Joe at a convention in Boston, I think it was right after 9/11. He had said, "I have something in mind for you after you finish *Origin*." I said, "What is it?" He didn't want to tell me what it was. I said, "Look, I'm not going to hold you to it. If you don't want to tell me, that's fine, but if you do tell me, it's okay. Don't worry about it. If it doesn't go through, it doesn't go through." So he told me it was a project with Neil Gaiman. I immediately said, "I'm going to hold you to it!" [*Laughs.*] So that's how it ended up that I did it.

*In a recent* Comic Book Artist *[issue 20] interview, you mentioned you felt very comfortable doing the research required of period-piece projects; for example, the research needed to do a war book. Was that part of the reason you were offered* 1602?

Very early in my career, when I was drawing the *Sergeant Rock* monthly book – it went to bi-monthly, probably in the mid-'80s – I would go out and buy all kinds of World War II books and World War II reference. I'd just get a kick out of sitting there, looking up this reference, and reading all about the time period and the history that I'm drawing. It gets your head involved in what you're doing. Now, with the Internet, it makes it a lot easier. You don't have to go to the bookstore all that much, there are places online you can go. I just like checking out what I'm drawing. With *1602*, there's so much history in that time period, it was so different as to what I had drawn before.

Really, before I even started, it took a long time to just get my head into it, into the setting, costumes, people, and the looks. It was a lot of fun, and I enjoyed doing it. It took a lot of time – it's been a year and a half that I've been working on it. I'm finishing it up now.

*As a kid, you weren't really a big super-hero fan, which is interesting, considering the work you're known for.*

If I liked the art, then I would probably read the story. I never really went to the comic shop growing up because my dad [Joe Kubert] would always bring home comics. But mostly what he brought home were DC Comics; he never brought home Marvels, because he worked for DC and was on their comp list. I remember reading and loving Neal Adams's *Batman* stuff. I didn't really look at the names of the artists, I just liked the artwork. Later on, I would know that, and say, "Oh, it's Neal Adams." I used to remember reading the Curt Swan *Superman* stuff, too, and I enjoyed that a lot. Maybe I used to read *Kamandi*, [but] it was mostly just the war stuff. It just caught on with me. Marvel stuff? I really never got exposed to it until I went to my dad's school, and with all the other students there – they're all comic fans – I just kind of got absorbed in the whole thing. That's when I got caught up with the Marvel stuff.

*I was wondering if your early interest in DC's war books and other non-super-hero titles influenced your recent work, which has featured super-heroes in historical settings.*

It probably has. I never really thought about it in that way, but it probably has.

*Were you also a history buff, growing up?*

I don't know if I was much of a buff, but I enjoy reading about it. I enjoy watching the History Channel, the Ken Burns things that are on PBS, *Modern Marvels* on the History Channel, those kinds of programs. I always check that stuff out.

*Origin had a unique look, for a mainstream super-hero project, which came from scanning your pencils directly into the computer. 1602 also has that look.*

We developed a style and a technique, between Richard Isanove and myself, that would work with it being digitally inked and digitally colored. What I *didn't* want were the pencils to look like pencils that were being done to be inked. And they shouldn't be – there should be tones in there; it should be done more like a painting, or a tonal drawing. (Before a painting is done you usually do a tonal drawing.) Instead of something with heavy solid blacks in it, I wanted the color to go on *top* of it, but I wanted to be able to see what was going on, in the shadow areas. That was the technique that we worked on. It's the same, basically, with *1602*. It's a little different in that it's tighter – I'm just rendering it tighter; the tones are rendered a little tighter. On *Origin*, the deadlines were a little tighter so there was a lot of fine drawing that I just didn't really have time to do. But in *1602*, I had the time to go in there with a sharper pencil and just play around a little bit more. That's pretty much the only difference between the two projects.

*At the time you were offered 1602, had you read much of Neil's work?*

I had read Neil's *Sandman* in the beginning. I should go back and re-read them, because it was so long ago.

*1602, as it progressed, changed from Neil's initial plan. He expanded the story as it went along.*

It was initially supposed to be six issues, and then we booted it up to eight. The last issue was double-sized, so you could say it is nine issues long. I think he had more of a story to tell. He had this story in his head that just couldn't fit into six issues.

*How would you describe Neil's scripts for 1602? I assume you were used to working from plots, since most of your career has been spent with Marvel.*

Traditionally, for most of my Marvel career, I had been working with just plots. Since Joe became editor-in-chief, I've mostly been getting full scripts, and I've really been enjoying them. Neil's scripts are great. They are very well thought out, they're phenomenal to read. He e-mails me the scripts, and I print them out; they're just a joy to read. He thinks it out, up and down, and sideways. A lot of times, you'll be sitting there reading it, and think, "How the hell did the guy think of that?" I'll call him on the phone and say, "That is just great," and I'll hear him on the other end saying, "Ah, thank you very much." [*Laughs.*] It just works out so well. The guy really knows what he's doing. It's a pleasure to work with somebody like that.

*How much of 1602's plot did Neil discuss with you before you began working on it?*

Before I started, he went over his whole idea with me, pretty much the whole outline of what he wanted to do. We were on the phone for so long when I first talked to him, the battery in my phone went dead. When we were going over the characters, I was jotting down his thoughts on the characters, what they should look like. And this was before I even put pencil to paper because I just really wanted to know his feelings on what these guys should look like, their mannerisms, what kind of clothes they would be wearing, what their backgrounds were at that time. I still have all those notes. It was an interesting experience, sitting down and going over all of it with him.

It was mostly me listening to him, to get his gist on it. He had this specific story in mind, he developed this whole thing as to what he wanted to do. I really wanted to stick closely to the vision that he had. He gave me a lot of direction with the characters and what he wanted them to look like. I would go and research all the costumes and things like that, and I would sketch them up and send it to him. Then we'd talk about it after he got them.

*Was there ever a case where Neil might have described a character a certain way, and, through your research, you found another way of depicting that character?*

I kept close to what he was looking for. If he had something else specific in mind, he would tell me, "Just change this a little bit," or "I picture that person with a longer beard," or "Why don't you put a goatee on that guy?"

*Which character design do you think worked best?*

I love Nick Fury. I think he worked out great. And I think Dr. Strange worked out well. And I'm very happy with Thor as well.

*Dr. Strange and Thor are the two major Marvel characters that seem to work best in 1602's time period... Were you aware that a lot of non-comics readers might pick up 1602 – Neil's audience of prose readers?*

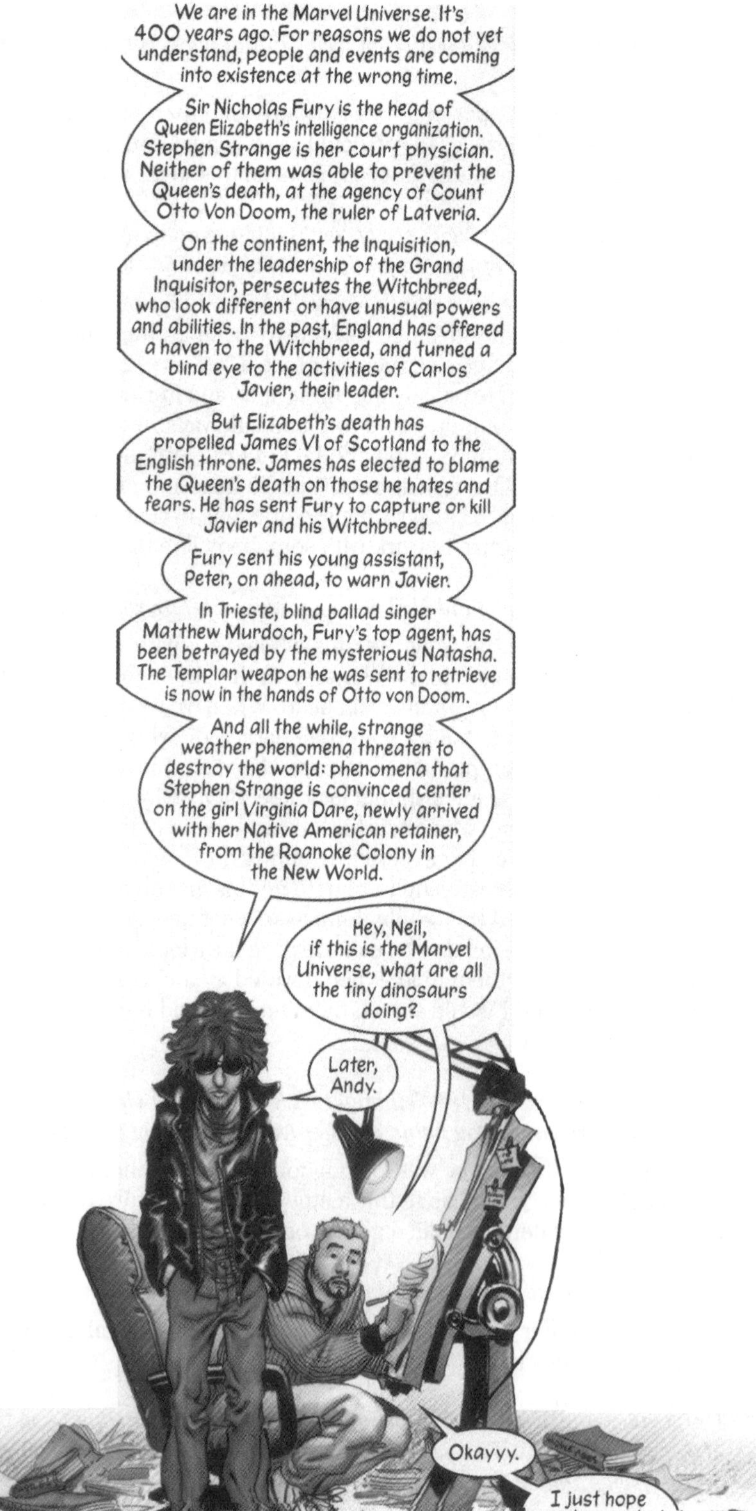
We are in the Marvel Universe. It's 400 years ago. For reasons we do not yet understand, people and events are coming into existence at the wrong time.
Sir Nicholas Fury is the head of Queen Elizabeth's intelligence organization. Stephen Strange is her court physician. Neither of them was able to prevent the Queen's death, at the agency of Count Otto Von Doom, the ruler of Latveria.
On the continent, the Inquisition, under the leadership of the Grand Inquisitor, persecutes the Witchbreed, who look different or have unusual powers and abilities. In the past, England has offered a haven to the Witchbreed, and turned a blind eye to the activities of Carlos Javier, their leader.
But Elizabeth's death has propelled James VI of Scotland to the English throne. James has elected to blame the Queen's death on those he hates and fears. He has sent Fury to capture or kill Javier and his Witchbreed.
Fury sent his young assistant, Peter, on ahead, to warn Javier.
In Trieste, blind ballad singer Matthew Murdoch, Fury's top agent, has been betrayed by the mysterious Natasha. The Templar weapon he was sent to retrieve is now in the hands of Otto von Doom.
And all the while, strange weather phenomena threaten to destroy the world: phenomena that Stephen Strange is convinced center on the girl Virginia Dare, newly arrived with her Native American retainer, from the Roanoke Colony in the New World.
Hey, Neil, if this is the Marvel Universe, what are all the tiny dinosaurs doing?
Later, Andy.
Okayyy.
I just hope you know what you're doing.

Gaiman and Andy Kubert, from page 1 of *1602* Part Five. Art by Andy Kubert. © 2004 Marvel Comics.

I was very aware that would happen. And I specifically designed the pages and panel layouts toward that purpose. I wanted to keep it as simple and straightforward as I could without making it boring. But I knew a lot of people that normally didn't read comics would be picking this up, and I didn't want to lose them. I kept the storytelling very straightforward, I wanted to keep it very clear; and I wanted the compositions to work as well as they could so people didn't have a tough time following the drawings, and where things go. One of the pleasures of working from a full script is that Neil writes in the dialogue so I can spot and leave enough room where those balloons go. I can design the panel and the page that way so balloons don't go over all the artwork and all the figures, so it's not difficult to tell what was going on.

*Has working on* 1602 *affected the direction of your career? For example, would you find it at all difficult to return to a traditional, contemporary super-hero book?*

To tell you the truth, I never really thought about that. I love doing super-heroes, I'd go back to it. I have no idea how I'm going to handle something until I'm actually sitting down, reading the script, working on the thumbnails, and figuring the thing out. The way I would approach a project, it's tough to say until I'm actually doing it and I know what the story is, I know who's involved, I know where the story is going. Would I approach it the same way as *1602*? Possibly.

*Are you interested in creating your own comics property? Do you have any ideas in the back of your mind?*

Definitely. I do have things on the back burner, but they're going to stay back there for a while, because Marvel keeps me pretty busy. Someday I definitely will go in that direction. I just don't know when.

*Do you ever worry about being perceived solely as a Marvel artist?*

I'm very comfortable with that. Marvel has treated me so well over the years. I have no complaints. I'm very comfortable with being considered a Marvel artist.

*Are you ever concerned that Marvel's present management could change one day? That those to whom you've remained loyal could leave the company?*

Since I've started working at Marvel, there have been four editor-in-chief changes (Shooter, DeFalco, Harras and now Quesada), three different owners, and I don't know how many presidents, publishers, and chief operating officers.

Every one of them has been very good to me, and I to them. For me to start worrying about a present management change now would be a waste of time. I concentrate on the work and the work ethic. Everything else, I have no control over.

*Of course, in addition to working for Marvel, you continue to teach at the Kubert School. How did you come to teach?*

It's something that my father and I had discussed. This is my third year of teaching, and we had been discussing it for a good few years before I started. This is a family business. And, of course, as in other family businesses, the father wants the kids to hopefully keep it running. That's basically what we're looking for. I do enjoy teaching. I find that while helping the students, I help myself. As I'm going over the students' work, it really helps me in my own thinking and in my own approach to drawing. Instead of doing things intuitively, I'm thinking things out more on my own.

*One of the best ways to learn something is to teach it to other people.*

You go over it step by step, and you're reasoning things. I never really did before. I was always more like, "This thing goes here and that thing goes there." But now as I'm discussing it with a student – "Okay, this figure goes here for this particular reason. The background goes here for that particular reason." In my own head, I'm thinking, "Oh, okay, there is a purpose for that background." My dad told me that would happen, and he was right. [*Laughs.*]

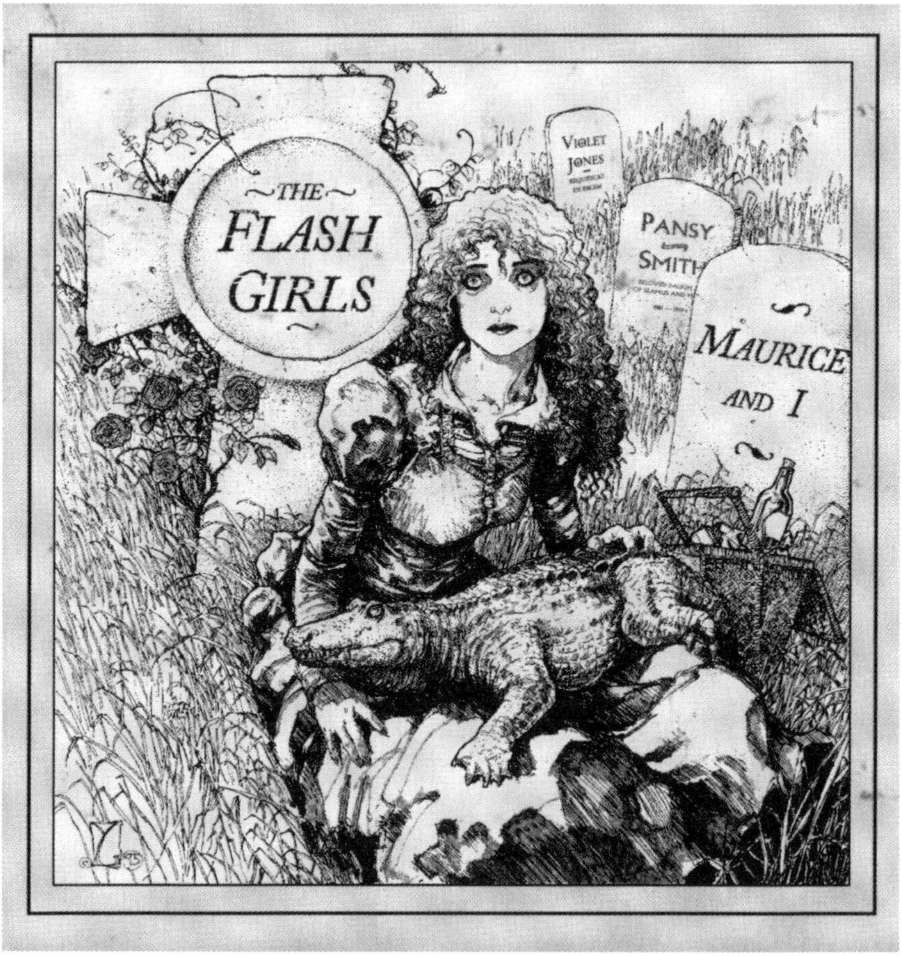
THE
FLASH
GIRLS
VIOLET
JONES
PANSY
SMITH
MAURICE
AND I

COVER OF *MAURICE AND I*, THE FLASH GIRLS' SECOND ALBUM. ART BY MICHAEL ZULLI. © 2004 MICHAEL ZULLI.

*The Flash Girls*

................................................................

# THE FLASH GIRLS WERE GAIMAN'S FIRST "HOUSE BAND."

THE DUO CONSISTED OF GUITARIST EMMA BULL (ALSO THE AUTHOR OF SUCH FANTASIES AS *THE WAR OF THE OAKS*) AND THE FIDDLE-PLAYING "FABULOUS" LORRAINE GARLAND.

TOGETHER, BULL AND GARLAND RECORDED THREE ALBUMS OF GOTHIC FOLK MUSIC – *THE RETURN OF PANSY SMITH AND VIOLET JONES* [SPIN ART, 1993], *MAURICE AND I* [FABULOUS RECORDS, 1995] (NAMED AFTER A NEW ORLEANS ALLIGATOR SKULL GIFT GARLAND RECEIVED FROM GAIMAN), AND *PLAY EACH MORNING WILD QUEEN* [FABULOUS RECORDS, 2001]. THEIR ALBUMS OFTEN FEATURED MUSIC AND LYRICS BY GAIMAN, AS WELL AS WRITERS LIKE JANE YOLEN AND ALAN MOORE.

THOUGH THE FLASH GIRLS WERE FORCED TO SEPARATE AFTER BULL MOVED FROM THE MINNEAPOLIS AREA – WHERE THEY WERE A PART OF THE MINNESOTA RENAISSANCE FESTIVAL – TO LOS ANGELES, IT WAS NOT BEFORE THE DUO HAD WON A SIZABLE FOLLOWING, AND A MINNESOTA MUSIC AWARD FOR "BEST WORLD FOLK GROUP" IN 1994. THE FLASH GIRLS ALSO APPEARED IN COMICS – IN DC'S *SOVEREIGN SEVEN* AND A CAMEO PANEL IN *SANDMAN* 73 ("SUNDAY MOURNING," ILLUSTRATED BY MICHAEL ZULLI, WHO CRAFTED THE COVER ART FOR THEIR LAST TWO ALBUMS).

WITH THE FLASH GIRLS ON AT LEAST TEMPORARY HIATUS, BULL CONTINUES TO WRITE PROSE FICTION, WHILE GARLAND PERFORMS WITH FOLK UNDERGROUND; WHICH SHE CO-FORMED IN 2002, SEVERAL MONTHS AFTER THE FOLLOWING INTERVIEW WAS RECORDED.

................................................................

*How did the two of you meet?*

Bull: Well, we met through Steve Brust, actually. Steve Brust is a fantasy writer from Minneapolis, and he found Lorraine out at the Renaissance Festival. All of his obsessions are so absorbing that his friends get sucked into them. So you're hanging out with Steve, and he's making hanging out at the Renaissance Festival – for which you are miserably overworked and thoroughly underpaid – look like the most fun you could possibly have for seven weekends out of the year. So I started hanging out with the people he was hanging out with, and I found myself in the most wonderful community of musicians and other creative people, and Lorraine was one of them. She started teaching me all these good tunes. That's how I met her. That's not how the Flash Girls formed, but that's how I met her.

Garland: We were even in another band together.

BULL: Oh, and wasn't that an experience.

Garland: The Merry Leprechauns.

Bull: Yes, we were called the Merry Leprechauns, and it was a fairly delightful experience because everyone else was shorter than us.

Garland: We hated it.

Bull: It was just abominable. But Steve was in it, and we liked Steve.

*I heard the Flash Girls formed at one of Neil's Guy Fawkes parties.*

Bull: That was the origin of the Flash Girls, right there.

Garland: It was late one night at Neil's first Guy Fawkes party. And we were sitting around the fire, and Em and I were pretending that we were rock stars. We had albums out and we were touring the world, and we were acting really big.

Bull: We were actually sitting out by this bonfire freezing to death, because we were in the upper mid-west and it's Guy Fawkes, which is typically in November. (I'm sorry, but I don't care what they tell you about solstices and equinoxes, that's when it is.) We were playing together. I was playing guitar and she was playing the fiddle, and we were doing all these tours and having a great time, and Lorraine was kind of teaching me new things and I was playing along, and we were talking about how marvelous we were, and how famous we were, and how incredibly cool we were.

Garland: And then her husband, another writer – Will Shetterly – got really mad. He lost his whole cool, and went into this rant, saying, "You don't seem to understand that if you guys actually became a band together you could do all this. There's nothing you could think about that couldn't happen."

Bull: He was really peeved. He said, "Quit wasting your time fantasizing and run with that, and do stuff." Will is one of those people who's always got a really good plan for all of his friends' lives. And sometimes they actually take him up on it, and it's a good thing. So we said, "Do we want to be a band?"

Garland: And we said, "Okay." Really it was the only way to make him stop, so we had to form a band.

Bull: But we didn't know what we were going to call ourselves. We were at an Irish pub in St. Paul, watching our friends perform, and they did a song that we'd never heard before called "Rockin' the Cradle," which has this line in it: *"Come all ye young men with a motion to marry and pray won't you leave those flash girls alone."* And "flash" is this word that means, well, maybe "no better than they should be," "a little bit con-artist," "a little bit snazzy," maybe "a little bit too high-toned to be completely dependable and reputable."

Garland: And we thought, how perfect!

Bull: We were sitting around the table, and we were digging the song, and Will said, "You could call yourselves that." And we said, "Flash Girls!" Will said, "You'll be the Flash Girls." But he said it in an Irish accent, because we were in the Merry Leprechauns.

Garland: We weren't really.

*You mean you were kidding?*

Garland: I'm so sorry.

*"A little bit con-artist," eh?*

Bull: But that will not be the last you hear of it. We could keep this up.

Garland: I always tell pretty much the same joke over and over again on stage. It gets things tuned *real* quickly.

Bull: Yes. There's very little dead time on stage when Lorraine tells a joke. We're right there. Do you want to tell him about how we actually came to make a CD?

Garland: We thought we would make a little demo tape, and we'd have something to sell at the Ren Fest.

Bull: Just a dopey little cassette, y'know? So we got into the studio and we did the first day of recording and then we went out to eat and had a couple of pitchers of beer...

Garland: Each! And it was like, "Let's just make a CD. Let's do the best thing we can do. Let's throw this puppy out into the world and see what happens."

Bull: Now, unfortunately, we had decided pretty much after we had laid down the basic tracks for all of the songs. So the attitude changed entirely after we had material down that we couldn't really afford to spend the studio time replacing. And let's face it, we just didn't know as much.

Garland: We were babes.

Bull: We just weren't as good at what we do. I mean it's not that I think we're fabulous at what we do now. This is a work in progress.

Garland: We listen to it now in little places and think –

Bull: "Oh, no. Don't go there! Aw, you went there..."

*Let's talk a little bit about Neil. Besides throwing the party at which the Flash Girls were formed, he wrote several of the songs on that first album.*

Bull: We have pillaged his output mercilessly. We figure, as long as he writes things that rhyme, we'll turn them into songs.

Garland: We turn stuff into songs that he doesn't even know is...

Bull: There was the "Herring Song" story. That was the best pillaging we've ever done. That's quite splendid. Tell him the "Herring Song" story.

Garland: When I first went to work for Neil, he was showing me how to move files around on my computer that he'd just got. I knew nothing, and so he created a file and he showed me how to move it around. A couple of months later, I said, "I've got a tune for 'The Herring Song.'" He said, "What are you talking about?" I said, "You know. You wrote one." I sang, "...*I was a tiny little girl, I ate my herrings with gusto...*" He said, "That wasn't a song." [*Bull and Garland sing*] "...*my bust was tight and my nose was long, and I drank my fortune away...*"

Bull: Yes. So Lorraine says to him, "Really, we have a tune for it." He says, "But it wasn't really meant to be a song, wasn't really meant to have a tune and be sung out in front of people." We said, "Uh, too late now." It was great. We just simply nabbed and ran off with it, sort of like a dog stealing your lunch.

*Was that the first song you did based on something Neil had written?*

Bull: No, "Tea Song" and "Post-Mortem" were actually the first ones and those are both on the first album, which is now thoroughly unavailable.

Garland: Neil was sort of sitting on the couch one night after a party, sort of strumming a guitar and singing "The Tea Song." I said, "What was that?" He said, "Well, years ago, you know..."

Bull: It's actually "Tea and Corpses," because otherwise it ends up sounding like the titles of *Friends* episodes, which always begin with "The one about..." Otherwise we'd have to make all the Neil songs "The 'something' song." We have to actually give them titles.

Garland: He gave me that and then he said, "Here," and he gave me a bunch of poems and lyrics he'd written.

*Previously unpublished?*

Garland: Yes. It was just stuff he'd written.

Bull: At the point at which we started doing this, *Sandman* was out and very popular, and *Violent Cases* was out, and *Signal to Noise.* And he'd done *Good Omens* with Terry Pratchett. But Neil was actually at the start of his career at this point. He had really just become a phenomenon in America.

*This was around 1992 or 1993.*

Bull: I wrote "Signal to Noise" as a song for Cats Laughing, the band that Flojo Russo and I were in. And Neil liked the song, and he liked the concept of the title. He called me up and said, "Can I use that as the title for a script I'm doing, because it's about the amount of noise in any information. That's one of the themes that's going on in the story." I said, "Excellent! I would be proud. That would be wonderful." And, in fact, in the first edition there's a note saying, "Thank you so much for the title." People keep thinking that the Flash Girls wrote the song in response to his graphic novel, but if you check the copyright dates, I think the song is copyright 1988, or something like that. Writers, and artists of all kinds, are always doing that, saying, "I want to put that in. Can I borrow that?" or "You inspired me to do this" or "Do you mind if I do something very much like your character, as an homage?" You get to steal from each other, with permission. It's really swell.

*Have most of the times you've collaborated with Neil been similar to the ones you've described, with the two of you taking something he's already written?*

Bull: There are times when he has words for which we don't have a tune yet, and we'll take them and do the tune. We've done that with a couple of his things.

*Who usually comes up with a tune?*

Bull: Sometimes he does, sometimes we do. He does about half the time. Sometimes there's someone else involved. What's the other credit on "Personal Thing"?

Garland: He had a friend many years ago who had written a tune, and he'd said it was a wonderful tune, except it needed to resolve differently. There needed to be one more little line on it, so he added the little line on it.

Bull: So the music was by the friend, and the addition and lyrics are Neil's. The story of the third album [*Play Each Morning Wild Queen*] was "Gee, let's do an album.

You know we haven't played together for five years, but that never stopped us before. Let's do an album." We had some stuff that was left over from our repertoire that we had never got to, that we had learned and started doing after the second album [*Maurice and I*]. So we had some stuff that we knew we wanted to put on the album – and then there's the rest of the album. And I had to move to Los Angeles; so it wasn't as if we'd been developing material for four years. I barely remembered how to play guitar for God's sake.

Garland: But I believed in this album, for I had a vision.

Bull: [*Laughs.*] But we really wanted to do an album. We said, "Look, let's see what we've got." I came out maybe three days before we were scheduled to go into the studio. I came out and settled into the spare room – actually it was the library – and we started going out to the summer house and playing some tunes, saying "Do we know this?" Lorraine comes up with this amazing sort of early music vocal group that does this ridiculous old English tavern song, "Nottingham Ale." She says, "We should do this." I said, "Yes, we certainly should." Lorraine said, "You've got these friends – The Tim Malloys, who are the roughest, toughest Irish band in the world – to sing drunken male chorus." I said, "Obviously we need that." There was a song! Neil came along and said, "Well, how about this?" And he played us "Personal Thing" on the piano. "Personal Thing" is the saddest song in the world really.

Garland: It's a love song from a ghost.

Bull: Yes. It sounds as if this is the kind of thing that's driving that ghost who can't leave the house; the one who makes the cold spots in the hall. It sounds as if that's the story behind somebody who's caught in this thing that they were never able to resolve, that they were never able to do anything about, and it's kept them here forever. It's a wonderful song. Yes, obviously that was going on the album. He played it, and it was one of those songs of which I pretty much learned the tune the first time he played it. The tune was *that* right – it had kind of an inevitability, it was just, "Of course, now I know that."

*How prolific is Neil as a songwriter? Does he write much without the intent of recording it?*

Bull: He writes all the time, as writers do. You never really know, because all of the sudden he'll go, "You know, I once wrote a song…" Or I'll be going through files or boxes and pull something out and go, "This is lovely," and he'll say, "Yeah, well…" "Yeti" he wrote when he was seventeen.

Garland: "Yeti" – off the second album – and he claims to be terribly embarrassed by it.

Bull: And yet every now and again he mentions wistfully that it's been a while since he's heard it. He's not embarrassed by it. He's very proud of it actually. It's a very silly song. And it's got that kind of Gilbert-and-Sullivan patter-song quality. It's a good'n. He's right to not really be as embarrassed by it as he says he is.

*But he writes some music specifically for the Flash Girls.*

Garland: Oh, yes. "I think I've written a Flash Girls song, " he'll say, and we'll listen to it.

Bull: There's nothing like having a house band. If you have friends who have a band, who think you write cool stuff, you're going to write more cool stuff with the likelihood of them using it, because they're going to want for that sort of thing.

Garland: When Emma had moved to LA, and we were a little geographically challenged, Neil said, "I miss having you guys around, because I write songs for you. I love writing these songs. It's very fun, a very nice outlet, and now that you're not performing them I don't have them."

Bull: Opportunity produces a lot of art. And there is some art that will be produced without the opportunity, that will be produced whether it's a good moment for it or not. But there's nothing like, for instance, knowing there's an editor at a magazine who likes your stories to get you to write stories. And having a house band, having a bunch of people who say, "We really like that song..." I think there was only one song [of Neil's] that I really didn't like. And that was a theological issue for me, it really was. It was really funny, really cool. Has anyone done it?

Garland: No one's ever done it.

Bull: There's no reason that someone shouldn't do it. It's just that I wasn't comfortable with it. It's an Adam-and-Eve song, and it's a charming take on that version of the Adam-and-Eve story with which I'm just not comfortable, which is "It's the girl's fault." And as funny as the song was, I just...felt weird about repeating it. But it was an entirely personal thing (to name another cool song). But it was entirely me, it was one of those things where it was "All right, we won't make you do the song. We really like it but we won't make you do the song." And I said, "Thank you."

Garland: He's got another one that's almost finished, that he's had for years and years, called "Old Nick at Night." At first, I said, "I'm not doing that song. It's sort of naughty." Now, as years have gone by, I say, "Why don't you finish 'Old Nick at Night'?"

Bull: As we get older, we get a little saltier.

Garland: I think that "Old Nick at Night" may well wind up as the one song we're sure about on the next album.

Bull: See, this is how our albums show up now. It's like, "Well, we've got a vague idea of where it's going." I'm trying to remember some of the other ones we didn't have until we started...and some of them mutated. Some of them were things that we had done live often, that became different.

*Neil mentioned he was in a punk band at sixteen. Do you know how long he was involved with that?*

Garland: Oh, for some years. I didn't know him then of course (at that time I was in junior high). But he was sixteen then, and I think, although I'm not quite sure, he was a singer, and they got pretty good; as I hear the story. There was some interest in them, and they had some gigs.

*They toured?*

Garland: A little bit. As much as sixteen-year-olds can get together.

Bull: You can do more of that in England, because England's smaller, but basically, you're still sixteen.

Garland: And you need to get your dad to pick you up afterwards.

*Has Neil ever performed live with you?*

Garland: Not as a musician. He does wonderful readings.

Bull: He's hormonally challenged that way. It would be tough for him to be a Flash Girl.

# FORMER FLASH GIRL "FABULOUS" LORRAINE GARLAND

TEAMED WITH TWO FELLOW RENAISSANCE FESTIVAL MUSICIANS – ACCORDIONIST TREVOR HARTMAN AND GUITARIST PAUL SCORE – IN 2002 TO FORM FOLK UNDERGROUND, GAIMAN'S PRESENT "HOUSE BAND." THOUGH THEY'VE ONLY RECENTLY RECORDED THEIR FIRST ALBUM – 2003'S AMUSING AND MACABRE *BURIED THINGS* [FABULOUS RECORDS] – THE STRONG REVIEWS IT RECEIVED FROM FOLK-ROCK CRITICS AND THE APPLAUSE THE TRIO GENERATE AT THEIR LIVE PERFORMANCES POINT TO A BRIGHT FUTURE.

GAIMAN – ALONGSIDE SUCH WRITERS AS JANE YOLEN AND THE MAGNETIC FIELDS' STEPHIN MERRITT – CONTRIBUTED THREE SONGS TO *BURIED THINGS*: THE BAND'S EPONYMOUS SIGNATURE TUNE; "GOING WODWO"; AND THE FAUSTIAN "THE BUTTERFLY ROAD" (WITH ITS EERIE CHORUS: "NOW THERE'S NO GOING BACK, AND THERE'S SOMETHING UNDEAD, IN YOUR MIND AND YOUR EYES, IN YOUR HEART AND YOUR HEAD. AND IF ANYONE ASKS HOW YOU FEEL, JUST SAY IT WAS PART OF THE DEAL...").

GARLAND, HARTMAN, AND SCORE ARE CURRENTLY WORKING ON THEIR FOLLOW-UP TO *BURIED THINGS*.

*What led to the end of the Flash Girls and the beginning of Folk Underground?*

Garland: Emma left and moved away to California, to La-La Land, and I was band-less for some years. I met Trevor, working in a belly-dance band together. (We weren't the belly dancers, we were the music!) And Trevor knew Paul his whole life.

*Lorraine, do you and Trevor go back before the Flash Girls?*

Garland: No. The Flash Girls had been broken up, or geographically-challenged, some years before I ever met Trevor, or Paul.

*How would you say Folk Underground's music differs from that of the Flash Girls?*

Garland: They're boys. It's definitely different working with boys than it was with Emma. Emma and I very much shared a brain, and it's hard to share a brain with boys.

Hartman: [*Laughs.*] I always thought Paul and I shared a brain for many years.

Score: We're still trying to figure out whose it is.

Hartman: [*Laughs.*] We differ from the Flash Girls in that there's a lot more you can do with three people singing, and three people all having their own instruments, than just two. So that's kinda helpful.

Score: We've got a really good live sound that's very full. The drums definitely add the low end. Vocally, we can do the nice three-part harmony, which is always really fun.

Garland: It's great seeing what kind of things come out of Trevor's head or Paul's head. It's a whole new direction, wilder than the Flash Girls ever were.

*Trevor and Paul, what was your background? Goth and folk, as Lorraine's was?*

Score: Our background is really very far away from what we're actually playing. But we have a very diverse interest in lots of different types of music. The way it came about is I knew I was going to be out at a festival, around these two, at the same time. And usually when you stay out there overnight on weekends, musicians get together and jam, so I got a hold of some Flash Girls CDs and learned some of the tunes off of them.

Hartman: At the time Lorraine and I were in the belly-dance troupe, and after all of the performances that day, I invited Paul to our dressing room and he started playing his guitar. Paul and I were working on some stuff together from before that, and we were thinking about just kicking out some music, doing a bunch of stuff like They Might Be Giants tunes or something, just for fun, and maybe playing some coffee shops. But that night, when Paul was playing some Flash Girls tunes…

Garland: I was really tired. I was actually saying, "I'm going to bed, I'm too tired, I can't stay up any more. We've got a show tomorrow. Forget it." And then they started playing one of my songs…ignored me. "Well okay, show me how does it go here, Paul? How does it go here?" And I said, "Wait a minute, wait a minute, no, it goes like this. This is how we do it." By the end of the night, we had a few songs down, and we started to play them the very next day at the festival.

Score: Well, when we played the very next day, that was a great effect. People asked us if we had a CD. This was the first time we played the songs!

Hartman: We'd been together for *less* than twenty-four hours, but… [*Laughs.*]

*Your first gig as Folk Underground was at Minneapolis's First Avenue, the club featured in the film* Purple Rain.

Garland: It was. In the main room, close to a thousand people.

Hartman: That was actually our first gig, after we decided on a band name and unified our direction.

Garland: It was six weeks after we had formed and it was an unusual spot for our first gig.

*One of your first Flash Girls gigs was also at First Avenue, Lorraine, when you opened for the late Warren Zevon.*

Garland: It was. I think our third gig. Our first two were at coffee shops. Sometimes, you know, you have a few drinks and it seems like a good idea.

*What was that experience like?*

Garland: I remember hanging onto a post, and everybody telling me how calm I looked. I thought, "I'm hanging onto a post because I'm about to fall over." All that was going through my head was, "Don't throw up, don't throw up." It was pretty scary.

*Regarding Folk Underground – apparently Neil wasn't crazy at first about the band's name.*

Garland: Not originally. He thought it was blah and boring. We told him, "No, it's like folk *under* ground, you know, dead things, buried things. They're dead."

Score: Not the sort of "Kumbaya" folk band.

Hartman: We didn't want that. We had a bunch of options we wanted to use before that, but we looked them up online, and all the ones we wanted to use were already taken, like Wake The Dead, Rogue Band, etcetera… We kicked around a few. Perhaps the selling point for Folk Underground was when we realized we could have t-shirts that had "FU" on them. [*Laughs.*]

Garland: And chant "FU! FU!" which they (the audience) have.

*Having heard you play live, I can say your music is both darker and funnier than the Flash Girls. Is that intentional?*

Score: I think it's intentional. There are times when we take it back a little bit, where we think, "No, that's too far."

Hartman: "That's too dark." Right.

Garland: Sometimes we have songs where nobody dies, so we actually kill somebody off just to… [*Laughs.*]

*Neil wrote three of the songs on your first CD,* Buried Things, *including your eponymous signature song.*

Hartman: Yes, he did lyrics and music for that one. And he did the lyrics for "Wodwo," which we stole.

Score: That was one we did without even realizing we were doing it.

Garland: I love the poem. It was published in Ellen Datlow's *The Green Man: Tales from the Mythic Forest*, in 2002, and I had it up in my office. We were kicking around song ideas and I thought, "This would make a great song." And literally, five minutes later, Trevor had written it.

*For your signature song, did you request "Folk Underground" from Neil, or was it his idea?*

Hartman: Neil offered because he wanted to make sure people knew it was things dark and creepy versus folky and lame. So he offered, and we said, "Great, by all means," inwardly thinking, "Hell, yeah!"

Score: I remember he came back with the first two verses of it, and with the musical content for it. We played with it for a while, and basically brought it back to him and said, "This is fantastic."

Hartman: "We need more."

Score: We said, "Can you write a third verse?" So he wrote a third verse, and it was just fantastic.

Garland: It's a wonderful song.

*The third song he wrote on* Buried Things – *"The Butterfly Road" – how did this one come about?*

Garland: That was one Neil had written and given to us, and then he went out of town, out of the country, and…

Hartman: It was kind of a vaudevillian tune that he had popping around in his head, and he already had the lyrics to. He gave it to us to do, and then promptly left the country. And so, having heard it in months previous in the studio, we cranked it out as best we could in remembering what he played for us. Turns out it wasn't exactly what was in his head, when he wrote it, so we'll hopefully be re-doing that one for him. But can anyone truly know what is lurking in Neil's head?

Garland: He's got some spoken-word CDs that are coming out every few months that Adam Stemple – who produced *Buried Things*, and all of the Flash Girls CDs – is producing, and I think the next one will have that version of "The Butterfly Road" on there.

Score: So there will be two versions.

Hartman: We like it and we think it's a great song. It's just the fact that it didn't quite match what Neil's original vision of it was.

Garland: Chris Ewen from Future Bible Heroes is also playing around with some of our songs, doing dance mixes.

*It would be interesting to hear his take on them… The Flash Girls contributed music to* Warning: Contains Language *[DreamHaven, 1995], one of Neil's spoken word CDs. Will Folk Underground also contribute to those?*

Garland: It's definitely in the plan.

*Most of your songs actually have a fair amount in common with Neil's fiction, in that they cheerfully subvert, in this case, traditional folk songs. Obviously through the lyrics, but also subtly through the music.*

Garland: I think it just comes from the process of working together and playing music that we think is fun to play. The Neil song, "A Girl Needs a Knife" [from *Maurice and I*], which the Flash Girls did, we're doing that now, and Trevor and I both sing it. Having a male vocal in there gives it a whole different feel, a whole different meaning.

*Trevor and Lorraine, you have an appealing dynamic in your duets. Sort of a Sonny and Cher vibe.*

Hartman: [*Laughs.*] I've never heard that one before. That's good. I can deal with that, I suppose. Speaking for myself, I never really paid attention to the lyrics much. I'm more interested in the music, and I think the lyrics came about being inspired by our name and which direction that was heading. It could also be because of the people we generally like to frequent with – people who are into science fiction, fantasy, and conventions, and who might have read Neil's books.

*Are the three of you fans of science fiction and fantasy?*

Hartman: Well, yes. I think that contributes to the morbidity. I'm into things like *Star Trek* and *Star Wars*, Japanimation, role-playing, and Paul is into…

Score: I'm into all that stuff, and the fact that my professional career is in science doesn't help any either. [*Laughs.*]

Garland: I think it frees you up, too, to admit, "Yeah, we're all geeks," so we don't have to come across as cool. We don't try to follow any kinds of trends or create a certain kind of music that will sell because of its appeal. It's just...kinda us.

Hartman: We're playing music for people who would rather have had Wookies on Endor than Ewoks. That's who our fans are. [*Laughs.*]

Score: We all have a naturally dark sense of humor, too.

Hartman: Right. We go with those lyrics, but, musically, we're all across the board.

Score: For me, a good song has to be interesting on more than one level. You can have a great song that's a driving melody, but if the lyrics are empty, that's not as good as it could be.

Garland: The one thing about this band was how quickly it got together. It was so intense – by the end of that first night, I knew we were a band. And that we *were* going to make this great music. It was just instant.

*You recently played your first gig with Neil, accompanying him as he read* Coraline *on Minnesota public radio. How did that go?*

Garland: It went wonderfully. Absolutely fabulously wonderful. Katherine Lanpher, the host of *Talking Volumes* (the name of the radio show), couldn't have been nicer and sweeter to us. Neil, of course, does this sort of thing brilliantly.

Hartman: He seems generally pleased, so that's all we can hope for.

*Lorraine, there's something I've been meaning to ask you – how does one become "fabulous"?*

Garland: If you believe it enough, it can happen. [*Laughs.*] Someone put it on an answering machine in California when I was out there on tour with the Flash Girls. It said, "If you're looking for the Fabulous Lorraine, she's down at Dark Carnival." Apparently forty people called that day and it stuck.

We're starting to work on some new Neil songs. I've got four or five lyrics to start working on musically. I could never come up with any tunes for them, but Trevor and Paul have got such great gifts for writing music.

*How long ago were these written?*

Garland: Some of these go way back. There's one actually from an early *Sandman* – or was it *Death?* – "My Name is Judy and I Died Back in '69." Of course, we'll probably have some more Jane Yolen on the next one, and we're actually messing around with an Alan Moore song.

*Regarding Neil's approach to writing music – he seems to experiment a good deal with songs. For example, with "Banshee," his initial idea was to write a song constructed as a pantoum, was it not?*

Garland: Yes. That one was amazing. It's just that form of poetry that hardly anyone knows.

*Line 1 and line 3 in one verse were to become line 2 and line 4 in the next verse. But apparently it evolved into something else when Neil added a tune.*

Garland: He had another one called "Sonnet in the Dark" that I always thought would be fun to do as sort of an a cappella number, but it was an actual sonnet. It was on the first Flash Girls CD [*The Return of Pansy Smith and Violet Jones*], which is thankgodfully out of print.

*Was Neil very pleased when Folk Underground formed, because he had a band for which he could write regularly once more?*

Garland: He said he'd missed it. In the few years when I wasn't playing in a band, he said to me a couple of times, "I wish you were in a band because I like writing songs. I like writing for you."

Score: When Trevor and I and Lorraine got together and started all this, Trevor and I had no *idea* about this whole side of Neil writing songs. We had no idea that it was...

Hartman: An option.

Score: [*Laughs.*] Yes. A source of creativity.

*How busy do you find yourselves?*

Garland: We keep getting the strangest gigs. The radio thing at the Fitzgerald Theater with Neil is a whole new level of venue. It makes me wonder what's going to happen next.

Score: It was hilarious – when we first got together, our big hope was "Yeah, we can play coffee shops on the weekends, and do gigs like that, where we just hang out and play acoustically and do our stuff!" And...we have yet to play in a coffee shop. [*Laughs.*] We played First Avenue twice and several other major theaters.

Hartman: We're going to keep doing weddings and pig roasts. [*Laughs.*]

Garland: My whole thing is: Life is short, just go for it. Take it as far as you can, as fast as you can, and enjoy the ride. We want to record more of Neil's songs, and see what exactly will happen next, and just hope people keep enjoying the music. The music is what is important. That *is* it in a nutshell.

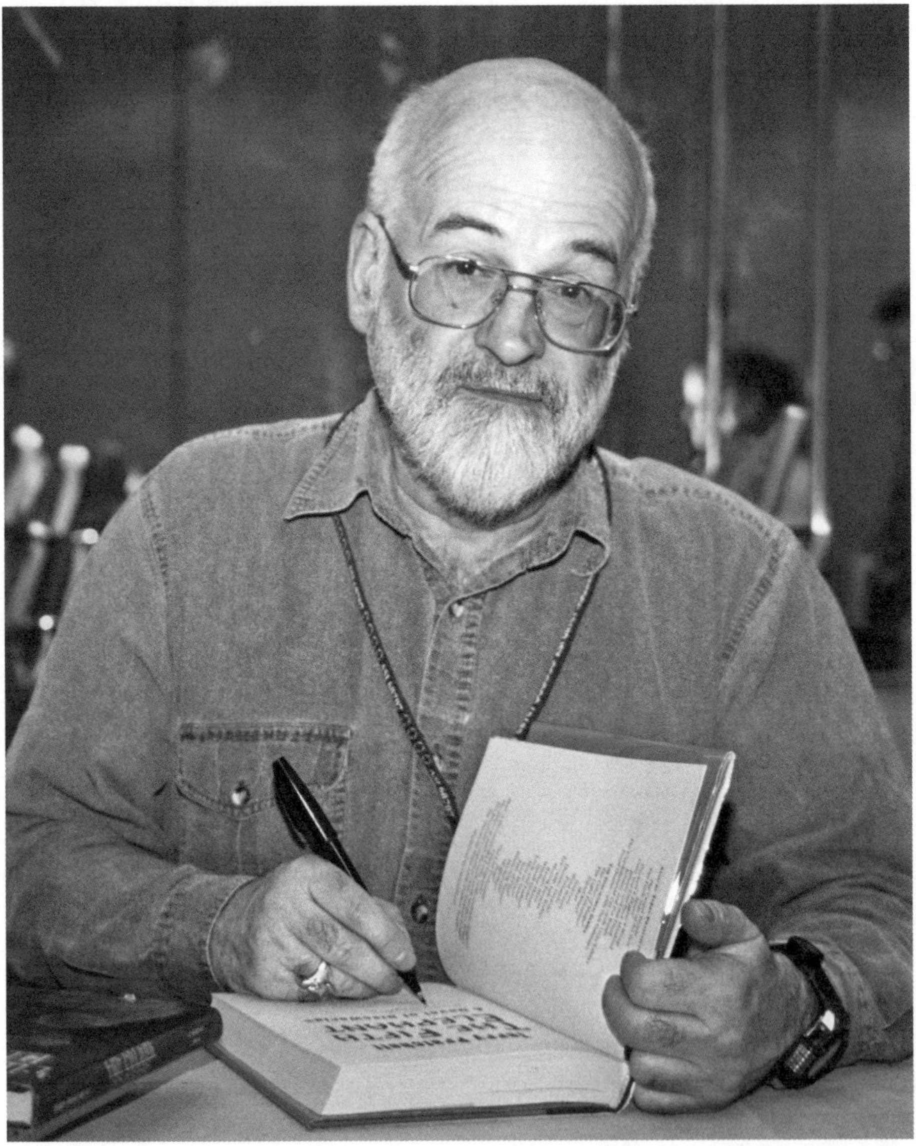

*Terry Pratchett*

..............................................................................................

# IT'S BEEN SAID THAT ONE TENTH OF ALL BOOKS SOLD
IN THE U.K. ARE FANTASY, AND THAT ONE TENTH OF ALL FANTASY BOOKS SOLD IN THE U.K. ARE TERRY PRATCHETT BOOKS.

PRATCHETT BEGAN HIS CAREER AS A JOURNALIST. HE WROTE HIS EARLY NOVELS IN HIS SPARE TIME BEGINNING WITH 1971'S *THE CARPET PEOPLE*. IN 1983, *THE COLOR OF MAGIC*, THE FIRST OF PRATCHETT'S MANY SATIRICAL *DISCWORLD* NOVELS, WAS RELEASED IN THE U.K. BY COLIN SMYTHE, LAUNCHING A PUBLISHING PHENOMENON THAT CONTINUES TO THIS DAY. THERE HAVE BEEN TWENTY-NINE *DISCWORLD* NOVELS PUBLISHED THUS FAR, EACH ONE FURTHER DEVELOPING ONE OF THE MOST FULLY-REALIZED WORLDS IN FANTASY LITERATURE.

IN 1990, *GOOD OMENS*, CO-AUTHORED BY GAIMAN – WHOM PRATCHETT HAD BEFRIENDED YEARS EARLIER – WAS PUBLISHED (BY GOLLANCZ). WITH ITS HUMOROUS TAKE ON THE APOCALYPSE, *GOOD OMENS* HAS LONG BEEN IN DEVELOPMENT AS A FILM PROJECT (THOUGH IT IS CURRENTLY STALLED) UNDER DIRECTOR TERRY GILLIAM.

PRATCHETT WAS MADE AN OFFICER OF THE BRITISH EMPIRE (OBE) IN 1998 FOR HIS SERVICES TO LITERATURE. AND HE ACHIEVED A LEVEL OF CRITICAL SUCCESS TO MATCH HIS COMMERCIAL ACHIEVEMENTS IN 2001 WHEN HE WAS AWARDED ENGLAND'S PRESTIGIOUS CARNEGIE MEDAL FOR THE FIRST CHILDREN'S *DISCWORLD* NOVEL *MAURICE AND HIS EDUCATED RODENTS*. THE BOOK'S SUCCESS HAS SPAWNED THE FOLLOW-UP NOVELS *THE WEE FREE MEN* AND *A HAT FULL OF SKY*. PRATCHETT'S NEWEST ADULT *DISCWORLD* NOVEL IS *GOING POSTAL*.

..............................................................

*Where are you from originally? Which part of England?*

It would probably mean very little to Americans, but I was born in Beaconsfield, Buckinghamshire, which was the town where G.K. Chesterton lived. That was why I started reading him, because my grandparents knew him. They weren't friends of his as such, but he was a guy they saw around the town. My grandmother described him as a big, fat man with a squeaky voice. But because he was a local author, she had some of his books, and I read those in my very, very early teens. That was another way into fantasy, because Chesterton wrote two – I think – of the most influential fantasy novels of the early twentieth century, which were *The Man Who Was Thursday*, from which half the spy movies you ever see eventually derive, and *The Napoleon of Notting Hill*, which is at the very root of fantasy, I think. Just as an aside, I imagine if you've spoken to Neil Gaiman, he may have mentioned Chesterton as well, because we're both fans of the man.

*One of his* Sandman *characters is based on Chesterton – Fiddler's Green.*

And we make a little homage to Chesterton in *Good Omens*.

*Who were some of the other fantasy authors who influenced you as a youth?*

"Influence" is kind of the wrong kind of word, because it's rather like "Ah, did you get such-and-such from so-and-so?" But from my point of view it was the normal ones – James Branch Cabell, Leiber, Tolkien, Vance. But there was a period from about the age of twelve to when I was about seventeen or eighteen where I just read *any* SF I could get my hands on, and I read incredibly fast. I don't read so fast now because I tend to read far more non-fiction; with fiction you can kind of skim.

*What made you want to write? Was it reading the work of these people?*

One of the very nice things about fandom is there is this tacit encouragement to write: if you go to cons and you're not a complete dork you can hang out with real writers. Certainly in the U.K., where they'll probably be in the bar and thirsty. You can edge into a group, and, again, if you're still not a dork, and you make the occasional intelligent comment, you become part of it, and then suddenly you think, "Hey, this is me talking to Arthur C. Clarke..." or whatever. And then, without any conscious decision being made, it just kind of creeps up on you that "maybe I can do this stuff as well." I know of no other genre or branch of literature where this sort of thing happens. Romance writers have something equivalent to conventions, and so do western writers, but I don't believe either of them can be attended by the readers as well.

*When you wrote* The Color of Magic, *the first* Discworld *novel, did you see the potential for a series of books? Were you already thinking several books ahead?*

The best answer I can give you is – not consciously. I'm no Tolkien. Tolkien planned a world in minute detail and then wrote the story. I do it the other way around: The stories create the world. Once the world has been created then, fine, other stories must obey the laws, but the characters and the story come first.

*As richly developed as Discworld is, the books never become a travelogue. It's always evident that the characters are at the forefront.*

A large proportion of the stories are set in a comparatively small area – Ankh-Morpork, for example – and quite a few of the stories have never gone outside the city. The city itself is now a major character within the series. I think it's a bit too easy just to get a bunch of guys together to make them go on a quest.

*Yes, any kid playing a role-playing game can do that.*

Oh, "You better have the wizard," you know, "Better have the dwarf, better have the elf..."

*Discworld works as satire, obviously, and has proven to be a flexible milieu. But has there been any subject that you would like to satirize, but felt wouldn't quite work in Discworld?*

The present-day in *Discworld* is set in an indeterminate time. I like to think it's sort of very late Georgian, with something like an industrial revolution going on... Some things are racing ahead. They already have a kind of mechanical version of the Internet practically, but they don't have steam. They have, in some respects, quite a modern political outlook, but they have no electricity, and some aspects of the society are still quite medieval. On the other hand, Ankh-Morpork has a small condom factory. Something of a first, I feel.

There was a thread on the Internet some time ago about "sexism" in the books, by which the vague term was meant: Not enough roles for women. Well, the Witches' books are just full of roles for women, and there's quite a few of them. But if books are set in something which resembles a pre-Victorian England, then the number of roles for women are limited by the very nature of the period. If you try to buck this by applying some kind of modern "equal opportunities" thinking, then you end up with a medieval southern California run by the Society for Creative Anachronism. It doesn't work. It rings false. But there are ways of making a virtue out of the restrictions, and I think I've done that in *Monstrous Regiment*.

There have been times when I've considered a subject and thought: "That's a good story, but it wouldn't fit in *Discworld*. I can't make it fit. It would change too much." Let's think, for example, "Hey, why don't we invent the railways?" Well, yeah, fine, but once you invent the railways, you have seriously changed your civilization and there's no going back. Now you've got the bulk movement of people and materials over long distances, cheaply, and you're beginning a huge upheaval. You can't have a medieval society with railways *continuing to be a medieval society*, even if you've got dragons heating the boilers. It's too easy for people to run away, news spreads too quickly, it's too easy to derail the Sheriff of Nottingham's train. Your society will change in a major way. Plenty of good stories there, but before long, your world is going to be unrecognizable.

*You co-wrote* Good Omens *with Neil. I spoke with him about that experience, and he said working with you was like going to college. He felt like a journeyman, and that you were a master craftsman, a "Wedgewood chair-maker," and he said he'd "never made a chair before," but that he'd "had some experience as a woodworker." What are your feelings about that collaboration?*

One person had to carry the book, because Neil still had *Sandman* to produce on a regular basis, whereas I could just put down that book in place of a *Discworld* novel. So one person had to be, for want of a better word, the "editor," and the custodian of the big pie. Broadly, I suppose you could say I could overrule Neil, on the basis that if it had been a comic he could have overruled me, but there was never any serious disagreement in *Good Omens*. There was never a fight or anything. It's true, though, that our relationship wobbled a little when a movie was first in prospect. I felt that what Sovereign was doing was completely and utterly disemboweling the story, and Neil, God bless him, thought, "Well, if we hang in there...if we kind of stay on the train, maybe we can steer it." And I would yell, "It's a train! It's on tracks!" That caused a certain coolness, I think. Anyway, it never happened. It goes on never happening.

There were certain rules. Jesus Christ couldn't appear, for example. And we were clear that no one must die because Adam Young was alive. But what I remember was that we both had tremendous fun. It's a one-off, too. Neil probably said to you that we couldn't possibly do something like that these days, that it would take a year for both of us to maneuver our schedules in such a way so that we would have the same time slot available. And, sadly, that's true.

*I read somewhere that the book first came about because you were both playing around with your modems and looking for something to do with them.*

No, it went like this: Neil wrote about half of a short story, which he showed to me and said, "I don't know how this ends." And I looked at it and I didn't know how it ended, and I put it away somewhere. But I kept thinking about it, and about a year later I phoned him up and said, "I don't know how it ends but I know how it continues." And he said, "Let's write it together." I still had the original copy, but Neil didn't, and it was actually *typed*, on a real typewriter, like your granddad had! I know I typed it out again on the word-processor, with alterations, and that became the baby-swap scene in the beginning. Everything else we just developed together.

*How did you first meet Neil?*

Neil was the first person that ever interviewed me as an author. A semi-professional magazine sent him to interview me – Neil was a freelance journalist – and we had a Chinese meal in Soho, and we just kind of kept in touch.

*How far back was that?*

...1985?

*You've had a lot of success on both sides of the Atlantic, and so has Neil, though I'm not sure how his work is perceived in England.*

I think we are kind of mirror images. I do well in the United States, there's no doubt about it, enough to be invited to cons and so on; and I sell pretty well. But none of my novels have sold as much as *American Gods*, I'm damn sure. In the U.K., I'm certainly bigger than him, although he's pretty established. But...so what? What are we counting and why? On *Good Omens*, the deal was that Neil got his name on first in the U.S. and I go first everywhere else. Of course both of us have noticed that Neil's gone after the biggest country but, hey, those small ones add up.

*Why do you think Neil has achieved so much success in this country?*

I don't think it has specifically to do with the American audience. It's very similar to why I've been successful. It's...texture, maybe, is a good word.

Look, when we were writing *Good Omens*, there was seldom a case where one of us came up with an idea, some weird historical fact that the other guy didn't know about. Maybe the other guy hadn't heard so much about it or something like that, but we both had a very similar background, which included absolutely *omnivorous* reading, and a delight in strange trivia. When you've been doing this throughout your late childhood and into your teens, you get a wealth of obscure but valuable material to draw on. And mine gets consumed into *Discworld*, and Neil brought this knowledge to graphic novels. I mean here's a guy that knows *lots of stuff*. He hasn't just looked it up, he *knows it*. It's the kind of stuff that you've known for so long, that you cannot remember ever not knowing it, and also you believe that everyone else must know it because you know it, you assume it's sleeting through the atmosphere! And it always comes as a shock to me when I find there are people that don't know things which I assume everyone must know, like tulipomania or floral clocks. I think that's got a lot to do with it – that very esoteric knowledge base, and the ability to draw on it. Then, of course, he was working in graphic novels, and brought that knowledge base to graphic novels. But I've always felt kind of against graphic novels, because I thought, "They have the drawback of not being movies and the drawback of not being books." I'm not surprised that Neil is now leaving that and doing other things. I think he'd much rather do a lot more movies.

*Why do you think that is?*

I don't know, we haven't discussed this… Because it's a bigger train set. Because you can do everything you can do in a graphic novel, but you've got sound! You've got movement! You've got the actual cadence of the dialogue; you've got this whole extra palette to play with. Now in a book, you've got some of that, because the reader is providing all the sounds in their own head. The comic book, or graphic novel, while it offers the false prospect of giving you more than the book has got, I feel it gives you less. And it gives you less than the movie. My reading of it is, "Do books and movies."

*I heard Neil was impressed Terry Gilliam had found a way to include your footnotes in his planned film version of* Good Omens. *He felt that Gilliam had got it.*

I thought the script was great. I was surprised at how much had been left in. We knew he'd got it, when, more than ten years ago, we met him in a club in Soho and he…well, he'd just *got* it. We know he wants to be involved. I don't think it's a foregone conclusion that it ever gets made, especially since 9/11. We have to assume it will never happen, even when the big stretch limo is pulling up outside the cinema. Assume it's not going to happen, that's the way to stay sane. It's never going to happen. And if you think it will, it won't.

*Are there any other people with whom you'd like to collaborate?*

I collaborated with Neil because things were exactly right. Neil was getting well-known with comics and graphic novels and I've always done well in books. We were both successful in a field that the other guy wasn't particularly interested in at that point, so jealousy was out the window. It's like working with an artist in a different discipline, you see – I'm the writer, you're the artist, we're not in competition. So if the book's successful, wow, that's great. So the whole thing happened in a very pleasant kind of way. I have, on occasion, discussed collaborations with other authors. In fact, Larry Niven and I discussed one and agreed that, while our working methods probably meant it wouldn't gel, either of us could do anything with all the things we talked about, because there's no copyright on ideas. But our approaches to writing probably wouldn't mix well.

Neil and I spent a lot of time on the phone. One of us would say, "I know how to make this scene work. What we do is…" We wrote the book, in fact, to see how it would go. But Larry is more of the school of "write it down and make lots of notes, plan it out, and then write the book." And my take is…in fact, I'm doing it at the moment – I'm writing draft *zero* of the next book, the one I write to see if it's going to *be* a book. I haven't written the ending, although I know certain bits in the middle. But at this point I'm open to new ideas, and willing to see they help the book move in the direction it wants to go, or whether I should put them aside and maybe save them for another book. I think Neil works the same way. It's less chaotic than it sounds. It's more like trying out riffs in the recording studio until you get the sound right…

We discussed *Good Omens II* when we were on tour. It was a great relief when we finally admitted to one another that we didn't actually want to do it, but we both thought the other guy did. It would have been doable, if ever we could have got together. (Half the time is second-guessing what the other guy's thinking.) I don't think it'll ever happen now. Any sequel to *Good Omens* that we write wouldn't be as good as the sequel that we didn't write. Besides, we're both hard at work on our own projects now.

*You mentioned earlier that you read a lot of SF growing up. Why do you think so many fantasy writers begin as SF fans? Is it simply because SF was more readily available than fantasy?*

Certainly, when I was a kid, there *was* a small amount of fantasy in a lot of SF, and SF won me over first, probably because I was interested in astronomy. Both SF and fantasy were toward the end of the bookshop. Not for nothing is my view of the classic specialist SF bookshop as one positioned with the tattoo parlor on one side and the porno cinema on the other. That's where you used to find the average SF bookshop. And that's where it belongs!

*Back in the ghetto?*

You know, it's funny you should say that. I mean it isn't a ghetto any more, not really. Oh, a lot of critics don't like it, but who cares? There's lots of people out there who have *grandparents* that read fantasy and SF. They're in every bookshop, sometimes even near the front. They're out in the mainstream now. You can tell by the way mainstream literary authors pillage SF while denying they're writing it!

*Why do you think* Discworld *has survived for so long?*

The reason that *Discworld* has survived is that it's changed. It began with funny wizards running around. Some of the more recent books have been quite dark and quite serious; and it's kind of grown up. People think, "He uses lots of puns." Well, I'm "He" and He uses *very, very* few puns, although there is a fair amount of wordplay. What I do use are paradoxes, which Chesterton loved, and perhaps also skewed-but-logical ways of looking at a situation. Chesterton said that what fantasy should do is take that which is everyday and therefore unregarded, and pick it up and turn it around one-hundred-and-eighty degrees, and show it to you again from a different direction, so that you see it with fresh eyes, for the first time – again. He took the view that the "normal" and "everyday" are by their very nature fantastic. I think an example he used in one of his stories was a street lamp.

*That was in* The Man Who Was Thursday, *wasn't it?*

I think so, but he used it in one of his essays, too – how magical a street lamp was because of the huge number of wonderful things that had to be achieved: the mining of the coal, the smelting of the iron, the cooperation of so many people over a long time. In order for a street lamp to come into being whole civilizations had to grow, whole ways of thinking had to change. Yet a street lamp – or a penknife, or a box of matches – are perceived as normal, everyday, boring, dull things, when really there are some of the most astonishing things in the world. That was the way Chesterton thought, and that's a good way for a fantasy writer to think.

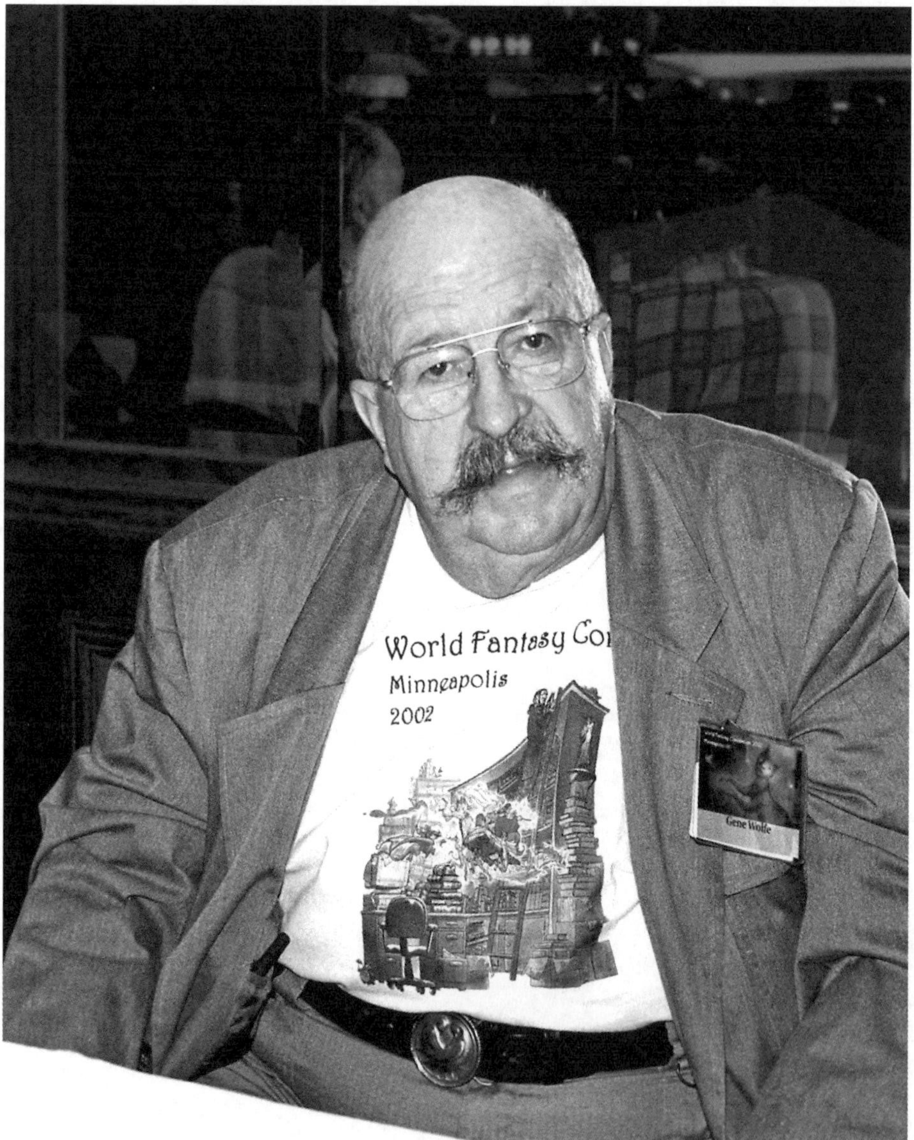
World Fantasy
Minneapolis
2002
Gene Wolfe

*Gene Wolfe*

GAIMAN HAS WRITTEN IN HIS ONLINE JOURNAL, "MY FAVORITE LIVING AUTHOR TO CORRESPOND WITH IN THE REAL WORLD IS PROBABLY GENE WOLFE, BECAUSE HE SENDS THE BEST LETTERS, AND HAS THE MOST PERCEPTIVE POINTS OF VIEW."

WOLFE IS WIDELY CONSIDERED ONE OF SCIENCE FICTION'S FINEST AUTHORS. SO FINE, IN FACT, THAT HE IS OFTEN THE WRITER WHOSE BOOKS SF WRITERS HAND TO THEIR NON-SF-READING FRIENDS WHEN THEY WISH TO SHOW THEM THE GENRE'S POSSIBILITIES. WOLFE'S FOUR-VOLUME *THE BOOK OF THE NEW SUN* IS REGARDED AS A MASTERPIECE, AND HIS LONG AND CELEBRATED CAREER ALSO INCLUDES SUCH NOVELS AS *PEACE* AND *SOLDIER IN THE MIST*, AND THE WORLD FANTASY AWARD-WINNING COLLECTION *STOREYS FROM THE OLD HOTEL*. HIS MOST RECENT NOVELS ARE *THE KNIGHT* AND ITS SEQUEL, *THE WIZARD*.

WOLFE – AN ARDENT SUPPORTER OF THE COMIC BOOK LEGAL DEFENSE FUND – COLLABORATED WITH GAIMAN ON *A WALKING TOUR OF THE SHAMBLES* [AMERICAN FANTASY, 2002] – THEIR MACABRE "TOUR BOOK," PUBLISHED FOR THE CHICAGO WORLD HORROR CONVENTION.

THE FOLLOWING INTERVIEW WAS CONDUCTED AT THE 28TH WORLD FANTASY CONVENTION IN MINNEAPOLIS. WOLFE WAS CELEBRATING HIS WEDDING ANNIVERSARY DURING THAT LONG WEEKEND, BUT SHARED SOME OF HIS TIME ON THE LAST NIGHT OF THE CONVENTION.

*Neil remarked in a recent interview [*Weird Tales *320] that at the end of the day he is probably "in the Stephen King camp" – a "storyteller." As opposed to a "risk-taker" like R.A. Lafferty, Robert Aickman, Avram Davidson, or Gene Wolfe. What is your opinion of Neil's work?*

I think he's brilliant. I think he's one of the best writers that I read. I respect him enormously. The thing that I always look at hardest – and whether other people reread Neil or not, I do – is the dialogue. I think he is a master of dialogue.

*How do you think he became such a master of dialogue?*

I don't think we can say anything in the way of training or experience – it's inborn talent.

*An ear for it?*

That's part of the talent. If you have that kind of talent then you have an ear for dialogue. That's the kind of thing that a playwright needs to have very badly, and Neil's got it. I recently saw *Neverwhere*. Have you seen the BBC *Neverwhere*? Listen to what those people are saying. When anybody does something that's really, really well, it looks so easy that there's no art to it. And Neil is like that.

*How did* A Walking Tour of the Shambles *come about?*

Somebody, I think it was Bob Garcia, got in touch with Neil and said, "I'd like you and Gene to collaborate on a book to be sold at World Horror." And Neil said, "Yes, I'll do it if Gene will do it." I thought, "Wow, Neil Gaiman! It would be great fun to work with him because I like Neil and I know that he is damn, damn good." And it was far easier than I expected and it was about three times more fun than I expected. It was a blast. Some people, I think, have enjoyed the book a lot, probably some have been disappointed in it; that sort of thing is inevitable. But we had a wonderful time writing it, and trying to top each other and make up fantastic stuff, and take some little thing that one of us had mentioned and blow it up into a major part of the book later on and so forth.

*Whose idea was it to do the book as a guidebook?*

Neil came up with a list of ideas that he thought we might want to do. One was a dictionary, one was a guidebook, one was an almanac, and so on. I said, "Well, let's do the guidebook." So if you want to give credit, credit Neil for coming up with all the original ideas. What I did was pick something out of this list that seemed to me to have more promise than the other things did. It seemed to me, for example, that an almanac would be awfully limited as long as it remained an almanac. And the dictionary thing has been done by a number of people already – I think Ambrose Bierce was probably the first one. He wrote *The Devil's Dictionary*, which is a very skeptical take on life and things.

*Did all of Neil's ideas have an Edward Gorey-Charles Addams feel to them? That sense of humor that filled the final work?*

Yes, that's certainly the kind of thing that we came out with, but I don't think that either of us knew for sure that that was what we were going to do. That's what worked out. He just started out by saying, "Let's do a dictionary or a travel book or an almanac, a guide to a neighborhood, or something like that."

*So the only common theme among these ideas was – since this was done for the 2002 World Horror Convention – the macabre?*

Yes, well, that's the thing. We could have done the same thing and done serious horror if that had been our bent. But we decided we would just have a lot of fun with it. And it was a lot of fun. It was, you know – the Cereal House, the Blind Man's House, and all that. The cover [by Gahan Wilson] is tremendous.

*Neil commented in his online journal that he'd always enjoyed Gahan Wilson cartoons and now he was able to* be *a Gahan Wilson cartoon.*

Yes, I think everybody does like Gahan Wilson cartoons. By the way, are you familiar with the radio play that they did of "The Tree is My Hat" at World Horror Convention?

*I've heard about it, but I haven't heard the actual play yet.*

It's out on CD, and if you want to hear it, you can get a CD of it. Larry Santorum assembled a cast, musicians, a sound effects man, and so on; and did that story of mine, "The Tree is My Hat."

*Has that one been collected yet?*

It isn't in any of my collections, it's too recent. It's going to be in the new one. In that radio play, Neil plays the Reverend Rob, the missionary. It takes place on an island in the South Pacific, and you have Polynesian natives, you have the Reverend Rob, who's an English missionary; you have the protagonist, who's basically a Peace Corps guy, who's been sent there.

*Was this recorded before a live audience at the World Horror Convention?*

Yes. The thing that started me off on it was that Gahan Wilson was the announcer for the radio show. He came out and did his best Boris Karloff impersonation, and announced the show and the cast and so on.

*Did you play a role in this production?*

No. I was just the author of the original story. The rights to the radio play belong to Larry Santorum, because I gave them to him. I said, "The radio play is yours. You write the radio play. All I want is credit as the author of the original story," which he has given me.

*You don't often collaborate with other writers, do you?*

This [*A Walking Tour of the Shambles*] is the only collaboration I have ever done.

*This is the only one? In your entire career?*

Yes, yes.

*There must be a number of people who have wanted to collaborate with you.*

I've had a few people ask, that were interested in collaboration. And once or twice I've tried to collaborate with somebody and it did not work out, and we dropped it.

*After this collaboration, do you think you might like to do another one, with Neil or with someone else?*

I might, yes. If it were Neil, I think I might be a lot more ready to, because I know that Neil and I worked together with very little friction. I think the trouble you get into is when you're working with someone who is far better than you or far worse than you, and then the more talented person tends to ride over the less talented person. That seems to me to be pretty much inevitable in collaboration. Sometimes you could get collaborators who have different strengths; that's the ideal obviously.

*Neil said he believes in something Alan Moore has said, that "the only true communication is between equals." I suppose that could be modified to "true collaboration."*

I don't know. I would have some hesitation about that. Obviously you're going to have to define what you mean by "equals," and what you mean by "true collaboration."

*As you said, a working relationship in which one partner doesn't completely dominate the other one.*

Yes, or dominate the other one to the point where the other one rebels. And, of course, if one partner is very dominant, the partner will start thinking, "Well, it's really about ninety-percent me, but I'm only going to get fifty percent of the credit, and fifty percent of the money. Not a very good deal for me, is it?"

*Yesterday, here at the World Fantasy Convention, you and Neil appeared on a panel together. Neil mentioned a couple of his* Sandman *stories and you instantly knew which ones he was referring to. There was a sizeable number of people on that panel, but I didn't notice any other panel member reacting as quickly to the stories Neil mentioned. And since you wrote the introduction to the* Sandman *collection* Fables and Reflections, *I guess it's safe to say you're a big fan of that series.*

Yes. I'm a big fan of Neil Gaiman's. I will read just about anything he writes, if I can find time to do it and if my eyes will hold up. I'm at the point now where I can read for maybe a half an hour or an hour; and I have to take a break because I can't see the print any more. When I was a young man, I could read eight hours a day. And it's no longer physically possible for me. And, of course, I have my own work to do.

*One of the things your work shares with Neil's is an interest in gods and in religion. Where do you think the two of you agree in your depictions of gods, and where do you think you differ?*

I'm not sure that we differ at all, to be honest. We differ theologically, but that's sort of a given.

*How do you differ theologically?*

Well, I'm a Christian, and I don't think that Neil is a Christian. I believe in the divinity of Christ. I don't believe that Neil does. Now, maybe I'm wronging him, but my guess is that he does not. But I think both of us agree in the existence of God, and in a God who is ultimately unknowable. If God has an infinite mind, then human beings are not capable of understanding that mind. And we're never going to be capable of understanding that mind. We can go five-hundred years into the future and have computers that are a whole helluva lot better, but they're still not going to be able to comprehend an infinite mind. We need to relate to God in a way that's satisfactory to both parties, and to adjust our behavior in a way that's satisfactory to God as well as us.

And I think Neil and I agree on those things. If Neil were an atheist or an agnostic, I would still like him and he would still be a heck of a good writer, but I don't think that we're that far apart.

I was a friend of Isaac Asimov's. Isaac Asimov would probably have considered himself an agnostic, although he might have called himself an atheist – that did not prevent us from being friends. But it did mean that we had some serious philosophical differences. It seems to me that you can almost define civilization by saying it's people who are not willing to hurt other people because the other people are different. We have to be willing to say, "Okay, he's not the same as me, and that's all right."

*You mentioned your belief in the divinity of Christ. One of the interesting themes in your work – particularly in such novels as* The Book of the New Sun *– is the concept of the messiah. The way that you tackle this concept is somewhat unique in that it's on an intellectual level. It works on an emotional level as well, but you don't allow your emotions to really ever block the intellectual examination. How have you been able to cultivate this discipline where so many other writers failed to do so?*

I'm not sure that it's anything that I have done; I think it's part of my character. It's innate. It seems to me that it is wrong to write propaganda that is not clearly propaganda. I teach writing from time to time, and you get a certain number of people who basically want to write what's basically propaganda for some cause or other. Or some church or other – I have a Mormon friend, and when he tries to write fiction, his characters lecture on Mormonism, when the lectures on Mormonism have nothing to do with the story, frankly. Someone asked Avram Davidson, "Why aren't any of your characters Jewish?" – because Avram Davison was a devout Jew; wasn't just Jewish, but was a *devout* religious Jew, an observant Jew. He said, "They all are." He wasn't pushing Judaism, but he was writing with what he was, which was a Jew. And I think I write as what I am. I think Neil writes as what he is. Because if you're going to be honest with the reader, that's what you do. The other thing is pretending, and maybe that's allowable in certain instances where, let's say, a man writes as a pretend woman, or a woman writes as a pretend man or whatever. Even so, I think the bedrock beliefs are going to come out, and the bedrock attitudes. I could easily write as "Jean Wolfe" and sell my stuff to a woman's magazine, let us say; and maybe I can fool the editors, but my attitudes are still going to be there, whether they are gender-specific or not.

*Your short stories are known for being very experimental. You're very willing to challenge the reader to decipher the meaning of your stories. Who or what are influenced this approach? I assume Borges was one influence.*

Borges, yes, absolutely. I like Borges, and certainly was influenced by him. I don't think there's any question that I've been influenced by Chesterton.

*Neil's very fond of Chesterton as well.*

Yes, and that's very odd. Because Chesterton, of course, was a believing Catholic and wrote very much from a Catholic standpoint. And Neil has also used him as a character, which I think is really neat. I've never done that, but I've no objection to Neil doing it, and I'm really happy that he did it. When I read through one of those books [*A Doll's House*] and I realized who this fat man [Fiddler's Green] is… that was nice. [*Laughs.*]

*It is interesting that Neil seems to get so much out of Christianity, among many other faiths.* Sandman *is certainly riddled with theological concepts from various religions. I think Neil has said something to the effect that it's often useful to study religion from outside the faith because you can be more objective about it.*

I think that writers tend to be outsiders, or people-with-one-foot-in-each-camp type of people. It seems to promote creativity, just in the human soul. If you assume that my group is right and the other groups are not really worth looking at very hard, you get very limited, and that doesn't make for good writing.

*Since we're talking about religion, "Murder Mysteries" comes to mind. In Neil's short stories one often sees – as one does in yours – that attempt to challenge the reader. It's perhaps most evident in "Murder Mysteries," which is one of his most highly regarded tales.*

Yes, one of the best stories I ever read.

*I think I can see some of your influence in that story. Are you aware of – or has Neil spoken to you of – how much he's been influenced by your work?*

He's read a lot of me. I know that. I don't know how much he's been influenced. I think we're all influenced, to some degree, by everything we read. I'm influenced, to some degree, by Neil; he's probably influenced, to some degree, by me. But if influence was all it was, everybody would be a writer, and it takes a lot of yourself. What do you bring to the story? And I thought he brought just marvelous stuff to that story. That's a wonderful story.

*Neil commented in that interview I mentioned earlier that if a person is reading a Gene Wolfe story and not "getting it," it's their fault somehow. "Go back and read it again," he says, "you'll get there."*

They may be working very hard. They're just not getting the answer. I'm an engineer by training, and I have good third-rate mathematical talent. I got very good grades in mathematics, up until I got into the higher reaches of calculus, and when I got up into differential equations, I hit the wall. My talent had carried me as far as it would carry me. And from now on, I was having a terrible time getting anywhere with it, because, as I say, I have good third-rate ability. Alice Bentley, who is a bookseller here in the huckster room, can handle high-energy physics. I couldn't do that.

*You could fool me, from the level of your writing.*

I might fake you into thinking that I could, because when you're writing you learn how to cram up on a subject, and learn the things that you need to know to write the story. I was asked, a few months ago, how much research I did before I began writing a story. The answer is "Almost none," because what I do is begin writing the story and then find out what it is that I need to know as I go through the story, and so I do the research in parallel with the writing, not reading twenty books and then sitting down and writing the story, but writing the story and stopping to *page through* twenty books to find the facts I want.

*When you write a short story, do you find you do most of the research while writing the first draft?*

Yes. But then I may see something else in a second draft that requires more research.

*How many drafts do you tend to do?*

At least three. And often more than three. Four or five – not uncommon.

*Are any of these handwritten?*

Sometimes the first draft is handwritten. After the first draft, I'm generally working on a machine. I had one little short story in the *New Yorker* once, and that's the story that I wrote in pencil on a lined tablet while I was sitting on a railroad train. It's called "On the Train," and it's about a somewhat surreal railway trip. I wrote it in the observation car of the train, going to the west coast.

*What do you ultimately hope readers and fans will get, and keep, from your stories?*

Wow, is that a heavy question... I would like them to better understand human beings and human life as a result of having read the stories. I'd like them to feel that this was an experience that made things better for them and an experience that gave them hope. I think that the kind of things that we talk about at this conference – fantasy very much so, science fiction, and even horror – the message that we're sending is the reverse of the message sent by what is called "realistic fiction." (I happen to think that realistic fiction is not, in fact, realistic, but that's a side issue.) And what we are saying is that it doesn't have to be like this: things can be different. Our society can be changed. Maybe it's worse, maybe it's better. Maybe it's a higher civilization, maybe it's a barbaric civilization. But it doesn't have to be the way it is now. Things can change. And we're also saying things can change for you in your life. Look at the difference between Severian the apprentice and Severian the Autarch [in *The Book of the New Sun*], for example. The difference between Silk as an augur and Silk as caldé [in *The Book of the Long Sun*]. You see?

We don't always have to be this. There can be something else. We can stop doing the thing that we're doing. Moms Mabley had a great line in some movie or other – she said, "You keep on doing what you been doing and you're gonna keep on gettin' what you been gettin'." And we don't have to keep on doing what we've been doing. We can do something else if we don't like what we're gettin'. I think a lot of the purpose of fiction ought to be to tell people that.

*To help them achieve a kind of Nirvana?*

Yes. To free yourself from the wheel, and you'll become at one with God or Brahma or whatever. Buddha? I don't know. Buddhists free themselves from the wheel of incarnation and become at one with the infinite. I've never been sure that that was absolute bunk. There's a little part of me that always suspects there's something going on there. I used to have a dog called Sir Lancelot, whom everybody called "Lance." I opened a door of a room when he wasn't expecting me to, and he was at another door trying to turn the knob with his front paws. And I thought, "Has he always been a dog?" It makes me wonder... There are things like that that you wonder about.

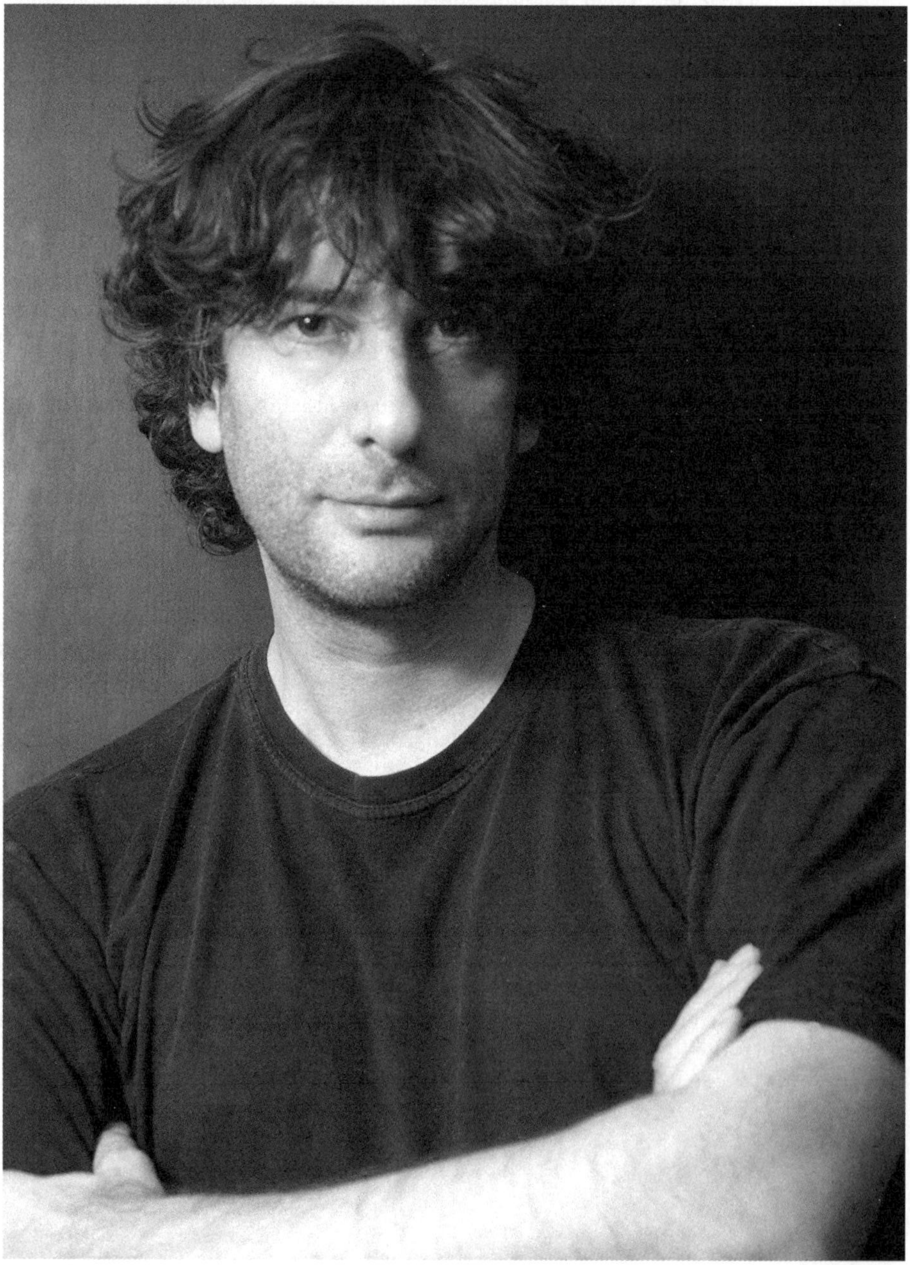

## IN THE INTERVIEW THAT FOLLOWS, GAIMAN SHARES A FEW

MORE THOUGHTS ON HIS COLLABORATORS, AND EXPLAINS SOME ADDITIONAL DETAILS OF *SANDMAN*'S CREATION AND DEVELOPMENT. HE ALSO COMMENTS ON THE DIFFERENCES BETWEEN HIS COLLABORATIVE AND SOLO WORK, AND REVEALS THE NAMES OF SEVERAL INDIVIDUALS WITH WHOM HE ONE DAY HOPES TO COLLABORATE.

*We began our first discussion by mentioning a few of the artists with whom you've worked. I'd like to hear your thoughts on several we didn't touch on last time, beginning with someone you've worked with since he began his career – Mark Buckingham. What did you first see in Mark's art?*

There was a lightness and a joy to Mark's art. What was weird was that Mark and I had actually been working together and I'd barely known it, because we'd been doing a bit of stuff for a sort of humor magazine that didn't last too long.

The Truth?

Yes, for which Kim Newman and Eugene and I were writing funny bits. There was a very odd series called "Around the World," and we would just pick a subject, "Finances Around the World" or "Sports Around the World," and Mark would illustrate that. There was one that Mark did – although I think by the time we got to the point with Mark doing this one, I knew who he was and was getting him to do it because it was Mark – which was "If Adult Products Were Properly Sold to Kids." We did a Superman parody, "Nicoteen." It began with "My x-ray eyes can see the damage these cigarettes are doing to your lungs..." and ended with Superman and Nicoteen walking off arm-in-arm, with Superman puffing on a fag and saying, "Oh my God, these cigarettes are great. These are cigarettes for men of steel," and Nicoteen saying, "Yep, and for girls and boys of steel as well!" It was a comic strip that Mark and I did. And, of course, we had the famous (this is all sort of Kim Newman rather than Mark, but I'll get back to Mark in a moment) article which proved that Jack the Ripper was in fact a glove puppet. [*The Truth* 12; October 20, 1988; pages 16-19]. I consider that famous because I was looking for something recently on Amazon.com, and found myself looking at one of those Amazon "Search Inside the Book" features at a page in a Jack the Ripper book where they pointed to our theory as an example of the kind of parodic lunacy that can occur. I was very proud. I e-mailed it off to Eugene and Kim, and said, "Look, we've made history."

But anyway, Mark had been illustrating a few of our things. I'm not even sure if they'd come out, and he was doing these odd little cartoony things – "Haemorrhoids

Rabbit" was one. We were at the Society of Strip Illustration, and Mark had some photocopies of a strip he'd done for the country-and-western issue of a comic he'd done called *Heartbreak Hotel*, a sort of comic/magazine. Bizarrely, it was an adaptation of that "Wild Side of Life" song – you know, "*I didn't know God made honky tonk angels…*" It ended up with some girl flying away. I looked at it and I thought, "This is actually completely the feeling, the emotion…" There was something lightweight and delicate and cool. I thought, "You know, I bet he could do *Miracleman*."

Alan [Moore] had asked me about a year before if I'd be interested in doing *Miracleman*. I'd been absolutely terrified, and said, "Yes." I hadn't really any idea of who to do it with. I don't think Dave McKean was interested. He'd said that he was interested in doing the covers, and he didn't seem like the right kind of artist to do *Miracleman* with. I wanted to do it with somebody who looked more classical and yet could go all over the place. I saw that art and said to Mark, "Hey, do you want to do *Miracleman*?" He thought I was mad or illusory, or possibly both, and said, "Yes," a lot, and he said, "Obviously, you can go and find a real person if you like and I won't hold you to this." [*Laughs.*] We went off and did *Miracleman* together. I think some of the best writing I've ever done and some of the best art Mark's ever done is because we just took such joy in going to odd places, and the sheer madness that makes you go, "Okay, well, let's do a comic that's a Warhol" ["Notes From the Underground," *Miracleman* 19] or whatever, was just an absolute delight.

*Mark also worked closely with Chris Bachalo, on the two* Death *mini-series* – The High Cost of Living *and* The Time of Your Life. *Chris was another comics artist who made his professional debut illustrating one of your tales, several years earlier, on* Sandman *12 ("Playing House"). What did you see in Chris's work that made you feel he was suitable for Death's solo debut title?*

That's a really good question… The trouble with your book is looking through it, and going, "Oh my God, memory is such a fallible thing." A lot of the time, I was reading stuff, thinking, "Oh my God, I remember this better than the person that's being interviewed." [*Laughs.*] And then sometimes I'd read it and think, "Ohhh, yeah…" Kim Newman was one – I kept thinking, "Oh my God, I remember that…"

Chris Bachalo. I remember the process of figuring out Chris for *Sandman* 12 very, very exactly. He'd sent in some samples, and they'd got onto the desk of Richard Bruning, who at that point, I believe, was art director at DC Comics. He looked at them and loved them, and he had passed them onto Karen [Berger]. There were two people, maybe three, who'd come in recently. We knew that we needed the fill-in issue. We knew that we needed the fill-in issue because the serial killers convention story ["Collectors"] was going to be double-sized, and we knew that Mike Dringenberg could not draw a double-sized issue and get it in on time, and Mike was a little bit behind as well, I think, at that point. So it was sort of an awful lot kinder to get… I think I'd always planned that 14 – the serial-killers convention issue – was going to be double-sized, and that 13 was going to be the Michael Zulli one ["Men of Good Fortune"], to let Mike catch up. Only, as we headed into it, Mike was a bit behind, and stuff like that. So it became apparent that somebody else would do number 12, Michael Zulli did 13, and then Mike Dringenberg did the double-sized 14, as it were. What happened then was just looking at these pencil samples; and there was something really cool about Chris Bachalo's work. There was something odd and interesting. He did a two-page sample, and there was a real visual imagination going on. He was so young and untried and this was his very first thing, but you could tell that he could do it, and he did. I loved writing the script for him, and I loved what he did.

After that, he did *Shade, the Changing Man*, and I remember Pete Milligan got him for that because they saw the work he'd done on *Sandman* 12, and everybody loved it and they gave him *Shade*. I think, partly, he got the [*Death*] job because he'd been doing this amazing stuff in *Shade*, not the highest profile of the proto-Vertigo titles. (This was all pre-Vertigo. But it was all the material that would eventually become Vertigo, and become sort of united under the Vertiginous banner.) But Chris had been working away. He was getting better and better, and I think part of it was just Karen wanted to give him something good. I loved his work, and I loved what he and Pete Milligan were doing in *Shade*. I loved the sort of cool visual style he brought to things. We got Mark Buckingham in because there was no way that Chris could have inked it in the time that he had. I don't think Bucky had ever inked Chris before, but it seemed like a fun project, and that was why. I loved Chris's work. I still do love Chris's work. We got back together again for the *9-11* story, "The Wheel." Again, I just loved what he brought to it. One thing that I tend to do with Chris, that I'll do with Michael Zulli, and I'll do it with Dave McKean and Mark Buckingham and with precious few other people, is I'll describe *loosely* what's happening on the page, but I'll write something much closer to a film script for them, and let them break it down.

*Death's appearance, as well as those of a few of her siblings, were originally designed by Mike Dringenberg, who is credited as one of* Sandman's *co-creators. How did Mike's sensibilities mesh with your own in developing those characters?*

The one that Mike did that, more than anything, I think, defined everything that he brought to it, and the one that really, in many ways, is Mike's – it's *not* mine – is Death. Everybody else began with me. In the case of Morpheus, actually doing drawings and sending them to Sam Kieth. They weren't very good drawings, but they were very much "This is what the character looks like" drawings. (Then I remember Sam did a sheet of faces, which were all sort of variants on this thing that I'd drawn and sent him. We all picked the same one, and, being Sam of course, he said, "Oh, you picked the Kevin Nowlan one." We said, "How do you mean the Kevin Nowlan one?" And he said, "Oh, no – *I* drew it, but I was thinking of Kevin Nowlan's style" – one of these lovely Sam things we got. Somewhere I still have the sheet of paper with all of these little Sandman drawings, all of these little faces, and one of them circled.) So Morpheus I drew first. Despair began as a cool photo that I found and sent off. I think Delirium, actually, was a photo, although that was one of those weird things of knowing what she looked like, and then suddenly running across some photo in the back of the magazine, and going, "*That's* her," and, again, sending that off to Mike. With Desire, I basically said to him – it was in the script – "Desire is kind of like Annie Lennox, done like a [Patrick] Nagel drawing." That was what we got.

Death was something else. I'd talked about Death in the outline for *Sandman*, and I'd mentioned that we were leading up to it, and in number 8 ["The Sound of Her Wings"] we would meet Death, and this is what she was like. And in my description for her, I think I was actually going for Nico, circa *Chelsea Girl* – that amazing ice-queen look – and I thought the blonde hair would be a nice contrast, and we hadn't had anybody who had that look in comics. And I sort of always considered the image – the cover of *Chelsea Girl* – to be one of the most beautiful things in the world. Also, I suppose, there was something about Nico when I met her that made me think of Death. When I met her, in real life, I was very aware of the skull beneath the skin. So

I think I'd mentioned Nico, and in conversation with Mike I said, "Look, we could go Nico, maybe we could go Louise Brooks…" and what was fun was Mike went with his friend Cinnamon. And he sent me this drawing – it was the "How would you feel about life if Death was your older sister?" drawing, and that line is Mike's. That was written on the drawing. He sent it in, and it just sort of turned up.

I've told, many times, the weirdness of that day. The drawing arrived in the morning. I took it up to the Society of Strip Illustration meeting that evening, when I was meeting Dave McKean to talk about *Sandman* covers. We went down to the My Old Dutch Pancake House, and were served by this *astoundingly* beautiful, skinny, long-dark-haired, American girl with an ankh on, who looked *exactly* like Mike Dringenberg's drawing. I mean not looked *sort of* like Mike Dringenberg's drawing, but looked like it to the point where I kept saying to Dave McKean, "Shall I show her?" [*Laughs.*] She was the kind of person that you meet, and you sort of…"fall in love with" are the wrong words, "have a crush on" are the wrong words…but are immediately just sort of besotted with. Dave and I would just sort of stare at her as she walked around the room [*laughs*] in that sort of pleasurable state of going, "Oh, she's wonderful…" Had she come up to us afterwards and said, "Now, I need you two to come with me and make war," we would have said, "Oh, okay. So it's off to war!" I kept saying to Dave, "Should I show her the drawing?" And he kept saying, "No, it's embarrassing. Shut up." So I didn't. In the morning, when the drawing had arrived, I wasn't certain. I looked at it and went, "Well, I *think* he's got it. I think this is really cool." By the end of that evening, I said, "Oh, yeah. That's Death. I know what she sounds like [*laughs*], I know how she moves, I know what it's like sitting there while she brings you a pancake. Great. I'm in there." I think that was part of that lovely sensibility.

My favorite thing about Mike Dringenberg was he was always the coolest one of the team. In this sort of wonderfully strange out-on-the-edge kind of thing. Mike knew every skate punk in Salt Lake City, which was fun. I'd have these marvelous conversations with him, where everything would somehow relate back to strange things that happened in Salt Lake City. Mike would tell me strange and interesting stories. But it was an astonishingly eclectic sort of time, that early *Sandman* stuff, with everybody grabbing every image that they could.

There is a joy to not knowing what you're doing, and being allowed to create something while you don't know what you're doing. Which is something that I kind of miss these days. I miss that freedom. The joy of *Sandman* was the freedom to fail. Nobody expected it to be successful, nobody expected it to last, nobody expected it to anything. Simply remaining in print and not being cancelled was such a huge success. We were just this odd little book these guys were doing that wasn't like anything else. I kept expecting that phone call from Karen saying, "You know, we just *really* aren't selling enough." [*Laughs.*] Then I would have said, "Oh, okay," and gone back to journalism or whatever. The one thing that I still look back at those early *Sandman*s and see – and it lasts through to about the middle of *Brief Lives*, when suddenly the world noticed that we were doing this thing – is not only the freedom to fail, but the freedom to do what people probably wouldn't like. To me the perfect *Sandman* moment was when I finished the first storyline. I had *Season of Mists* in my head at that point, and it was quite obvious from having finished the first *Sandman* storyline that the story that everybody loved the most was the Hell one ["A Hope in Hell," issue 4]. The thing that everybody wanted to see was the big Lucifer rematch, and stuff like that. I had a whole story in my head. As far as I was concerned there were two things I could do: I could either do this thing that I thought might be called *The Doll's House*, which, basically, the Sandman would barely be in, and it certainly wouldn't be particularly user-friendly, and I'd have old African folk tales, the serial-killers convention, and a weird historical thing going on. Or I could do this thing that I thought would probably be called *Season of Mists* or *Suppose They Gave an Inferno and Nobody Came*. I could do that thing, and everybody would love it. The decision to go off and do the one that probably people wouldn't like, and to put off the one that everybody would love until the end of year 2, for me, was the most important thing in *Sandman*, and sort of signaled what we were trying to do. And the terms in which we were trying to do it.

*Since we're talking about those early days – Sam Kieth is also credited as a co-creator of* Sandman, *and the book's penciler for its first five issues. How did your collaboration with Sam influence those that followed it on the book?*

I don't know that I can answer that question, just because I don't know that it did. On the one hand Sam is a genius, and that was why we wanted him. There was something so primal that I responded to, and it's that thing that people have responded to in everything he's done since, most clearly in *The Maxx*. On the other hand, at the time when he took on *Sandman*, I think it became very clear that he was moving in one direction and I was moving in another. I could either not do this thing that I wanted to do with *Sandman*, or I could just do stories that Sam would like to draw. And wherever I could, I'd do the kind of stories that Sam would like to draw, particularly with *Sandman* 4, where it was like, "Okay, let me just give Sam stuff that will make him happy." When you say, "Okay, it's a double-page spread. Can we have about a hundred-thousand demons? The entirety of Hell turned up, a double-page spread. Several miles away we have a little rock peak with Lucifer and Sandman standing on it. All around them are demons, millions of demons from horizon to horizon, and every single demon is different." Most artists, at that point, would just go out and drink for a while, and they'd make little wax models of you and start to stick pins in them. Sam was so happy with that, that he inked it himself [pages 12-13]. He didn't just pencil it, he inked it.

But I know we were happy when he quit. Not because I don't think that artistically it wouldn't have worked for the book, but he was miserable. He was *so* miserable. He was miserable on a daily basis. I'd phone up and I'd ask, "How are you doing?" and he'd be sad. He was not enjoying it. He cheered up immensely when he quit. I know he quit during issue 3 ["Dream a Little Dream of Me"]. (Karen and I had this strange set of conversations, which went "Who do we get to pencil?" And I said, "Well, why not get Mike Dringenberg to pencil?" And she said, "Oh, okay. Who do we get to ink?" I had been looking at *The Question*, and I'd loved Malcolm's inking. I said, "What about Malcolm Jones?" She said, "Oh, I love Malcolm's inking. Hang on a sec… *Malcolm, do you want to ink* Sandman?" [*Laughs.*] She went walking down the corridor and she came back and said, "It's okay, we got Malcolm.") But the reason I knew it was issue 3 was that Mike Dringenberg's tryout pages (because he still had to do a tryout page) were two pages from issue 3. Issue 3 is the Constantine one. He just drew the two pages where Constantine and Morpheus turn up at the empty house, and Morpheus magicks the door open and they go in. It was lovely, a completely different feel to what Sam was doing, but completely consistent at the same time. So that was what happened with Sam. I was so happy afterwards that Sam went on to achieve fame in his own right, because I think if he'd merely been celebrated for having been in on the start of *Sandman* [*laughs*], I don't think that would have made him very happy. But I thought it made him very happy that he got to do it himself.

*The role of a comic book's letterer is often overlooked. Yet you've frequently mentioned* Sandman's *letterer, Todd Klein, as an important part of the book. How do you view Todd's role?*

Todd is a genius, and he's a genius per the definition I read once many years ago, of genius as "an infinite capacity for taking pains." Todd completely has that. Later, I think, he regretted it. Partly because I'd bring in a character, we'd do one scene, or even one panel (as in *The Doll's House*), he'd pick a lettering style on the basis that he was never, ever going to have to do it again, and then I'd bring the character back. And Todd was suddenly suffering at having to sit there. And he always did.

The thing of doing the Sandman's lettering in upper and lower I think was me. And white on black, I think, was Karen. That wasn't Todd, and it was a major pain in the ass – doing white-on-black lettering for the major character for the whole thing. Because everything had to be then photocopied, reversed, cut out, pasted back down. I sort of have this theory that comics lettering is something that you hear rather than you see. When it's done really well, it goes in through the ears almost rather than the eyes. I don't know if that's true or not, but at least it's the way that I like to think. I felt like that was how Todd did it, too. So I could come up with lettering styles in the scripts that would suggest ways that people would talk. My favorite was probably Delirium's, where I said, "Can we get bigger and smaller again, and change the size?" And he did. He came up with this lovely sort of slightly wobbly style that got larger and larger and smaller and smaller. Just complete magic. You sort of know what she sounds like from that. Todd is an unsung genius of lettering.

I think it's interesting that when he went over to computers, finally, he remained just as good. Working with him on *1602* was a delight. There were things that neither of us were completely keen on. I didn't like the fact that, from Marvel, suddenly there came the edict that everything had to be upper-and-lower-case lettering. It was sort of arbitrary. But the fun thing with *1602* was, because Todd was doing it on a computer, we suddenly found color at our disposal. You could say things like "Okay, the Invisible Girl talks in transparent word balloons," and you could do that, which is marvelous.

I love it when Todd gets attention, I love it when Todd gets awards. I sometimes find myself wishing that Todd hadn't decided that he wasn't going to write any more. Todd started out as a writer (or as a number of things, but one of them was a writer), and he stopped. He said it was me and Alan [Moore], lettering our stuff [*laughs*], that made him decide he would never be that good, so he wasn't going to do it. I look at what he does in *Promethea*, I look at what he did in *Sandman*... The other thing I should also say is that Todd had the function of a sort of... I guess "assistant editor" is the wrong way of putting it, but I'm not quite sure what the right way of putting it is. He was secondary proofreader, secondary editor. He, as much as anybody, would change my spelling to American style, or not change the spelling. He would pick up goofs. It was unusual for goofs to get past him.

*A colorist's role, like that of a letterer's, can be sometimes overlooked. How do you view Daniel Vozzo's –* Sandman's *most frequent colorist's – role?*

Danny was the third colorist that *Sandman* had. The problem that Danny had – as I saw it for much of the *Sandman* period, particularly the hell that was *Brief*

*Lives* – was just that he wasn't in control of the entire color process. These days, it's Danny and it's Danny's computers, but the color separations were very distinct from the coloring. Our first colorist, Robbie Busch, was good and enthusiastic, but I don't think he ever really worked out. We went from him to Steve Oliff, who did "Midsummer Night's Dream" [issue 19] and the succeeding three or four issues, and was amazing. Steve Oliff was fantastic. I don't remember if it was just that he was too expensive or whether he quit, because he was still doing all the Image stuff at the time, but he left. Which meant that Danny Vozzo took over, in the middle of *Season of Mists*. As I remember, the color separations were being done in Ireland. Danny took over, and, on the one hand, it was wonderful to have somebody that I thought was completely reliable, completely solid. On the other hand, it was frustrating because we had these Irish idiots. *Brief Lives*, in particular, had more coloring errors, and more sort of coloring mishaps, than you would imagine. It's the only one where we actually got permission to do some recoloring, and to recolor, after the collection came out. I think the first collection may still have some coloring errors, because they said we could recolor. Then it was like, "Well, you can do three recolorings, and that's it," or whatever, for budget. Then gradually we were allowed to go back in and color a few more things. But it would be things like… Dream would have a blue broach around his neck, and they'd decide to color it red. And we're saying, "No, he doesn't have a ruby. If there's one thing he doesn't have wrapped around his neck, it's a ruby. The ruby was destroyed." That would be the coloring people. It was as frustrating for Danny as it was for us. Then we got new separators. The Android people came in with *Worlds' End*. Suddenly you could really start to see what Danny was doing – it just started looking prettier and meatier. It wasn't filled with horrible little goofs as *Brief Lives* was.

Danny was with us all of the way through, and I love his coloring. We talk a lot about recoloring the first couple of *Sandman*s, to just make them more consistent with the rest. (What tends to happen is that the Powers That Be at DC say, "Yes, yes, yes, yes, yes, yes, yes, yes, yes – hang on – that will cost money.") Did Danny tell you that he actually got his wife through *Sandman*? There's some cool little by-products of having done *Sandman*, that in some ways have nothing to do with having done *Sandman*, and in some ways they're lovely places where life coincides. The idea that a *Sandman* fan would ring up Danny Vozzo, and say, "You are coloring *Sandman*, and it's my favorite comic" – and now they're married and they have a lovely daughter – makes me feel like I had something to do with the world.

Danny's amazing. A really nice colorist, especially toward the end. As I would get later and later, and as Marc Hempel would get later and later – or other artists – the colorist and the letterer become the sort of buffer zone of "You've got twenty-four hours to turn this around, because everyone else is late, and we have to catch up." Todd always does. And Danny always did.

*Karen Berger edited* Sandman *throughout its run. She is one of the many editors with whom you've worked, in a variety of media. Others include Stephen Jones, Ellen Datlow, and Terri Windling. This may be a broad question, but what do you believe constitutes good editing?*

Well, the editors you've mentioned are different kinds of editors. So for a Steve Jones or an Ellen Datlow or a Terri Windling, what constitutes good editing, at least with me working with them, is they are very good at actually two things. One is these are people with very high standards, so you're going to try and give them your best work because you know it's going to go into something with good work. And they have a very good eye for what they like. In Terri and Ellen's case they're very good at coming to me and saying, "We want, specifically, 'X,'" which is normally, "Can you do us a three-page poem?" or something. And I'll say, "Okay, yes."

The thing that Karen really did with *Sandman* was just believe in what we were doing, which sounds like such a cliché, but what we were doing in *Sandman*... It's very weird these days. We're now in 2004 – it's been seventeen years since I started writing *Sandman* (which makes me feel old). I know I said this during this interview, but people forget how unlikely... People forget how different what we were doing was, because lots and lots of things have come along since then. It's not even that they've borrowed anything from us. It's more as if we went into the forest and we bulldozed a whole area where nobody had ever been before, then lots of people would come along and go, "Oh, cool, you can build in this area of the forest." The one that I still cite was the biggest fight that Dave McKean and I had with Karen. When we won it, we could have won everything. Because she, at that point, understood it and was completely willing to go with it: which was just the idea that [Morpheus] wouldn't be on every cover. Because Dave had done some *Swamp Thing* covers, and he had to draw Swamp Thing on the cover of every issue. And then Dave did all of the first twenty or thirty *Hellblazer* covers, and he had to draw John Constantine on every issue so people knew it was a John Constantine comic. With *Sandman*, we got to say, "Now, the first thing is, he'll be on the cover of number 1. He may be on a few covers from time to time after that. But he won't be on every cover." And Karen was sort of like, "Well, how will people know?" We said, "Well, it will say 'Sandman' in big letters at the top." That was the biggest battle, that was *the* battle, really. And when she said, "Yes," on that, it was like she got it. And, from that point on, mostly what she did was keep everything working for us within DC. She was our ambassador. She was our representative.

She sent me one script back to change, and I am so glad she did, because I won the World Fantasy Award with it. It was the only script that she really didn't like, which was "A Midsummer Night's Dream." She wasn't a Shakespeare buff, and she didn't get it, which was fine, and she sent it back and said, "It needs more heart. Right now it's a bunch of people acting." All I did was put in the scene with Hamnet Shakespeare, his son. I think he's dressing the actors who play the actresses, and he's talking about his dad. It's just a page of how, even if [Hamnet] died, [his father] would just make a play of it. He doesn't really think his dad's there or involved or functioning as a father, whatever he is – he's this sort of absent presence. It's really sad that it wasn't there in the first draft. I'd been so pleased with myself for doing this huge, clever, complicated thing, with all this wonderful dialogue and all these cool faerie folk, and all this stuff happening on all these different levels – and all these great things for Charlie Vess to draw – that I'd sort of forgotten to give this story a reason for existing. In many ways, those panels, are its reason for existing. They are the heart of the story. So that is, from what people would probably think of as an editorial point of view, Karen's editorial input into *Sandman*. In terms of sending me something back and saying, "It's not good enough. Can you rewrite this?" [*Laughs.*] I think that was it, in the whole thing. On the other hand, Karen was the person, who, when I couldn't decide whether or not to do something, I would phone up, and say, "Okay, now I can end this story in way 1, way 2, or way 3 – which do you like best?" I'd talk with her pretty much daily, just checking in. Every now and then she'd make me do outlines of what would happen next, and I'd sort of list stories, and things like that. Less and less as time went on – she just sort of basically let me do whatever I wanted, once it became apparent that I seemed to know what I was doing. But Karen was great. I don't think that I could have done *Sandman* without her, on the basis, mostly, that I needed somebody there who got what it was that I was trying to do, and what Dave was trying to do, and what the artists were trying to do. And would stand up for it and champion it.

And also whenever it came to picking an artist, deciding who we were going to do, that was always me and Karen. Sometimes it would be Karen. Sometimes she'd say, "What about Stan Woch? He wants to do some more comics, and he called me the other day." I'd say, "Oh, great," and we got the Lady Joanna Constantine story ["Thermidor," issue 29]. Sometimes it would be me saying, "Hey, I ran into somebody," or "Hey, I like John Watkiss's work. Could we do one with John Watkiss?" – he did the Marco Polo story ["Soft Places," issue 39]. There were some strange ones in there. The funniest, of course, is Michael Allred, whose work I loved, doing one of the best-ever *Sandman* stories ["The Golden Boy," issue 54], and who Karen had rejected. He had done some tryout pages. It would have been around eighteen months into the *Sandman* run.

*Colleen Doran mentioned Allred [said he] was considered for "Façade" [issue 20].*

I don't think he was particularly considered, but that would have been about the same time, because the tryout pages he did would have been from number 17. If I remember, they were from "Calliope." Normally, tryout pages were just from the latest script I'd written, so that nobody could have seen what the other artists did. (Which is why I can tell you that Sam would have quit early on in number 3. Mike wouldn't yet have seen what Sam did on those pages himself. Karen would have just sent him pages to draw, pages 13 and 14 of *Sandman* 3.) Michael Allred did some tryouts from "Calliope," and Karen said, "No." She basically said, "No, you are not yet ready for primetime." What's interesting is Mike Allred credits this with making him get very good very fast. Because the anger and the fury and the hurt at being rejected (and I loved his stuff; I would have said "Yes" like a shot), he said, got him "very good very quickly." He took all that and channeled it into a sort of "I'll show you" kind of mindset, and rapidly became a superstar. And then came back for ["The Golden Boy"].

I don't know that being "considered" for "Façade" is necessarily exactly the right word. He was definitely trying out. I don't know if he was trying out *for that* or just trying out at that time. I don't think we ever quite got it as solid as "He's trying out for 'Façade'." Also, to be honest, I think that "Façade" was, in my head anyway, Colleen's pretty much from the beginning. (She was doing some kind of tour of the DC offices. We were introduced, and she walked out, and then she came back in again a minute later. She said, "Hang on, we were just introduced. You're the Neil Gaiman who does *Sandman*?" I said, "Yes." She said [*impersonating Colleen*] "Oh my God, I love that. Oh my God, I love that." It was wonderful. [*Laughs.*] I said, "Oh, good, do you want to draw one?" I don't know if I said, "Do you want to draw one?" at *that* moment. I think I just said, "How lovely," or whatever, and then thought, "You know, I really like Colleen's stuff."

I had this story in my head that was just sort of an image of this woman who was shedding faces, and using them as an ashtray, and wanted to die. I wanted to try and write about points of view. In the sense that I knew that, for most people, superpowers...it just depends on how you look at them. As a kid reading comics, I had never believed self-pitying characters. The ones who sit there and said, "Oh, if it wasn't for the fact that I'm cursed to have this super-strength and look funny, she would love me." So part of what I was trying to get into was "What would it mean to have these powers and for them to be a curse?" Great, you're absolutely immortal and indestructible – what does that mean if you have somebody who just doesn't want to be there any more? The idea of this woman, talking to nobody… I'd actually planned for lots of cool Sandman scenes in her dreams, because I'd spoken to Colleen, and Colleen really, really, really wanted to draw Morpheus. I should say, where Colleen is concerned, the thing that I feel worst about is that she drew two full issues of *Sandman*, and none of them had him in, except for one panel in one [*A Game of You*, Chapter 3, "Bad Moon Rising," issue 34] where I only basically threw him in because I realized that we were actually getting to the point where Colleen would have drawn two full issues without him at all. [*Laughs.*] So [on page 20], I had her draw a Sandman during the conversation with the ladies, that was really not something that the story called for. It was more embarrassment on my part, and knowing that she would rip me unmercifully, as the only artist to draw two full issues of *Sandman* in which he didn't appear.

*There was another artist who did not draw the Sandman in a comic, but depicted him in a series of illustrations that accompanied your prose. I'm speaking of Yoshitaka Amano, who illustrated* The Dream Hunters. *What did you appreciate in Amano's work?*

Oh, I love Amano's work. I think I love the combination of classicism and alien. But just from a point of view of the work, there's an incredible beauty going on there. And it's not only beautiful, but…

*Slightly unnerving?*

Yes, and I think it's the oddness that I love. And the fact that when you sit and you look at Amano's stuff, it's always very different. There's a weirdness to it. I responded to the first thing of his I ever saw. [Vertigo editor] Jenny Lee was saying, "What about Amano for the *Sandman* poster?" She sent me a few pieces of his art. I said, "Well, this is very nice, yes." I didn't really think about it very hard. And the poster came in and it was just like, "Oh my God, I love this. This is alien. And it's cool-alien, and it's different-alien." It just made me happy.

*Amano strikes me as something of an iconoclast, as do a number of your collaborators. Alice Cooper, for example. Can you describe the experience of developing, with Alice,* The Last Temptation?

It was wonderful. It was incredibly pleasant. My favorite memory of working with Alice is sitting in a hotel room in Phoenix, Arizona. A heavy-duty storm was rolling in, and it was a storm heavy enough that the hotel phoned up and told us to turn off all the power. Which meant that all the electric guitars and everything had to be unplugged, and we just turned off all of the electricity and went out and sat on the balcony and watched this storm rolling in from the mountains. And Alice told me the story about the time that he met Elvis Presley. Elvis showed him his karate skills. It was just so cool, sitting there, watching the storm roll in, listening to the story. [*Laughs.*] That was one of my favorite moments with Alice. The Alice moments that were so cool were just sort of doing fun things with Alice.

On Groucho Marx's eightieth birthday, he sent Alice his white circular vibrating bed, with a note saying he didn't think he'd be getting any more use out of it. And Alice didn't know what to do with it, and eventually wound up giving it to Paul McCartney as a wedding present, because McCartney had announced he had a round room, everything was going to be round. So it was a round bed for his round room. [*Laughs.*] These sort of wonderfully strange, magical stories... It wasn't that Alice didn't have rock-'n'-roll stories, but what was really cool was he got to hang with Mae West and with Jack Benny and play golf with Bob Hope, and all this kind of stuff. I said, "Why were you meeting all these people? They were cool, but why were you friends?" He said, "Well, I knew that if I could be a rock star, there was nothing special about being a rock star [*laughs*] so I thought I'd meet my heroes." I loved that. I loved that sort of attitude. Alice is just a delight. He's a terribly, terribly nice man. My favorite bit of Alice was just sort of creating the Showman persona for him, and the way that he took the character on tour, had the costume made and took it on stage. *That* I loved. I thought it was great.

*Alice isn't the only rock star with whom you've worked. You wrote short prose pieces to accompany each of the songs on Tori Amos's* Strange Little Girls *album. And you helped develop the personas she adopted for those songs.*

Well, the personas was an odd kind of thing. I was staying down with Tori and Mark, her husband, in Florida for a few days. We were playing records, and we were sort of developing the core list of the *Strange Little Girls* songs. She already knew a bunch of songs she wanted to do. And then a bunch more, over the next few months, were brought along by various collaborators, male collaborators. We were her little group. But this was just me and Mark as the sort of core group saying, "What about this song? What about that song?" and drawing up these a-lists and b-lists, and seeing what she responded to, and what we responded to. During that period of time, I remember Tori had a Cindy Sherman book, a sort of big Cindy Sherman retrospective that I had borrowed from her bookshelf and moved into my bedroom and was reading through. At one point, I was just flipping through this, and I simply thought, "Oh, why don't we do this? This would work." Then I went back to Tori, and said, "What about doing a Cindy Sherman with this, and just taking on identities?" She said, "Oh, yeah. Yep, we'll do that."

I knew that she had the wonderful make-up artist she used to use, Kevyn Aucoin; because he'd just done a couple of portraits of her and various other people as the people they wanted to be. He'd done one of her as a Cherokee princess, and one of her as Mary, Queen of Scots [in *Face Forward*]. So I'd seen those photos around the same time. Then we met together with the Cindy Sherman, and I said, "Kevyn can make you look like anything. Why don't we do that?"

*I'd like to touch on your work with Gene Wolfe. When I spoke with Gene, he said you are the only writer with whom he has collaborated, on* A Walking Tour of the Shambles.

If I'd known that, I never, *ever* would have dared do that, I want you to know. [*Laughs.*] I cheerfully assumed that Gene must have done this with dozens of people. If somebody had said, "You get to be the only author Gene has ever collaborated with," I would have just said, "No." [*Laughs.*] But luckily I didn't know that until I read the interviews in your book. I didn't have any kind of stage fright.

It was fun. It was Bob Garcia's idea. Gene and I were both going to be Guests of Honor at the [2002] World Horror Convention in Chicago, and Bob phoned up and asked if we could collaborate on something together for him. I actually thought that we were being asked for something for the program booklet, and I think maybe Gene did, too. [*Laughs.*] I don't think either of us had actually [thought] that this was a separate sort of project, or a booklet, or a chapbook. I was immediately incredibly intimidated, because I think Gene is the finest writer of short stories out there. And I knew that if we could figure out a format for it then we could make it work. I also knew there was no way that we would be able to do an obvious, narrative short story, because what Gene does is very strange and subtle and beautiful, and he knows what he's doing when he starts. He's a better short story writer than I am, might be a better short story writer than pretty much anybody currently working and living. I didn't want to get on the phone with him and go, "All right, there's this girl in a restaurant and…why is she there?" In fact, to be honest, I'm not really sure how I'd collaborate on a short story with somebody. It's hard to imagine. I did it with a novel [*Good Omens*]. But short fiction, if you've got it all in your head, and you've got the shape of the story in your head, then there's not really much reason for collaborating. By the time you've collaborated, you might as well have written it.

So then we got on the phone. We were tossing a bunch of ideas at each other. I think I listed things to him. I said, "We could do a dictionary, we could do a tarot deck, we could do a gazetteer, a travel guide…" He said, "I've done a dictionary," being Gene. [*Laughs.*] He said, "Let's do the travel guide." So that was it really. That was where it all came from, that was what he wanted to do. But then we talked about it, and what was lovely was, because it was fundamentally plotless – even though it developed a kind of plot, the plot was more *evolved* – I wrote four pages and sent them to Gene, and, a week later, five pages came back. (Because Gene is so much cooler than I am.) And then I wrote another four pages and got another five pages back. It was wonderful. And then we were writing jokes for each other and using each other's bits. I loved it. It made me smile. And it was a place where we could intersect, and we could do those wonderful Charles Addams sort of things. I think the best thing about it was that the cover was done by Gahan Wilson.

*I thought it might be appropriate that the last of your collaborators we discuss should, again, be Dave McKean, since he was the first we discussed, in our first conversation. You recently worked with Dave more closely than ever before, on the film* MirrorMask, *which you scripted for him to direct. What challenges did this present?*

The biggest challenge of *MirrorMask* was the weirdest, actually. Just the fact that, suddenly, after sixteen years of mostly collaborating from a distance… There was one point, actually, where we collaborated together, where we did a comic for Bryan Talbot's birthday, a birthday present for Bryan Talbot. We were on a signing tour for *Black Orchid*, I think, and we did it in Dave's hotel room late one night. The only thing on TV at that time of night (the *only* thing – every other channel was dead) was the pay-per-view porn channel. This was a little hotel in somewhere like Manchester and they'd cut out the porn. This sounds like a joke, but it's completely true. Dave and I did this, collaborated on this thing, with this movie playing. There was a film on, and it was twenty minutes long because they cut all the rude bits out. It was apparently a film about a bunch of tourists who go to Greece, pair up, gaze into each other's eyes longingly, go into rooms together… You cut to the pounding ocean surf, and then they'd come out looking happier. This was the thing on the porn channel at two o'clock in the morning while Dave and I did Bryan Talbot's birthday present. [*Laughs.*] But that was pretty much the only time we'd ever collaborated in the same room.

The first weird thing was Dave and I were in the same space. We went and stayed in Jim Henson's old house in London for ten days, which has not been changed since Jim died. They hadn't changed the wallpaper or anything. It was very, very strange. We spent two days butting heads, which was the first time in our entire artistic collaboration that we ever butted heads. It was this huge argument about methodology, because Dave, as a writer, wanted everything nailed down before he started. Everything: every scene, every beat, everything. And my attitude was "I want to know enough about the story – how it begins, how it ends, and a few cool things in the middle – to get going with. And then I want to find out who these characters are, and what they do and all that, by writing it." Dave kept telling me that that was unprofessional and wrong. He kept saying it was like beginning a drawing with the eyebrow, and how you have to sketch out the drawing first. I think part of it is just confidence and how long you've been doing it. Dave is a really good writer, but he doesn't do a lot of writing. If I were drawing a cover for somebody's book, I would sketch the cover first, and then I'd draw the cover. If Dave is doing the cover for somebody's book, which he does quite often for me, he'll show me a doodle on a napkin, and say, "Well, there'll be some lettering up here, and there'll be some fizzy stuff, and down there something will go 'wiggy, wiggy, wiggy.'" And I will nod, having no idea at all about what he's talking about. [*Laughs.*]

*Are there any individuals with whom you've not yet worked, but with whom you would one day like to?*

Let's see…good question…I've never worked with Barry Windsor-Smith. We tried to do it once and we kind of failed, which was probably a good idea, because the story wasn't terribly good. Eventually Michael Zulli came and drew it ["How They Met Themselves," in *Vertigo: Winter's Edge* 3], and it didn't really work very well anyway. But I'd love to work with Barry. I love Barry's work. I think there's a real sort of magic, and, again, that intersection, between classical art and comics. You can see somebody for whom both [Edward] Burne-Jones and Jack Kirby are equal influences. So I'd love to work with him.

*How about in the medium of film, which you've been delving deeper and deeper into?*

Well, I'd love to do something with Terry Gilliam. I don't really care what. I'd just love to do something. I think Terry's a genius, and he's a terribly nice guy. Whether one day I will actually get to do something with him or not, I have no idea, but I would very much like to.

I'd like to do something with Peter Greenaway. But the trouble is Peter Greenaway is one of those people like Jonathan Carroll – there's partly an urge to collaborate with them, but there's partly a huge urge just to see what they're going to do next. I love Jonathan Carroll's work – I think Jonathan Carroll is one of the coolest, smartest, most interesting writers out there. I think he's amazing. I don't really want to collaborate with him, because I want to read what he does. Lots of the people whose work I really love… Art Spiegelman is probably a fairly good example. There's somebody whose work I love, and who I have no particular desire to collaborate with. Because why would I collaborate with Art? I want to see what he's going to do. Ditto Will Eisner.

I'd love to do something with the Hernandezes. I've been an enormous fan of the Hernandezes for many, many years. I don't know really – there's so many cool people out there.

*With* Endless Nights *you worked with several significant new collaborators.*

I did. The big one that we never got to happen on that was Moebius, which still makes me kind of sad. I wish I'd got to write one for Moebius. But on the other hand, I got to write a Manara story for [Milo] Manara. [*Laughs.*] That made me happy.

The reviews of *Endless Nights* which were accurate but I felt missed the point were the ones where they'd say, "This feels like Mr. Gaiman is taking a backseat and letting the artists reign." I thought, "Yes, I am actually. That was sort of the idea of this, to find a bunch of artists whose work I love and then have them do the thing I love them doing." That was so much the idea. Also, knowing that we were going to have this large format, and knowing that I was going to be in a full-color printing process, the very idea of which was alien seventeen years ago when we started *Sandman*. It's like, "Absolutely, let's go ahead and see what I can do with Miguelanxo Prado or with Milo Manara."

*With all of your experience in collaborating, do you find it more difficult to write prose in a solo environment?*

I don't know about making it more difficult, but you lose things. One of the best impetuses for making deadlines for me is knowing that if I don't make deadlines, somebody else is not going to be able to pay their rent, if you see what I mean. I'm beyond those days when "If I miss the deadline, *I* won't be able to pay my rent." The knowledge that if I miss my deadline the letterer may not be able to eat that week [*laughs*] is silly enough to get me hitting deadlines, or at least getting close. The continuous feedback is lovely. Whether you're collaborating on something novel length or whether you're collaborating on comics, continuous feedback is great, and you have somebody to talk to about the art that you're creating. You have somebody who can say, "Hey, I love that character. Are they going to come back?" And you know that you only created that character because you couldn't have these two scenes butting into each other so something had to happen between them, but never intended this character to come back. You suddenly say, "Okay then. That could work."

*American Gods* was weird, but I'm only starting to realize how weird it is trying to do *Anansi Boys*. Because the way that I wrote *American Gods* was I went away for eighteen months, essentially. I physically went away for six weeks, then came home for Christmas and New Year's, then went away for about three or four months. But at that point I just sort of got myself a cabin and went down every day. I didn't talk to anybody, I didn't do anything else. *American Gods* was this solo thing of such weirdness that, by the end of it, I'd lost all social skills. I'd forgotten how to talk to other people. It became this place where I lived where Shadow and Wednesday were much more real to me than anybody else, and it felt more like I was writing down what had happened to them than that I was creating anything. I certainly missed the daily human interaction. I missed the little monthly deadlines. On the other hand, I'm no longer anywhere near as good at doing that stuff as I was. One of the things that I would have loved while I was doing *1602* – in a perfect world, I would have written the whole thing, and then done a second draft. Which is what I'm really enjoying doing with *Anansi*. I wrote half a book, and then typed it out, and changed little bits along the way as I figured out what I was doing. Not huge things, and not noticeably, but places where I had one idea about one way that I wanted to go and then I thought, "You know, actually, I think this goes somewhere else." Things like that. And I really wished that I'd had that in *1602*. There were places where I decided to do things at the beginning because I thought they were cool ideas, and by the time I got to the end it was like, "You know, that really wasn't a cool idea." In a second draft of *1602*, I wouldn't have had well over thirty leads. I kept going, "Where did I think that it would be a good idea to have thirty characters in a two-hundred-page thing who all had stories and all needed resolutions?" [*Laughs.*]